Murder

Mapped Out

PUBLISHING

First Edition published 2020 by

2QT Limited (Publishing)

Settle, North Yorkshire United Kingdom

Copyright © Nigel Hanson 2020

This is a work of fiction and any resemblance to any person living or dead is purely coincidental. The place names mentioned are intentionally fictional and have no connection with any similar or identical place names.

Cover Design by Charlotte Mouncey with illustrations from istockphoto.com and All-free-download.com

Printed in Great Britain by Ingram Spark UK Ltd

A CIP catalogue record for this book is available from the British Library

ISBN 978-1-913071-72-1

THE WISSTINGHAM MYSTERIES

A CRIME SERIES

BOOK 1

Murder Mapped Out

NIGEL HANSON

To my wife Pat, for her unending patience,
while I tapped away on the keyboard.

Chapter 1

Light from the street lamps sparkled in rainwater puddles dotted along the otherwise dark, deserted quayside. From the windows of some of the terraced houses opposite, occasional fingers of light slipped through partly closed curtains and stretched across the street. The lit cobbles were shining, iridescent in the rainstorm that lashed against the man's face. Hands plunged into pockets, he leant into the wind that blustered against his raincoat. From the harbour below came the metallic Morse pinged out by the steel cables on the masts of yachts yawing at their moorings.

As he neared a larger pool of light that shone on the wet road, he made out a faint hum of voices that came from a building across the road. He crossed, pushed open the scarred pub door and went in.

Inside, he paused for a moment as his eyes adjusted to the light, then peered through the fug of the smoky room. The hubbub of voices immediately subsided as eyes turned briefly on him. Then the faces, mostly tanned and weathered, turned back to their drinks and companions and the babble started up again. The drenched man cast around the room, with its solid wooden furniture and hard chairs. He spotted a solitary drinker seated in the far corner, his wiry frame and chiselled features little changed over the years since their last meeting.

The newcomer threaded his way towards him, through the closely spaced tables.

'Harry,' he hailed him with a grin on reaching his friend. 'It's been a long time.'

The other man rose slowly. His reptilian eyes, which had lazily watched Smudger's approach, remained fixed on him. Harry's lips pursed in a conspiratorial smile. He extended a soft hand, three fingers of which were adorned with large gold rings.

'Smudger, me old china!' he said, 'So you found it after all this time? It's been too long. Sit yourself down. What'll it be?'

Smudger shot his friend a fleeting scowl.

'Smudger it was, and Smudger it'll always be,' Harry insisted, and was accorded a grudging shrug of resignation. Yet again, Smudger wished he had never told Harry about his nickname.

'I'll have the usual,' said Smudger, upon which Harry went off to the bar.

'So how's tricks?' Smudger asked as they chinked glasses.

'Same old, same old,' his companion sighed. 'Doesn't get any easier. Not as easy as we had it in Germany, that's for sure.'

Smudger smiled at the recollection of their army days.

'How did you find me?' he asked.

Harry chuckled and tapped his nose.

'You know me, my old mate. Eyes and ears everywhere. All part of the job.'

His 'old mate' eyeballed him.

'And?' he asked.

Harry sat back and appraised his friend. Unfazed,

Smudger returned the stare.

Harry leant in close to him and spoke in a low voice.

'Got something I need you to help me out with. It's big, it's long-term, and it needs to be secure and hush-hush. I need someone I can really trust and just the right location.' He leant back again and cast Smudger a searching glance through slitted eyes. 'That's unless you've gone straight on me.'

His smile wavered until Smudger slowly shook his head and said,

'I've not changed. I miss the old days.'

'They were good times, weren't they?' Harry enthused. 'It'll be just like then.' He waggled his finger to invite Smudger closer, glanced quickly to each side then outlined his proposal. 'It's babysitting gold bullion while its owner's doin' a stretch. Could be twelve years, if he's a good boy, but knowing him I don't reckon he will be.'

Smudger knew better than to ask if it was the proceeds of the Cavendish job, news of which had been plastered all over the papers. Best not to know.

'There'll be four deliveries then nothing more,' Harry continued. 'Nothing in or out after that. Payment will be monthly. There's seven grand a year in it for you.'

When Harry finished, Smudger let out a low whistle.

'It's as safe as the Bank of England,' Harry assured him. 'And after that, we can branch out into other things. But it has to be stored in the right place. Safe, secure and well away from prying eyes.'

Smudger's eyes darted here and there as he racked his brains in search of *the right place*. After what was, for Harry, an agonising wait, he gave a faint smile as his friend mentally found a location.

'You got somewhere, then? Are you in?' Harry asked eagerly, then relaxed as Smudger nodded.

'Yes, I reckon I've got just the right place, well tucked away. But,' he added quickly, 'we'll need to cut someone else in on it.'

Harry frowned and his face contorted as if he had trapped wind.

'What for? I want to keep this as tight as possible.'

'He has access all over the place,' Smudger explained. 'It wouldn't be safe if he wasn't in on it. But don't worry. He'll do what I say and keep his trap shut.'

'I want to meet him, first,' Harry insisted. 'And see the place.'

'Not a problem. I'll set it up.'

Harry motioned to their empty glasses.

'Your round, I believe. I reckon we've got something to drink to.'

Smudger winked and headed to the bar.

***

Commander Selwyn Fitzgerald forked his last piece of sausage then continued to read his newspaper. After a while he glanced down at his plate and frowned in surprise when he saw he had finished his breakfast. He glanced across at his wife Georgina, who passed the toast rack to him with a bemused smile. He returned the smile, buttered his toast and reached for the marmalade dish while, not for the first time, Georgina set about coaxing their eight-year-old son Felix to finish his breakfast.

Georgina folded her napkin neatly and set it down next to the copy of *Vogue*, delivered that morning.

'So what have you got on today, Bumble?' she enquired.

'Not a lot, really,' Selwyn answered.

'What about the quarry inspection?'

He finished his mouthful of toast before he replied.

'Lucian's got that in hand.'

'And the new security fence at the paddock?'

Another pause.

'Vincent will deal with that,' Selwyn assured her. He ate a last morsel, after which his tongue set off on an exploration of his mouth.

'Then what *are* you going to do?' Georgina challenged and peered at him over the top of her glasses.

His eyes narrowed for a moment as he pondered the question.

'Not too sure at present,' he admitted. 'I'll take Mustard for his walk and think about it on the way.'

He smiled at the look of exasperation on his wife's face.

'Well, you won't be treasure hunting all day,' she warned him, as she carefully folded her glasses and set them on top of the magazine. 'Don't forget it's half-term. You can take Felix out on the lake later.'

Selwyn rose, wiped the corner of his mouth with his napkin and leant over towards her.

'I love you, Georgie,' he declared. He turned to his son and winked. 'And you, little man,' he added. The boy smiled back at him.

'And I love you too, you rogue,' his wife replied. 'But mark my words – one of these days someone or something's going to shake you out of that cosy complacency of yours.'

'They'll have to catch up with me first,' he retorted lightly. 'There's the luck of the Fitzgeralds to contend with.'

'Thin ice, Bumble. Thin ice,' Georgina warned. 'Don't be too long out.'

'I won't,' he promised and, with a broad grin, he headed out of the room.

***

On his stroll through the estate grounds, his beagle alongside him, Selwyn sniffed the air and looked about with a rapturous smile.

'A good wife, if a bit spirited, a gorgeous son, good staff, all this – and, of course, you.' He stooped to pat the dog. 'What more could a chap ask for?'

Mustard did not deign to answer. Now unleashed, the dog trotted off and his master sauntered after him.

OCTOBER 1987

'Fuck it!' Lionel Pitt hissed, as he crouched in the dark at the last of his empty snares. There had been nothing for three nights now. Behind him, the strident bark of a distant fox pierced the rustle of the wind through the trees.

The demoralised poacher shouldered his empty bag, rose slowly, listened, then glanced around before he shone his torch at the ground ahead. He crept forward but froze after a few paces at the sound of an approaching vehicle on the old quarry road. Pitt switched off the torch, squatted down and watched the van drive slowly past. It came to a stop by a large barn. As its door opened, a shaft of light shot across the road.

Pitt was tense. He had seen the vehicle the previous week, also in the pitch-black early hours of the morning.

It approached slowly on sidelights, from which he assumed something shady was going on. He had even thought of keeping clear of the Wisstingham estate altogether, but the cooking pot needed to be filled and cigarettes did not come cheap.

He stared in the direction of the vehicle. It was bad enough working this new patch of woods without unpredictable goings-on. Pickings had been meagre, even worse than at his old stamping ground on the other side of the lake.

Each to his own, I suppose. The whole fucking world's at it, one way or another, the poacher reflected gloomily.

As he stooped to creep away, Pitt heard lowered voices. He crouched down again and watched as the vehicle's sidelights went out and a light appeared inside the back of the van. A smartly dressed man, someone clearly in authority, stood at the open door to the barn.

He looked up and down the road, then approached the van, from which two others emerged.

'Where the hell have you been?' he demanded. 'You should have been here over an hour ago. I'm supposed to be going out.'

'Sorry, mate. Traffic,' the driver replied, with little conviction or regret.

A stab of alarm shot through the poacher as his mobile phone started to ring. He fumbled to shut it up and cursed under his breath. Pitt always put it on silent before he went out. His guess was that the button must not have been clicked back properly. The poacher looked up anxiously. There were signs of movement at the barn, but no one seemed to have heard the sound. The man in charge had disappeared. Presumably he was inside the barn.

Motionless, the poacher waited until the two men

pushed the barn doors closed and climbed back into the cab. Now there was only a narrow shaft of light that seeped from the building.

Twinges of pain crept up Pitt's legs from having crouched so long.

I'm getting too old for this game, he thought. There was no sign of the bossman, and gradually the poacher's pain was overtaken by a deep unease. The van's engine started, but Pitt's instinct told him something was not right. Around him, it all was too quiet. The background noise of the woods that he was so used to was missing.

There was a rustle behind him. Pitt tried to get up but his legs resisted.

'Well, well, if we haven't got a visitor,' came a sardonic voice.

Pitt swivelled to see the bossman tower above him. His hand twitched a length of pipe, as if calculating where to land the first blow.

'Get up,' the suit growled.

Pitt abandoned any thoughts of trying to talk his way out of his predicament. He tightened his grip on the heavy stick he always carried and swung it in a low arc that connected with the man's leg.

'Bastard!' the man bellowed in pain. He raised the pipe. The poacher lurched forward, his head connecting with the bossman's stomach as the pipe swung down and missed him. The winded man sagged. Pitt rose and bounded off through the woods. Behind him he could hear the thrashing of the scrub and the oaths of his enraged pursuer.

The undergrowth gave way to more open terrain, which enabled the poacher to make some ground. He stumbled into a hollow by a large sycamore, where he crouched and listened while he tried to get his breath back. His heart thumped, but there was neither sight nor sound of his attacker.

Pitt squatted there and gulped mouthfuls of air, his whole body aquiver from the adrenalin rush. After what seemed like an eternity he straightened, then turned back into the densest part of the woods. He moved towards the quarry road and Wisstingham. The van had long since gone.

The poacher's hands trembled and his legs ached, but he breathed a sigh of relief as he neared the road and relaxed his grip on the stick.

Suddenly, from behind a tree, the bossman stepped out, the moonlight reflected in his eyes. Pitt lashed out again with the stick and landed a blow on the man's arm that brought a yelp of pain.

The terrified poacher made to escape but the pipe was already scything through the air. It crashed onto his skull with a sickening crack. Pitt gasped, then sank to his knees. His body crumpled then finally toppled sideways.

The killer stared at the motionless form. Around him was darkness and silence, as if the creatures of the night had borne hushed witness to the murder. Grim-faced, he took out a torch and shone it on the body. A glint of light reflected from the eyes, frozen in a final stare.

'Blasted poacher!' the suit muttered. His eyes closed briefly in pain before he scanned his surroundings in search of witnesses. Thinking hard and fast, he shone the torch back on the body and then around him to get his bearings. There was only one thing for it: to throw the corpse down the old pit, if he could find the bloody thing again. He would get the pit covered over and no one would ever find him down there.

Angered by the inconvenience, he set to work.

***

Lucian Fitzgerald paced back and forth across the bedroom floor at Wisstingham Hall. Each time he passed the window, he paused to anxiously scan the drive, the lawns and the trees beyond, then the one corner of the stable block visible from his room.

'Oh, Christ! What a mess. What a bloody mess!' he muttered, rubbing his brow as he continued to pace. 'What the hell am I going to do?'

He dropped into the chair in front of the mahogany writing desk commandeered from the study when he had taken up residence at the Hall. With his head sandwiched in his hands and his elbows plonked on the desk, Lucian stared at the blank laptop screen.

His thoughts drifted to his early childhood and the death of the boy. If he felt he had gone through hell then, it was nothing compared to what he felt now. Painful though it was, there was only one thing he could do before retribution would surely descend upon him.

For more than an hour he sat at the desk and carefully formulated his plans. Then he turned on the computer to start to give them some substance.

NOVEMBER 1987

Breathless from her flight down the Hall's imposing staircase, Georgina rushed along the corridor towards the dining room, the marble floor reverberating to the clatter of her heels. She paused momentarily to catch her breath and threw open the heavy doors. Once inside, she glared along the long dining table at the solitary diner seated at the far end, his face eerily coloured by the sunlight that filtered through the stained-glass window.

'He's gone, Bumble!' Georgina announced. Her tone and her arms akimbo signalled a demand for an explanation rather than the delivery of information.

Selwyn peered round the edge of *The Times*, his lined brow wrinkling at the unwelcome urgency his petite whirlwind darling had blown into the room. He regarded her round flushed face, curvaceous figure, and large hazel eyes, fixed resolutely on his.

'Who's gone?' he drawled as he reluctantly lowered the paper. 'Where's Felix?' he added, as an afterthought.

Georgina marched up to her husband.

'Lucian of course, your unreliable half-brother. Who else?' she bristled. 'As for your stubborn offspring, Felix is confined to his room until he's cleared up the mess he made.'

'Headmistress's study job, eh?' Selwyn smirked, but only briefly. 'Maybe Lucian's gone out early, gone up to town or something,' he offered, lamely. Georgina's eyes widened, always a danger sign, indicating that he would have to do better. He adopted a different tack. 'Good Lord, a bloke's entitled to go off now and again without all this fuss, isn't he? Have a word with Mrs Soames. She's bound to know where he's gone.'

A rustling, backhand slap to the back of his newspaper jolted Selwyn quickly back to the gravity of the situation and he abandoned the now crumpled *Times*.

'I'm telling you, Selwyn, he's gone. Totally. Lock, stock,

and barrel. *Everything's* gone.'

'Everything? What do you mean, everything?' Her husband's eyebrows rose as he grappled with the implications.

'I went to call the lazy devil – the agent's due this morning, in case you'd forgotten. There was no reply. Lucian didn't respond when I shouted so I peeped into his room. His bed hasn't been slept in and all his stuff's missing. The cupboards and drawers are virtually empty.'

Selwyn's mouth fell open, which he quickly corrected as Georgina's eyes narrowed.

'Oh,' he murmured. He offered nothing more, merely swallowed hard.

With a groan, his exasperated spouse abandoned any hope of meaningful conversation and stormed off. Her shout of,

'Mrs Soames!' echoed loudly down the corridor.

Heavy jowls accentuated by his downturned mouth, Selwyn stared glumly at the open door.

'Can't have gone,' he muttered irritably. 'How's a chap to run the ruddy place on his own?'

With a heavy sigh he discarded his napkin, folded the crumpled paper and, after a rueful glance at his unfinished breakfast and another at his watch, he set off ponderously in pursuit of his adorable but sometimes frighteningly feisty wife.

***

Vincent Monaghan glanced irritably from his *Daily Mirror* to the ringing phone on the table beside him, but made no attempt to answer it. Mary closed her eyes for a moment then, sighing inwardly, she walked over to pick it up. Unsmiling, she dutifully held it out to her husband as she mouthed,

'The Commander.' The estate manager jabbed at the television's volume control, slurped some tea from his mug and grabbed the phone from her.

Several minutes later, unnerved by the call, he strode briskly from the stable yard towards the Hall. His piercing pale blue eyes were mere slits against the cold wind. Vincent's mind raced. Where the hell had Lucian gone – and why? And did Fitzgerald now know their secrets?

'If he does, that bugger's screwed me good and proper,' Monaghan muttered darkly, while he frantically considered what strategies he should adopt.

As he passed the rear of the Hall, with its turrets and leaded mullioned windows shadowed in the morning sun, he glimpsed the portly Commander through the French windows.

Vincent pushed open the studded side door and snatched off his cap. Once across the east corridor, he knocked on the drawing room door and went in. Selwyn was standing by a large leather-topped table packed with family photos. He was gazing up at the ceiling and fidgeting impatiently while Georgina straightened his cravat.

'Take a seat, Vincent,' Selwyn called out, with a vague gesture to the red chesterfield. 'Did Lucian give you any inkling at all that he was going?'

The estate manager shook his head.

'Well, it's a rum do,' the Commander muttered. 'Fellow didn't say a word to anyone. Not a peep. Didn't even leave a note. Just incredible!' All the time his stare remained fixed on the estate manager.

After two years at the Hall, the Commander's relentless stare was a trait that Vincent was accustomed to. At first he had found it intimidating but eventually had come to realise that the Commander's thoughts would invariably have drifted off elsewhere. He was staring at something or someone he didn't even see.

Selwyn wandered over to the French windows, palmed away some condensation and peered out. Thin wisps of mist still hugged the lawn. Several crows perched in the branches of the large sycamores whose remaining golden leaves hung limply, soon to join the amber carpet below.

'So, what's to be done, Bumble?' Georgina demanded. Her fingers drummed on the magazine she had discarded by her side. She knew that using his nickname in front of others would irritate her husband, but at least it might stir him into action.

Broken from his reverie, Selwyn twitched and frowned.

'Haven't the faintest idea,' he mumbled, his eyebrows raised and his mouth set in its hangdog expression. 'We'll just have to wait till the blighter gets in touch, and meanwhile get stuck in. How does this affect you, Vincent?' he asked.

If only you knew, thought the estate manager.

'Well, from the stables side there's no problem. The quarry – that was very much between him and Mac. On the woodlands, we'd decided which trees need to go and I think he still had to meet Fred Ferris about the coppicing.'

Conscious of Georgina's dwindling patience, Selwyn quickly marshalled his thoughts.

'All right, you deal with the woodlands and I'll sort out Ferris,' he instructed. 'Get a report from Mac on where things stand and get back to me by lunchtime. Anything else that springs to mind, let me know. Let's jump to it then, shall we?' he added briskly, to mollify his wife. 'Oh,

I nearly forgot to ask. How's Mary?'

Vincent turned at the door, a slight frown flitting across his brow.

'Just fine, thank you. She says thanks for the flowers.'

Selwyn caught Georgina's quizzical glance.

'Good. Excellent news for you both, eh?'

'Yes, it was a surprise after all these years,' the manager remarked, with less enthusiasm than Selwyn had expected.

'Well, our best wishes.' As the door closed, Selwyn resumed his baffled contemplation of the garden.

'Flowers, hmm? It must be nice to get flowers,' Georgina commented icily.

With a wince, Selwyn cleared his throat and turned, but before he could come up with a reply, his wife had moved on.

'Of course, if Lucian's really gone, Bumble, it'll put paid to your treasure hunting.' She patted the vacant seat beside her. 'You'll be far too busy for that.'

Selwyn was only too well aware that Georgina had long ago resigned herself to the countless hours he'd spent – and would doubtless continue to spend – on his obsessive quest to recover the missing family fortune.

'I'm not going to give up on it, Georgie,' he warned. 'I'm close, I know I am. It's here somewhere. When I find it, we'll be able to restore this place to its former glory. No more scrimping and scraping to keep it up to snuff.'

She smiled indulgently at his eager face and patted his knee.

'All well and good, my little sailor. I know it's your dream, and I don't mind your pursuit of it, up to a point, but right now the priority is to fill the gaps that Lucian has left behind. I'm sure it'll be easier when we've got on top of things.'

Any response was curtailed by the appearance of the apple of both his parents' eyes and the scourge of Mrs Soames, the housekeeper. Felix stomped sulkily into the room and demanded breakfast.

***

Smudger had been surprised at how relaxed Harry had sounded over Lucian's disappearance, to the extent that he wondered if Harry knew more about it than he was letting on. When you supped with Harry, you supped with a long spoon. That had been Smudger's reading of the man since he had first met him.

The one main concern that Smudger and Harry shared was that, with Lucian gone, the Commander might take a greater interest in the estate's outbuildings, particularly the barn. At first Smudger had half-expected Harry to decide to close down the operation when he heard the news. However, after some discussion he had said,

'I don't see why you can't handle it without Lucian,' to which Smudger had agreed. 'Of course, if you think the Fitzgeralds are getting too close, that'll be a different story. Unless you can buy them off,' Harry had cautioned him. 'I'll leave it up to you, as long as you think you can handle it. I'm sure you know that failure's not an option in this game.'

DECEMBER 1987

'Hang on,' Selwyn whispered tersely into the handset before laying it on the desk. He padded to the open doorway and glanced up the hallway, then softly closed the door.

'"Sorry," just doesn't cut the mustard, Lucian,' he resumed. 'It's been three weeks since you skedaddled without a word. Where are you?' The Commander's face coloured crimson at the reply. 'Hong Kong?' he bellowed, almost apoplectic. 'What the bloody hell are you doing there?'

Eyes narrowed, Selwyn glared across his desk as he listened. Lucian's reply did nothing for his pallor or his blood pressure.

'Stifled?' he eventually exploded. 'I wish you were here – I'd ruddy stifle you, believe me. When are you coming back?'

He held the receiver in front of him and stared at it, incredulous at what he had heard. Alternating between spluttering disbelief and fuming exasperation, he voiced his displeasure.

'You didn't even have the decency to tell us all this and that you were going. Now you expect me to run this place on my own *and* financially support you? Lucian, you're bloody selfish and totally irresponsible. How the hell are Georgie and I supposed to cope?'

The lively dialogue continued for several minutes, Selwyn more the listener than the listened-to. Finally, with a deep sigh of resignation, he demanded a few moments to think. He placed the receiver back on the desk and stared as he considered his options, his tongue off on another oral expedition.

Realising that there was no way he was going to persuade Lucian to return, Selwyn frowned. His anger grew at his half-brother's selfish abandonment of him.

Stiff upper lip. Where's that Dunkirk spirit? Selwyn could almost hear his father whisper in his ear. Eventually, the disconsolate Commander picked up the handset and spoke in a calmer, more measured tone.

'All right, I'll set up a regular payment. I've no idea what either of us will inherit when Father finally goes. What I send you comes off your share of the estate. The conditions are that you don't come back, certainly not without my prior agreement, and you don't communicate with anyone here. If you do, the payments will stop. Understood?'

Selwyn listened, then shook his head vigorously at the reply.

'Those are the terms, Lucian. Take them or leave them.' With a final nod, he reached for a notepad and jotted away before he said a less than heartfelt goodbye.

There's something he's not telling me. What the hell is it? Selwyn thought, as he replaced the receiver and left the room.

***

DS Stone jingled the loose change in his trouser pocket and stared gloomily out of the rain-spattered window. Outside, across from the police station car park, the sou'wester-clad council workmen were struggling to put up the Christmas lights. Over his shoulder, Stone addressed DC McBride.

'So what you're suggesting is that we turn up at the home of one of the most influential people in the county and insist on trampling all over his land to look for some ne'er-do-well whose wife hasn't a clue when or why he went missing. If he's missing at all.'

The thought of turning out in such weather was not an

appealing one.

'But there was no sign of him at Penston Woods, so perhaps he moved on to the estate,' McBride argued with waning conviction.

'At this rate, we could end up searching the whole flaming county just because of one of your whims. I'm not going to propose to the inspector that we go to the expense of a full manhunt at this stage. Do some more digging,' Stone ordered. 'Find out when Pitt really was last seen. Quiz the wife again, if necessary, or get Pelman to do it. She seemed to have a way with the dreadful harpy.'

'So no search, then, sir?'

Stone afforded the question a tired sigh.

'Much as it goes against the grain, the last thing the DI will want to do is to upset the Commander,' he affirmed. 'He's well in with the top brass – weird handshakes and trouser leg stuff, if you catch my drift.'

McBride's smirk clearly showed that he did.

'For now, we'll concentrate our resources on other lines of enquiry,' Stone instructed, with a final jingle.

By the following afternoon, the weather had not improved and neither had Stone's mood.

'So, what've you come up with, McBride?' he demanded.

'The wife's checked with all their relatives and friends but there's been no contact. She now says that Pitt's gone off twice before without a word to anyone. There's some old navy friend who he disappeared with on a bender for a few days, but she doesn't know who or where.'

'Bloody hell! We've been wasting our ruddy time,' his boss exploded. 'Why the hell didn't she tell us this before?'

'She didn't think it was relevant. It seems he did it after they'd had a big row.'

'I'll be having a bloody big row with her,' Stone growled. 'That's it, then. Post the usual missing persons' notices and leave it at that.'

'No search of the estate then, sir?'

'Not bloody likely. There'll have to be a lot more before I take that upstairs.'

FEBRUARY 1988

The Monaghans' stone cottage fronted onto a large square courtyard. In one corner, a cobbled passageway led to a road that ran alongside the lawn at the back of the Hall. Opposite the cottage was the stable block. The courtyard's other two sides comprised storage buildings and workshops which, at the far corner of the yard, straddled another cobbled passageway that led to the paddock and training course. A stretch of dense woodland bounded by a high security fence separated the course from the council's recreation fields, which were on land leased from the estate.

Several weeks after Lucian's departure, as noon chimed on the Victorian clock above the stables, Vincent arrived home with Pilsbury, his black Labrador. As he heeled off his mud-spattered wellingtons, the estate manager peered through the porch window into the kitchen and watched the two figures seated at the table. The Commander idly fingered the handle of his coffee mug as Mary chewed at a fingernail and dabbed her eyes with the handkerchief that he had passed to her.

The Commander took her hands in his, leant forward and spoke. As Vincent entered, his wife sprang up and, head bowed, began to busy herself at the sink.

'Vincent,' Selwyn exclaimed breezily, also getting up. 'Just called to see if you were in. Failed on that score, but all was not lost. Had one of Mary's excellent coffees.'

Vincent's hands slowly balled into fists at his sides.

'So I see. What can I do for you?' he asked, and forced a smile.

'It's budget time again,' replied Selwyn. 'How are you fixed for a meeting early Thursday morning?'

Vincent's eyes flitted from his boss to his wife's still-bowed head.

'You could have rung me to save yourself a journey,' he suggested.

'Oh, I needed some fresh air,' said Selwyn.

Vincent eyed him again then nodded.

'Thursday will be fine. I'll have the figures ready but I don't expect you'll like them,' he warned.

'Well, we'll see on Thursday, eh?'

Selwyn donned his duffel coat and gave Mary a smile. With her back tight against the sink, she smiled back weakly. With a nod, he bade them goodbye and headed out into the courtyard, followed by Vincent, who watched thoughtfully as his boss headed back to the Hall.

JUNE 1988

'We've called him Sebastian,' Mary whispered as she gazed down at the puckered red face in its cocoon of sheet and blanket.

'Fine name. I like it.' Selwyn smiled approvingly as he

sat by the bed in the cottage hospital and studied the boy. 'June's a good time to be born. All the summer ahead of him.'

The new mother rocked the sleeping infant and stared fretfully out of the window.

'Is everything all right, Mary?' Fitzgerald queried, with a gentle touch on her arm. She glanced at his hand and anxious expression, then gave a brief, tired smile before she looked away to hide her trembling lips and moistened eyes.

Selwyn turned his attention back to the baby and studied the child's face. As he did so, the door opened slowly and Vincent crept in. When he caught sight of the visitor, Vincent's smile faded. Selwyn rose and, having extended his congratulations to the new father, took his leave, pondering on the Monaghan household and the change he had noticed in Vincent's demeanour.

In the meantime, the father took hold of the infant and scrutinised his face while the baby's minute fingers flickered into slow and random animation.

'Penny for them?' Mary offered at last, but any further exchange was curtailed by Sebastian's lusty cries. As his wife fed the child, Vincent stared fixedly across the room until his brooding was eventually interrupted by the matron's arrival.

Chapter 2

Smudger stared at the neat piles of new banknotes stacked on the table in front of him. His thoughts were still in turmoil. The meeting and the celebration with Harry had gone off well, as Smudger had expected – at first. The bullion had gone and the payout was generous.

'We're going into the antiques and art business, my dear friend,' Harry had announced, with a viperous smile, after the first few drinks. 'A bit more risky than the bullion. It'll mean deliveries and collections maybe a couple of times a week, but I reckon you'll be able to handle that, eh?' Over more drinks he outlined the new operation in detail, together with the rewards it offered.

Smudger had been in no position to decline. He had come to realise long ago that you didn't turn down any suggestion that Harry put forward, let alone any instruction. The Wisstingham location was as safe as ever, and the operation sounded a good and very profitable one.

It was what had happened later that evening that had come as a shock to Smudger. He'd never expected that, not in a million years. All this time, he'd never had an inkling. It had been the drink, of course. They hadn't been on such a bender since their early days together in Gibraltar. There was a lot to be said for sober inhibitions. And it was the shock, that Smudger had been unable to hide, that had wounded Harry.

How the relationship with Harry would go on from here remained to be seen. They had parted civilly but on strained terms. Maybe time would sort things out.

Smudger exhaled loudly, closed his eyes for a moment then stared once more at the banknotes before he gathered them up to put them safely away.

MARCH 2008

The painting stood unfinished on the abandoned easel, framed by an idyllic view of the blue sky, the distant rolling hills of the Downs and, in the foreground, the lake. Selwyn contemplated it then inclined his head for a different perspective of the canvas.

'Perhaps it's an abstract,' he muttered, then tutted as he began to screw the tops back on to the tubes of paint.

He wandered into the lake garden and sat on the bench at his favourite spot. Across the lawn the grass glinted, wet from the morning frost that was now almost completely thawed by the sun.

In the naked branches of the sycamores, the outlines of several crows' nests were visible, and the birds' harsh caws were resonating in the still air. At the top of the nearby rise above the trees was a tall stone folly that gave magnificent views over the estate and the landscape beyond. Erected by an ancestor, Sir Henry Fitzgerald, it had been built to commemorate Wellington's victory at Waterloo.

Selwyn wondered how many of his predecessors, who now lay cold in the family vault, had also sat here and looked out at the same scenery, which had changed little over the centuries. Their achievements, evident in the Hall and the grounds as well as the family history, were a constant goad to him, a reminder of how little he had achieved. True, he had made the old gravel quarry a commercial success, and by shrewd management had greatly enhanced the reputation of the stables, but Selwyn viewed these achievements as barely maintaining the status quo. They only kept the estate intact and solvent. The Hall's restoration, the stables and the estate hungrily gobbled up any profits. Even the extensive research he had carried out to hunt down the missing family fortune had so far come to nought.

'As you're the eldest, I'm handing over the reins to you, Selwyn,' his father had informed him, shortly after Felix's birth. 'With my health, I can't manage things as well as I should. It needs younger blood. Lucian's agreed to join you here. I'm sure that between you you'll make the place thrive.'

Lucian's practical and moral support had indeed proved invaluable, despite his dislike of the countryside and his occasional obstinacy. Selwyn had known very little about his half-brother before his arrival at Wisstingham. His widowed father's early separation from Lucian's mother, and subsequent reticence on that chapter of his life, had seen to that. Even after Lucian took up residence, Selwyn had learnt little more. Lucian had proved very reserved, almost secretive by nature. However, Selwyn soon came to realise that the chap had expensive tastes, which were often a bone of contention.

Seventeen years he's been gone and not a word, Selwyn reflected. He had thought of Lucian often, presuming he was still in Hong Kong, although he could be anywhere. The bank transfers had long since stopped. For all Selwyn knew, Lucian could have even come back to England.

Selwyn wondered what he was doing now, though it was doubtful Lucian would have speculated about him, had the roles been reversed. Charming, attractive and intelligent, there was little doubt that the absentee brother would have landed on his feet.

Selwyn had been very bitter at first. Times had been hard, and still were. However, his feelings had mellowed – unlike Georgina's. It appeared that Lucian had kept his part of the bargain and not contacted anyone on the estate but there remained an emptiness about it all, made worse by not knowing why he had left.

The surface of the lake, still as a millpond when Selwyn had arrived, now rippled from the oar strokes of a dinghy that approached the jetty. A young man stepped lightly out and tied the boat to a mooring ring, which raised a smile of affection on Selwyn's lined face.

Felix walked slowly towards the garden, stopping now and then to gaze about him at the scenery. He lifted his face to the sky and breathed deeply. A look of intense pleasure played on his round face, which was flushed by the morning chill that had not yet been chased away by the sun.

'What a great morning, Father,' Felix exclaimed, as he dropped down onto the bench. He leant back, clasped his hands behind his head and stretched out his legs. 'It's idyllic out there when it's like this. Pity you weren't with me,' he enthused.

'I thought you were painting. I would have come out with you, if I'd known.'

'Oh, I got fed up with it,' Felix replied, giving the easel a dismissive glance. 'It looked so good out there. *Carpe diem* and all that.'

'You've got your mother's impatience,' Selwyn observed.

'You should get on the lake. You'd enjoy it. The exercise would be good for that dodgy ticker and you'd get rid of some of that paunch.' The young Fitzgerald grinned and a glint shone in his eyes. Selwyn gave him a light punch on the arm and they sat in companionable silence, taking in the panorama.

'Painting not for you, then?' Selwyn ventured, after several moments.

Felix grimaced.

'Can't seem to get the hang of perspective.'

'And the writing? Have you abandoned that?' The question was awarded a brief scowl.

'I'm still at it. I had a short story published,' Felix volleyed defensively.

'Not enough to keep body and soul together, though, is it?'

Felix stamped irritably on a passing ant, but Selwyn persisted.

'I really think it's time to settle to something.'

His son sat upright on the bench and scowled. Selwyn raised his hands submissively.

Yes,' he continued hastily, 'I know you do things on the estate, but you need to be more involved. Don't forget all this is going to be yours to deal with one day.' Selwyn wanted to tell him not to sulk but the scowl was already in place and there were other subjects he still needed to broach.

'Very well, enough said. Change of subject. What would you like to do on your birthday?' he asked.

Felix sat quietly for several seconds before he eased out of his mood.

'Oh, nothing fancy. Perhaps a quiet meal out.'

'I think your mother had a party in mind. It's been ages since we did anything like that. You could have all your friends over.'

Felix screwed up his face.

'I'd rather go to the pub with them.'

'Are we invited?' Selwyn asked.

Felix snorted.

'You are kidding, Father? It just wouldn't be your scene.'

Selwyn fell silent. He and Georgina had hoped the birthday would enable them to meet some of Felix's friends, to whom they had never been introduced but about whom they had heard some rumours. Not all of them good.

'Your mother and I have heard a few unsavoury snippets about some of the young blades in Hopestanding. I trust you've not got in with the wrong crowd, have you, Felix?' Selwyn ventured cautiously.

Felix stood up. His lips tightened as he inhaled deeply and glared angrily at his father.

'Are you serious? There's nothing wrong with my friends. I don't go around judging yours. Anyway, the way you keep me short of cash, I'm hardly able to get in with anybody at all, let alone the *wrong crowd*, as you put it.'

Selwyn stared ahead in silent frustration.

'Listen,' he murmured eventually. 'It's only natural that your mother and I should worry about you and the company you keep, considering we never meet any of them. On the money side of things, times are hard and we do what we can.' He was about to remind his son about the university education and gap year he had enjoyed and to ask what it had all been for, but that would be like showing a red rag to a bull.

'Well, it'll suit you if I don't have a big do, won't it?' Felix retorted.

'I'll let *you* tell your mother about that,' sighed Selwyn. He groaned as his mobile rang, an unwelcome interruption to a meeting he had tried to engineer for some time and which, for him, was far from a resolution.

'I think you'd better get back right away.' Georgina's voice sounded tense.

'What's happened?'

'Just come back,' she said and rang off.

The beautiful morning and further conversation were both abandoned as the duo set off briskly for the Hall.

***

'It's from Hong Kong,' Georgina handed Selwyn a letter. She fingered her bottom lip and watched him closely as he opened and read it.

He wiped his brow, reread it, then sank down onto a chair and stared blankly ahead.

'Well?' she prompted.

Tight-lipped, Selwyn glanced from her to Felix.

'It's from Lucian's landlord,' he replied, the surprise in his voice reflecting his incredulity at what he had read. 'He says that according to the Hong Kong police, Lucian's missing, presumed dead. Off a ferry.'

Georgina let out a low moan and clasped her hands to her mouth while Felix sat down and bowed his head.

'Oh my God! Poor man,' she murmured, taking the letter from Selwyn. 'Perhaps it's a mistake.' Then she rallied. 'Perhaps it's not him at all,' she said, after having read it. 'Anyway, why wouldn't the police have contacted us directly?'

'Perhaps the landlord never told them about us,' Felix suggested.

'I can't think why not,' she replied, her hand now on Selwyn's shoulder.

'It's Lucian we're talking about,' said Selwyn. 'Perhaps things weren't straightforward. I'd better go there and find out what's happened.'

'Not on your own, you won't. Not all that way,' Georgina decreed.

'We'd better discuss it over dinner. I need to think about this,' Selwyn replied with a finality that ended the conversation.

***

That afternoon, Selwyn took Mustard for a long walk in the grounds. He had refused his wife's offer to accompany him, and on this occasion she knew better than to insist. There were times when even she could not hold sway over him.

It was during their exchanges when they changed for dinner that Selwyn felt marginalised by Georgina's decision-making. She would not countenance his going to Hong Kong on his own and was determined to go with him. She was insistent that Felix could be left to run the estate in their absence, despite Selwyn's assertion that their son couldn't even run a bath.

'It'll get him away from that playboy lifestyle,' Georgina suggested.

'You've got a point there, I suppose,' he conceded.

'And he'll have Vincent to support him. Our son's got

hidden depths.'

That's what worries me, Selwyn thought, his brow knitted as he pondered the argument. However, he offered no further objection, at which his wife shot him a questioning glance.

What she did not know was that Selwyn had already contemplated – and mentally cringed at – the changes he might face, were he to return from the trip with Felix, having left Georgina in charge. Furthermore, to try to wrest power from her afterwards would prove the Devil's own job.

At dinner, Georgina announced 'their' plans.

'Felix, I'll go with your father to Hong Kong. If we were away for about a month, do you think you could hold the fort with Vincent's help?'

Selwyn made to speak but she ploughed on, silencing him with a look.

'We don't know how long it will take to sort things out, but hopefully a month should be enough. If it's much less, I thought we might as well combine the trip with a holiday, since we've not had one for years.'

'That's fine by me,' Felix agreed. 'Of course I'll manage.'

Despite the confidence of his reply, Selwyn remained uneasy and quiet.

'You'd only be an email or a phone call away if there was anything I needed to consult you about,' Felix said reassuringly.

Selwyn stared at him but, in the absence of a better plan and in answer to his wife's raised eyebrows, he gave a resigned nod.

Georgina lowered her gaze.

'Then that's all sorted out,' she pronounced, with a smile.

'When we get back, Felix, we'll do something special for your birthday.'

Selwyn and his son exchanged glances.

***

Vincent stared coldly at his sobbing wife then placed a hand on her shoulder, the firmness of his grip one of control rather than of consolation. He shook her slightly.

'Snap out of it, woman. Lucian didn't mean that much to us,' he chided her.

Released from his grip, she sank into a chair as he moved off to stare impatiently out of the window. He despised weakness in any shape or form. In fact, he reflected, he had come to despise *her*.

Mary sniffed and lowered her eyes to the handkerchief she was mangling in her lap. She shot him a furtive glance. Vincent had conveniently forgotten his desperation when he had been sacked from his last job for beating a stable boy. Had it not been for Lucian's intervention, Mary doubted her husband would ever have found another position.

'I never promised you that life would be a bowl of cherries,' snapped Vincent. 'Though with Lucian on our side, I did expect we'd get our feet under the table, especially when the estate's passed on. That's what he promised me and that's what I'm entitled to. Some of this is mine – or it should be,' he argued. He glared at his wife. 'Oh, for Christ's sake, Mary, stop it. It's not as if I'm losing my job. What was he to you, anyway?' A note of distrust had now crept into his voice.

'Nothing, nothing at all,' she sniffed and looked up to return his stare. 'But why shouldn't the Commander know Lucian was your cousin?'

His puckered eyes weighed her up.

'Because when Lucian recommended me, he said Fitzgerald wouldn't want one of his relatives working here. A "complicated family thing", he reckoned. If I told the Commander now, he'd probably ditch me for having deceived him, especially since Lucian did.'

'Not after all these years, surely?'

'These people have long memories. There was a lot of bitterness when Lucian's mother split up with the old man.'

'But he thinks highly of you.'

'Maybe he does but you can't trust 'em, none of 'em,' Vincent snarled. 'Especially Fitzgerald,' he added darkly.

Mary could see the envy and hatred glistening in her husband's eyes but she refused to kowtow.

Vincent felt his control slipping away. His temper rose. Mary normally knew her place, but today she was different.

'Well, woman, you got something more to say?' he growled.

'Yes, I have,' she exclaimed, taken aback by her own sudden assertiveness. 'You said before that Lucian was a bad lot and that he was deceitful, couldn't be trusted. Well, maybe he was, but why take on so about the Commander? He's been nothing but kindness and a friend to us.'

'You stupid bitch! You don't know a bloody thing,' Vincent sneered.

Mary broke down at the viciousness of his reply. She hung her head and started to whimper.

'Oh for God's sake, woman, shut up,' he snarled.

'I can't stand this, any more,' she spluttered, through her tears. 'I don't know what to expect from you from one moment to the next. You never used to be like this. I don't know who I'm living with sometimes.' She recoiled at the sight of Vincent's bared teeth and cowered as he advanced towards her, but he was stopped in his tracks by a voice from the porch.

'Hello, Mum, what's for tea?' asked Sebastian, who had appeared in the doorway, gawky in his well lived-in school uniform. Even Pilsbury, who had skulked under the table, made no effort to greet the boy. Sebastian's smile faded at the sight of yet another confrontation.

'That's right, just barge in on a conversation, you inconsiderate shit,' Vincent shouted, as he turned on the boy, balling his fists. Mary clasped a hand to her mouth.

'Sorry,' muttered Sebastian, who bolted for the stairs and the sanctuary of his bedroom.

'And don't you stay up there, you lazy sod,' Vincent barked after him. 'There's the stables to clean out, so get changed and get to it. And get that bloody bedroom tidied up. It's a disgrace, you little pig.'

The corner of his lip rose at Mary's barely audible sigh.

'You're too soft with him. That boy needs to pull his weight. Some hard discipline is what the little sod needs,' he snapped.

Even more than you've been doling out to him over the years? she yearned to reply, but knew better than to say it and retreated to the sink.

Vincent moved towards her but was interrupted again, this time by the phone's ring. Thin-lipped, he picked up, listened then slammed down the receiver.

'He wants me at the Hall, the lazy bugger!' Vincent spat.

'Wouldn't think to come over here, unless of course he fancied one of your *coffees*,' he added with a sneer, and thrust his face close to his cowering wife's.

With a last withering look at the head now bowed over the washing-up bowl, he cursed and stormed off.

'No doubt he'll be all sweetness and light as usual when he gets there,' Mary muttered grimly, drying her hands. As she climbed the stairs to find her son, she had to admit to herself that Vincent had been right about the bedroom.

Chapter 3

The door to Penrose Cottage swung open and Alexander Penn's generous frame filled the opening. As he wiped a pair of wire-rimmed spectacles, his piggy eyes peered out from a ruddy face framed by a mop of white hair, with matching beard and moustache.

'What?' he demanded gruffly.

Before him, with his back to Wisstingham Common, stood a young athletic-looking tall, slim man with a tie loosely knotted round his neck and his suit jacket hanging casually on his shoulders. He ran a slender hand through his tousled mop of short, curly hair and grinned as his uncle struggled to identify him.

'Good Lord!' Penn finally spluttered, the glasses now in place. 'It's our Martin.' His eyes and face crinkled in delight, and a broad grin exposed the gap between his two front teeth. 'Do come in, my dear boy,' he urged and squeezed to one side, shouting, 'Aunty! It's Martin come to see us.'

Martin Brightside smiled as his happy uncle pumped his hand and ushered him to the sofa. He took in the surroundings then his eyes settled on a frail, stooped lady who had shuffled into the room and was frowning at him.

'It's Martin, our Julia's son,' Penn boomed.

Aunty Hilda frowned some more then suddenly

42

broke into a smile, with a vague shake of her hand, as her memory finally made the family connection. She extended bony arthritic hands to their visitor.

'Martin,' she murmured shakily, as he bent to kiss her cheek. 'How lovely to see you. Just look at you. My, my. Would you care for some tea, my dear?'

She set off for the kitchen and Penn subsided into his sagging armchair. He leant forward, shirt buttons straining across his bulging midriff.

'I'll probably have to go and help her,' he confided. 'I'm afraid dementia's setting in. Sometimes she's fine, but...' he tailed off.

'I'm sorry I didn't warn you,' Martin apologised. 'I had to visit a company in Hopestanding yesterday and I'm on my way home, so I thought I'd just call in and say hello before I set off back home.'

Penn's smile faded.

'Nonsense, I'm delighted you're here. You can't go off so soon. Stay the night and go tomorrow. There'll be less traffic on a Sunday.'

Martin hesitated but, since he did not have to leave the UK until the following week and in view of his uncle's insistence, he agreed.

'So how are things at the school?' he asked.

'Much the same as the past seventeen years. Nothing much changes apart from the curriculum.'

'I'd have thought with English and history there'd be little to change.'

'Don't you believe it. After some of the things that have gone on, we've concluded that the lunatics are running the asylum. Still, I'm not going to change now. The school's close by, it's very nice living here and Aunty and

I get along quite well.'

At Hilda's call, Penn lumbered into the kitchen and returned with a heavily laden tray.

'Aunty says to excuse her. She's just gone for a lie-down,' he announced.

'Weren't you doing some work on the local history?' Martin enquired.

Penn smiled, as the conversation turned to his great passion.

'Yes, the history of Wisstingham, the Hall and its family.'

'Sounds interesting. Tell me more.'

'Well,' said Penn, needing no persuasion, 'if you really want to hear about it…' But he did not wait for a reply and immediately began.

'The Fitzgeralds have been here since the early sixteenth century. They own the manor house and its grounds, which include a paddock, a racecourse, stables to go with it, a quarry, around forty acres of farmland that stretch from Wisstingham towards Hopestanding and nearly the same area of woodlands. Now during the Civil War the area was overrun by the Royalists but the Fitzgeralds were accused of being loyal to Cromwell, do you see?'

Martin nodded, slowly.

'Well, some members of the family were arrested and the Royalists occupied the Hall. This is where we come to the interesting bit. It's rumoured that the family fortune was hidden away before the Royalists rode in, for fear of confiscation should the area be taken over. But before anyone could do a proper search for the treasure, Cromwell's forces recaptured the area.'

Martin frowned.

'So what happened?'

Penn looked uncomfortable and ran a hand over the back of his neck.

'Ah, well... Unfortunately, the Fitzgeralds that were arrested ... erm ... well, they died. Darnedest thing. A fire broke out in the prison while they were there. So, if they hid the treasure, they took the secrets of its location with 'em.'

Martin winced.

'Aye, quite,' agreed Penn. 'Later, during the Restoration, the surviving Fitzgeralds had their lands and titles and all reinstated, but no trace of the treasure has ever been found despite many a search over the years.'

'Where does the estate boundary end in relation to the village?' asked Martin.

'It's almost a small town now,' corrected his uncle, and pointed through the window towards the public footpath and the cycle track next to the road. 'Those fall within the estate, together with the recreational grounds beyond. The land is leased to the council at a peppercorn rent and every ten years the estate has the right to terminate the lease, though it's never happened.'

'And how far does the town extend?'

'Well, it was originally made up of two communities. D'you know Frogsham Bay?'

Martin gave a quick head shake.

'Old fishing village,' Penn explained briefly. 'So, Frogsham Bay and the old village of Wisstingham. What's interesting is that we're blessed with three pubs: the Happy Rat, which the fishing families and lifeboat men patronise, the Phantom Hound, where most of the village's businesspeople go, and the Ferret and Wardrobe, where you'll mostly find the true Wisstingham villagers.'

Alexander gave his nephew a sideways glance. 'You're a cartographer, Martin. D'you think there's a chance you might be able to search out some old maps of this area?'

Martin thought for a moment then nodded.

'I reckon I might,' he replied, with a smile. 'There's a chap I know who specialises in maps around the time of the Civil War. I'll have a word with him.'

'Splendid,' Penn exclaimed, heaving himself to his feet with a grin. 'Now, if you fancy it, this is where the history lesson turns practical. What do you say to sampling at least a half in each of those hostelries, while we observe history and some of the inhabitants in action?'

Martin needed no second invitation and was up in an instant. Within minutes, they were on their way across the common towards the first watering hole, the Happy Rat.

MAY 2008

Felix stood under the Hall's imposing portico and watched the taxi's slow approach up the long, gravel drive. He skipped down the steps to greet the arrivals, smugly reflecting on how well he had managed the place during their absence.

Selwyn climbed out of the cab and, without a smile, motioned his son to open the other door for his mother. Felix's cheery expression vanished as Georgina, deathly pale, emerged slowly and hesitantly. With only a flicker of happiness at seeing her son, she grasped his arm as he shot a questioning glance at his father.

'Your mother's not well. We think she must have picked up something in Hong Kong,' Selwyn explained.

'Anything further on Lucian since your email?' Felix

asked, as they slowly mounted the steps with their delicate charge.

'No, there's been no trace of him. Anyway, we'll talk inside. Let's get your mother sorted out with the doctor first.'

Georgina leant heavily on her son's arm and laboriously continued her climb up the steps, followed by the taxi driver with the cases. Selwyn paid the fare and glanced across to the regiments of daffodils, their tips tinged yellow, though their signal of spring brought him neither a smile nor any apparent comfort.

JUNE 2008

'It's not good news, I'm afraid,' Selwyn warned his son as they walked towards the kitchen garden. 'The hospital's confirmed it's a virus she undoubtedly caught in China.'

Felix halted and stared at him for a moment then cast his eyes to the ground as the news sank in.

'She is going to be all right though, isn't she?'

'They don't know.'

'Jesus! When *will* they know?'

The Commander squared up to him.

'Felix, I don't know,' he replied irritably. '*They* don't know. They do know that some people have died from it. There are more tests they have to do. She'll be kept in isolation for some time yet, I think.' Selwyn turned and walked on a few paces as Felix frowned and watched him. Then his father stopped, returned and took hold of his son's arm. 'I'm sorry, son. I didn't mean to bark. I'm just so worried. It's very exasperating, not knowing. I feel so helpless. I don't know what I'd do without her.'

Felix hugged his father, a rare sign of affection.

'It'll be all right, Father. It will be,' he said soothingly and looked reassuringly into Selwyn's glistening eyes.

Selwyn gave him a tight smile and they carried on walking. After a while he stopped and turned.

'When your mother's back with us, I'm going to want to spend as much time as possible with her. That means I'll need you to carry on running things. I'll still be here, of course. How do you feel about that?' He was nervous about asking this of his son and still harboured some reservations but the place was still standing, after all, and Vincent had been full of praise for how well Felix had coped. Anyway, it would be good experience for Felix as the estate's future owner. He knew that Felix wanted to travel, but that could come later. Right now, he would give his son the reins, if he was prepared to take them up.

'Yeah, I'm happy with that,' Felix replied.

Selwyn breathed a sigh of relief and they walked on in silence, each occupied with their own thoughts on the subject.

JULY 2008

Vincent leant up into the cab and reached for his mobile. At first he had not been inclined to answer it, but he relented.

'Vincent Monaghan,' he answered, gruffly. His tone reflected the mood he was in. The drive from Wisstingham had been a nightmare.

'Vincent, it's Felix,' came the reply. 'I want to see you right away.'

'I'm afraid that's not possible. I'm at Lingfield. Just got

48

here. I did tell you.'

'Damn, I'd forgotten,' said Felix, 'Then I want a meeting with you the minute you get back.'

Vincent frowned.

'What's it about?' he asked.

'The old barn and what's in it,' replied Felix. Vincent felt a chill run down his spine.

What the hell do I say? was his first panicked thought. Then from somewhere inside he could hear a voice tell him, *If in doubt, say nothing.*

'Oh,' he replied, 'Yes, I'll come to see you as soon as I get back. I must go – they want me to move the van. I've caused a jam.'

He rang off, locked the cab door, then went off to find a strong coffee and to make an urgent call. Until now he had never understood just what a cold sweat really was like.

***

News had indeed travelled fast. From the initial telephone call from Felix, to Smudger's call getting through to Harry it had taken less than an hour. At first, Harry had been delighted to hear Smudger's voice. It had seemed an absolute age since they had parted under very strange circumstances. Since then, not a day had gone by when Harry was not tempted to call him, if only to establish what Smudger's attitude was towards him now. But he had resisted the temptation and consequently kept himself in a purgatory of worry and speculation.

What Smudger had gone on to tell Harry, however, was definitely not something he had wanted to hear.

So, the young boss of Wisstingham had discovered the

operation and was going to either can his estate manager, hand him over to the police or give him a roasting. It all now depended on whether this Felix chap could be bought off or scared off. If he could be bought, all well and good. They would cut him in and keep a close eye on him. If not, they would have to threaten him with being done in, unless he gave them sufficient time to close the operation down and get out. Under those circumstances, he might even be prepared to say nothing more about it, then act the innocent if the Bill ever caught on. As long as the guy did not tell his father in the meantime…

Harry dearly wished he could be at the meeting with this Felix guy. No matter. The estate manager would be well primed.

'It all depends how greedy the little bastard is and if he's got any balls,' Harry murmured to himself. He lit a cigar then sat back in his chair and watched the blue smoke curl up into the air.

He smiled as his thoughts returned to Smudger's call. Yes, things were going to be all right between them, he reckoned.

***

Felix leant well back in his father's leather chair with his feet on the edge of the desk. His unblinking eyes switched back and forth from the paper clip he was reshaping, to Vincent, who stood silently waiting for a response. As the new boss considered the estate manager's proposition, his eyes finally came to rest on the postcard from Hong Kong that lay on the floor, next to the wastepaper basket.

The monthly amount that Vincent had been authorised to offer had proved too much for Felix to turn down. The criminality and the danger of the enterprise – dealing in stolen antiques and jewellery – would normally have had Felix running a mile, but it had been going on unnoticed for four years, right under both his father's nose and his own, until he had decided to take a good look round the estate and discovered the barn's contents.

Vincent said that he was low down in the chain of command, but he was the one taking all the risks. All Felix would be doing was renting Vincent the old barn for whatever he was using it for.

Felix thought about the money: a regular income, cash in hand, some of which he could plough into the estate and keep the finances healthy, to keep his father off his back, and enough for himself. He glanced at the postcard again. At last, he would be able to hold his head up in Hopestanding. Anyway, the old man never took an interest in the barn or anything near it. The old quarry road was never used now, and it was far enough away from the Hall, obscured by the woods.

Felix glanced again at the postcard and the paper clip, then looked up at Vincent who was watching him through anxious eyes.

'I'm not opposed to taking a risk,' Felix said. 'It's all a question of how much it's worth to take it. If you see what I mean.'

Vincent told his young boss how much more he would receive if he was totally involved. Felix pondered briefly and was swayed by his greed. Hell, why shouldn't he be fully involved? There would be a bigger slice of the action. And there was a way in which Felix thought he could really enhance the operation to bring in more money. He even wondered whether he should charge Vincent from the date when he had taken over from his father, although that might be pushing his luck a bit.

The question was, could he trust the man? He studied him. The chap had always been straight with him and they seemed to get on all right. The proposition was just too good to turn down. He smiled at the estate manager, rose, and tossed the paper clip in the general direction of the bin.

'It sounds good to me, partner,' Felix announced with a grin, extending his hand. 'I'm in all the way. What's more, I reckon I know how we could improve things. We could discuss that, eh?'

Vincent smiled and nodded and they shook hands. As the estate manager reached the doorway, Felix called to him,

'Better get a new lock to replace the one I broke, Vincent. And pretty quick, eh?'

***

With a self-satisfied smile, Jez Fellowes checked his hair in the rear-view mirror, adjusted his tie and tugged down his waistcoat. He emerged lithely from the Porsche Boxster and tugged at the waistcoat again. Twirling the keys round his fingers, he crossed the car park towards his office, with a couple of pauses for a backward glance at his new acquisition.

Fellowes House, originally built as Hopestanding's only brewery, boasted four floors which surrounded a cobbled courtyard that had been used originally for loading, storage and cooperage. A corridor ran along the court- yard's internal perimeter on each floor, giving access to the building's numerous rooms. Each corridor, with an open aspect onto the courtyard below, was accessed by stairwells at the four corners.

Jez wiggled his fingers at the receptionists and entered the shiny steel lift. He reflected on how far he had come since he had first started at his father's small and grimy sheet-metal works in Dublin. He recalled school holidays spent working there for his thrifty parent amid the odious dirt and acrid smells of steel and welding.

Hopestanding Electronics had been in a state of near collapse when Jez, newly graduated and emboldened by a hefty parental loan, had bought the company. Since then, following substantial refurbishment, a cash injection and some fatherly advice, together with an overhaul of the company, business had really taken off. Most of the offices were now let, and his own IT, electronics and security company subsidiaries were flourishing.

Jez had just logged on to the system when his mobile rang.

'Hi Jez, it's me.'

'Felix, how are you doing, dude? I've not seen you for weeks.'

'Been busy. I'll fill you in later. Right now, I have a proposition for you.'

'If there's a profit in it, fire away.'

'Of course there is, I wouldn't waste my time ringing you otherwise.'

Jez smiled at the banter, sat back and listened while he inspected his impeccably manicured fingernails.

'I've got involved in something that needs some sharp Internet development,' Felix explained.

'Then I'm your man. When do you want to meet?'

'How about the Phantom, say five o'clock tomorrow?'

Jez tapped his keyboard and peered at the screen.

'Yeah, that's fine. I'll see you then.' After he had rung off, Jez grinned and rubbed the tips of his thumb and two forefingers together. 'Money, money, come to Jezzy,' he muttered.

SEPTEMBER 2008

Once outside the cottage, Vincent paused at the kitchen window and glared in at Mary, who was sitting at the table in floods of tears. At her side, with a comforting arm around her shoulders, stood Sebastian, who cast an icy stare back at his father. Vincent sneered, stooped to attach Pilsbury's lead and strode angrily away.

He tugged his cap forward and headed through the dreary September drizzle towards the folly, yanking the lead impatiently whenever the Labrador dallied. Beyond the lake garden he continued past the boathouse, where the waves lapped on the edge of the shingle, which crunched underfoot.

At the quarry road, he slowed his pace and turned back towards the Hall. Here, Pilsbury was allowed to dally and inspect the shrubs and trees that dotted the rise. Before the climb to the top, Vincent unleashed the dog and left him to nose around the grassy knoll.

Vincent mounted the folly's spiral staircase. It smelt dank, and the stone walls were cold to the touch. At the top he sat on the wooden seat, sheltered below a circular canopy, and looked out over the bleak landscape, misty with rain. He filled and lit his pipe, took several deep draws and sat back. A shadow of a smile emerged as his melancholy abated temporarily.

He pulled out a hip flask from his jacket pocket, took a swig, then stood to survey his empire of the moment. As always, his gaze came to rest on the Hall. His bitterness at Lucian's desertion and how it had affected him resurfaced. Vincent was now profitably involved in the stolen antiques operation – doing very nicely it was too, with its regular, clandestine deliveries to and from the barn on the disused quarry road. And Jez's technical involvement had proved a bonus. However, he and Lucian had known each other since boyhood, and their destinies had been bound together ever since *that day*.

As if the desertion were not bad enough, Vincent had also come to realise that Smudger's hold over him ever since *that day* was something he could not fight against, try as he might. Smudger's will was by far stronger than his own and would always prevail.

Lucian had promised his support and a share in the estate, which would have left Vincent well provided for. With Lucian gone, that pledge was now nothing more substantial than the smoke that curled upwards from Vincent's pipe. Lucian had no interest whatsoever in the stables and had assured him that the Commander would be persuaded to let him take over their management and retain any profits they generated. This promise had also long since curled heavenwards.

Vincent's initial uncertainty as to whether or not Sebastian was his son had grown with the child. Starting as a tiny seed, it had germinated in the barren soil of his and Mary's deteriorating relationship and their repeated failure to have a child through those early years. Now, the burgeoning plant's tendrils were strangling his very heart and soul. Vincent's whole being was being gradually, increasingly, invaded by its roots, ripening the bitter fruits of uncertainty, suspicion and hatred. As was his every thought.

There were moments of lucidity, when he could hack and tear away at the vegetation and glimpse the soul of the man he had once been. The man who had loved, courted and laughed with the slender beauty whose soft lips and brown eyes had once smiled on him as she drew his pints at the village inn. In those moments, Vincent would smile and remember how he had gazed in admiration at the sheen of her long black hair, and grin when he had succeeded in bringing a flush of embarrassment to her already rosy cheeks with one proposition or another.

But those glimpses faded quickly, as had their happiness, when the doubts and suspicions of Mary's true feelings had started to creep in. Then the darkness would descend once more and the plant's stealthy growth would tighten round his withering heart and mind.

His suspicion that the Commander had had an affair with Mary was in no way diminished by the apparent love and affection Fitzgerald showed to his own wife. On the contrary, Vincent firmly believed that a casual affair with the wife of one of the members of staff was just the sort of thing Fitzgerald's kind would pursue. They had the power and money to get away with it and Vincent loathed them for it.

The sound of a car horn from somewhere near the quarry drew his attention. He scanned the area and made out the edge of a car through the trees. He hurried towards the shrubbery and reached the clearing and the car. Its windows were opaque with condensation. He memorised the registration and stealthily approached the driver's door, grabbed the handle and jerked it open.

Inside, precariously astride a half-naked man was an even more naked girl, who screamed as she scrambled to disengage herself and recover her clothing. The man swore and flailed like an upturned turtle, unable to do much more, being semi-prone and still covered by the panicking girl, who frantically threw open her door and struggled to clamber out.

'I won't ask what you're doing. That'd be too obvious,' Vincent sneered. 'What I will ask is this: what makes you think it's all right to do it here on estate property?' He frowned as he struggled to recall the girl's familiar face. Now slightly more decent, she sat sideways in the passenger seat, her head lowered as she hastily fumbled to put on her remaining clothing.

'Here, you're Jeremy Sand's lass,' Vincent exclaimed.

'Oh, God! Please, please don't tell my parents,' she pleaded. 'Dad'll kill me if he finds out.'

'He'll probably kill you too,' Vincent remarked to the red-faced man, who had now pulled up his trousers and buttoned his shirt. 'What's your name?' Vincent demanded. He was quite enjoying this. 'And don't give me a false one. I've got your registration number.'

The man stared at him, his expression a mixture of anger, guilt and defiance.

'Clifford Caines,' he muttered, resigned to not making any attempt to brazen things out.

'I need your address and phone number,' Vincent demanded.

'On your bike!'

Vincent weighed up the situation. He had enough

information for what he needed.

'All right, just get off the estate and stay off,' he ordered, his stare as cold as an iceberg.

Caines slammed his door, started the car, revved the engine and drove his sobbing, damp and crumpled passenger away.

With narrowed eyes, Vincent watched the car disappear.

'This is a turn-up for the books,' he muttered as he took out his mobile and punched in a number.

Before a week had gone by, Smudger had ensured that the fate of Clifford Caines was well and truly sealed.

FEBRUARY 2009

Selwyn tucked the scarf closer round his neck as he trudged across the cobbled yard, his breath forming puffs of condensation on the biting air. The soft crunch of the snow compacted underfoot was the only sound in the courtyard as he plodded through the thick white carpet to the stables. From the stone tower came the sunlight's dazzling reflection off the deep pillows of snow mounded on the ledges, and the normally green copper cupola was now also a brilliant white under its blanket. In the stables, clouds of steam from the breath of the patient horse nearly obscured Vincent's head as he groomed its mane.

'Good morning, Vincent,' Selwyn called. He pushed open the stall door and turned down the radio that hung in its case from a nail.

'Good morning, Commander,' came Vincent's breezy reply as he looked up, smiled then continued to brush.

'How's Mrs Fitzgerald today?'

'Pretty much the same, I'm afraid, though she's glad to be home. It's been a long haul and I'm not sure how much good the convalescence has done her.'

Vincent stopped and studied the Commander.

'I'm sorry to hear that,' he replied, then resumed his work.

Selwyn leant against the door frame and watched the methodical grooming. He felt a strange relief at being almost inconspicuous. Georgina's illness, and the complications that had arisen from it, had steadily drained him of his resolve to soldier on and maintain an appearance that everything was business as usual for the sake of the staff. His loneliness, born of the practicality of his and Georgina's nightly isolation from each other, sometimes crowded in on him until he felt he would smother under it. Every morning he had to brace himself to appear the solid, dependable, unflappable husband and leader, no matter how scared he was of losing his beloved wife.

To add to his burdens, the year had been a lean one for the estate. Only half the stables were occupied, with little prospect of new enquiries for accommodation. One or two good wins were badly needed to turn things round.

'I'm beginning to think we're on a hiding to nothing,' he commented, eventually.

'Don't give up, Commander. Wisstingham Biscuit is coming along nicely. I reckon next year could be our year.'

'You say that every year, but we always end up with a loss,' Selwyn countered, gloomily. 'At this rate, I won't be able to hold out much longer against opening the Hall to the public. Had the blasted council on about it again this morning. I'm damned if I'll do it,' he continued, now on a roll. 'Dash it all, a fellow's home is his home. Don't want a lot of strangers and weirdos trampling all over the place and me having to keep doors locked and hurdle over rope barriers everywhere I go.'

At this unexpected outburst, Vincent turned his head to hide a wry smile.

Still incensed by the topic he had raised, Selwyn decided to change tack.

'How's Mary?' he enquired.

'All right,' Vincent replied guardedly, shooting him a quick sideways glance.

'And Sebastian?'

'OK, I suppose.'

'What's he going to do next year? College?'

'There's no way we'll afford that.'

'So what, then?'

Vincent shrugged and patted the mare.

'He'll just have to get a job somewhere, if someone'll have him.'

'What's he interested in?'

'No idea,' Vincent shrugged. 'Mary would know better. He likes computers, but I suppose all youngsters do.'

They fell silent. Selwyn groaned inwardly at Vincent's reticence and apparent lack of interest in the boy. He watched pensively as the unconcerned estate manager carried on brushing.

'What if I offered to fund him through college?' he ventured.

Vincent stopped and turned to stare across at the Commander, his expression clouded in suspicion.

'Why would you do that?'

Thrown by the reply, Selwyn shifted uncomfortably. He felt obliged to return the cold stare, aggrieved that his offer had not been better received.

'He's a bright lad with a good head on his shoulders and he's part of the estate family. I'd like to see him do well.'

'That's not something you do for the other employees,' Vincent argued.

'No, but you're a highly valued member of the team and I believe Sebastian would benefit from it.'

Vincent remained motionless, still staring at Selwyn.

'There's no strings attached,' the Commander added, fighting to suppress his exasperation. 'In fact, if he were so minded, he could reciprocate with some occasional assistance with the admin work at the Hall.'

At the mention of this, Vincent paused in thought. His demeanour changed. He looked Selwyn in the eye, for a moment and then gave way to a smile.

'Well, thank you, that's very kind of you, Commander,' he replied. 'Mary will certainly appreciate that.'

APRIL 2009

On the lawns at Wisstingham Hall, swathes of daffodils and narcissi had replaced the earlier kaleidoscope of crocuses, which had gone over, heralding the end of winter. The branches of the trees were in bud and in the woods, dead leaves, which had lain throughout the winter, were obliterated by carpets of bluebells. Nature was astir while, at the Hall, activity of a more electronic nature was afoot.

'Father, meet Jez Fellowes,' Felix greeted Selwyn as he popped his head round the doorway to the study, which was now Felix's office. The Commander hardly ever ventured there, contenting himself with a table in the library for those infrequent times he involved himself in estate business. They were a distraction from the time he spent caring for Georgina whose health, despite the best efforts of the hospital, continued to decline as a result of the complications that had set in through the virus.

Selwyn's puzzled frown vanished as a head of black hair, slicked back from a broad forehead, rose from behind the top of the desk. It was accompanied by a broad smile that revealed a set of very white teeth.

The men shook hands and Felix described Jez's ownership of 'Fellowes IT' and his installation of the Hall's new computer and software system.

'We're just down the road from the college,' Jez explained.

'Oh, that's where our estate manager's son has got a place for this year. He's doing IT and business studies. All a black art to me, this computer stuff,' Selwyn admitted. 'I can use a spreadsheet and Word, but that's about it. Nothing flashy whatsoever.'

Jez smiled politely.

'It's a good course,' he commented. 'Vincent's already earmarked one of our work placements for Sebastian.'

It was true. Vincent had been at pains to convince Felix and Jez that it would be wise to keep Sebastian close and under their observation in his computer activities.

'Oh, you know the Monaghans, then?' Selwyn exclaimed.

Felix frowned and shot Jez a warning glance, just as the Commander's attention was distracted by Mustard's arrival.

'Small world,' Selwyn remarked. He stooped to stroke the beagle. 'Well, I'd better take this little chap for a walk and let you get on,' he added.

Felix and Jez returned his smile in silence.

'As you were,' Selwyn added, feeling somewhat superfluous and awkward. He turned to go and the faithful hound padded off eagerly in front of him.

Chapter 4

The doorbell's deep ring echoed through the entrance hall and down the corridor to the kitchen, from where the flustered, head-shaking Mrs Soames bustled forth, dabbing her hands on her apron.

'I'm coming, I'm coming, 'old yer 'orses,' she muttered, shuffling along the dimly lit passageway. 'As if a body's got nothing better to do than taking on as a doorman.'

She threw back the iron bolts, turned the large key, and cautiously pulled the heavy oak door slightly ajar. Outside stood a corpulent white-haired man clutching a battered briefcase. Small round eyes blinked at Mrs Soames through wire-rimmed glasses. His toothy smile faded on seeing her scowl.

'Good morning,' he said. 'I'm Alexander Penn. I rang Commander Fitzgerald this morning and he suggested I should call round.'

As there seemed to be no prospect of the door opening wider, he pressed on.

'The Commander did ask me to come over right away.'

Mrs Soames peered at him suspiciously as she weighed him up before she slowly opened the door.

'You'd better come in, then,' she said, with more than a hint of reluctance. 'Mind you wipe your feet.'

After so doing, Penn trailed dutifully behind her as she led him slowly past faded tapestries, portraits and polished dark wooden doors, the sight of which restored his smile.

With a gentle knock on the drawing room door, Mrs Soames pushed it open and stood in the doorway, her backward frown signalling that Penn should approach no further.

'Commander, there's a gentleman,' she halted momentarily to consider this characterisation, 'a Mr Benn—'

'Penn,' Alexander corrected her from behind, which attracted another reproachful, glance.

'Mr Penn,' she continued. ''E says as 'ow you asked 'im to come and see you.'

'Ah yes, thank you, Mrs Soames. Please show him in,' came a cheerier voice from within.

Mrs S, of ample proportions herself, stood well aside to admit the rotund visitor then, refreshments ordered, she set off back to the kitchen.

'Folks as what are expecting of a clean and tidy establishment and a good meal tonight, using a body as a doorman and a footman. My Mrs F would be 'avin' none of that, if she weren't all laid up,' she enlightened the corridor, with a roll of her eyes for good measure.

Once introduced, Selwyn led the historian to the chesterfield, onto which Penn collapsed. He looked appreciatively round the room then at the Commander, seated opposite.

'Thank you for coming,' Selwyn said, eagerness twinkling in his eyes. 'You mentioned something about a map?'

'Yes,' Penn replied and fumbled to unbuckle his briefcase, then reached inside it. From its dark interior he produced a folded map and cast around for somewhere to spread it out. 'I recently found this in the course of my research,' he continued, as Selwyn led him to a plan table. 'Well, actually, it was my nephew who found it. It dates back to before the Civil War and covers a large part of your estate. I thought you might be interested to see it.'

'Yes, indeed,' Selwyn readily agreed, then eagerly scanned the map, which they proceeded to pore over together for several minutes.

Penn pointed out the Hall and some of the original buildings that had subsequently been built over, which surrounded the familiar outline of the courtyard.

'It doesn't cover the land that is leased to the council, but it does reach close to the boundary,' he explained. His shirt buttons strained as he stretched over the table to prod something with a stubby forefinger. 'This is one feature that might be of interest, though.'

The Commander stared intently at the outline that had been pointed out and started to stroke his mouth and jaw slowly, deep in thought.

'I can't think of anything that exists there,' he observed. 'What do you reckon it might be?'

'It looks too small to be a building, but it might possibly be a well or some sort of pit.'

Selwyn's tongue started off on a dental excursion, his mind now in top gear as he contemplated the possibility of the lost family treasure lying buried there.

'If you were interested in pinpointing the location, I could arrange to get the map copied for you,' Penn offered. 'It wouldn't cost a lot.'

'I'd greatly appreciate that.'

'You would keep me in the loop, though, regarding anything interesting you find?' the historian pleaded.

'Of course, my dear chap. Of course I will,' Selwyn reassured him.

***

The kitchen had been a hive of activity since Georgina had first mooted the idea of a picnic, much to Selwyn's surprise and delight. Although it had been a last-minute decision dictated by whim and weather, Mrs Soames had nevertheless risen splendidly to the occasion. Finally, her plump red hand rested on the open lid of the wicker hamper that dominated her kitchen table as she anxiously studied its contents.

'This has got me in a real tiswas and no mistake,' she muttered to herself as she rummaged through the basket and took a second roll call of the various pots and neatly wrapped, carefully labelled packages.

'Mrs Soames, it's just a picnic, not an expedition up the Andes,' Selwyn reassured her, after an examination of the fare from over her shoulder. 'You've catered for us admirably.'

An exhaustive rundown of the hamper's contents duly delivered, the housekeeper lowered the lid and fastened the hasps, her brow still furrowed about what she might have missed.

'If you'd be so kind as to oblige with the cool box, Commander, I'll take the hamper out to the car,' she said.

'No need for that, Mrs S,' Selwyn replied. 'Sebastian will give a hand.'

Like a genie, Sebastian appeared and made light work of hoisting the hamper onto his shoulder, to the housekeeper's great consternation. He was cautioned severely to take great care in its transport. He nodded and picked up the cool box with his free arm. With a teasing, tottering gait and a wink at Selwyn, he headed to the entrance hall, followed by the uneasy Mrs Soames, who mentally promised him a whack of her tea towel once the hamper had been safely loaded.

Minutes later, with Georgina settled comfortably in the Jaguar, Selwyn took the wheel and drove slowly to the lake garden. Their send-off by the waving housekeeper and cheering Sebastian added a touch of grandeur to the occasion.

The rug spread and the folding chairs erected, Selwyn led his wife gently from the car to the picnic area. Their arms were clasped round each other's backs, more for the frail Georgina's support than the impression of romance they would have presented to an onlooker.

'I hope you've no dishonourable intentions in offering a fair damsel strong drink on this picnic, good sir,' Georgina warned with a coy smile and tired but twinkling eyes, when Selwyn lifted the champagne from the cool box. 'I'm no pushover.'

'No, I don't believe you are,' he murmured, as he gazed lovingly at her pallid but happy face.

Georgina looked about her and slowly, indulgently, took in the surroundings: the fuchsias, heavily laden with lantern flowers of reds, purples and pinks, blooms bursting on the dwarf rose bushes, and the sun glinting brightly off the folly's weathervane, set above the green copper dome, which appeared to be almost illuminated.

She turned her head skyward, closed her eyes and inhaled deeply to capture the garden's fragrances. Then she watched Selwyn and his strained expression as he wrestled with the champagne cork. That brought a chuckle as she remembered similar varsity occasions at Oxford. Treasured memories of idyllic summer days spent punting on the Cherwell floated into her mind.

They chinked glasses and, as they sipped the wine, they drank in each other. Then it was Georgina's turn to take charge as she systematically unwrapped packages and placed their contents on plates.

'This really was a capital idea of yours, Georgie,' Selwyn remarked over a chilled Chablis as they watched a flight of geese land on the lake, the sunshine reflected in the ripples that fanned out across its surface.

'Yes, I'm so glad we did it,' she agreed. 'I just wanted to be with you, away from the Hall and everybody. Our little escape.'

They sat in a contented silence and worked their way through Mrs Soames' numerous delicious offerings.

'I'm concerned about you, Bumble,' Georgina eventually observed.

'There's nothing to be concerned about.'

'Yes, there is. Something's not right, I can tell. What is it?'

'Nothing, old girl,' Selwyn insisted, giving her slightly too broad a smile.

'I might not be well, but I've not lost my marbles,' she cautioned. 'Don't you come all stiff upper lip with me, Bumble.' Her eyes widened, ominously.

He did not want to spoil the moment, but he knew her tenacity.

'Is this why you suggested the picnic? To ambush me?' he asked.

'Not at all,' she reassured him, though her sheepish expression suggested otherwise. 'Well, not totally. So, out with it!'

'Well, Georgie, if you must know, things don't seem to be quite tickety-boo with the estate. Despite what he says, I get the impression that Felix is leaving undone those things that ought to be done, and doing those things which ought not to be done, to quote my old house prayer. Nothing for you to worry about. It'll all get sorted,' he hastened to assure her.

'Are we solvent?'

'Oh yes – and that's the surprising thing, all things considered. I glanced through the accounts and found some income that I haven't got a clue about. I'll have to go into it in more detail.'

'Have you spoken with him?'

'No, not yet.'

'You must do. Have you spoken with Vincent?'

'Yes. He reckons everything's been going swimmingly. That's another thing. He seems changed, seems so ruddy morose most of the time.'

'I don't think things are all that good at the cottage.'

'I'm sure you're right. The fellow doesn't seem to have any interest in Sebastian, or even in Mary.'

'Can't you have a word?'

'Tried to broach it already, but the fellow doesn't want to know. It's awfully difficult.'

Georgina fell silent, her brow knitted.

'Selwyn, you're just going to have to take over running things again,' she announced after a while.

'It's not as easy as that. Felix has to get the experience and if I just bulldoze him out of the way, that's not going to do much for his morale, is it? You know what he's like. I'd never get him interested in being involved again.'

'Well, the place has to be run properly,' Georgina argued.

'That's got to be the priority.'

His head slightly to one side, Selwyn gazed silently at her for a few moments and smiled.

'You're my priority, Georgie,' he declared, fighting back a tear.

She sniffed then closed her eyes. When she reopened them, they glistened.

'Now don't you go all soppy on me, Bumble,' she admonished him.

'But you…'

'No buts, my little matelot. The place has got to be looked after. If Mrs Soames can't manage to look after me on her own, you'll have to get a carer in.'

Selwyn knew that look. Further protest would be futile. What's more, he knew what she was saying made sense.

'All right, my love, we'll do what you say and I'll have words with Felix. Just don't you worry about a thing. You're all that matters to me.'

Georgina pursed her lips in a smile then, distracted by the sound of the wind rustling through the trees, glanced in the direction of the folly. She turned back to Selwyn and gave him another smile, but it could not mask her weariness.

The calm of the day had been chased away by the wind. Their moment had gone. Selwyn sensed Georgina's desire to return to the warmth of the conservatory. He sprang into action and, within minutes, the laden car was back at the Hall.

SEPTEMBER 2009

The Commander frowned at the pile of rusted and redundant machinery.

'It'll all have to be shifted, Vincent,' he instructed. 'I can't think why Lucian wanted it put there in the first place. He'd have been better storing it in one of the old sheds. Hell, there's certainly enough space available.'

'That was the last thing he told me to do just before he disappeared,' Vincent stated. 'When do you want it gone by?'

'They're due on-site the middle of November, so you'd best get it cleared by the end of next month. Just get a scrap company in.'

Vincent nodded and watched as Selwyn re-examined the survey company's quote.

That he had been refused permission to extend the survey to the land the council leased from the estate was a source of intense frustration to Selwyn, who had no illusions about how protracted his negotiations with the council would be. For now, he would have to content himself with this small piece of the jigsaw, doubtful though he was that anything would come of it.

***

For nearly as long as the Fitzgeralds had occupied Wisstingham Hall, the neighbouring Beckworth Farm had been handed down through generations of the Middleton family. Hector Middleton, the farm's current occupant, had so far shown no sign that he would continue the family tradition, having remained a bachelor throughout his thirty-seven years. From his lifestyle, he appeared destined to remain so.

The farm lay to the north of the Wisstingham estate, contentiously bounded by land sandwiched between the two that was occupied by the estate but to which the

Middletons had laid claim for several generations. The inherited duty of each Middleton had been to seek the restoration of this land and to consider themselves at war with the Fitzgeralds until its ownership was restored. This state of affairs did not make for good neighbourly relations.

Economically, the farm would have foundered years earlier had it not been for Hector's development of its large and picturesque lake as a camping and fishing attraction. Over time, the lakeside tent sites had been transformed into timber chalets, available for hire. As a schoolboy, Sebastian had secured a summer holiday job at the centre. Because of his abilities and his keenness to work, he had developed such a good relationship with Hector that, when the farmer finally discovered just who Sebastian was and where he lived, he still kept the boy on. Though he was not handsomely paid, Sebastian's greater reward was being allowed to fish the lake free of charge during the quieter periods. He therefore spent as many evenings there as he could, and Hector sometimes joined him.

One balmy September evening, Sebastian arrived and unloaded his fishing tackle. As he was about to set off for his usual spot, a buzz of conversation and laughter proved too much for his curiosity. When he rounded the corner of the house he found a barbecue in full swing.

He was about to leave when Hector's call from the behind the barbecue halted him.

'Sebastian, excellent timing. Come and join us,' he shouted, his craggy face lit up by a broad grin, a beer bottle in one hand and a spatula in the other.

Those present turned in curiosity towards the new arrival. Sebastian looked hesitantly down at his fishing apparel and cast an embarrassed smile at the onlookers. After he had stowed his fishing gear by the wall, he headed towards Hector, acknowledging the nods and smiles of those who greeted him.

'I'm really not dressed for this,' he told Hector who, at first glance, was standing in bra and pants, with beads of sweat on his weathered forehead.

The farmer dismissed the comment with a wave of his hand and wiped his large muscular hand on the bra portion of his apron before he shook hands.

'It don't matter. It's good to see you. It's all a bit last-minute, anyway. A celebration of my cousin's new job at the library.' He leant forward. 'She's already badgering me to join,' he confided, in a lowered voice. 'She'll try to get me reading books next. Can you imagine it? Me and books!' He let out a belly laugh at the thought, wiped his nose with the back of his hand and turned to the smoking sausages. 'Go and get yourself a drink,' he said with a sniff. 'I'll introduce you to her later.'

Glass in hand, Sebastian began to circulate diffidently. Introductions were made to the other guests, who were mostly farming friends, suppliers and local shopkeepers. Eventually alone, he gazed out on the orchard beyond the garden. The bronzed apples glinted in the late afternoon sun.

'I don't think we've met,' came a soft, deep voice from behind him.

Sebastian turned. His mouth inadvertently gaped as he found himself staring into large, almond-shaped dark hazel eyes framed by shiny chestnut hair, which hung long and straight on each side of an oval face. He stared for a little longer than such a meeting would properly merit.

'Nice teeth,' the girl commented.

Sebastian's mouth closed, instantly.

'I'm sorry,' he muttered to the pink, smiling lips. 'I'm Sebastian Monaghan.'

'No need to apologise for that. I'm Amanda Sheppard,' she replied, her slender hand held up limply, awkwardly high for a handshake. She took in his boyish face with its thick lips, prominent cheeks, innocent eyes and, above them, the unruly shock of curly brown hair.

'So, Sebastian – or do I call you Seb? What do you do?' she asked.

'Sebastian's fine,' he replied. 'I've never really liked Seb. I always think it sounds medicinal. As for what I do, well, nothing much.' He wished he could boast he was a racing driver or pilot and was disconcerted by the eyes that seemed to bore into his. 'I've just graduated at Hope-standing College.'

'In?' continued his inquisitor.

'Business studies and computer technology,' he replied limply.

'Ah, the shoulder-bag-and-laptop brigade, eh? Do you live locally?'

'We live at the Hall. My father's the estate manager.'

Silence reigned as they sipped their drinks and stared at the orchard.

'What about you?' Sebastian eventually ventured.

'I live in the village with my grandmother. I've just started as librarian in Wisstingham.'

'Oh, you're Hector's cousin,' he exclaimed. She gave a

curtsey. Sebastian regarded her for a moment.

'Yes?' Amanda enquired.

'It's just that I'd have expected a librarian to look paler.'

She leant her head closer to his.

'I've taken my dust jacket off for the occasion,' she whispered confidentially and winked. He blinked, uncertainly.

'Hector talked about you earlier,' she continued. 'I think you must be either lucky or special.' She peered at him as if trying to determine which.

'How do you mean?'

'You seem to be the only person from the estate that he has any time for. Fortunately, I'm distant enough not to be involved in the dispute.'

'What dispute?'

'You've rather nice lips, did you know that?' the librarian observed, after what seemed a painfully long time, during which Sebastian became increasingly uncomfortable. He blushed and glanced down at his feet, the tips of his ears on fire. Before he could conjure up a reply, she placed her hand gently on his arm.

'I'm sorry, I didn't mean to embarrass you. It's a fault of mine – doubtless not the only one,' she muttered as an aside. 'I just come out and say what I'm thinking before weighing up what I should say, if anything at all.'

'That's quite all right, and thanks for the compliment.'

'Don't mention it,' came the casual reply. 'You were asking about the dispute. Well, it goes back yonks over land that really belonged to our family, but through time and use was taken over by the Fitzgeralds. There's been enmity over it ever since. I think the dispute's become more important than the land itself. If Hector ever managed to get hold of it, he'd probably go grey wondering what to do with it.'

'Are you quite close to him?' Sebastian asked.

She looked towards the barbecue.

'Oh, about twenty metres, I'd guess.' Straight-faced, she turned to eye him.

'No, I meant—' Sebastian broke off. He caught the merest hint of a smile. Now it was his turn to stare and size her up. Unlike him, she showed no sign of discomfiture and gazed back before wrinkling her nose at him. 'You're quite a character aren't you?' he observed.

'It has been said,' Amanda replied. 'And the answer's yes, I suppose we are quite close. Hector's always looked out for me like an older brother. Always keeps an eye on me and makes sure he knows where I am.'

There was a shout from the barbecue of,

'Food's ready, come and get it,' at which the guests shuffled forward and further conversation between them ceased, until Sebastian's later departure.

'It was lovely to meet you,' he told her as he shouldered his fishing basket. 'I hope I'll see you again.'

'You will if you visit the library,' she replied with a smile. 'If you're not a member, you should join. There's no charge and you get a choice of picture on your membership card. The elephant's quite sweet.'

'I knew it. The barbecue's turned into a recruiting campaign,' Hector's jovial voice broke in from behind her. Sebastian said his goodbyes. With a toothy grin, the farmer waved a beer bottle in farewell while Amanda stood alongside him and smiled thoughtfully as she watched the departing angler.

'Are you thinking what I'm thinking, John?' the newly promoted Detective Inspector Stone murmured to his colleague as they watched the bones and the remnants of clothing being carefully lifted from the pit.

'The poacher?' Detective Sergeant McBride replied, his gaze fixed on the activity around the body. He just longed to say, 'I told you so.'

'Hmm,' Stone murmured. His memory homed in unhappily on the occasion many years ago when he had refused McBride's suggested search of the estate for the missing man, a refusal that seemed to have boomeranged back on him.

Further off, beyond the taped cordon, the Commander and Vincent stood and watched in subdued silence.

'That old scrap must have been there for about twenty years,' Selwyn commented. 'Had you any idea the pit was there when it was dumped, Vincent?'

Vincent shook his head.

'Not a clue,' he replied.

Selwyn stared thoughtfully in silence for a few moments.

'So it must have been a coincidence that Lucian asked you to move the stuff there,' he said at last.

'I expect so,' said Vincent.

With a sideways glance at his sergeant, Stone moved off to join the pathologist who was kneeling to examine the remains.

'Year of death?' the DI asked.

The pathologist let out a snort.

'You are joking,' he replied. 'Well, it certainly wasn't last year. I'd hazard a guess at more than ten years but don't hold me to that.'

'And cause of death?'

'You know that'll have to wait. But, as a guess, I'd say it was this blunt-force trauma to the skull.' He pointed to a large fracture.

'Could it have been from falling in there?' Stone asked, pointing to the opening to the pit.

'I wouldn't think so. There must have been some real force behind it. However—'

'Yes, I know, it'll have to wait for the autopsy,' came Stone's tired interruption. 'Make sure that we get photos of the inside of the pit, then get it sealed off.

'We'll need to get the team in again first thing tomorrow,' he instructed McBride, who had just joined them. 'For my money, I reckon we're looking at murder here,' he added and gave McBride a knowing glance. 'Now for His Lordship,' Stone muttered under his breath, as he headed off in the direction of the two spectators.

Chapter 5

The tranquil darkness of Bishop's Wind was suddenly pierced by a shaft of light as the door to one of the mews cottages was flung open. From inside, the sound of a party in full swing blared forth into the night. A man teetered unsteadily on the doorstep before lurching out onto the path. His arm reached out in vain for support from a tree, but having severely misjudged its distance, the drunk fell sideways with a muffled cry, rolled onto his back and lay gazing upwards at the night sky.

He hiccupped then giggled.

'Thersh no stars tonight, not a one,' he observed, as his head oscillated in search of them.

'Hardly surprising, as it's started to rain, you idiot,' his companion commented, then bent to help him up. 'Come on, Jez, up you get.' Once his friend was unsteadily back on his feet, Felix pinioned his shoulders and manoeuvred him into the street as the door slammed shut and the mews was plunged back into darkness.

'I'll take you home,' Felix sighed.

'Again Kathleen,' Jez sang and sniggered. 'Anyway, you can't.'

'I can and I will.'

'Can't, I've lost my keys.'

'Oh shit! Where've you lost them? Are they back in there?'

'Nope! Must have left them in the apartment, hee hee,' Jez replied.

Felix groaned, and the guided walk halted as he considered what to do. He had a key to Jez's place but it was back at home.

'You'll have to stay at the Hall tonight, then I'll take you home tomorrow morning.'

'You're a real pal,' said Jez. 'To be sure, to be sure.'

'Yeah, yeah, you eejit,' Felix muttered, and bundled him into the rear of his estate car.

'Felix, you're not fit to drive,' Jez warned, from the darkness of the rear seat. 'Better let me take over.'

'No bloody way!' Felix snorted, and started the car.

They left Hopestanding behind. By the time they reached the Wisstingham road, the rain was torrential, bouncing off the tarmac. In the car all was quiet.

Minutes later there was a chuckle from the back.

'I thought you were asleep,' said Felix.

'Nope, but I've found my keys,' Jez mumbled.

'You idiot! We're too far along now. I'll carry on.'

The storm intensified. Felix wiped away the condensation, peered through the windscreen and cursed himself for not having replaced the wiper blades. From ahead, the full-beam headlights of an approaching car dazzled him.

At that instant, Jez loomed up, clasped both hands over Felix's eyes and shouted,

'Guess where we are!' As he grappled wildly with the hands, Felix shook his head.

'Get off, you fucking idiot!' he yelled.

The sound of the other car's horn added to his confusion and panic. He lurched his head to one side to free himself from the hands, swung the steering wheel and narrowly missed the oncoming car, which sped away, its horn still blaring.

He struggled to regain control of the car and jammed on the brakes. Jez, who had thrown himself against the back seat, was now flung forward and his head collided with the back of Felix's. The brakes screeched and the car skidded wildly out of control. With a squeal of tyres, it careered off the road and hurtled down a shallow verge. There was the sickening sound of crumpling metal and shattering glass, accompanied by a scream of pain. Then all was quiet, except for the drumming of the rain on the roof.

After several moments, the rear passenger door creaked open and Jez tumbled out onto the ground, gasping for breath. He rolled onto all fours, struggled to his feet and staggered to the edge of the road. After looking round in vain for help, he stumbled back to the wreckage and halted, afraid to look. Then he clasped his head in his hands.

'Oh Jesus! Oh Jesus!' he repeated, as he edged to the front of the car. Agonised, he peered through the gaping hole where the windscreen had been. A branch lay across the bonnet, protruding inside the car.

Jez peered in then recoiled.

Felix's last moment of agony was fixed on his bloodied and motionless face. His eyes stared, unseeing, up into the branches of the tree that had killed him.

Jez crumpled to the ground and was sick. Ashen, but sobered by the horror of it all, he burst into tears, his face contorted in anguish. In his terror he looked wildly around him then, flinging his arms wide in despair, he tottered away.

***

In Hopestanding, tired and on his way home, Vincent drove through the virtually empty streets. The storm had subsided into light rain and the Wisstingham road was deserted, except for a solitary figure that plodded its way in the opposite direction, a jacket held over its head.

Poor bastard, Monaghan thought. *Rather him than me.*

A few minutes later he stopped as he spotted the rear of an estate car, lying on an incline off the road.

'Christ! It's Felix's!' Vincent gasped, having recognised the registration.

By the dim light of a nearby street lamp, he could make out the front of the car, which was crushed into the trunk of a large tree. He went cold as he hesitantly approached the car and jerked his head away quickly at the sight that met his eyes. His pulse raced as, with shaking hands, he shone the light from his mobile through the open rear door. There was nothing there, other than a wallet that lay on the seat. Inside it Vincent found Jez Fellowes' driving licence and a small polythene packet containing some white powder.

He glanced around, pocketed them both and returned to the Land Rover. He sat for several minutes, his eyes glued to the wreckage, deep in thought and his mouth set firm. Finally, he returned to the vehicle, closed the rear door and tapped in 999 on his mobile.

***

'Give the Commander a hand. Jump to it, lad,' Vincent

prompted his son as he brushed away a crumb from his black tie.

Sebastian stepped forward and took Mrs Fitzgerald's arm as she hesitantly lifted her foot onto the first tread of the staircase. He was about to speak but Selwyn gave him a slight shake of his head, so they mounted the stairs in silence. Once his wife was safely in her bedroom, Selwyn called back his helper, who had paused at the top of stairs to study the generations of Fitzgeralds set in their frames on the lofty walls.

'Quite an awe-inspiring family line-up,' the Commander commented drily, as they regarded them. 'Rather a hard act to follow – and feeling much more so now.'

'I can imagine,' replied Sebastian as his eyes switched from one portrait to another, before he turned to face the Commander. 'I'm so sorry about Felix,' he offered, 'it must be so hard—'

'It is, my boy. It really is,' Selwyn interrupted him, his voice faltering. He gazed at Sebastian for a moment, a look of desperate, silent appeal on his face. Then he inhaled deeply, squared his shoulders and pulled himself together. 'But life has to go on and there's others to think of and do things for,' he continued, his voice now steady. 'That's the nature of it all. Thank you for helping Mrs Fitzgerald. It's all been too much for her, I'm afraid.'

'I'm glad to help. If there's ever anything I can do, you only have to ask,' Sebastian replied.

'Funny you should say that,' said Selwyn. 'How are things going?' he added, glad to steer the conversation in a new direction. 'You're full time now with Fellowes Industries, I hear.'

'Yeah, it's OK, though the pay's not great. I'm hoping it'll improve after my probation period.'

'So can you manage, financially, if that's not too rude a question?'

'Yeah, I'm OK. There's also what I get from my part-time job at the Mazawat cafe.'

'Quite a busy fellow. Looks like that puts paid to what I was going to ask you.'

'Which was?'

'Well, with Felix gone and everything else I'm tied up with at the moment, I was hopeful that you might take a look on his computer and let me know where he was up to.'

'Sure – but would next week be all right? I'm likely to be away on a job.'

'That'll be fine. In fact,' Selwyn continued, with a gesture that they should go downstairs, 'if you could spare the time, I'd really appreciate your continued involvement here. I'd pay you, of course.'

Selwyn paused on the stairs and Sebastian, who had gone down a couple of steps, also stopped and turned to look up at him, his delight with the proposition evident from his smile.

'I'd feel cheeky about being paid after all you've done for me, but I'll certainly do it.'

'It doesn't say much for a business course that encourages its students to say they'll work for nothing,' Selwyn commented with a wry smile.

'I must have been off sick when they covered that.' Sebastian grinned. 'If that's the case, I already had half a mind to give up the cafe anyway.'

'Then let's speak later in the week.'

Selwyn caught sight of Mary, who stood alone near the

doorway. Her husband was some distance away in deep conversation with Mac Bilton. Mrs Soames bustled in and out of the room to keep the buffet trays replenished and in good order, as well as maintaining a sharp eye on the cutlery.

'I must speak with your mother,' said the Commander, giving Sebastian a parting pat on the shoulder.

Vincent, who had been watching Sebastian and the Commander, finished his conversation and threaded his way through the mourners to join his son.

'There's no sign of Jez,' Sebastian commented, after he had scanned the room.

'No, I'm surprised he's not here. What was the Commander talking to you about?'

'He asked if I'd look at Felix's computer. I said I'd do it when I get back. And he wants me to help out in the office.' Sebastian's enthusiasm was barely containable.

Vincent fastened his gaze on the Commander, who was now deep in conversation with Mary.

'I reckon it's a good idea for you to keep involved, boy,' he replied. Then he wandered off to make a call on his mobile.

The afternoon wore on and the guests drifted away until eventually only Mrs Soames was left, ferrying back and forth from the kitchen. Selwyn, whose offer of help had been adamantly refused, sat in a fireside chair, nursing a glass of single malt and staring into the flames. He mused grimly that from being a naval commander, he was now the responsible officer for trying to row a lifeboat to safety with only one other ailing member aboard, the other lost to one of life's savage storms. As the images of earlier days with Georgina and Felix flooded his mind, he shifted his position in the chair lest Mrs Soames should see the tears that now coursed down his face or the heave of his chest as he sobbed quietly.

Eventually he rallied and his thoughts turned to the more recent past. The last two weeks had been hellish. On top of Felix's death, there had been the discovery of the poacher's body and the relentless questions from the police.

'Who, other than the person whose land he was on, would want to murder a poacher?' the DI had asked.

It seemed that Selwyn's reply, that he and his staff did not even know that the wretched man was working his land, had hit home with Stone. There was, however, the question of the convenience of the pit to hide the body and who might have known of its whereabouts. On this, they had reached a stalemate, Stone's contention being that the estate staff would be the most likely suspects. Selwyn's response was that a disgruntled poacher who frequented the estate might well have known of it, and not been amenable to his territory being invaded by someone else.

The line of questioning regarding Lucian and his whereabouts had rapidly arrived at a cul-de-sac once Selwyn had told the DI that his stepbrother had travelled abroad at about that time and was now dead. However, the manner of Lucian's departure was a can of worms that Selwyn had decided not to open, although it had left him with a nagging uncertainty about whether there had been more to Lucian's disappearance than he had understood at the time.

So, the murder case had been left open pending further

enquiries, the DI's final promise being that he would get to the bottom of it. The site, although it had been thoroughly investigated, remained cordoned off. Selwyn felt that was more out of the DI's spite than for any practical purposes.

***

The following evening, after he had dropped off some invoices in the study, Vincent was on his way back down the corridor when Selwyn called him from the drawing room doorway.

'Got a few moments, Vincent?'

'Certainly, Commander.'

'Then come and join me in a snifter.'

'It's a bugger how things work out in life,' Selwyn lamented, after they had been drinking in silence for several minutes. 'Lucian and Felix both gone, my parents gone, and Georgina fading away a little more every day.'

Vincent moved uncomfortably in his chair, lost for something meaningful to say.

'I've given a lot of thought to the situation over the last few days,' Selwyn continued. 'Since I took on this place, I've often wondered whether my father left me an estate or a millstone. Not that I'm ungrateful, you understand, but it's a big responsibility, keeping things going.'

'Perhaps the stables will have a better year,' Vincent suggested.

His remark was met with a sideways glance and a doubtful frown.

'Maybe they will. What I'm trying to say, Vincent, is that I have no living relatives to leave everything to other than Georgina, and I'll be damned if the state's going to be allowed to grab everything. So, on the assumption that Georgina doesn't survive me – a hateful thought but a realistic one, I'm afraid – I'm minded to leave the estate to your family if you want it.'

Vincent's eyes widened. He exhaled as if he had been punched in the stomach and stared at Selwyn, astounded at what he had just heard.

'You've put a lot of good work in here, Vincent, and made a real contribution,' his boss continued. 'I feel that you and your family deserve it more than anyone else I can think of. However, I should warn you that it's not as glamorous as it might seem. Also, I'd stipulate that the entire estate could not be disposed of within fifteen years or it would all automatically revert to the National Trust. I don't want you to say anything now. Go away, discuss it with Mary and have a really good think about it.'

'I will – and thank you, Commander,' muttered the still-winded estate manager as he rose to his feet.

'A couple of other things before you go,' Selwyn added.

'Yes?'

'Georgina doesn't need her car any more. It's not worth anything and only gathering dust, so we thought Sebastian might like to use it. It'd be better than that flatulent motorbike that he rides, when it's not spread about in bits on the garage floor. Tidiness isn't exactly his strongest suit, is it?'

Vincent shook his head.

'Anyway,' continued Selwyn, 'the insurance will cover him until it runs out and he can keep it garaged where it is. The keys and the documents are on the desk.'

'Thanks again, Commander. That'll make his day.'

Selwyn fixed his gaze.

'He's a good chap, Vincent.'

'Hmm,' came the lacklustre reply.

Selwyn waited for something more, but in vain.

'And the other thing?' Vincent prompted.

'Oh yes, there's a box of papers and files on the desk. They're all I could find of Felix's things. I've not looked through them, just bundled them together. I can't face them. Not now. Can you pass them to Sebastian to look through? Tell him to bin anything that's not important and bring back whatever he thinks I should see. He can file the rest. I know he won't be able to get on to it immediately.'

Vincent let out a deep sigh, at which Selwyn looked across at him.

'Are you OK?' he asked with a frown.

'Yes, I'm fine,' came the quick reply. 'I'm just so taken aback by your offer. I'll make sure Sebastian gets the papers.'

'Good – but don't burden him with them tonight.' Selwyn winked. 'Let him test drive the car instead.'

Vincent smiled his total agreement.

Alone once more, Selwyn wondered if he had done the right thing. He had really wanted to leave everything to Sebastian, but the lad would be unable to cope with it all for the foreseeable future. It would need Vincent's continued involvement in running the estate, to ensure success. Anyway, the will would be worded in such a way that Sebastian could not be disinherited from future ownership and, in the meantime, Selwyn was determined to teach him everything he could.

***

As he strode away from the Hall, Vincent could not believe his luck. Since Felix's death, he had wracked his brains about the various scenarios that were likely to unfold when the Commander reassumed the management of the estate. Selwyn would look through Felix's things and unwittingly take the lid off the Pandora's box of their criminal activities, the stolen antiques racket in operation at the estate, right under his nose. For each scenario, Vincent had calculated his strategies and responses.

In the small office at the stables, the midnight oil burned into the early morning. The desk was strewn with photos, files, and papers as Vincent sifted through the contents of the box he had brought from the Hall.

In the early hours of the morning he locked some of them away in the desk drawer, where they would remain until they could be transferred to safer premises. He placed the remaining papers in the box, which he tucked under his arm, then set off into the darkness back to his cottage.

Jez would already have been busy on Felix's computer files from the safe distance of his offices. Something to do with a network, he had tried to explain to Vincent.

Wonderful thing, technology, Vincent thought, as he crept into the cottage.

JANUARY 2010

Selwyn gazed down at the back of the bald head that was just visible in the darkness of the pit. He had been uncomfortable with the arrangement, but there it was.

This was the first day when it had not been bitterly cold or pouring down and, although Vincent had had to go off to the race meeting, Selwyn was determined not to delay matters any further. The site had been released by the police and Selwyn badly needed something to take his mind off the horrors of the past two months.

So here he was with Fred Ferris, who had obligingly offered to assist. The man was digging away in the pit in search of whatever it was that the GPR survey had said was there, and what Selwyn's metal detector had positively screamed at that very morning, before Fred had started work.

Surely to goodness, the man must be down three or four feet by now, Selwyn thought, as shovelfuls of earth continued to arc their way from the pit onto the adjoining ground.

'Any sign yet?' Selwyn shouted, not for the first time, after he had tried in vain to curb his impatience.

The sound of digging stopped. Fred straightened, turned, and gave the Commander a smile that cast doubts on the wisdom of the question. Selwyn quickly held up his palms. Fred bent back to his task, and the Commander vented his frustration with a kick at a nearby clump of bracken.

If it had been a gunshot, the sound of metal on metal could not have jolted the Commander more. He hastened to the edge of the pit and peered down, just as Fred's beaming face emerged.

The next thirty minutes seemed to pass like so many hours as Selwyn paced, then stood at the edge of the pit, then continued to pace again, all the while at a loss to know what to do with hands that were as restive as his tongue.

Finally, a dirty metal trunk appeared over the edge of the pit and landed at an angle on top of the heaped fresh earth. Selwyn's brow immediately furrowed, not only at the trunk's appearance but also at the apparent ease with which it had been handled. There had certainly been no sound of any exertion on Fred's part, so whatever was in the trunk had little weight to it.

With a sinking heart Selwyn slowly, almost reluctantly, approached it. Fred clambered out and, with a quick glance at the Commander, who nodded his approval, bent to unfasten the lid. As it creaked open, Selwyn took a deep breath and peered in on the contents.

Chapter 6

Felicity Bevidge strained to hear over the hiss of the coffee machine frothing the milk.

'I said have you got anyone lined up for this weekend now Sebastian's left?' her cousin Gwen Chase shouted over the high counter.

'Not yet, but I'm seeing someone tomorrow.'

For four years the cousins had run the Mazawat cafe, an enterprise that had caused many sage and grey Wisstingham heads to shake when it first opened its doors. After a slow start with depressingly few customers, the tasty confectionery, the wide variety of quality coffees and the friendly staff – particularly Gwen – had established a regular clientele. Not least of the place's attractions was the opportunity to catch up on local gossip, to such an extent that the cafe had become as essential a part of the village's communications network as the post office, newsagents and general store.

'Man-mad,' one of the cafe's elderly customers would sourly and regularly mouth to her friends, after being served by the much younger of the two, the irrepressible Miss Chase.

Far from objecting to such accusations when they came to her attention, Gwen looked upon them as a badge of honour.

'Mind you,' she would say in her defence, with a defiant

toss of her blonde curls, 'I'm not easy. I'm not unfaithful or indiscreet, and I won't go for married men or idiots.'

Following this, she would flounce off with a grin and her tray. This creed rather restricted the amorous options available to her in the village so, when they came her way, she was never backward in coming forward. Furthermore, being generously endowed in the upper-body region, her 'coming forward' was the first thing that her unsuspecting prey became aware of.

The male who undoubtedly topped Gwen's desirability list – and had done so since she had first set eyes on him – was Sebastian Monaghan. During the years that he had worked part time at the cafe, she had employed every female wile in her arsenal to ensnare him, but to no avail. To Gwen's frustration, theirs remained a close and humorous friendship, despite the kisses and embraces she had secured on occasions such as Christmas and birthdays. A lesser woman would have conceded defeat by now but not the indefatigable Gwen, whose motto appeared to be 'Always bounce back', something she appeared to practise physically around the cafe, to the delight of its male customers.

***

'It's the mayor,' Gwen hissed to Felicity over the counter one Monday, as a smartly dressed woman entered and cast an appraising glance over the cafe and its customers.

Councillor Miriam Cheyney chose a table next to the large bay window, through which she watched a group of sombrely clothed people who had gathered on the pavement outside. Other than for occasional, muted exchanges, the assembly waited in silence, as more people slowly gathered on the opposite side of the road.

Presently, a tall well-built man, smartly dressed in a dark morning coat and black top hat, paced slowly along the centre of the road, his stride measured with an ebony staff. Behind him walked a pair of plumed black horses that drew a shiny black-lacquered carriage, at the front of which sat a black-liveried coachman. The glass sides of the carriage were ornately framed in an etched scroll pattern. Within lay an oak coffin topped by a large oval wreath of white flowers. The carriage roof was covered by numerous wreaths and a host of other floral tributes. Behind the carriage purred three black limousines followed by a procession of other, less sombre-coloured cars.

In the cafe there was an instant cacophony of chairs scraping on the floorboards as the customers stood in respect. Miriam followed suit. All was then still and quiet in the room, apart from the rustle of some of the ladies who rummaged in handbags for handkerchiefs or tissues. As the last of the vehicles passed the onlookers outside slowly dispersed, though small groups lingered to chat.

Within minutes, the funeral seemed to have drained the cafe of its earlier social atmosphere and the room gradually emptied of customers, except for the mayor.

'Such a tragedy for the Commander,' she commented to Felicity, who had arrived to clear an adjacent table.

'Yes, she was a lovely woman, his wife.'

'And he's quite a striking man,' Miriam observed, as she paid her bill and fixed her pensive gaze on the deserted street.

***

As the heavy door swung slowly open, the look of apprehension on Alexander Penn's face faded as he observed the housekeeper's beaming smile.

Mrs Soames had been the unwilling spectator of the Commander's steady decline for more than a month since her mistress's much-lamented passing.

''E's wastin' away. Wastin' away,' Mrs S had muttered tearfully to herself on many occasions as she shuffled off to the kitchen with tray after tray of virtually untouched food.

Much against her better judgement, and very much on her boss's insistence, the Hall's shopping list had started to include more regular orders of the Commander's preferred whisky – and those were only the 'official' bottles that Mrs Soames knew had entered the building.

'I really don't know what to do about him, Sebastian. I really don't,' she had confided despairingly one day, over a cup of tea in the kitchen. ''E just sits in 'is chair by the window, starin' out. Won't say a word unless 'e 'as to. 'E really needs buckin' up, but I don't know what to do about it and that's a fact. 'E's lost all interest in life.'

Sebastian had pondered for several moments over the housekeeper's dilemma before he responded.

'Well, there is one thing that might just snap him out of it. That chest he discovered.'

So, at the risk of losing her job, the very next day Mrs Soames had casually enquired whether the Commander wished her to get rid of 'that dirty old box'.

'What?' Selwyn virtually exploded, his face wreathed in incredulity.

'Well, it's been sat there these past few weeks,' the brave woman explained. 'I just thought as 'ow it was maybe redundant, like.'

Selwyn soundly disabused her of such a notion and she was dismissed to her kitchen, but not before she had fired off a final,

'Well, it don't look like anything's going to happen to it and it's only gatherin' dust, if it's possible for it to gain any more.' With that, she had waddled down the corridor with a hopeful smile, having seen in her boss the first signs of any interest for many a week.

***

'I appreciate your coming, Alexander,' Selwyn greeted the rotund historian, a faint spark of eagerness apparent in his eyes. 'As I mentioned earlier, I've come across something I'd like you to look at.'

'I'm sure if there's anything I can do to...' Penn replied. His voice petered out as he caught sight of the trunk on the floor, its lid raised and its contents reminiscent of the props of some cheap pirate movie.

'I found it in the pit your map indicated,' Selwyn resumed. 'Bloody awful event that turned out to be,' he declared. 'You probably heard about the body that was found. Still not been laid to rest. The case, I mean,' he added with a rueful glance. 'Well, maybe not the body either, for all I know.'

Penn gave a slight nod.

'Anyway,' said Selwyn, 'at first I hoped it'd be the missing family fortune.' He threw Penn an embarrassed glance. 'You've probably heard of my quest to find it, though some say it's more of an obsession.'

The historian's eyes and face creased up in an understanding smile.

'Turns out,' Selwyn continued, 'that it's a load of old maps and documents. Maps I can read, but I can make neither head nor tail of the writing on the other things. As an expert, I thought you might be able to give them a once-over and shed some light on what they're about, or at least point me in the right direction.' With his eyes locked on Penn, Selwyn sat back with his arms draped over the sides of his chair and his hands gripping the chair arms as if he were about to set off on a fairground ride.

'Well, I'd be delighted to take a look…' Penn began, but faltered as Selwyn suddenly leant forward and frowned at him.

'Of course, it all has to be hush-hush,' the Commander interrupted. 'What you find, I mean.'

His visitor hesitated. This had seemed like a heaven-sent opportunity to enhance his own project.

'I was hoping you would permit me to make some mention in my local history of the town and the Hall,' he suggested.

Selwyn stared at him, and his tongue set to work on his molars and bicuspids.

'Hmm,' he murmured, after a very pregnant pause. 'It depends on what all this turns out to be,' he said, with a glance at the trunk.

They stared at each other until Penn tried to break the impasse.

'Suppose you let me know what you'd let me publish once I've gone through the stuff and picked out what would interest me?'

'Sounds good to me,' Selwyn agreed. He rose, approached his guest and thrust out his hand.

Penn heaved himself up with a grunt and the two men shook hands on the arrangement.

MAY 2010

Throughout the morning, the sun had battled with leaden clouds that scudded over Wisstingham, its sporadic rays bringing brief cheer to the cold February day. A shaft of sunlight pierced the gloom of the Monaghans' bedroom as it streamed briefly through the leaded window and fell on the bedridden figure.

The face, pale and shrunken like the body, was motionless.

As Vincent unlatched the creaky wooden door, the eyes flickered open, nervously followed him round the room then watched him put down the tray and draw up a chair. He lifted Mary into a sitting position, spread a towel around her neck and in silence began to feed her soup from a bowl. Afterwards, he wiped her mouth then started to feed her grapes.

'You used to do this for fun once upon a time,' she murmured in a dry whisper.

'We used to do lots of things for fun once upon a time,' he replied drily.

'When we were in love,' she croaked.

'Which didn't last long for you,' he countered, the bitterness thick in his voice.

'Longer than you ever believed. It was your suspicion and obsession that drove us apart.'

'I had good reason.'

'You had no reason,' Mary replied in a tired whisper. 'I told you that often enough, but you never believed me. You became distant, unkind and cold.'

'You always fancied other men.'

Her head sank back onto the pillow. She tried to catch her breath while he put the bowl aside, careless of her emotional and physical exhaustion.

'I used to see you with Masterson at the pub,' Vincent accused. 'You two were always laughing and larking about. Why do you think I was so keen to leave and come here?'

Mary closed her eyes and sighed.

'You know why you came,' she murmured. 'You lost your job and Lucian got you in here. He said you'd both get control of this place. He had all those big ideas about persuading his father to favour him, rather than the Commander. He might even have succeeded. Lucian was a sweet-talker, all right.' She turned her head away, wearied of the exertion and memories.

'Ah, the glorious *Commander*,' Vincent snarled. 'One of the rich and powerful. They can have everything they set their eyes on.' He lowered his head close to hers. Mary's eyes narrowed as she cowered away from him.

'He's always been fond of you, hasn't he, Mary?' he hissed. 'Always been cosy and friendly, like. You were unfaithful. You've always been unfaithful,' he railed, then sat back. 'You've lied and lied and lied,' he continued, his voice now raised. 'Your lies have been as cancerous as the thing that's killing you now.'

Red-faced, he fell silent, his hands trembled. There was no reply. The only sound was the ticking of the mantel clock over the fireplace. He bowed his head. His whole frame shook.

'You were wrong, so wrong,' Mary whispered and tried to place a hand on his, which he instantly withdrew. 'There was never anything between me and Reg Masterson, or anyone else there,' she pleaded.

'*There*,' Vincent emphasised the word, his anger rising. 'But not *here*. That doesn't include here.'

She drew her hand back to her breast.

'You've always been so possessive,' she murmured. 'You turned away from me. Never wanted me. You said I was always plotting against you. You see plots against you everywhere.'

'Ha! Plots. The biggest plot lives right under this roof, doesn't he? Doesn't he?' Vincent roared, jumping up. 'That boy's not my son, though you've tried to pass him off as mine.' He glared at his withered wife. Seeing no response, he leant over and frenziedly shook her frail form. Tears began to course down her ghostly face. 'He's not mine. He's not mine, is he?' Vincent raged, incandescent.

Mary bleated in pain.

'Stop, stop, please,' she begged, in a barely audible whisper. 'No, he's not yours, he's a Fitzgerald,' she exclaimed. 'I—'

But Vincent would listen no more. With a cry of rage, he stumbled blindly towards the door. Wildly lashing out at anything within range, he blundered through the cottage and collided with Sebastian as the distraught man lurched outside into the yard.

'She's in there, the bitch. Get to her, you bastard!' Vincent snarled, then wiped his sleeve across his mouth and staggered away.

Terrified, Sebastian dashed to the bedroom. His mother

lay awkwardly across the bed, panting for breath through her sobs. As he tried to comfort her, she feebly drew his head close to hers and, with laboured breath, whispered something he could not make out. She reached under her pillow, took Sebastian's hand, and held it limply. Then she gently pressed something metallic into his palm with her other hand.

'Rest easy. I'll get the doctor,' her son said soothingly. But by the time the anguished son returned, the only sign of life and motion left in the room was the ticking clock.

***

A gentle breeze caressed Sebastian's face as he stood by the open grave. The clear blue sky mocked the desolation of his day. Overhead, the new leaves on the branches of tall sycamores, uniformly spaced against the cemetery's stone wall, filtered the sunlight, some reaching the rows of stone and marble gravestones.

Beside Sebastian stood Vincent. Grim-faced, he stared down at the coffin, its polished surface throwing back the light from the sun's intrusion. Sebastian glanced across at the other mourners before his eyes came to rest on the Commander, who stood to attention in a long black coat, his lips pressed tightly together, black kidskin gloves stretched tightly over the knuckles of fists that were clenched at his sides. Sebastian could not help but reflect how different the man looked in contrast to his normal, casual dress. Selwyn caught his gaze and offered a fleeting, reassuring smile.

At the appropriate moment, Vincent bent down to pick up a handful of dirt, cast it carelessly onto the coffin and looked away as he did so. With a nod to the vicar but never a glance at anyone else, he strode off, leaving Sebastian to accept the graveside condolences of the mourners and to thank the vicar for his ministrations.

Eventually, only Sebastian and Selwyn remained. The Commander placed a firm hand on Sebastian's forearm as he shook his hand.

'I'm so sorry, my boy. Your mother was a very special lady,' he sympathised.

'Thank you, Commander. I'm glad you're here. I'm afraid my father—'

Selwyn raised a hand to silence him.

'I trust you're coming to the Phantom?' Sebastian asked.

'I am indeed.'

After one last look at the grave, they walked off to join the groups of other mourners who were huddled in conversation outside the church.

***

In the Phantom Hound pub, his hands spread wide on the business end of the bar, leant the landlord, Oliver Mann. His gleaming eyes surveyed the funeral party as they entered. Those with drinks to order crowded the bar, while friends and partners drifted off to find tables in the adjoining room. The few customers already present stared at the newcomers with interest, those at the bar grudgingly conceding as little space as the propriety of the occasion demanded. With a broad, toothy smile, Oliver scratched his bushy ginger beard and his muscular arm set to work to pull away smoothly at one of the beer pumps.

'Millie, put the nail varnish away and get yourself in here, lass,' his deep voice boomed, followed by an explosive laugh for the benefit of his locals, who grinned at him over their drinks.

A curvaceous redhead scurried in from the back and gave her husband a mock scowl and a backhander on his rump before smiling indulgently at the crowd and enquiring who was next. Without the slightest interruption to his beer pulling, Mann let out a deep-throated chuckle and cast a sideways leer in his wife's direction.

In the course of his conversations with the wake's various guests, Sebastian found himself obliged to listen patiently to the proprietor of the local hardware store, who was tediously holding forth on his pet subject of Lamson tube systems.

'Absolutely fascinating,' came a voice from behind Sebastian. He turned to see the oval eyes and mischievous smile that had filled countless moments of silent contemplation since his first sight of them.

'Do you really think so?' the shop owner asked, as a glint appeared in his eyes.

'Well, not really,' Amanda admitted. 'Not in itself. But I should think if you introduced them in your shop, they'd create loads of interest and custom, if only out of curiosity. In your shoes, I'd sound out some of my customers.' She motioned with her eyes to the groups of people nearby. He stared at her then glanced around the room.

'Market research,' she whispered.

'Well, I'd never actually thought of...' Words failed him as his imagination started to run riot. With hurried thanks to Amanda, he nodded to Sebastian, gave his arm a squeeze of condolence and moved smartly away.

'You're quite wicked,' said Sebastian, who had broken into a warm smile at the cheery librarian. Her company was a welcome, if temporary, relief from the unhappiness of the occasion.

'I'm glad you noticed. But you looked in need of rescue and anyway, I wanted to speak to you.'

He stared at her and observed how elegant she looked in black.

'I was very sorry to hear about your mother, Sebastian,' she said, in her soft, chocolaty voice. She placed a consoling hand on his arm for a moment, the brevity of which he regretted.

'Thank you. Can I get you a drink?' he asked, wishing his mother could have met this beauty.

'No thanks, I've got one in the other bar. I'm with a couple of friends,' she replied.

Sebastian was about to speak when the formidable proprietor of the beach shop bore down upon him with her ample bosom and sympathy. As she verbally burst upon him, he glanced helplessly over her shoulder at Amanda, who was on her way back to the other bar. She turned to give him a brief wave, paused to take a card from her pocket, held it up in one hand and pointed at it. He smiled at this fresh invitation, then apologised for his inattention to the affronted and scowling Mrs Prendergast.

Amanda rejoined Alexander Penn and his nephew Martin, to whom she had been introduced earlier.

'Sorry about that,' she apologised. 'I had to offer my commiserations. It's the funeral of one of the people from the estate,' she explained to Martin.

'Did you notice if the Commander was there?' Alexander asked.

'Yes, he was talking to a bald man with an egg-shaped head and a moustache.'

'That sounds like his quarry manager, Mac Bilton,' Alexander observed with a chuckle.

'Must feel funny to have a moustache. I wonder if they take a lot of cleaning,' Amanda mused, which aroused Martin's curiosity.

'That's something you've got to get used to with our Miss Sheppard,' Alexander explained. 'She tends to come out with whatever is going through her head.'

Far from being offended, Amanda smiled.

'Sorry, Martin. Alex is quite right, it's a bad habit,' she admitted. 'So tell me, where do you live?'

'A seaside town called Lytham St Annes. Quite a gentle place, really. Lots of retired people,' Martin replied.

'And you work there?'

'No, Canada at the moment.'

'Bit of a commute, but never mind. What do you do?'

'I'm a cartographer.'

'Building carts eh? Only joking. I know it's maps, really.'

'Yes. I'm working on contract in Quebec.'

'And how often do you get home?'

'About every three months, though sometimes I'm back on business in between. How do you know my uncle?' Martin queried.

'Amanda and I work quite closely together sometimes,' Penn cut in. 'She helps me with my research and, more often than not, can get me the books I need.'

'In exchange for which he sometimes takes me out for a drink or a curry, which is very enjoyable and probably totally at odds with the council rules concerning bribery. But so far I've avoided arrest,' Amanda added.

'I don't think a king prawn curry's likely to get you thrown in the Tower,' observed Alexander. 'Anyway, it's not a bribe, it's just taking my girlfriend out,' he added, winking at Martin. 'But, to more serious things. While I've got you together, there's something I need to ask you both.'

'If it's more than twenty pounds, I'll need a cash machine,' Amanda warned.

'Nothing to do with money,' Penn assured her. 'It's about my research. Amanda, I want to ask you something. If anything should happen to me, would you be prepared to go through my papers and find the best home for them, either with the appropriate bodies or individuals? You're probably the only person locally who'd understand what most of them mean.'

'Of course I would, Alex – but not for a long while yet, I hope,' she replied, somewhat taken aback by the prospect.

'And that leads me to ask if both of you would be prepared to act as my executors,' Penn continued.

'Seems like you couldn't have chosen a more fitting occasion to ask that,' Martin remarked, with a glance across to the other room where the mourners had now launched an attack on the buffet. 'But I'm quite prepared to do that, of course,' he added.

'Me too,' agreed Amanda.

'Then that's all settled. Thank you both. Now, who's for another drink?'

'Not for me, thanks,' Amanda replied. 'I need to get back to the library to see how far the decorators have got on. We must have everything back in place for Monday's reopening.'

'So tell me, is there a decent Chinese in the village?' Martin asked Amanda as Alexander lumbered over to the bar.

'Well, there's Qwik Qwak. Their curries are fantastic and, as you might guess, they specialise in duck dishes.'

'I don't suppose you'd care to join me there this evening?' he asked, in as throwaway a manner as he could muster.

'Well, I don't know when we'll be finished at the library but a gal's got to eat sometime, so yes,' she replied, standing up to leave.

'Why don't we meet up here for a drink first, say seven o'clock?' Martin suggested.

'That's fine – but only if we go Dutch,' Amanda insisted. 'I wouldn't want my boyfriend to get the wrong idea.' She nodded in Alexander's direction, then smiled and waved to him as he turned to look at them from the bar.

'Dutch and seven o'clock it is,' Martin agreed.

After she had said goodbye, Amanda paused to take one last look at the funeral party but there was no sign of her potential new recruit.

'She's a grand lass,' Alexander commented later as he quaffed his pint. 'You could do a lot worse than her, Martin.'

'Matchmaker,' Martin replied, though the suggestion was one that had already flitted across his mind.

***

'Damn, I've left my scarf,' Sebastian exclaimed as he took off his coat.

Vincent, who had stooped to put some logs on the fire, merely grunted then sat down in the fireside armchair. Left alone with his thoughts, he watched the growing flames with a furrowed brow.

After he had eventually retrieved his scarf from under one of the seats in the pub, Sebastian glanced around the now familiar surroundings. The remnants of the buffet were gone, and the empty room was a stark reminder that his mother's funeral was already fading into the past. He sat down to gaze into the ebbing fire and pictured the burial plot where he had stood those few hours earlier.

How cold and silent it'll be now, he thought. *How dark that tight space in which she's lying, the ravages of nature's decay already started.* He drew comfort from the grave being in a pleasant corner of the churchyard, near the canopy of a large chestnut tree. There was a bench close by, on which Sebastian imagined he would sit, many times in the future.

He reflected on the wake. Yes, it had been satisfactory, but how much better it would have been if his father had not adamantly rejected the Commander's offer to hold it at the Hall. That had puzzled Sebastian. Furthermore, he could not understand why his father's attitude towards the Commander had changed so much. Sebastian was certain that the Commander and *his* attitude to Vincent had not changed. Although his father still appeared friendly and accommodating towards his boss, behind his back it was now a very different story.

As his mother's dying moments strayed into his thoughts, Sebastian dug into his pocket and pulled out the silver locket she had pressed into his hand when she had desperately tried to tell him something that he could not make out. He opened it and looked at the two monochrome photos of his mother on one side and his father on the other, evidently taken in happier times.

The shifting embers alerted Sebastian to his whereabouts. As he was about go, he checked his watch and looked across to the other bar. There, dressed in the same elegant coat he had seen before, was Amanda. At her side stood a man who was laughing, presumably at something she had just said. Sebastian felt a stab of jealousy tinged with a feeling of betrayal, though reason dictated he was not entitled to the latter. He hurried outside and caught sight of the couple as they sauntered casually down the street. They stopped outside the Chinese restaurant, studied the menu posted in the window, then went inside.

With a groan, Sebastian pocketed the scarf, which he wished he had never forgotten, and trudged home, kicking moodily at anything in his path. Back at the cottage, unwilling to be alone with his thoughts, he joined his father by the fireside.

'Found it, then?' Vincent asked.

'Yeah.'

They both gazed into the fire in silence.

'There'll need to be some changes,' Vincent announced eventually as he leant forward to feed the fire with another log. 'We're going to have to pull together to keep things going. You'll need to do more in the cottage.'

Sebastian briefly closed his eyes and shook his head ever so slightly. The prospect of the two of them rubbing along together was not an appealing one. Unfortunately for her, his mother had often been the buffer between them. All too often she had come off worst from her husband's invective and fists. On one of the rare occasions when Mary was out of the cottage, Sebastian had squared up to his father over his treatment of her and received a painful beating. What had hurt him more than the blows was the way his father had seemed to enjoy giving them.

Vincent looked across to Sebastian.

'I reckon I'll be away a lot more this next year,' he said, as if he had read Sebastian's thoughts. 'Fitzgerald's hell-bent on entering the horses for as many meetings as he can.'

'How are things going?'

'Not so good. He even talked about closing the stables if things don't improve next season.'

'Do you think he will?'

'Dunno. It's the one passion left in his life now, so I reckon it wouldn't come easy to him.'

'How's Wisstingham Prancer coming along?'

Vincent cast him a searching glance.

'So-so,' he replied warily. 'We'll see what sort of a showing he has.'

He did not intend to share his bigger game plan with Sebastian, whose closeness to the Commander was now a concern. Nor was he prepared to share all the other thoughts and plans he had conceived since Mary's death. More than anything, the widower had brooded heavily on what she had told him and its potential consequences. Clearly the Commander was unaware that Sebastian was his own offspring. As long as that remained the case, all was well for Vincent's claim on the estate. That Mary might have confided her secret to someone else was an unknown that he would have to live with.

Vincent believed that if the Commander were to discover that Sebastian was his son, undoubtedly the boy would inherit. That might put Vincent in a favourable position, if only through Fitzgerald's feelings of guilt. However, there was no certainty of that, and the crumbs from Sebastian's table would certainly not satisfy Vincent's hunger. Besides, he and the boy were not remotely close, and he could not rely on Sebastian to do him any favours if he was to inherit everything. Too much water had flowed under that bridge. Sebastian might well cast his cuckolded father completely aside, particularly if he discovered who his real father was.

'What'd happen to you if the Commander did close the stables?' Sebastian asked.

Vincent stared unblinkingly into the fire.

'Dunno. He'd have to find buyers for the three horses first. There are a few rounds to play before we get to that, I reckon, and there's plenty of other work on the estate that I'd be needed for. I'm not thinking of packing my bags just yet.'

With both men absorbed in contemplation of the future, silence descended on the room.

For Vincent, there were indeed a few rounds yet to be played. He recalled the previous October's discussion with Fitzgerald, when they had thrashed out the following year's budget. Vincent had intentionally kept quiet about the promise Wisstingham Prancer showed as a future winner, because he intended to buy out Fitzgerald's share in the colt at an advantageous price, then bring him on for the following season. Moreover, Vincent was increasingly confident he could persuade the Commander to let him take over the stables. Through his contacts, Vincent believed he could attract other owners to stable their horses at Wisstingham. Given Prancer's success, his winnings, stud fees and further stabling would generate very substantial profits.

Buoyed up by these thoughts, Vincent smiled to himself as he rose to go to bed and left Sebastian dozing in his chair.

Chapter 7

Penn briefly halted his passage down the corridor from the entrance hall. He turned and observed Mrs Soames' disapproving glare, followed by a shake of her head as she shuffled off in the opposite direction.

Her initial pleasure at the historian's visits seemed to have faded completely. For weeks now, the library had been effectively out of bounds to the housekeeper's hoover and duster. Not that any official instructions had been issued. It had been more a case of the cluttered nature of the room defying any attempts to clean it. Every table and surface was covered either with unfurled maps, weighted down at their corners, or with scrolls of varying sizes of yellowed, ancient-looking parchment. Other rolls of documents were separated into small piles and scattered around the room, their logic known only to the roly-poly historian. In pride of place in the centre of the room sat the grimy, battered metal trunk in which the new inhabitants of the library had once resided.

His briefcase propped against a table leg, Penn burst into an appreciative smile as he surveyed his temporary fiefdom and gently closed the door. It was not a gentleness born out of respect for the room and its contents, but an attempt to avoid giving the Commander an indication of his arrival. Selwyn's constant interruptions to enquire about progress had proved both tiresome and interruptive.

The historian realised, however, that he would soon be obliged to offer something of interest on his findings. He had kept quiet for as long as he could, his visits limited to evenings, weekends and the school's Easter break.

Alexander turned to one of the piles of documents and began to sort through them. For that day he had selected one of the smallest to work on. As the minutes ticked by, he became more and more riveted until finally, with a long exhalation of breath, he sat back and stared at the document. He rubbed a hand over his mouth.

'Good Lord,' he murmured, then hastily secreted the document within its pile at the sound of the door handle being turned.

'Back for more, my dear chap?' Selwyn said as he entered the room. 'Is Mrs Soames keeping you provisioned?'

'Ah, yes, Commander,' Alexander confirmed, though she had long since abandoned that duty. 'I'm well looked after, thank you.' He had no stomach to incur her further displeasure through a report of any negligence.

'Any joy?' Selwyn asked.

'Nothing so far,' Penn lied with a smile, and placed a chubby hand and forearm on the pile next to him.

'Oh,' muttered Selwyn, whose jowls sagged in tandem with his spirits. He moved towards the pile of documents, as if he intended to examine them.

'I say nothing,' Penn hastened, 'but I did come across an interesting map that covers the other part of the estate and the village.' He led Selwyn to it, unfurled on the plan table. 'You can see the outline of two buildings on the area within the estate boundary.'

His smile restored, Selwyn bent to study the map.

'Fortunately,' continued Alexander, 'the courtyard

buildings and the Hall are shown. From these, it should be possible to triangulate the positions of the other buildings – depending on the map's accuracy, of course.' He straightened and cast a triumphant smile at the open-mouthed Commander.

'What sort of buildings do you think they were?' asked Selwyn.

'It's difficult to say, though the fact that nothing can be seen of them now would indicate they were either simple storage structures or maybe timber dwellings, perhaps to accommodate some of the workers.'

'And is there any indication of when they disappeared?'

'At this stage, no. Although from this other document, here,' Penn picked up one up from an adjacent pile, 'I reckon they existed in 1639. This appears to be an inventory taken of the entire estate in that year. Unfortunately, although individual stores and buildings are listed, we can't say for certain which is which. But, by the number of them, it would appear they are included.'

Selwyn eagerly leafed back and forth through the documents then looked at Penn who, with a broad smile of self-satisfaction, drummed his fingers on the edge of the plan chest.

'So where do we go from here?' Selwyn asked. The expression on his face suggested he knew full well where he would like to go: directly to the land in question, with a bulldozer. The flames of his quest to find the family treasure appeared to have been well and truly reignited.

Penn glanced around the room.

'I think I need to plough on with the rest of these and we'll see what else turns up.'

'Capital,' Selwyn enthused. 'Then I'd better leave you in

peace.' Despite the sentiment, he seemed reluctant to go. Penn gazed expectantly at him. 'All right, as you were,' the Commander finally conceded and left.

Penn waited for the footsteps to recede down the corridor. Furtively, he extracted the document and map he had been working on earlier, rolled them up and deposited them in the dark confines of his briefcase. Although confident he understood what was written on the document, he needed an expert opinion. If he was right, they would both be a bombshell both for Commander Fitzgerald and for Wisstingham.

***

Not a week had passed before Mrs Soames found herself, no less irritated than before, once again having to answer the doorbell. When she discovered the identity of the visitor, however, her demeanour changed dramatically. With the sort of smile she would wear if she had just been awarded a Michelin star, she pulled the door wide open and, with her head bowed in deference, admitted Wisstingham's mayor, Miriam Cheyney.

The housekeeper, much disconcerted by the floury appearance of her apron, scuttled in front of the dignitary who, as most visitors did, cast glances of approval from side to side at the Hall's decor and furnishings.

With frequent backward glances to check on the mayor's safe passage, Mrs Soames arrived at the drawing room door, rapped on it, then flung it open and announced in a loud voice,

'Commander Selwyn Fitzgerald, the Lady Mayor, Miriam Cheyney.' Then, with an obsequious smile, Mrs S took orders for refreshments and scurried off to the kitchen.

Selwyn tried to hide a smile as he watched her depart then advanced to greet his guest.

'On behalf of myself and my colleagues at the council, I should like to express our sincere condolences at your recent loss, Commander Fitzgerald,' the mayor announced. Her eyes lingered on his.

'That is greatly appreciated, thank you,' Selwyn replied, and invited his guest to be seated.

After the sad exchange of information on Selwyn's loss had been exhausted, the mayor got down to business, a trait that the Commander both noted and admired.

'I should explain that I'm not here in my capacity of mayor, but as the Councillor with Portfolio for Leisure Tourism and Cultural Services. A bit of a mouthful, really. Since your enquiry related to the recreation area, it fell into my domain.'

Selwyn nodded.

'Your call was very interesting,' she continued. 'If I understand correctly, you want to carry out some exploratory work on the estate land leased to the council. Am I right?'

'In a nutshell,' Selwyn replied, eyeing her keenly.

'Well, I've had some preliminary discussions with the council officers and my colleagues, but I'm afraid there's not much of an appetite to interrupt the land's present recreational use. We'd need to have a clearer picture of the nature of the work and the timescale involved. Also, how it would affect the land.'

Selwyn outlined Penn's discovery and showed her the map.

'Initially I'd like to see if there's any sign of the buildings through a ground scan,' the Commander explained.

'That would only take a few days and I'm told it wouldn't involve much, if any, excavation.'

'That might not present too much of a problem but, if the buildings were located, what then?'

'Well, the next stage would be to do some trial excavations.'

'Now that's where the council might have some difficulties,' the mayor warned. 'It's not that we would *want* to be difficult,' she hastened to reassure him with an indulgent smile, 'but if the council couldn't show the community some benefit, having taken the land off them, so to speak, I doubt it's a project we could run with.'

Selwyn's jowls drooped and the mayor struggled to hide her amusement at his endearing hangdog expression.

'Even though it's estate land?' he parried.

'On lease to the council,' the mayor reminded him. 'As I said, if there were some visible benefit for the community that would be quite a different story.'

'Surely a dig for seventeenth-century buildings would bring a lot of interest and visitors to the village. Put the place on the map, so to speak,' Selwyn argued.

The mayor frowned.

'I doubt that would be a big enough attraction to appease the locals. Now, if you were to decide to open up the Hall to the public,' she mooted, her eyebrows raised, 'I'm sure that would be totally different. The excavation could even feature as an aspect of the estate in action, to enhance its history. Who knows – there might even be a grant available for the work. Though not from the council,' she added hastily.

The mayor crossed her long legs, and Selwyn did not fail to notice how shapely they looked. She smiled sweetly at him and affected to pat an odd wave of brown hair back into place, though it had never really strayed at all.

Selwyn broke into a smile.

She's really given her strategy some consideration, he thought, with sneaking admiration. Here was another agenda. It was a long time since he had last enjoyed some tactical negotiations.

'Ah, that old chestnut,' he exclaimed and wagged his forefinger at her. 'I wondered when we would get around to that.'

He stood, walked over to the window and made a point of looking out over the garden. Whether the mayor stood or remained seated would tell him quite a bit. As he had anticipated, she rose and joined him.

'Selwyn, if I may call you that, it's such a beautiful Hall with so much history. Just think how it would put Wisstingham on the map, as well as bring in a healthy income for you. Won't you consider it?'

He turned and contemplated his adversary. He wondered whether to play his trump card but decided to keep it for another occasion.

'Perhaps for the purposes of this meeting we're getting too far ahead of ourselves,' he suggested. 'All I'm seeking at present is agreement to carry out the ground scan. If it doesn't come up with anything, the rest is academic.'

There was a pause, then finally the mayor agreed.

'If you can give me more details on the timing, duration and impact of the survey, together with a risk assessment, I'll get one of our officers to look at it and put a paper together,' she offered. 'It should come under delegated powers, so it's the public notice that would take the time.'

Their meeting concluded, Selwyn escorted her to the

entrance hall. All the while, his guest cast her eyes about, from the panelled ceiling to the small tables topped with Chinese patterned lamps, then to the suits of armour and the highly polished wooden floor.

'This really must be a beautiful place to live in,' she observed as she stopped to gaze up the wide staircase, its richly patterned runner framed at each tread with gleaming brass stair rods.

Selwyn resisted the temptation to offer the mayor a guided tour, which he felt sure she was hankering for. It would not be wise to give her more food for thought on the subject of opening up the Hall. He shrugged.

'I suppose it must be, although, as with all things in life, one becomes accustomed to it and tends to take it for granted,' he replied casually. 'I'd be delighted to show you around on another occasion.'

'I'll be sure to take you up on that,' she replied.

Selwyn watched her drive off in her white BMW convertible and smiled at his enjoyment of the preliminary skirmish with this attractive woman – though he really would have to google 'risk assessment'.

***

Wisstingham's library was unassuming in its external appearance and carefully designed to be in keeping with the adjacent premises. Only the sign above the mahogany front doors gave an indication of the building's purpose.

Lucky enough to have found a parking space, Sebastian sat in his car opposite the building and stared at it, hesitant about whether or not he should cross its threshold. He had heard nothing from Amanda since the last time he had seen her, though there was no particular reason why he should have. He had mulled things over repeatedly. With the unsettled nature of his home life and the bitter experience of his parents' relationship, did he really want the further uncertainty of a relationship with her – or with any other woman, for that matter? His jealousy when she had walked off with the other guy, and the way she repeatedly invaded his thoughts, weighed heavily in that debate, together with the question of whether or not the librarian would even want to be involved with him.

He got out of the car, crossed the road, paused, then finally entered the building.

At the library counter, a wispy young woman was busy checking out a customer's books, but there was no sign of Amanda. Seated at one of the tables nearby was the man he had recently seen at the Hall.

Sebastian scanned the room. He was about to leave when he heard a familiar, chocolaty voice behind him.

'This is a members-only club, sir. I'm afraid you're trespassing and I'm going to have to call security. There could even be a custodial sentence involved.'

He turned to see the smiling face and eyes that were ever in his thoughts.

'Of course, if you were to enrol within the next three minutes, we'd be prepared to drop all charges,' Amanda continued.

Feeling like an awkward schoolboy, Sebastian could only mutter 'Hi.'

'Hi,' she murmured with a smile. She hoped her delight at seeing him was not too obvious.

'Well, I suppose you've got me bang to rights,' he admitted, aroused by the way she was gently biting her bottom lip. 'Where do I sign up?'

'Follow me,' she instructed. 'If you're very good, we'll even let you play with the books – though I should warn you, we don't do comics.' She gave him a wink and led him to the counter.

While she processed his card, Sebastian could feel the butterflies in his stomach.

It's now or never, he thought as he leant closer towards her to ask for a date.

His intentions were stymied by Alexander Penn.

'OK to use the photocopier, Amanda?' the historian interrupted.

Sebastian looked aside in frustrated silence.

'That's fine, Alex. Monica will take the money,' Amanda replied with a nod in the direction of the wispy girl.

'Who's he?' Sebastian demanded.

'That's Alexander Penn, teacher and local historian of this borough,' Amanda replied, with an inward smile at the testy note in Sebastian's voice.

'Ah, that's probably why I've seen him in the library at the Hall.'

'Yes, he's got some sort of a research project there. He seems to be very excited about it but he won't let on what it is.'

She held out the card and Sebastian took a silent gulp, still in mental rehearsal for his next words.

Amanda turned to watch the historian.

'I'd better follow him. He's not very mechanically minded,' she confided, then set off in pursuit.

'Why, hello mate. Finally got to you, did she?' came another familiar voice. Sebastian closed his eyes momentarily in further frustration then turned to face the newcomer.

'Hello, Hector, how are you? Yeah, she certainly did,' Sebastian replied and held up his card. 'Got you to join too, eh?'

'Not on your life. I've just come to copy a grant application,' replied the farmer.

After a few pleasantries, Hector asked where Amanda was. Sebastian pointed in the direction of the corridor, where she had now reappeared. Something seemed wrong, however. With an anxious frown, she beckoned the two men to join her.

'Alex has come over all giddy. Can you help get him into the office?' she said in a low voice.

In the small photocopier room, Penn was leaning with his back to a desk, both hands clasped firmly onto it for support. The two men took hold of his shaking arms, followed Amanda to the office and helped him into a chair, where the ashen-faced historian continued to gasp for breath.

Within minutes an ambulance had arrived. After examining the stricken man, the paramedics stretchered him into the vehicle and drove off to hospital, despite his protestations that he felt better.

'All right if I go and get a copy of this?' Hector asked Amanda, once the crisis was over.

She nodded.

'Don't forget to pay at the desk,' she called after him.

'You never told me joining the library would be as exciting as this,' Sebastian commented.

'Just wait till you actually find a book to take out,' she replied.

The butterflies were back, but Sebastian seized his chance.

'Would you like to go out for a meal sometime?' he blurted out.

'Yes, I'd love to,' Amanda replied without hesitation. 'I thought you'd never ask.'

'How about Friday at Mauro's?' he suggested. Now it was his chest that was nearly bursting.

'That'd be fine.'

'I'll pick you up at seven, if that's all right.'

'Seven it is.'

They swapped mobile numbers then stared at each other in silence.

'Then I suppose I'd better go and find a book,' Sebastian ventured, just as Hector reappeared and held out two ancient-looking documents and some other sheets of paper.

'I found these at the photocopier. I assume they belong to the big guy,' he said, and handed them to Amanda. She glanced at them then started to read the notes.

Hector seemed agitated and cast Sebastian an impatient glance. Amanda had become quite engrossed in the documents.

'I supposed I'd better be off, then,' the farmer said reluctantly, eyeing Sebastian, who clearly was not going to take the hint to go.

'Yes, bye,' came Amanda's perfunctory reply. She did not even look up.

'I'll give you a call,' her cousin promised.

'Mmm,' she murmured.

'And I'll go and find a book,' Sebastian added, after Hector had gone. 'I'll see you on Friday.'

'Yes, bye,' came the same distracted reply.

As she continued to peruse the old documents and

cross-reference them with Penn's notes, the librarian's eyes widened and her mouth slowly gaped open.

***

Two hours later, there was a frantic phone call from Alexander.

'Don't worry, they're safe,' Amanda assured him. 'How are you? What have the doctors said? Are they keeping you in?'

Even as she spoke, her eyes were drawn irresistibly back to the documents that lay on her desk.

'All right,' she said, finally. 'Tell me all about it when I see you. I'll call round this evening with your stuff.'

***

'What was the problem?' Amanda asked later that day as she sat with Alexander.

'Apparently, I might be diabetic,' he replied. 'They've taken blood samples. At least my ticker's OK.'

'Not lost its tock, then? I suppose that's something.'

'Thanks for your help at the library and for these.' Penn patted the documents.

'I couldn't help but look at them,' Amanda admitted. 'And once I started to read your translation, I just couldn't stop. I'm sorry.'

'No need to apologise. I felt exactly the same when I came across it.'

'So, is it right that the estate land leased to the council was given to the village in exchange for other land?'

'Not only that, but also some of the land within the current estate boundary, next to the council's lease. Of course, it all needs to be checked out. There must be another document – the copy belonging to the village. Maybe it's in the town's archives. Of course, it could be that the document was never enacted,' Penn continued, 'though the seal would seem to indicate otherwise. The strength of the argument lies with the estate's present use, if any, of the land that the transfer document exchanged. I need to find something about that land's original ownership and use. The problem is that it happened around the time of the Civil War. What with the area being taken and retaken by the two sides, who knows what really happened?'

'But this is incredible,' Amanda gasped. 'The council may have been denied access to land it has owned for nearly four hundred years. They could have a field day – and, knowing some of the councillors, I wouldn't put it past them. Does Commander Fitzgerald know about this?'

Sheepishly, Alexander admitted that he did not.

'If I told him, he'd have demanded the document back and would probably have destroyed it,' Penn said in his defence. 'Similarly,' he continued, 'if the council got to know about it, it would no doubt be taken out of my hands and all sorts of hares would be set running.'

'Nothing as small as hares. Giraffes, maybe. So you're going to research it yourself?'

Penn smiled and nodded.

'Exactly! I've waited for years for a break like this. I'm not going to give it up to someone else.'

'Well, if you need any help, you know where I am,' Amanda offered, getting up to leave.

'I might well have to take you up on that,' Alexander replied.

The following day Hector rang the library.

'Amanda, about that map and that document I found at the photocopier...' the farmer said. 'The notes say that some of the Fitzgerald land *really* belongs to the council, right?'

'Hector, that's nothing to do with you,' his cousin insisted.

'Oh, come on, Amanda, don't get indignant. I'll bet you read it too.' She fell quiet. 'So tell me, am I right?' he persisted.

'Yes,' she replied, irritably. 'But it's confidential and you mustn't breathe a word about it to anyone. Understood?'

'Thanks, Amanda, I don't intend to make it public. Bye,' Hector said cheerily, which left Amanda with a distinctly uncomfortable feeling.

Chapter 8

'Heavens, it's a while since I was last here,' Penn remarked, as he and Clifford Caines ambled along the canal towpath. Though very different in outlook, their shared appreciation of the canal, coupled with the years they had taught in the local school, had formed a unique friendship and bond.

'Must be at least three months,' Caines replied. He took a last draw on his cigarette then flicked the butt into the canal.

Penn's eyes flashed heavenwards.

'I do wish you wouldn't do that,' he complained, with a pained expression. 'It hardly shows a good example as a teacher.'

'Fusspot,' Clifford retorted. 'It's not as if it's an old bike or a shopping trolley.'

Penn shot him a withering look then shrugged his shoulders. Suddenly, he halted as his head scanned the length of the canal.

'Did you see that?' he exclaimed. 'It was a kingfisher.'

'No, but I've seen them before,' came the nonchalant reply. 'Seen one, seen 'em all.'

'This canal's wasted on you,' Penn lamented, with a slow shake of his head.

They reached *Merryweather 2*, and Caines stepped nimbly aboard the narrowboat, reached for a bunch of keys from his fleece, unfastened the sturdy padlock then opened the doors to the cabin below. He turned to help

Penn, who clambered precariously onto the small deck.

'There are times when I envy your life on the canal,' the historian admitted, once seated inside.

'It has its moments,' Caines acknowledged and reached for a whisky bottle from inside a cupboard.

'I've been told to lay off the stuff,' Penn warned without much conviction when his colleague offered him a glass.

'Go on. One won't hurt you.'

'Well, maybe just one.'

The afternoon drifted slowly and pleasantly on. The sun gradually went down in harmony with the level in the whisky bottle. His earlier, fleeting resolve having deserted him, Penn chattered on, effusively.

'Oh, I'd love to live on the canal,' he enthused, his sparkling eyes now slightly glazed.

Caines raised a cautionary hand.

'It's fine when the weather's good, Alexander, but the late autumn and the winter are killers, believe me. I wouldn't be here if there was an alternative.'

'Are things no better, then?'

'Far from it. It just gets worse and worse. There's no chance of getting back with Esmie,' Caines lamented. 'But in fairness, she does help me out with money. It's the other bitch who screws every last penny out of me. And on top of that—' He stopped suddenly.

Alexander looked at him, clearly concerned for his friend.

'On top of what?' he prompted.

'Nothing,' Caines insisted. 'That's quite enough about me. What else is happening in your world? What haven't we covered? You haven't told me how your research up at the Hall is progressing.'

Penn gave a little snigger and shook his forefinger.

'Can't tell you,' he whispered, and wrinkled his nose.

'Oh, go on. I've confided all my woes.'

Alexander hesitated, then leant forward and put a finger to his lips.

'Well, all right, but it's all hush-hush. Not a word, now.' He gave a warning frown to his friend, who nodded his agreement.

Penn proceeded to describe the discovery of the map from the papers in the trunk, then, after he had stressed its secrecy, the discovery of the transfer document. Their significance was not lost on Caines.

'So what happens now?' Clifford asked.

'As it's half-term next week, I'm off to London to get them both checked and authenticated. Providing they're genuine, I'll then try the old parish records, to see if there's any mention of them and the reciprocal transfer of the other land. Once all that's exhausted, I suppose I'll have to present my findings to the Commander.'

'Who's going to be pretty pissed off with you, I reckon,' observed Caines.

'Yes, I suppose so.'

'What if he just tears them both up and denies their existence?'

'I'll have copies of them certified and keep them back, just in case.' Penn peered at his watch. 'Goodness, is that the time?' he exclaimed and grabbed for support as he rose. 'I'm going to have get my skates on.'

Caines bade him goodbye and held his colleague's arm as Penn tottered off the boat and set off to make his unsteady way homeward along the towpath.

***

Roused from his catnap, Selwyn yawned as a puzzled-looking Mrs Soames entered the room.

'Hector Middleton's asking to see you,' she said. 'Should I tell him to make an appointment?'

'No, no, Mrs S, I wouldn't be able to contain my curiosity. Show him in, please.'

Hector entered, the arrogant smirk on his pockmarked face a change from the customary scowl he usually afforded the Commander.

'Good afternoon, Hector, do sit down,' Selwyn greeted him.

The farmer shrugged off his jacket, slung it casually over a chair and dropped onto the sofa. He splayed out one leg and raised an arm to clasp the back of his head.

'I won't beat about the bush, Fitzgerald,' he blustered. 'You know what I've come about.'

'I don't believe I do, but if it's about the land, you might as well have saved yourself a trip. There's no change in my position.'

Hector broke into a grin.

'Well, there's something here that I reckon will make you change your mind,' he replied adding, 'old boy,' in a sarcastic drawl.

Selwyn refused to rise to the bait. He watched as Hector withdrew some papers from his pocket and passed them over. The Commander looked through them, then started to examine them in more detail. The smile on the farmer's face widened as he watched Selwyn's reaction. Finally, the Commander stared at the farmer with an expression of complete incredulity.

'So from that,' Hector said, revelling in the moment, 'it's pretty evident that some of the land you think you own, you really don't. Now, by my reckoning, the area of land involved is a lot more than that land of mine you refuse to give up.'

Selwyn looked down at the papers, then slowly lifted his eyes and fixed them on his adversary.

'Where did you get these?' he demanded, almost in a whisper.

'That's for me to know and you to find out,' Hector said, to goad him.

'And what do you want?'

'Very simple. You play ball with me and I'll play ball with you. If you're not interested then I'll spill the beans to the council and put them on to the person who has the originals.'

'That's not much of a deal. If the person who has them decides to go public or tell the council, it's all up anyway.'

'Leastways you've got a chance. If you agree to what I propose and I tell you who's got the originals, you should be able to persuade them to part with the documents.'

'And what do *you* want out of this?'

'You release half of the land that should be mine and I give you a name. Then, if you or I succeed in getting hold of the original documents, you release the other half.'

'What if I don't get the originals but they never come to light?'

'We'll give it three months. If nothing's said or done by that time, you release the rest of the land to me.'

'I'll need time to think about it.'

'You don't have that luxury.'

'Two days,' Selwyn insisted.

Hector thought for a moment.

'Very well, two days. And after that, we meet to look at the boundary,' he conceded.

133

After he had safely delivered Aunty Hilda to stay at a friend's house during his absence, Penn drove on to Hopestanding station. With plenty of time before his train was due in, he walked across to the Railway Arms to sample one of the guest beers the pub boasted. He sank down into a seat and, as he took a long draught from his glass, an almost seraphic smile lit up his face.

In a dark corner of the pub's public bar slouched Julian Steele. He glanced again at the address on the piece of paper his mate Mickey had given him earlier that week. Granted, they had both been fairly pissed when Julian had told him the name of the person whose address he wanted to find out. But Mickey could be trusted, could he not? After all, he worked at the town hall.

As he rhythmically kicked the underside of the empty chair opposite, Steele otherwise occupied himself with muttering comprised of various combinations of the words 'bitch', 'woman' and 'magistrate'.

'The fuckin' bitch even named her poxy house after herself,' he muttered. 'Penrose fuckin' cottage!'

He had already cased the cottage, which fronted the common. That night, he planned to have his revenge on the detested Ms Alexandra Penrose, the magistrate who had sent him down for receiving and who, according to Mickey, was safely away on holiday.

***

'Perhaps you'd care to join me for lunch here at the Hall,' Selwyn invited the mayor over the phone. 'I could give you a guided tour.'

'I'd be delighted,' she replied and punched the air with a clenched fist, a look of triumph on her face.

He wouldn't be offering that if he still didn't intend to open the Hall, she thought. She believed the fish was on the hook. All she had to do now was play it and reel it in.

Selwyn had pondered hard and long about whether he should lead the mayor to believe he was now receptive to her proposition of opening the Hall. On the one hand, to do so would reveal his hand and weaken his negotiating position. On the other hand, with the threat of the documents, of which he had now seen copies, coming to light, time was totally against him. He desperately needed to move quickly to survey the site and move on to the excavation. The Commander's hopes of finding the lost family treasure had never been higher, so he could ill afford to waste time in protracted negotiations.

The other argument for showing his hand was to lull the mayor into a false sense of security. If she got used to the idea of his being prepared to open up the Hall, his subsequent reluctance or refusal to do so would throw her off balance. That would make her desperate to recover the position and, he thought, more amenable to compromise. Anyway, Selwyn still had the ace up his sleeve.

Hector's threat had vanished, at least for the present. Two days after the farmer's visit, after further reflection and in a calmer frame of mind, Selwyn had pointed out to him that the council could never have a valid claim on the land without the original documents. Furthermore, if Hector was to turn up the documents, then Selwyn would be willing to negotiate with him, but if Hector publicised them the farmer could say goodbye to the disputed land forever.

More of a problem was the person who held the originals. Selwyn strongly suspected it was Penn, but attempts to contact him had met with no success. If the documents did become public knowledge, it would certainly scupper his chances to excavate the site. More than that, their discovery would have savage repercussions for the estate, which would lose a considerable area of land.

After further deliberation, Selwyn had decided that since the documents had not already surfaced, either Penn – assuming it was him – was not satisfied with their authenticity, or he still had not decided what to do with them. If Selwyn had correctly judged the historian's character, it was unlikely Penn would do anything before he had the decency to contact him first. If he did not have the documents, Selwyn would only add fuel to the fire by alerting him to their existence. Therefore, much as it went against the Commander's instincts, he had decided not to try to get in touch with the historian again, for the present.

***

'Oh my God!' Alexander exclaimed, as he stared at the devastation in front of him. The living room floor was strewn with books, papers and smashed ornaments. Drawers gaped open, and the historical prints that had decorated the cottage walls either hung askew or lay smashed among the debris. Chairs and coffee tables lay on their sides, and the standard lamp leant at a crazy angle against the sofa. Penn gazed despairingly around him but resisted the temptation to enter the room or move on elsewhere.

Thank goodness Aunty wasn't here, he thought as he phoned for the police.

While he waited for them to arrive, Alexander carefully opened the front door, walked round the outside of the cottage and peered into the rooms through the windows, to see what other damage had been done.

DS McBride snapped his notebook shut as his colleagues finished their work and prepared to depart.

'Well, sir,' he addressed Alexander, 'it looks to be either a case of vandalism, or someone came to look for something and, unable to find it, they resorted to vandalism to hide their motive for the break-in. I think we're just about wrapped up here so, if there's nothing else you can add, we'll be on our way. If you contact the station, they'll give you the crime number and any other information you need for your insurers. I'll be in touch with you and if there's anything that occurs to you, please give me a call.'

He handed Penn a card and left.

Alexander lowered himself onto the sofa. He was tired and angry. Tired from the journey from London and angry, that aside from all the mess he now had to sort out, he had Amanda to thank for the betrayal of his confidence. There was no other explanation. He would confront her as soon as possible, but there was something more urgent that clearly needed to be done before that.

***

'My dear fellow, how delightful to see you. Do come in,' Meredith Jewson, the manager of Hadwins Bank, greeted Penn the following morning.

Seated with his briefcase clasped firmly on his knees,

the historian peered across the desk at his old public-school friend.

'My, my, it's quite some time since I last saw you,' Jewson observed, after he had ordered some tea. 'Let me see now, that'd be when we got to the final.'

'I believe it was,' Penn replied, though cricket could not have been further from his mind.

'So what can I do for you, Alexander?'

The historian described the break-in and his need to keep certain documents secure.

'I thought you might be able to look after them for me, just for a short while. I'd be most grateful.'

'Not at all, my dear chap,' Jewson agreed. 'I'll keep them safe with my own papers in the vault. That'll save you having to open an account and fill in all that tedious paperwork.'

Half an hour later, Penn emerged from the bank a much-relieved man. He would have felt happier still had it not been for the next visit on his list, to which he was not looking forward at all.

***

Amanda screeched to a halt at Middleton Farm and finally tracked down her cousin in the barn. There was hot fury in her stomach, and that was all. She had not been able to face her packed lunch after Alex's stormy visit to her office. He was pent-up with accusation and rage that needed to be passed on.

'Well, well, what brings my favourite librarian out here?' Hector asked, his smile cut short as she bore down upon him.

'To ask you a few questions,' she replied, her eyes almost

pinpricks. 'Who did you tell about those documents?'

'N-n-no one,' he stammered.

'Don't give me that bullshit, Hector. I know you. Who did you tell?' Amanda insisted.

'What does it matter to you?'

'What does it matter to me?' she fumed. 'A very good friend of mine's home has been broken into and ransacked by someone looking for them. Alex reckons it's all my fault. So who did you tell?'

Hector backed away, looking distinctly uncomfortable as Amanda advanced on him.

'Commander Fitzgerald,' he admitted. 'But I never told him who had the documents.'

'He'll have guessed it was Alex!' she exploded. 'Alex has been working up at the Hall for weeks, you numbskull.' She glared at him. The way she leant forward looked as if invisible arms restrained her from actually assaulting him. Never before had Hector seen his cousin in such a state. 'You've just about ruined everything, jumping into something that doesn't concern you and tramping about in your thundering great wellingtons!' she railed, then gave way to a shudder.

'I'm sorry, I just thought—' Hector began.

'No, you didn't think. That's your trouble, Hector. You don't think. You just blunder around and cause mayhem. Well, keep your big nose out of this business.' Without waiting for a reply, the angry librarian gave her timorous-looking cousin a final glower then stormed back to her car.

***

Clifford Caines stared blankly at the narrowboat's small

table and the pile of homework books on it that were still waiting to be marked. They had only been back at school for a week after the Easter break, but already he felt jaded.

When his mobile rang, he glanced at the display. His stomach began to churn as he recognised the caller's number.

'It seems you've forgotten about our arrangement, Caines,' came Smudger's icy greeting.

'I'm sorry, things have been really tight. I'll make it up next month,' Caines promised, rising bile caught in his throat.

'That's just not good enough,' warned Smudger.

Clifford clasped his forehead as he furiously tried to think what to say next.

'Caines, are you there?' the caller demanded, after several moments of silence.

'Yes, I'm here,' Clifford responded, unable to articulate anything more. He felt like a rabbit trapped in the glare of oncoming car headlights.

'If you can't pay me now, you certainly won't be able to after you've lost your job and the police are on your case,' Smudger threatened. 'So what's it going to be?'

'Wait! I can pay you something now, but not all of it.'

'It doesn't work that way. It's all or nothing. Isn't that clear enough for you?'

'*And* I've got something for you,' Caines offered.

'What's that?'

'I'll need to meet you.'

'First things first. How much are you going to pay now?'

'Five hundred,' Caines offered and closed his eyes in hope.

'Not enough. You're wasting my time,' Smudger snapped.

'I can scrape together six hundred but that's all.'

Caines listened anxiously through the agonising silence.

'Bring it with you to the usual place tomorrow evening – and you'd better have something good, or else.'

'I'll be there,' answered Caines, in fearful resignation.

***

The following evening, Caines sat and glared as Smudger counted the banknotes, pocketed them, then smiled at his wretched victim.

'You're bleeding me white,' he moaned.

'The wages of sin,' taunted Smudger, with a shrug. 'So, what have you got for me?'

Full of self-loathing that he was about to betray his friend's confidence, the teacher revealed what Penn had told him. His blackmailer stared at him impassively as he juggled the implications and likely consequences, should the details of the transfer document and the map become public knowledge.

'Well?' Caines asked, embarrassed by the silence.

'Who else knows about this?' Smudger demanded.

'No one, as far as I know.'

'And Penn definitely has the document?'

'That's what he told me,' the teacher confirmed. He shuffled his feet as silence reigned again.

'Very well, I'll let you off the rest,' the blackmailer conceded. 'In fact, there's something else I need you to do. Do it and I'll let you off the next three months' payments. Do it well, and maybe we can come to another arrangement for the future.'

'What d'you want me to do?' Caines asked, his eyes narrowed in suspicion.

Smudger outlined the task.

'I can't do that,' the teacher spluttered. 'I'm not up for that.'

'Take it or leave it,' replied Smudger. 'But if you leave it and can't pay up, I don't reckon much of your chances of another teaching job, let alone avoiding jail. *And* I dread to think what the girl's father will do to you. I'm told he's very possessive of his daughter, and he's got a wicked temper.'

Caines fell silent.

'All right. I'll do it,' he murmured eventually.

Smudger smiled and gave his instructions to the miserable man.

Once Caines had slunk out of the pub, Smudger absent-mindedly started to pick apart the beermat on the table in front of him. From what Caines had told him, it appeared that all the estate land the council currently used – and more besides – was not actually owned by the estate but by the council. And since the old quarry road and the barn were only a stone's throw away from the boundary, it was highly probable that these also belonged to the council. Not that Caines was aware of the barn's particular significance.

For Smudger, this placed the most lucrative antiques operation in jeopardy, which was something he was not prepared to let happen. To be on the safe side, the barn would be cleared for now and the operation suspended. When the document and the map had been obtained and the historian silenced, Smudger would wait until the dust had settled. A smile briefly hovered on his lips as he rose to leave and reflected on how useful a victim Caines had proved to be.

***

With her elbows propped on the Mazawat's counter, Gwen cast a curious sideways glance at the woman with the Cleopatra-style hair, who was seated at the back of the cafe. Although she was a new customer, Gwen felt sure she had seen the woman before, though she could not remember where.

'Who's that?' Gwen whispered over the counter to Felicity, and jabbed a forefinger in Cleopatra's direction.

'Librarian,' her cousin mouthed, while she poured a coffee. As the bell rang, she looked up to see Sebastian enter.

Gwen's eyes lit up. It seemed ages since she had last seen him. About to rush forward, she noticed Cleopatra wave to him, her smile and body language speaking volumes – at least to another woman.

With a broad grin, Sebastian went to join the librarian, oblivious to Gwen's frown. He took Amanda's hands into his.

'Hi,' he murmured. 'Sorry I'm late. Been here long?'

She shook her head and watched him take off his fleece as he explained that he had been held up in a meeting.

Ignoring Felicity's warning glance, Gwen breezed over to their table.

'Hi, Sebastian, I've missed you,' she pouted. 'Life's been very dull around here without you. What've you been getting up to?' She gave him an alluring smile, and watched for the librarian's reaction from the corner of her eye.

Amanda completely ignored Gwen's presence and held Sebastian's gaze while she asked him what he would like.

His eyes flitted uncertainly between the two women before they settled back on Amanda.

'I'll have a latte,' he said.

The librarian continued to hold Sebastian's gaze as she said,

'He'll have a latte, waitress, and a cappuccino for me, please.'

Gwen's smile vanished. She looked at Sebastian, who was still enraptured by his companion, then flounced off to the counter and shouted the order to Felicity who, having watched the whole encounter, was having great difficulty in concealing her mirth.

'Looks like you've got a fan club there,' Amanda observed.

Sebastian shrugged.

'I used to work here part time.'

'You must have looked good in a pinny. We'll avoid the question of the job description and move quickly on,' Amanda teased. 'How's the Commander?'

'Got rather a lot on his mind at the moment, I reckon.'

'Problems?'

'One or two – and that's just those that I know about.'

Amanda studied him as he looked round the cafe.

'You know a lot, then?' she asked.

'He takes me into his confidence and I keep my eyes and ears open,' Sebastian replied.

'I'm beginning to wonder if you're a bit of a dark horse, Sebastian. I hope I've not got myself involved with someone shady.'

He puckered his lips and winked at her.

'Stick around with me, kid, and I'll show you the world,' he offered, in a very dubious American accent.

'Well, I suppose that's got to be better than Hopestanding on a wet Wednesday night,' she replied.

Gwen arrived with the order. She presented the latte to Sebastian with a ravishing smile and her eyes rested on him fractionally longer than was necessary for good customer relations. She dumped the cappuccino unceremoniously in front of Amanda and threw her a disdainful glance before she stomped away.

Bemused by the performance, Amanda leant forward.

'So tell me, what's the latest?' she whispered. 'I'm like a field of corn, all ears.'

Sebastian described how the Commander's survey of the playing fields had revealed the remains of two buildings buried there. He also mentioned that the mayor had been invited to lunch at the Hall, which the Commander had made a big thing of and driven Mrs Soames up the wall.

'She's probably on the ceiling by now,' he conjectured.

'The mayor? She's my ultimate boss.' Amanda frowned and started to nibble her bottom lip. 'I wonder what that's all about. She's been going through all the departmental budgets to find spare money. She's obviously got some project in mind that needs funding.'

'Hey, why don't you come to the Hall?' Sebastian suggested. 'I could introduce you to the Commander. I'm sure he'd give you a guided tour of the place. Then I could cook you a meal at ours.'

She smiled at his eager puppy-dog expression.

'Wow! A man of many talents. What about your father? Wouldn't he mind?'

'Not if we arrange it for when he's away at one of the race meetings.'

'Sounds great, but I wouldn't want to be around when Lucrezia Borgia's there.'

'Who?'

'The devious Mayor Cheyney.'

'Is she that bad?'

Amanda affected a little shudder.

'I wouldn't trust her as far as I could throw her. She's a politician through and through, though they say she's been very successful with her own Internet business.'

'How about family?' Sebastian asked.

'I think you're rushing things a bit,' Amanda kidded. She smiled as he coloured. 'But if it's the mayor you're talking about, she's happily divorced with no kids.'

'You throw me with that deadpan humour of yours,' Sebastian muttered, his face still flushed. He scratched his head. 'I've never come across anyone like you,' he added.

'And *you're* supposed to be showing *me* the world? Perhaps I ought to get off at the next stop.'

'I'd rather you didn't,' he pleaded. The humour of their exchange had suddenly given way to seriousness.

She looked into his eyes and placed her long, slender fingers on his clasped hands.

'Yes,' she said, 'I think I'd rather like to stay on a little longer.'

'Good,' he replied, studying her face. He sensed a little unease on her part. 'You never talk about your home and family,' he said.

'There's not a lot to tell, really. Nothing very interesting.'

'Go on.'

'OK, you asked for it. Welcome to the Sheppard guided tour. I live with my grandmother, who needs a lot of looking after. My father left us several years ago, after Mum died, and we've never heard from him since. My only brother Stevie lives in Southampton and works as an entertainer on cruise ships. That's about it, really. Please don't forget the driver when you leave the coach.'

'What about you?' he prompted.

'Well, I like cooking, baking bread, reading and searching for antiques. I dislike crowds, technology, noise and spiders, especially hairy ones.' Amanda watched him, defensively.

'No, you the person,' Sebastian persisted. 'You always seem so self-assured and confident.'

She lowered her head then threw him a sheepish glance, like a small child who had been caught out and was trying to discern how bad things were going to be.

'It's all a bit of a front really, particularly the humour,' she admitted. 'Something of a defence mechanism. I'm not all that good with relationships – I suppose I'm frightened of making a commitment and getting hurt.' She looked down at his hands, which were still clasped on the table. Hers no longer rested on them.

'Then let's just take things gradually,' Sebastian whispered.

'Sounds like a plan,' Amanda murmured with a smile and reached out for his hands again.

Chapter 9

Ever since Hector's visit, Selwyn had slept badly and on the big day of 'the meeting', he rose bleary-eyed and feeling exhausted.

'Come on, Fitzgerald, get a grip on yourself,' he muttered to his reflection in the shaving mirror. He pictured a wide-eyed Georgie standing behind him, ready with a pep talk.

'Right, Bumble, there's a lot riding on this meeting, so buck up and don't let the side down. The last thing you want is for those ancestors of yours to glare at you every time you go up and down the stairs.'

That he would never hear himself called that nickname again, which he had acquired at Oxford and which Georgie had quickly and permanently latched on to, hit him with a blow of sadness. In the mirror he saw the reflection of his faithful beagle, sitting in the doorway and who still regularly wandered around the Hall in search of his mistress.

'Still not bad-looking,' Selwyn muttered to his reflection, when he was dressed and ready to greet the day.

Accompanied by the dog, he went downstairs, picked up the newspaper from the salver on the bureau and headed to the dining room. Mustard veered off to the kitchen for his breakfast, his first outing already made earlier that morning, following Mrs Soames' arrival.

'Everything tickety-boo for lunch, Mrs S?' Selwyn enquired, as she carried in his breakfast. A roll of her eyes told him that it was.

'Lord bless you, Commander, don't fret yourself. Everything's all organised good and proper,' she affirmed.

'You do know I shall probably take her on a tour round the Hall?'

'Yes Commander,' Mrs S sighed, with a shake of her head at his needless concern. 'Everything's taken care of. You just enjoy your breakfast.' She shuffled off and he was left to bury himself in *The Times* and his full English.

When he heard the doorbell finally ring, Selwyn, who had been pacing up and down in the entrance hall, hastened to open the door and greet the mayor. Her chauffeur departed in the mayoral car to other duties until such time as he would be recalled to the Hall.

Miriam looked stunning in a black knee-length dress edged in red, perfectly matched by her scarf and lipstick. Her wavy chestnut hair framed an oval face that lit up with a broad smile as she took his hand.

'Mayor Cheyney, delighted to see you again. Welcome back to Wisstingham Hall,' the Commander greeted her and vigorously shook her hand.

'Thank you, Selwyn. I'm so pleased to be here. Do please call me Miriam.'

He led her through to the drawing room, where they sat by the window.

'I see you've changed things around since I was last here,' she commented with a nod of approval.

'Yes, I thought it was time for a change. It struck me how ridiculous it was not to have some of the seating nearer the windows with a view over the lawn and grounds.'

'It's really quite beautiful.'

'In the spring, the lawn's a mass of crocuses, then daffodils and narcissi. Later, beyond the lawn, we have the summer wildflower meadow. It's a first-rate display.' Conversation ceased as the housekeeper arrived with a tray that bore a bottle of champagne, an ice bucket and two glasses. Mrs Soames smiled at the mayor as she backed her way out of the room.

'A toast, to the results of your survey and the future of the Hall,' proposed Miriam, raising her bubbling glass.

'To the survey and the Hall,' Selwyn echoed as they chinked glasses.

If the mayor had been impressed at what she had seen so far of the Commander's ancestral home, she was positively bowled over when they adjourned to the dining room for lunch. She enthused at length about the room. By the time they got to the cheese course the conversation, which had carefully skirted serious matters and centred mainly on exchanges about each other, took on a more serious note.

'Now that you have the survey results, what do propose to do?' asked Miriam.

'To dig some trial holes, of course, and see exactly what's there,' Selwyn responded enthusiastically.

'Which brings us back to the council's problem in granting permission,' she replied, watching for his reaction. She paused for a moment then continued, 'Unless, of course, the whole thing could be seen in a larger context of promoting the Hall to the general public.'

Selwyn let out a sigh and rubbed his chin.

'You must see how reluctant I'd be to lose my privacy by opening the Hall, let alone the problem of the costs involved,' he argued, with a peek across the room to the panorama outside.

'Yes, I can certainly see how hard it might be,' Miriam empathised. 'Obviously there would be areas of the Hall closed to the public. And as to finance...' she paused, 'I believe there might be grants available for the set-up costs.'

Selwyn cast aside his napkin, looked briefly at Miriam then rose and walked to the window, where he stared out of it in silence. The mayor's anxious stare followed his actions.

'All that would take time,' he replied eventually, returning to the table. 'There would be an awful lot of spade-work to be done. I wouldn't want to wait for all that to happen before work could start on the excavation. Shall we adjourn somewhere more comfortable?' he added, before Miriam could say anything.

The mayor neatly arranged her napkin and rose. Over coffee, she leant forward, her hands clasped together and her eyes fixed firmly on her host.

'The problem is, Selwyn, I really don't think the council would be prepared to countenance the excavation without some kind of assurance about opening the Hall. I do hope you can appreciate our position.'

'Oh, I can, but it seems to me you expect an awful lot in exchange for an agreement to let me to dig a few holes in the ground.'

'Which would involve depriving the residents of the use of land they've been accustomed to for years.' As she spoke, Miriam sensed their imminent arrival at an impasse.

'Surely you must realise I couldn't possibly commit to opening up the Hall without knowing what I'd be getting into,' Selwyn argued, 'both financially and in terms of how it would impact on the day-to-day life of the estate.'

'Oh, good gracious, I wouldn't expect that. But I can't see why there's such an urgency to start the excavation work. That could surely follow on as the Hall was being opened up. An added point of interest.'

'That's the priority I have,' Selwyn insisted, his tone now brittle. 'So how can we unlock this?'

'I really don't think we can,' Miriam replied, and shook her head.

'After all, the excavation will be on estate land,' he reminded her. He reckoned now was the time to play his ace.

'Which the council leases,' she pointed out.

'At a peppercorn rent,' Selwyn emphasised.

'But which it nevertheless holds as its own,' Miriam contended.

'Until such time as the lease comes up for renewal,' Selwyn volleyed.

Miriam frowned, her lips tightened on a faded smile.

'In seven months' time,' Selwyn pointed out.

Miriam's eyes widened.

'Oh, you wouldn't do that!' she exclaimed.

'I certainly wouldn't want to, Miriam, but this is important for me. If necessary, I would.'

They looked at one another as if the encounter had turned into a staring contest, until the deflated mayor sank back into her seat and fingered her bottom lip.

'Is that what you want me to take back to the council, Selwyn? Please give me something more positive than that,' she urged.

The Commander got up and wandered over to the window. Miriam's eyes never shifted from him as he silently stared out for a while. The tension was unbearable. She looked across the room at a painting depicting a cavalry charge, reflecting that she was negotiating with an officer who was doubtless well-trained in tactical manoeuvres, albeit naval ones.

Selwyn resumed his seat and finished his coffee. All the while, the mayor's eyes were fixed imploringly on him.

'This is what I propose,' he eventually said. The mayor's hopes rose at the conciliatory tone in his voice. 'I declare to you my firm intention to open the Hall, subject to having satisfied myself on all the financial and logistical issues. That is on the understanding that the excavation work can proceed at any time from now, subject to the timescales for public notice. You could put that forward, together with my expectation that the council will actively support me in my investigations and in a search for financial support. Then, if your colleagues aren't prepared to play ball, you can point out that there are only seven months left on the lease and that you believe I'd refuse to renew if they said no.'

Miriam's face brightened at a possible way out for both parties that avoided total confrontation. Knowing the sway she held with the council's deputy leader and the PR job she could do on the tourism benefits, she felt confident she could swing it. She beamed at him.

'I think we have an understanding, Commander Fitzgerald.'

'In that case, Lady Mayor,' he replied with a grin, 'I think it would be appropriate to proceed with a tour of my home.'

***

Pilsbury cowered under the table as Vincent stormed about the cottage and bellowed in rage. The dog's eyes were fixed on the closed kitchen door, from which his gaze diverted only whenever his rampaging master approached. While he did not understand the reason for Vincent's behaviour, nor the shower of expletives that accompanied it, the Labrador knew that each day around that time the door would open and Sebastian would walk in. The hiding place was therefore both one of safety and an opportunity for escape.

Before that could happen, however, the storm gradually blew itself out, though it left a trail of debris. Cushions, papers, photographs and anything that had been to hand lay strewn about the living room and kitchen. One lasting manifestation was the look of pure hatred in the eyes of the hound's master. Vincent now lay slumped on the sofa, his face flushed as he muttered obscenities at the crumpled DNA analytical laboratory report he had retrieved from the floor and spread out on his knee. As he read it again, his attention was diverted by the sound of a vehicle. Sebastian was back.

Vincent rose, quickly stuffed the report into his pocket, then scurried around and tidied the place up as best he could. The boy would be a little while yet if he followed his usual pattern of a visit to the stables.

Pilsbury bounded out when the kitchen door eventually opened. He gave scant attention to the usual show of affection from his other master. That in itself was a familiar warning sign to Sebastian, who scanned the shambolic room. There was no sign of his father. Then Vincent came downstairs and glowered at him.

'Don't cook anything for me tonight. I'm out,' he growled.

'And hello to *you*. What sort of a day did *you* have?' Sebastian muttered, as Vincent brushed past him. 'What's been going on?'

At the door, his father spun round.

'What's that you said, you little shit?' he snarled, and balled his fists.

Sebastian, though nervous, stood his ground and squared up to him.

'Just what I said. A bit of civility wouldn't go amiss. It's not the nicest of welcomes one could hope for. And just look at the place. What's happened? What's the matter? Have you had some bad news?'

Vincent's eyes narrowed.

'What the fuck do you mean by that?' he demanded.

'Nothing, but something's clearly bothering you.'

Vincent's fists tightened again but then he thought better of it and relaxed his hands.

'You mind your own fucking business, you gobshite,' he retorted and, with a final glare, he turned and strode off. The kitchen door slammed shut behind him.

***

'Can you get it please, Aunty?' Penn shouted from the top of the staircase over the loud ringing. He paused for a reply then lumbered downstairs and headed for the phone, just as Aunty Hilda called from the kitchen,

'Did you say something, Alexander?'

'No, Aunty,' he panted back as he lifted the receiver. 'Hello, Alexander Penn speaking.' He listened to the caller's introduction and started to bite at his fingernail. 'It was never my intention to keep the map and the document,' he began, before his explanation was interrupted. He grimaced as he

155

continued to listen.

'Well yes, of course I will,' he finally replied, his expression now brighter. 'I'll see you at the folly about four o'clock. We'll get an excellent view of the land from there.'

**

'I must say, I'm surprised Commander Fitzgerald isn't here himself,' Alexander observed, as the two men climbed the folly steps. 'With all due respect, I can't understand why he's delegated this to you. Do you have something to show that you're authorised to act on his behalf?'

'No,' replied Smudger, 'I don't need anything. He doesn't want to have anything more to do with you, on a personal basis, so he's asked me to deal with the matter, and that's all you're getting. That it's me you have to deal with is an indication of just how angry he is about it all. So if I were you, I wouldn't push my luck by asking for pieces of paper,' Smudger replied, curtly. Though still dubious, Alexander did not feel brave enough to prolong the argument. Not at this stage, anyway. At the top of the folly, Smudger looked out over the grounds and landscape beyond.

'So from here, I assume we can see the all the land in question. You've got the documents, of course,' said Smudger.

'No,' Penn panted, still almost bent double to catch his breath back. 'They're locked away safely.' Smudger rounded on him,

'I don't believe you,' he exclaimed. 'You must have them. I told you to bring them. What's the bloody point of coming here without them?'

Penn straightened in alarm and took a hesitant step backwards.

'If it's the land you want me to point out, there's no need for the documents,' Alexander explained. 'I can show you everything without them. I traced it out the last time I was here.'

The historian gingerly approached the parapet, to search for the landmarks, then warily began to point out the boundary, while Smudger stood alongside him, visibly ill-pleased. Penn gave him a quick sideways glance and noted his agitation. Trying to keep his own rising alarm under control, the historian pressed on.

'The boundary runs from just to the right of the little bridge, takes in that old barn, then goes between the trees that bound the bridle path and the other bank of trees on the edge of the recreation fields, just skirting the race-track. Then it finishes to the right of the road junction.'

Smudger's eyes were fixed on the barn, where the boundary would cut the old quarry road, alongside it.

'Those documents are estate property. We need them back immediately,' Smudger demanded.

'I never intended to keep them from the Commander, but they needed to be authenticated. I'll return them to him personally, this week.'

'I've told you, it's me you have to deal with,' Smudger snapped. 'And that's from him.'

'With all due respect, I'll have to put them in the Commander's hands,' Penn tried to insist. Smudger, who had shifted his gaze back to the barn, now turned to face to the increasingly fearful Penn. The venomous expression on Smudger's face set alarm bells ringing with him. Perspiration started to form on Penn's brow. He reached hesitantly into his pocket for a handkerchief. Smudger's eyes flashed as he watched him.

'You bastard, you've got them on you after all,' he exploded, and moved forward. Petrified, Alexander backed away. Smudger grabbed at his jacket and tried to reach into the pocket. Alexander tried to resist by seizing his attacker's arms. With a lunge, Smudger flung the terrified Penn against the wall. Half his body now hung perilously backwards over it. Smudger wrenched his arms free, reached down and grabbed Penn's legs. Then, with a grunt, he heaved upwards, overbalanced and toppled the screaming man over the parapet.

There was a sickening thud, which instantly gave way to silence. Smudger stared down at the body, which twitched for a few moments, then was still. He raced down the stairs and crouched over the corpse. After a rapid glance round to see if there were any witnesses, he searched Alexander's pockets. Having found nothing, the murderer muttered a final curse then slunk away, empty-handed.

***

Vincent scrambled down the rise through the thin morning mist and bounded over to the Hall, with the dog's lead trailing loosely in his hand. Pilsbury ran ahead of him, both interested and confused at the turn of events.

The estate manager burst through the side door, ran down the corridor, and came to a halt at the foot of the staircase just as the Commander, who was halfway down the stairs, stopped and frowned down at him.

'Good Lord, Vincent, what is it, man?' he demanded.

'Body by the folly,' Monaghan panted. 'Nearly missed it

in the fog. I was out walking the dog. He found it.'

'Oh, my sainted aunt!' exclaimed Mrs Soames, who had hastened from the kitchen and started to wring her hands.

'Who is it?' the Commander asked as he hurried to the phone.

'It's that history fellow.'

Selwyn stopped in his tracks.

'Good God!' he exclaimed.

Within twenty minutes, three police cars were parked haphazardly on the drive and the forecourt and the place was alive with activity. A small tent had been erected over where the body lay and the area taped off. A sergeant was seated in the study, taking down Vincent's statement, while Selwyn paced the drawing room floor.

'Bad business,' he muttered to himself. 'Can't think what the fellow was doing there. Not a peep out of him over the past few weeks. It's a rum do.'

The sergeant looked round at him and paused in his questioning of Vincent while Selwyn outlined Penn's work at the Hall.

There was a knock at the door.

'There's a pothogist 'ere,' Mrs Soames announced.

'Pathologist,' corrected the sergeant, who rose and headed to the door, closely followed by the grim-faced Commander.

By midday the body had been removed and most of the police officers had departed. The pathologist's preliminary findings were that there appeared to be no superficial injuries to the body other than those consistent with a fall. The rest would have to await the results of the post-mortem.

***

Clifford Caines was waiting at Folkestone. He nervously tapped his fingers on the steering wheel as he scanned the car park and the terminal building for signs of officialdom. When the electronic sign indicated that the letter *K* passengers should proceed to board the shuttle, he heaved a sigh of relief, started the engine and headed slowly towards the passport and security booths while trying desperately to control his rising panic and his breathing.

***

After a gruelling journey from Montreal, Martin finally reached Wisstingham. Despite the late hour, Amanda had waited for him at the cottage, although Aunty Hilda had long since gone to bed.

The librarian, Martin maintained, had been an 'absolute brick' in looking after the distraught old lady, who in her weaker moments repeatedly demanded to know where Alexander was. Amanda, however, felt anything but a brick and had passed anxious moments and sleepless nights agitated about whether she should inform the police about the map and the transfer document. There was nothing to show them, and to mention it at such a late stage would most likely bring down the council's wrath upon her. She might even possibly lose her job through gross negligence and duplicity. It would also point the finger of suspicion at Commander Fitzgerald as the one person who would not wish the documents to see the light of day. After all, Penn had died on his land. Furthermore, Amanda had convinced herself that

Alexander's death had simply been an accident. He had probably gone to the folly to look at the lie of the land and fallen. So she had kept quiet, despite occasional niggling feelings of guilt and doubt.

The view of the police, however, had not been so relaxed about the death.

'Two unexplained deaths on the same estate, eh, McBride?' Stone had observed with a sniff.

The file on Pitt's death had never been closed. Immediately after the DI had returned from the scene of Penn's death, he called down to the records department for the file on the poacher to refresh his memory.

The police investigation of the folly and the surrounding ground had not come up with anything of consequence. Neither had the examination of Penn's body or his clothing established any signs of a struggle or violence. Furthermore, once the historian's recent medical history had been obtained, attention had turned to the possibility of his fall having resulted from a blackout similar to the one he had nearly suffered at the library.

The height of the folly's parapet wall was considered marginal, in terms of the likelihood that Penn could have fallen while he leant over it. From interviews with people who knew him, there was nothing to indicate that he had any enemies, nor that he might have contemplated suicide. All these factors would receive due consideration at the inquest – though DI Stone remained doggedly convinced that foul play should not be ruled out.

***

Clifford Caines devoured the salami and cheese baguette, only breaking off at intervals to cram handfuls of crisps into his mouth. He had stopped at the last service station before Calais but almost driven straight back on to the autoroute after he had spotted three gendarmerie vehicles parked there. However, he was famished. Desperate to get back over the Channel, he had driven non-stop from Bar-sur-Aube, where he had stayed the previous night.

At the terminal, his anxiety level had nearly shot through the car roof as the woman at passport control seemed to take a disproportionate interest in him compared to how quickly she had dealt with the car in front. He felt his ears burn as she quizzed him on where he had come from and what he had in the car. She was probably just bored and wanted a bit of a diversion, the teacher tried to reassure himself, as he drove to the holding lane. But even the guard, who had walked along the train scanning the details on each label dangling from the rear-view mirrors, had given him a once-over, or so he had thought.

Caines scrunched up the plastic baguette wrapper and threw it into the passenger well to join the other debris that had accumulated during his journey. His frayed nerves frantically sought some distraction. The time on his watch had already been adjusted and the speedom-eter changed back to miles per hour. In the mirror he noted the bags under his eyes, and his weary expression. He had hardly got any sleep in the hotel, whose facilities, he had concluded, were as medieval as the town itself.

Once on the M20 he put his foot down, impatient for the safety and familiarity of his narrowboat. *He* would have to wait until tomorrow.

Desperately in need of sleep, Caines cursed the weather and the mud as he struggled with the padlock on the boat, thankful that it was nearly a full moon. In the dark confines under the canopy, he missed the business card that had been poked through the awning three days earlier, which had fallen on to the deck.

'Bastard thing!' the weary man muttered, once he was inside the boat and had located the mobile he had left behind in his hasty departure. He had been totally lost without it. He plugged it in to charge, took a long swig of water, then made up his bed and fell into it, exhausted. The world would have to wait until tomorrow to tell him anything it wanted him to know or what he had missed.

What the world wanted Caines to know, in the form of the overlooked business card, was that he had to contact Detective Inspector Stone immediately on his return. The mobile's list of missed calls and messages also wanted him to know that his friend Alexander Penn was dead.

The next morning he sat bowed over a mug of tea, weighed down with guilt and fear. He glanced at the business card and shivered, expecting the constabulary's rap on the door of the narrowboat at any moment.

Totally demoralised, Caines felt his life had plummeted into a criminal abyss. Never before had he felt so alone and so vulnerable to the maggots of people who now chewed away not only at his worldly possessions but also at the remnants of his ever-dwindling pride, his hope, his very soul. Wearily, he washed and dressed, skipped breakfast, then started to make some calls and texts.

***

It was the beginning of a busy day, which had started badly with a long wait in the interview room at the police station.

'He's been here quite a while,' WPC Pelman warned DI Stone as they strode down the corridor at the station.

'It was bloody Hadwins Bank. Had to wait ages,' Stone complained. 'Jewson, the bank manager, keeled over with a stroke or something. Took ages while they stretchered him out. Staff were running around the place like Henny Penny.'

'That's my bank,' Pelman exclaimed. 'Poor Meredith. He's such a lovely soul.'

Stone rolled his eyes and the conversation ceased as they had reached the interview room.

Caines found himself obliged to answer a barrage of questions from the surly DI, who was still annoyed at having his day off disrupted. Where had Caines been, and why had he gone away? Where was he at the time of Penn's death, and who could vouch for him? Did he know of anyone who had a grudge against the deceased?

Stone paused in his questioning to turn to his colleague.

'It's not the school holidays, is it?' he asked.

'Not that I know of,' replied the WPC.

Caines bowed his head and admitted he had called in sick and played truant from his work.

'I desperately needed a break. I just had to get away somewhere – anywhere,' he claimed.

The officers stared at him dispassionately for several agonising moments before Stone moved on.

'Is there anything you feel we should know?' he asked.

Caines pondered for several seconds before he decided that silence was his only option.

'No, nothing,' he muttered finally, though with little conviction.

The officers exchanged glances.

'Are you sure?' Stone demanded. 'It took you a while to think about that.'

'That's just what I was doing,' the teacher replied, his temper frayed. He and the DI stared at each other until Stone eventually conceded that he had no more questions for the present.

'I'm not convinced,' the DI muttered to the WPC, as they stood outside the interview room watching the exhausted Caines trudge away. Stone jingled the coins in his pocket.

'Hasn't got a single witness to where he was and he looks guilty as hell,' he sighed. 'We'd better start checking. Start with the hotel he was staying in. How's your French?'

'Rusty GCSE,' his colleague replied with a grimace.

'Well, give it your best shot. If you have problems, get on to the college – they've been pretty helpful in the past. Something smells very rotten about this.'

With one last glance at the disappearing figure, he set off, jingling, towards the canteen.

***

Alexander Penn's cremation service was well attended and the wake was held in the Phantom Hound, where Sebastian had said farewell to his mother. Because he had not known the man, Sebastian had decided not to attend the funeral, though his real reason was a wish to avoid seeing Amanda and Martin together.

She had waxed lyrical about what a 'nice chap' Penn's nephew was. It seemed evident to Sebastian that his relationship with Amanda had somehow cooled. She frequently cancelled arrangements to meet, allegedly because of her grandmother. More than once he suspected she had got cold feet and he had recalled how she had told him about her fear of getting hurt in a relationship.

Tempted though Sebastian was to go to the pub and watch the proceedings from the public bar, he stayed at home, tormented with mental images of the couple engrossed in the enjoyment of each other's company.

The next day, his morning started badly when the car broke down on his way to work. While waiting for the breakdown service, his thoughts turned to Amanda, and to Penn's funeral. And again he imagined her, radiant and happy with Martin at her side. By the time Sebastian arrived at Fellowes House he was in no mood for work or anything else the day might throw at him.

There followed one calamity after another, which culminated in total misery and dejection by the time he finally left Hopestanding in the early evening. He decided to call in at the Mazawat, as he occasionally did. That way he could at least postpone his arrival at an increasingly unhappy home. The cafe was deserted, with only Gwen standing idly by the counter. Presumably Felicity was in the storeroom.

'Sebastian,' Gwen called as he trudged through the door.

His return greeting of 'Hi,' was cheerless.

'Oh, my poor lamb,' she exclaimed, 'what on earth's happened? You look like you've got the cares of the world on your shoulders.' She stood in front of him and placed her hands sympathetically on his shoulders.

'It's been a bloody awful day,' he sighed.

'Come on, let me make it better,' she said as she clasped

the back of his neck and pulled his face down to hers. Gripping his head tightly, she gave him a lingering kiss at the very moment that Amanda reached the door. Rooted to the spot transfixed, as she stood outside the cafe, she looked on open-mouthed at the couple. Her vision blurred as her eyes misted over and the unhappy librarian turned and set off for home.

'Woah!' Sebastian exclaimed and pulled away as Gwen showed no sign of breaking off. 'I love you dearly, Gwen, but not like that! Thanks for the sympathy. I feel much better. I think.'

'We aim to please,' she replied with a satisfied grin. 'You can't blame a girl for trying, and it's not as if there's any harm done.'

Chapter 10

'Since it's my last night, how about a Chinese?' Martin suggested to Amanda. They were seated side by side at the dining table, surrounded by heaps of Alexander's papers. Box files were stacked neatly alongside the sofa, which had been monopolised by ring binders.

'Yes, that would be nice,' Amanda replied in a monotone. She placed a document on the 'Offer to Hopestanding Historical Society' pile.

'Only if you want to. Somewhere else, if you prefer?' he offered, having sensed her lack of enthusiasm.

'Qwik Qwak'll be just fine,' she agreed, and managed a smile.

'I'll need to go and see Aunty first,' he warned, and threw a despairing glance at the mass of documents yet to be sorted through. 'I feel guilty at leaving all this for you to deal with.'

'It's not a problem. I promised I'd do it and it'll be interesting to see what Alex found, though I am concerned there's no sign of the transfer document or the map. I thought we'd have come across them by now.'

'I don't imagine I'll get any joy but I'll ask Aunty if she knows anything about them,' said Martin.

Amanda cast her eyes around the room and tried to assess how long it would take to deal with Alex's accumulated work. She would certainly need to transfer much of it to her own home, but only if she could ensure Nan would not interfere with it all, when Amanda was at the library. She started to compare the two characters of her grandmother and poor Aunty Hilda, who was now bereft of Alex's support.

'What's going to happen to Hilda?' Amanda asked. 'Is there any other family who can look out for her?'

'No, I'm afraid not. I've looked at homes here and in Hopestanding, but there are waiting lists everywhere,' replied Martin. 'Mrs Gant says she can stay with her until something comes up. I'll keep the cottage on so I can use it as a base when I'm on leave, either to have her here, to give Mrs Gant a break, or to visit her when she does get a place in a home.'

They went back to the paperwork. Martin's task was to sort out the chronology and the subject matter, Amanda's to determine what linked with what and to decide their ultimate destination.

'Martin, if I do find the documents, what do you think I should do with them?' she asked, after several minutes.

'I haven't the faintest. Uncle did say he'd leave you to decide.'

'I suppose it all hinges on whose property they are,' she surmised. 'Since they really belong to the Commander, I should give them back to him – in which case that's probably the last the world will ever see of them.'

'What if you gave them to him but kept copies and told him you'd inform the council about them? Maybe they'd find their own copies.'

'Sheppard the shifty librarian,' Amanda muttered, with the first hint of amusement that day. She glanced at the grandfather clock. 'If we're going out, I'd better get home to see Nan's all right and get ready.'

'So, seven at the Phantom, then?' he prompted.

'Fine. I'll see you there,' she replied. With a last rueful glimpse at the room and its contents, she rose and set off for home.

Martin slowly took in his surroundings. He wandered around the cottage and tried to decide if he could be happy living there. Though small, it was cosy and in a prime location. The town itself was charming and had enough to offer, since Hopestanding was nearby. Yes, he felt he could be happy there, but it all hinged on how his relationship with Amanda might develop. He weighed the pluses and minuses: his prolonged absence in Canada; the inquest; Amanda's involvement to help sort out the estate; the uncertainty of Aunty's future. There was enough to keep Amanda involved with him, but he could not afford to go away again without having told her how he felt and, more importantly, found out what she really felt about him.

Later, when Amanda arrived at the pub, one glance at Martin's expression told her that things did not bode well.

'Not good news,' he announced, as they sat down at their usual table. 'Fortunately I caught Aunty in one of her clearer moments. A few days after Uncle died, she came across a file labelled "Wisstingham Hall".'

'I didn't see that,' Amanda interrupted.

'No, she rang the Commander to tell him she had found the file and did he want to go through it for anything that belonged to the estate. He came for it the same day.'

'Oh no!' groaned Amanda, a hand clasped to her forehead. 'Well, that's messed things up. He must have the documents. That's the end of that.'

They finished their drinks in subdued silence. Amanda's recurring thoughts on the subject prodded her inner demons back to life. Should she have mentioned the documents to the police? Was it possible that they had anything to do with Alex's death? Had the Commander been involved?

'I didn't mention the documents to the police after Alex died,' she admitted to Martin. 'Do you think I should have done?' She watched anxiously as he mulled over the question.

'I don't think that would have done much good,' he replied finally. 'And it might well have caused you some trouble. I don't think the police could have got anywhere, if the Commander had denied any knowledge of them, which he would have done if he was involved.'

She breathed more freely and smiled at him.

'Come on,' he said, on seeing this new sign of cheer. 'I'm hungry. Let's go eat, shall we?'

As they strolled to the restaurant, Amanda reflected happily on his reassurance. He glanced at her and she returned his smile then linked her arm in his – just as Sebastian's car drove past. That driver cast an anguished stare at the seemingly happy couple.

'That really was delicious,' Amanda later complimented the proprietor, as he cleared away their plates and offered them a drink on the house.

Martin leant back in his chair, nursed a brandy glass and decided to take the plunge.

'Amanda, I'm very fond of you,' he declared.

'I was getting that impression,' she replied, and met his gaze.

Not for the first time, the librarian had caught him off guard. She read his concerned expression as he considered his next words and came to the rescue.

'I'm quite fond of you too, Martin, but I wouldn't want you to hold out any hope that it's more than a sisterly affection, or that it's likely to develop,' she warned.

Martin pursed his lips.

'Well, that's me told in no uncertain terms,' he observed.

'I don't imagine you'd want it any other way.'

'You're right, I suppose. Is there someone else?'

'I thought there was, but not now,' Amanda murmured. She stared down at the tablecloth and idly pushed a grain of rice around with her finger. Then, she looked back at him, and brightened. 'So, if you're in the market for a sister I'm your girl,' she announced, with a flourish of hands and a flashing smile.

Martin's dejection turned into a chuckle at his companion's infectious charm and humour.

'You really know how to spoil a guy's birthday,' he accused.

Amanda's eyes widened and her jaw dropped, as her hand went up to her mouth.

'It's not your bir—'

'Gotcha!' Martin grinned. 'If you'd been anything of a sister, you'd have known that it's the twenty-fourth of February.'

She poked her tongue out at him and landed a playful slap on his arm.

'That's not fair,' she pouted. The edges of her mouth rose in the ghost of a smile. 'I'm only an apprentice sister. In fact, I've not even been adopted yet.'

'You have now,' Martin declared. 'Who wouldn't want to

adopt you as a sister if they couldn't have you as a lover?'

As they left the restaurant, she looked up at him and they once again linked arms.

'Come on, big brother, walk me home,' she said.

He kissed her on the forehead and they started to stroll away. Across the road, a cold, grim and desolate watcher emerged from the shadows and slouched off homewards.

***

'God bless us!' Mrs Soames exclaimed, feather duster in hand, as she caught sight of the Commander sashaying out of the drawing room and along the corridor. 'If it wasn't autumn I'd say it was spring, I would indeed.'

Selwyn caught sight of her and instantly assumed his customary gait as he approached with a sheepish smile.

'Expecting the mayor for elevenses,' he said. 'I'll let her in when she arrives and let you know when we're ready.'

'But not with the bell pull,' she teased.

His smile faded.

'You mean it's broken?' he exclaimed,

'No.' She smiled.

His sense of humour returned.

'You're pulling my leg,' he accused, wagging his finger at her. He walked off with a slight swagger. The house-keeper remained where she was and, after a few paces, he predictably returned. 'Got any of those lovely short-breads of yours?' he asked.

'Right as not there's some left. I'll put them out.'

He flashed her a grin and set off for the drawing room, humming.

Mrs Soames would have said that it was just one of those days. The Commander was happy; she was happy; the sun shone, and all seemed right with the world. *She* even hummed as she continued with her morning's chores.

Unable to settle to anything, Selwyn set out from the Hall and sauntered down the front steps. He took in the rural vista, turned down the side of the building and, at the garage block, passed through the gateway to the walled kitchen garden, there to inspect the vegetable beds. He had just reached the fruit bushes when he heard the welcome, gravel-crunching sound of a car on the drive. Selwyn hurried back to the Hall just in time to see his guest draw up.

'Lovely to see you again, Miriam,' he greeted her as she stepped out of the car.

'And you too, Selwyn,' she replied, her eyes and smile evidently in full agreement.

He leant forward and kissed her on both cheeks.

'*Ooh la la*! How very continental,' she remarked, as they started up the steps.

In the drawing room, Selwyn walked over towards the fireplace and smiled to himself as he tugged the bell pull.

When she waddled into the room, Mrs Soames gave a slight curtsey, the large tray precariously balanced as she did so.

'As a mayor, I'm not important enough for such an honour,' Miriam gently tried to explain.

'Well I reckons you should be, ma'am,' the housekeeper replied loyally. 'I've always been a stickler for respect for them in 'igh office. Old-fashioned it might be, but that's just 'ow it is with me.'

'It's good news and bad news, I'm afraid, Selwyn,' Miriam

announced, once they were alone. 'The council's agreeable in principle for the exploration work to go ahead, but only if there's a firm commitment on your part to open the Hall.'

Selwyn let out a sigh of exasperation.

'That's totally unreasonable,' he exclaimed. 'We've been through all this.'

The mayor shifted in her seat.

'They believe it's really up to you to show some progress on looking into the funding and availability of grants,' she explained. 'Also, they believe that a start on the excavation work should coincide with a *public* declaration of intent to open the Hall, with a press release to cover both events at the same time.'

'And are they not bothered by the possibility that I might not renew the lease?'

She cleared her throat.

'There's a close divide between those who want to avoid that at all costs, and those who would view non-renewal as a direct threat to the community. Their argument is that if you're prepared to do that, and make the estate so unpopular with the town and the council, then go ahead and see what future cooperation the estate gets from the entire village.'

Selwyn stared at her and tapped his fingers on the armrest.

'And what do you think?' he asked.

'My proposal is that we take a three-month period to move things forward. Our offices will assist in the search for sources of funding, and actively support and sponsor any applications. At the same time, you'll look into the best and most practical way the Hall could be opened to the public: what would be needed, the costs involved, and the revenue opportunities.'

'And at the end of the three months?'

'We'd have a far better indication of the feasibility and whether you'd be prepared to commit to the project.'

Selwyn rose and wandered over to his customary vantage point at the French windows. On balance it seemed a reasonable compromise, which would only involve a delay of a further three months. If the transfer document and the map were going to surface, they were likely to do so before the end of the three months' notice he would need to serve anyway. If not, another three months would not make much difference.

He turned to see Miriam's eyes fixed on him, her hands clasped in her lap as if in prayer.

'This means a lot to you doesn't it?' he observed.

She glanced down to her hands for a moment, then looked up in silent appeal.

'Yes, it does,' she murmured with a slight catch in her voice. 'I have to admit that politically it would be the crowning achievement to my year as mayor and a great plus for next year's election campaign. From a personal point of view, it's something that I feel very strongly about.'

'Then I think we should try and make a success of it together. I'm going to need a lot of help, though.'

Her fingertips shot to her mouth and her eyes closed.

'We'll need to visit a fair number of stately homes to pick up ideas,' Selwyn suggested, feeling strangely uplifted. 'However, we might have problems with what we're allowed to do to the building where it has to be converted. Could be a bit tricky – listed building and all that guff.'

'Don't worry too much about that,' said Miriam, buoyed up by the moment. 'You'll have the full support of our planners and architects. I think visits to other stately homes is a great idea.' The schoolgirl happiness that had instantly engulfed her faded as she observed his cheery expression disappear. His eyes were focused on the family photos displayed on the table. He then turned his gaze to the window and there were a few moments of awkward silence before he rallied.

'No time like the present to get some ideas down,' he said, in a businesslike manner. 'That's if you've got the time?'

'As much time as we need,' she offered.

Seated at a table, they jotted down ideas and action points to be developed and pursued, with only a pause for the Commander to ask Mrs Soames to rustle up some sandwiches for lunch.

'I'll ask Sebastian to put these on to the computer,' he said later, as he leafed through the sheaf of papers their brainstorming session had yielded. 'Then he can email them to you, together with the information you need about the Hall.'

A date for another meeting was agreed and the Commander escorted Miriam to her car. As he waved her off, his haunted smile lingered long after the BMW had disappeared from view.

***

Saturday was usually the best day of the week for Sebastian, but today he trudged dejectedly after the scampering Pilsbury and Mustard on a late morning walk. After breakfast he had narrowly avoided a row when he refused to respond to Vincent's allegation that he was backsliding on his domestic responsibilities. Such disputes on almost any subject had become a regular feature of life at the cottage. Vincent frequently accused him of being self-centred and lazy.

Sebastian did all he could to distance himself from his father's mood swings and frequent open hostility, but today's glorious weather and the beauty of his surroundings had done nothing to lift the young man's spirits. Nor had the antics of the two dogs.

At the bridle path beyond the woods, Wisstingham Prancer was being walked out for the morning's exercise in the paddock. Sebastian stopped to admire the horse before he crossed to the track leading to the lake jetty. There the dogs splashed along the shore and chased the ducks, which took irritably to the air before they landed on the lake, where they quacked their disapproval.

At the lake garden, he sat down and looked up towards the folly. The recent events that drifted through his troubled mind were suddenly banished by the chimes of the stable clock. The Commander had asked him to attend a meeting. He would just make it if he returned immediately.

'Interesting times ahead,' Selwyn announced as they sat in the conservatory. He went on to outline the proposal to open the Hall to the public. 'Strictly confidential at this stage,' he stressed, and handed Sebastian the notes from the previous day, then proceeded to explain what he needed done. 'You know how you've constantly badgered me about the computer not being up to snuff,' Selwyn said, with a smirk. 'Well, I'm giving you the go-ahead to put in a new system. It'll need to have the capability to look after all the business accounts and paperwork if the Hall *is* opened.'

His grey day suddenly brightened by this piece of welcome news, Sebastian said,

'Right on!' and punched the air.

'I'll also need someone full time to run the business end of the show. Do you think you'd be interested?' Selwyn asked.

'Yeah, dead right,' Sebastian hastily replied, eager to hear more.

His evident enthusiasm made the Commander smile, but there *was* no more. Sebastian continued to look at Selwyn, waiting for him to say something, but the Commander merely stared back, deliberately expressionless except for a faint twinkle in his eye.

'Well?' Sebastian pressed him. 'Aren't you going to fill me in on what you want from the system?'

'That's up to you, my dear boy,' Selwyn drawled. 'You're the business and computer boffin. It's for you to come up with some ideas and proposals for me. And, of course, a budget. You've got a blank canvas to work on.'

Selwyn motioned with his eyes to the laptop, which lay open on the adjacent table. His new project manager stared at him for a few seconds as the magnitude of the task and its opportunities started to dawn on him. With a rub of his hands, and a grin at the Commander, Sebastian seated himself in front of the blank screen and flexed his fingers.

'I'll see you later, then,' Selwyn said, and walked off, a wry smile on his lips.

***

Vincent was the next person to be brought into Selwyn's confidence about the project. His brief was to come up with security proposals for those areas of the estate that the public would be denied access to, which would still enable the estate, and particularly the stables and paddock, to function.

In the days that followed, as the small project team grappled with aspects such as a cafe, toilets, a souvenir shop, car parking, a ticket office, a first-aid room, staff quarters and stores, as well as safety and security, the enormity of the venture unfolded. They juggled with forecasts, estimates, calculations and spreadsheets, as well as Internet usage. So, it was some time before Sebastian was ready to go through his proposals with the Commander.

'Now you're sure you can handle this project and all it entails?' Selwyn asked, with an apprehensive frown.

Sebastian assured him that he was, though he omitted to mention that he had already run his proposals past Jez, who had promised every assistance – though since Jez's company would probably supply the hardware and software at preferential rates, this was only to be expected.

For the Commander, despite the excitement that surrounded the project and its development, the question of the whereabouts of the transfer document and the map preyed on his mind. They were not in the file he had collected from Penn's cottage, so the fear that they could turn up among the historian's papers remained a real and ever-present one. If they were to come into the public realm, the estate would lose not only the land already leased to the council but also a significant tract of other valuable land. Should the family fortune be buried on that land, the opportunity to search for it would be lost to Selwyn, as indeed would be the treasure itself.

What Selwyn did not know was that, despite Amanda's thorough search of Penrose Cottage, the documents remained elusive.

'Either the Commander's got them, Alex passed them to someone else, or they've been secreted somewhere,' she told Martin during one of his telephone calls to her. 'There's nothing at Penn's bank, and the pipsqueak acting manager was as much use as dandruff. What's more, they've no idea when – or even if – the manager will return to work. I haven't got a clue where else to look.'

'We'll just have to see if they turn up,' Martin concluded.

'Rather like the tooth fairy,' Amanda replied gloomily.

***

Smudger felt distinctly uneasy. There was nothing tangible, just a gut feeling. The trade in stolen antiques was going well, especially with the brilliant job Fellowes had done with the dark web. Harry, who had now branched out into Europe, was more than satisfied with how it was all going. However, it was the uncertainty over the missing documents that troubled Smudger.

The barn was undoubtedly within the boundary of the land that the map showed, and the last thing he wanted was for it to attract any interest. He had recognised from the beginning that their good fortune would not last forever and his sixth sense now told him that something was about to happen. Smudger had developed contingency plans for closing down the operation with Jez, though he had kept some aspects to himself. They had to be ready to move, and move quickly.

The latest development of a new computer system for the Hall was a godsend. It would now be much easier to launch the next crucial stage of his plan. Jez was overjoyed at the news, which he said sorted out the logistics of the task Smudger had set him.

'It couldn't have turned out better,' was his comment. When asked what his plan was, Jez replied, 'I'll create two identical computers: one for my office to feed what we need on to it, the other for the Hall. I'll set up that computer so that it can be accessed remotely. Then, at the right time, we'll remove the remote access, swap them over and let the files tell their own story. What's more,' he continued, 'as a bonus, I'll recommend the installation of security cameras at the same time, which I'll offer at a big discount. If the Commander buys the idea, I'll programme the system to give us our own coverage. If not, we can still plant some bugs and one or two small cameras.'

'What about the costs?'

'I'll factor it all into the other work.'

'Don't over-egg the pudding,' Smudger warned. 'He mustn't go for other quotes. If necessary, you'll have to go in at a giveaway price.'

'Don't worry. I've already got Sebastian on side, if Fitzgerald proves to be stubborn,' Jez confirmed.

***

Amanda studied the paperwork she had just found in her in tray, wrinkled her nose and made a phone call.

'Sylvia, did you drop off these requisition sheets?' she asked.

'Yes,' came the cautious reply. 'Councillor Cheyney told

me to pass them back to you.'

'Really? Did she say why?'

'No.'

'All right, thank you.'

The librarian made another call and, within minutes, was barging through the front doors of the council offices. With a fleeting smile at the receptionist, she marched down the corridor. The wood-panelled walls echoed to the sound of her purposeful tread on the tiled floor.

At the mayor's parlour, Amanda rapped on the oak door, pushed it open and informed the secretary she was expected. She impatiently scanned the rows of photos of previous mayors on the walls while the mayor was called. Another rap, and the librarian stood bristling in front of Miriam Cheyney, who was seated at her desk, engrossed in a report.

The mayor slowly raised her head, gave an indulgent smile and motioned her visitor to sit.

'Why have the requisitions been sent back unapproved?' Amanda queried, barely able to impart any civility to the question.

'The library budget has to be cut back,' the mayor replied, oozing charm. 'Marcia should have told you before she went on leave.'

She looks like one of the bloody Stepford wives, thought Amanda, as she glared at the mayor and angrily brushed a wisp of hair away from her face. The further clarification she waited for was clearly not going to be forthcoming.

'I didn't hear anything. Why is the budget being cut?' she asked.

'It's not a permanent cut. It won't affect the budget for

next year,' the mayor assured her. 'It's just that we need some money for a new project. All my other departmental budgets are in the same position. The library service is not alone.' Her cold, hard stare brooked no further discussion or argument, a message Amanda refused to read.

'What is this project and how much of my budget's been taken?' she demanded.

Miriam settled back in the chair and rested her hands neatly in front of her on the edge of the desk. She gave Amanda a patronising smile, though her eyes were humourless.

'The project is going to be an exhibition, Miss Sheppard, and that's all I'm prepared to tell you at this stage. As for the budget, I would remind you that it is not *your* budget. If it is anyone's budget, it belongs to your superior, Marcia Pincher. I trust that clarifies matters.' She started to reread the report, evidently expecting the troublesome librarian to leave.

'Where will the exhibition be housed?' asked Amanda, who ignored her cue and remained seated.

The mayor leant forward, widening the spacing of her hands on the desk as if to rise in anticipation of conflict.

'At present, the conference and workshops room has been earmarked for it.'

'Why am I not surprised at that?' Amanda murmured, and threw the mayor a withering look.

'It should encourage a lot of visitors to the library, with an inevitable spin-off of new membership,' Miriam asserted.

'As long as we've got enough books to go round,' Amanda bristled.

'I don't think you appreciate your position,' the mayor

replied and finally got to her feet in indignation. Amanda also stood up, no less incensed.

'With my book budget raided and my top floor taken from me, all without any prior consultation, it looks like a pretty precarious position to me, with not much of it left,' she volleyed.

'Yes, well...' The mayor hesitated. 'There's clearly been a breakdown in communication. I shall have a word with Marcia on her return.'

They faced each other in silence, the atmosphere electric.

'Thank you for your time,' Amanda said finally, without a hint of sincerity. She barged through the doorway and stormed through the parlour. On seeing the librarian's demeanour, alarm spread across the thin face of the mousy secretary,

'A bit like working for a pirate, really,' Amanda muttered as she stomped down the corridor.

Chapter 11

His case packed, Selwyn draped a scarf round his neck, picked up the camera from the bed and sallied forth to the landing, humming the theme to *The Waltz of the Toreadors*. As he made his way down the staircase, the sound also drifted down to a bemused Mrs Soames, whose duster was in mid tickle of the armpit of a suit of armour.

'Lord love a duck,' she murmured to herself with a smile, 'if 'e ain't been like a spring chicken all mornin'.'

He deposited the case by the door and spotted the housekeeper's amusement, so the Commander threw her a broad smile before he sauntered towards the library, still accompanied by the bullfighters.

'Have you time for a coffee, Commander?' Mrs Soames called after him.

''Fraid not,' he called back over his shoulder, then turned. 'The mayor should be here any moment now.'

'Where is it this time?' asked the housekeeper.

'Haven't the foggiest. She's got it all in hand. Three places, I believe. I'll give you a call when we arrive.' Selwyn had taken Mrs S into his confidence about opening up the Hall, with an assurance that her position and duties would be secure and arranged to her satisfaction.

'Strikes me it's not before time, too,' had been Mrs Soames' surprising response. 'What this place needs is a bit of life and activity. Mind you, if I catch any of them kids mucking the place up they'll be for it, you mark my words,' she had threatened, her ample arms parked assertively across her matronly bosom.

'When will you be back?' she asked. The steel gauntlets were now on the receiving end of the duster's attentions.

'Probably Friday. I'll let you know,' he promised.

Further dialogue was halted by the mayor's arrival. Within minutes, Selwyn and his luggage were aboard and the car sped away. The Hall was left in relative stillness and silence, save for the creaking of armour.

The peace was short-lived, however, broken by the arrival of a white Fellowes IT Industries van, with a consignment of the new computer system. Jez and Sebastian emerged from the Transit van, threw open the back doors and immediately disrupted the cleaning routine as they ferried a procession of boxes to the study. With an alternation of tuts and shakes of the head, Mrs Soames and the duster criss-crossed the entrance hall as if to deliberately disrupt the flow of traffic and thus signify her resentment of the intrusion.

To make matters worse, a larger Transit arrived, from which two men in overalls appeared, and within minutes the invasion of the Hall was well and truly under way. Ladders, toolboxes, dust sheets and drums of cable were unloaded and hauled in to the hallway, together with the mandatory battered radio which, being the first thing to be carried in, was soon blaring out music.

Realising the hopelessness of her position, Mrs Soames glared at the occupying workmen and effected an orderly retreat to the kitchen in a cloud of ill-tempered muttering.

***

With Miriam behind the steering wheel, the open-top BMW careered along the country lanes, headed north.

'I thought Hiddleton Hall would be a good place to start,' she shouted above the roar of the engine. She shot a swift glance at the Commander and broke into a wry smile at his evident discomfiture at their speed. 'Not too fast for you?' she yelled, enjoying the feeling of power and superiority the situation gave her.

'No, not at all,' he retorted, then forced an unconvincing expression of ease before he turned to watch the countryside as it hurtled past. His eyes widened as Miriam patted his thigh reassuringly. Selwyn stared for a moment at the spot where her hand had been before he hesitantly returned her slightly mischievous smile.

A sudden and unexpected frisson of excitement disturbed the Commander's equanimity as he began to wonder just where this trip might possibly be taking him. This was immediately followed by feelings of guilt and betrayal of Georgina. There was no doubt he found the mayor attractive, but did he want things to go any further with her? Was he ready for that? Was he reading more into this briefest of physical contact than he should?

Had it not been for that smile, Selwyn would not have given it a second thought. Their earlier trip to view two other stately homes had been most instructive and useful, conducted throughout on a strictly business footing. True, they had enjoyed the time they spent together. The two of them had got on well and there had rarely been a lull in the conversation.

Selwyn's mind wandered to thoughts of Georgina and their conversations, when her health had been failing.

'Don't you dare become a crusty old widower,' she had

instructed him. 'You're too good a man for that, Bumble. Make sure you find a good woman to look after you and make you happy.'

She had taken his hand in hers, the thin, heavily wrinkled fingers that looked as old as his grandmother's. Georgina's decline had left her frail and permanently tired as she gradually wasted away, despite the best treatment and care. Through all this, her patience and resolute endurance had been inspirational. On numerous occasions, it had been very difficult for Selwyn to hold back the tears until he had left the room.

'There could be no one to match you,' he would respond. Then he would receive a gentle smack on his hand and a disapproving frown, though a rather sad-looking smile would inevitably follow.

'Time for a coffee, don't you think?' Miriam shouted, and cut across the Commander's thoughts. He nodded and they swung into the car park of a village pub.

This was purely a business trip and nothing more, Selwyn reminded himself as he climbed out of the car and followed the mayor into the dark interior of the Castle and Bear pub. The place looked deserted as they made their way to the bar. The yellow glow of the wall lights was reflected in the beaten copper-topped tables, in sharp contrast to the heavily worn maroon carpet and dark wooden beams.

A chubby freckled face suddenly appeared from under the bar top, at which Miriam let out a squeak of alarm. She lurched backwards and bumped against Selwyn, whose instant reaction was to grab her arms to steady her. She cast him a backward, embarrassed glance as the girl drew herself up to her full short height behind the beer taps.

'Sorry, m'dear,' the round face apologised, with a grin. 'What can I be doin' for yer?'

'We wondered if you might oblige us with some coffee,' Selwyn asked, over Miriam's shoulder, oblivious of his hold on her arms. The barmaid glanced at this apparent embrace and muttered an 'Ah', whereupon Selwyn abruptly removed his hands, stuffed them firmly into the pockets of his Norfolk jacket and noisily cleared his throat.

'Why certainly,' the barmaid replied. 'Just sit yerselves down somewhere and I'll bring 'em right up.' She disappeared down a dimly lit wood-panelled corridor as the travellers settled on a table by the window.

'Quaint place,' Selwyn observed with affected nonchalance.

Miriam busied herself in a search for nothing in particular in her handbag.

'Yes, it's an interesting place,' she replied a little too hastily. 'I reckon we should reach Hiddleton at lunchtime. That'll give us an opportunity to see what their cafe has to offer.'

'Where are we staying?' asked Selwyn, who began to scrutinise a dog-eared menu. His eyes settled on the special of the day: home-made steak and kidney pudding with creamy mash and mushy peas, his favourite meal. He started to salivate, checked his watch, then frowned at what he saw.

'Hope the cafe will be up to snuff,' he added. His next query as to whether they would get there in time for lunch was overtaken by the return of the buxom barmaid.

'Them shortbreads is home-made,' she announced proudly, and pointed to the generous pile of biscuits overflowing a small plate. With a knowing smile to Miriam and a wink at the now discomfited Selwyn, she waddled away.

'I do believe she thinks we're an item,' Miriam whispered with a smile.

Selwyn cleared his throat again.

'I asked where we're staying,' he reminded her.

'Why, at Hiddleton Hall, of course. We might as well learn as much as we can about how the place operates and what it offers.'

Selwyn's unease returned. Since that first flush of enthusiasm, second thoughts had crept in about the advisability of staying guests at his own Hall. He had grave concerns about how intrusive it could prove and this was perhaps a suitable moment to express his reservations.

'I must say, I've been having some doubts about opening up the Hall for accommodation,' Selwyn declared. 'I've come to the conclusion that the place really wouldn't be suitable.'

Miriam paused only for a second as she poured out the coffees, her eyes fixed on the cups. She offered the plate of biscuits to Selwyn, without any hint of surprise or emotion.

He sheepishly took a shortbread and glanced briefly at his companion. Relieved that she appeared not to have been too put out by his statement, Selwyn dunked the biscuit in the coffee and savoured eating the wet part.

'Tricky blighters for dunking,' he observed. 'All depends on the amount of butter in the mix. Once managed six seconds.'

Miriam looked across at the overgrown schoolboy and his mischievous smile. She tried unsuccessfully to suppress her own smile, then frowned in annoyance at herself. She sat bolt upright in her chair.

'I know we've a long way to go with the feasibility study, but why do you think that?' the mayor said in a challenging tone, her voice deceptively calm.

'I just think it's impractical and out of the question.' His hand waved vaguely in the hope that this would dismiss the subject once and for all, but her unwavering stare indicated otherwise. With a slight incline of her head, Miriam waited for him to continue.

'There's a total lack of facilities. Place would be a nightmare to change round.' Selwyn now warmed to the argument. 'I reckon we'll have a devil of a job to get the relevant permissions from the listed buildings wallahs, which would probably delay everything. Not to mention what the fire and the health and safety people would have to say.'

There, top that! the Commander's triumphant smile seemed to say.

'You're not getting cold feet, are you, Selwyn?' Miriam asked. The note of warning in her tone sounded uncomfortably reminiscent of Georgina's.

'No, not at all. I just think that, at best, the accommodation side would be too much too soon. Maybe it's something that should be considered at a later date, if the initial phase proved successful and profitable.'

'Well, I suggest we park that thought for now,' Miriam replied. 'Though I don't think we should dismiss it from our minds completely. Let's see how Hiddleton and the other places have organised things. Then we'll see what our architects have to say about your place. Naturally, I'll need a tour of the bedrooms when we get back.' She raised her eyebrows ever so slightly and gave him an innocent smile.

Selwyn's self-assurance instantly morphed into confusion. Was this innuendo, or was he misreading the situation? And if it *was* innuendo, was she serious or just playing with him? He checked that Miriam had finished her coffee then stood up abruptly.

'I think we'd better be getting on our way, don't you?' he suggested. Without waiting for a reply, he escaped to the bar to settle the bill and wondered, as he did so, just how bumpy an emotional ride this trip was going to be.

The onward journey passed in virtual silence. Selwyn was preoccupied with thoughts of his search for the missing family fortune. Though his eyes were fixed on the passing countryside and villages, he took in none of it. His musings were preoccupied with what he was prepared to do and how much he might have to spend to open the Hall.

It struck him for the first time how much of a gamble he was embarking upon to find something worthwhile in the planned excavation. Suppose there was nothing there? Even if there was, what if the documents came to light and he lost both the land and anything that was buried in it? What if he was unable to prove that any treasure he unearthed had actually belonged to his family?

He had little idea about how much expense he was letting himself in for. Once grants had been awarded, the work had been undertaken and the public had been given licence to rampage all over the ancestral home, there could be no turning back. He would find himself dodging round the Hall and grounds like a fugitive recluse.

With an inward shudder, Selwyn glanced at Miriam, and reflected on how the mayor had proved herself a formidable opponent through their various discussions. Had she really taken a fancy to him or was she just using her feminine wiles to gain an advantage? Ordinarily Selwyn would have brushed aside such thoughts. It was the anticipation he had felt that morning, when he waited for her to arrive, and the thrill of that touch on his thigh that had unsettled him.

Any further thoughts on that score were, however, shelved as they rounded a bend and the Hiddleton road sign came into view.

***

Amanda set the coffee mug down on the desk and eased back into her chair. After a bruising meeting with her boss earlier that morning which had left her with the distinct impression that her job was being undermined, she was in two minds about whether to type out her resignation. If it were not for her grandmother, she would clear off tomorrow. Sebastian was now clearly a thing of the past. After his initial attempts to contact her, which she had not responded to, there had been no phone calls or messages, nor had he tried to call at her house. And Amanda was firmly resolved she was not going to chase him.

'There's nothing left for me here,' she moaned to her mug.

'Think yourself lucky you're not losing your job,' Marcia had told her after giving her a dressing-down. 'If it hadn't been for my not having told you, and for your inexperience in how things are run at the council, Cheyney would have made me give you your marching orders.'

March? I'd have run, Amanda had thought, and tried her best not to smile at the mental image it conjured up of her wide-hipped boss and the glamorous mayor being bowled over in her own mad rush for the door. Marcia had readily agreed that it would be a good idea for Amanda to take some leave. It would mean that they did not have to face one another for a few days. Also, it would keep Amanda out of the mayor's way. With the librarian's instinctive forthrightness and present injured feelings, goodness knows what might happen if they met.

So, with her leave booked from lunchtime, Amanda sat at her desk and paid scant attention to the letter she had reread twice without having taken in its contents. Although the phone's ring served as a welcome distraction, she glared at it and wondered whether or not to answer. Any further contact with Marcia or, God forbid, the unbearable Cheyney, could well tip her composure over the cliff. She picked up and listened, then broke into a smile.

'I wondered if you were busy this weekend and if not, whether you'd like a short break at the seaside. Buckets and spades aren't compulsory,' said the familiar voice. Martin explained that he had returned on business, would only be there for a few days, and hoped to tackle some of the outstanding paperwork regarding Alex's estate.

Since Martin's invitation was the perfect solution for where she could spend her leave, and with the assurance that her host had no ulterior motives, Amanda happily accepted.

'Nan will just have to be content with the neighbour for a few days,' she muttered as she was about to leave.

At the door she turned to glare at the phone as it rang. In case it was Martin again, she returned to answer it, though her good mood deserted her as she listened.

'Amanda, it's me, Hector,' came the farmer's voice.

'I'm glad you've realised who you are,' she replied. 'What do you want, Hector?'

'Have you come across that historian's papers, the ones that I gave you? I hear you're dealing with his things.'

'It's got nothing to do with you,' she replied, irritation now etched on her brow.

'Oh, come on, Amanda,' Hector pleaded. 'They could mean everything to get the problem of that land sorted out.'

'I don't care. The two things aren't related – and, in any case, those documents are not mine to give. For what it's worth, I don't have them anyway. As far as I can make out, the Commander's got them now.' There was a lengthy silence. 'Hector, are you still there?' she asked.

'Yes,' came the glum reply.

'I'm sorry I snapped,' Amanda apologised. 'I've had a lousy morning. I really can't help you. Look, I was going to ring you anyway. I'm going away for a few days, so will you keep an eye on Nan for me, please?'

'Where are you going?'

'Lytham St Annes.'

'What for?'

'I'm staying with someone.'

'Who?'

'Martin Brightside, if you must know,' said Amanda, her

impatience mounting. 'Now I really must go, Hector.'

'OK,' he muttered. 'I'll look in on Nan. Don't worry. Have a nice time and let me know when you're back. Are we still friends?'

'Of course we are, nitwit,' she told him, her smile returned. 'And thanks, Hector.'

She hung up and headed for the door, thankful to leave work and Wisstingham behind, and happy at the thought she would soon see Martin again.

Chapter 12

'That's your fourth, Hector,' Oliver cautioned, as he placed a pint of bitter in front of the glowering farmer.

'Just keep 'em coming. I'm not driving back. I'll leave the Land Rover here and get a taxi.'

'It looked like you'd already had a few before you got here. Anything wrong?' The landlord recalled the time when the farmer had had to be poured out of the pub after the burial of his dog.

Hector merely shook his head and clumsily lifted his forefinger to his lips. He stared in silence across the beer pumps, then into the other crowded bar, and absent-mindedly fingered the dimples on his glass.

'What's goin' on?' he eventually queried as Millicent passed him with a round of drinks.

'Quiz night,' she called back.

'Oh, Christ! Not that again,' Hector complained. He took another large mouthful of his beer and turned to the customer who had just sat down next to him. 'A lotta smart alecs come quizzing,' he whispered to his neighbour, and pointed to the other bar.

The other nodded politely.

'You here for the quiz?' Hector asked.

'No, I'm meeting someone on business,' came the dismissive reply.

Hector studied the newcomer and screwed up his face then continued to peer at him.

'Don't I know you from somewhere?' he asked. The

stranger shrugged. Hector shook his head in resignation and gave the man a conspiratorial smile. 'I've got a bit of business to do as well,' he confided with a wink, which received a polite but embarrassed smile.

Hector gently patted his jacket pocket as he stared at the other man.

'Could've got me some land. My land, this,' he added, in a whisper and patted the pocket again. 'But that bastard Commander won't play ball,' Hector moaned. 'Uses it as his land but it's *our* land. Always been our land.'

Oliver scowled across from the beer pumps at the sound of the farmer's raised voice. Hector put his finger to his lips in apology, straightened in his seat and stared into his glass for inspiration.

'So,' the drunken farmer eventually continued, as he turned back to his now curious companion and applied another pat to his pocket, 'I'm going to get some of his land taken off him with these.'

He leant closer.

'Actually it's what the council uses, but more besides and I'm going to the papers with it,' he confided, in a whisper. He drew away and stared at his now distinctly interested neighbour and put his finger to his lips again.

The neighbour glanced at his watch.

'You won't get *The Chronicle*'s offices at this time,' he warned.

Hector frowned, then shook his head in resignation. The stranger stared back at him and leant closer.

'Are you talking about the Hall?' he asked. Hector nodded. 'So what exactly have you got in there?' queried the man, his gaze focused on the pocket.

Hector's eyes narrowed as he smiled and tapped the

side of his nose.

Try as he might, the stranger could not get anything more out of the farmer, who was now tight-lipped and trying to catch the landlord's attention.

Oliver approached and leant over the bar.

'You've had enough, Hector,' he said in a low voice. 'I don't want any trouble.'

Hector craned his head forward, his face nearly in contact with the landlord's.

'Then order me a bloody taxi,' he whispered. He stood up, wobbled, then walked unsteadily outside. In the car park, he leant against one of the parked cars to fumble for his cigarettes. He lit one and, between draws, stared about him.

After several minutes, Sebastian's voice came from nearby.

'Hector, are you OK?'

'Sebastian, old mate! I'm absolutely fine,' Hector slurred and threw down his stub.

'You're not driving?' Sebastian cautioned.

'No, got a taxi. I'm off home to fish. Come with me.'

'I reckon bed would be a better place for you.'

'I'm going fishing,' the farmer insisted truculently. 'You're welcome to come. Don't bother to get your gear, though, I've got plenty.' He hiccoughed and Sebastian grabbed his arm to steady him mid sway.

'Anyway, I wanted to ask you something,' Sebastian began. 'Do you…?'

The arrival of the taxi, which sent water spouts out in all directions from the potholed car park, put paid to the question as they quickly stepped aside. Hector lurched towards the cab door, opened it and swayed perilously with one foot in the car and the other in a puddle. Sebastian heaved him inside. He was about to speak when the farmer slammed the door and leant forward to talk to the driver.

Sebastian stepped back as the taxi set off and gave a snort of annoyance at the hand that waved vaguely from the rear window.

In the pub, after he had enquired of the landlord as to who his inebriated companion had been, Jez Fellowes headed slowly out to the car park, where he glanced around after the man, then reached into his pocket for his mobile.

***

Sebastian grabbed his fleece from the bedroom and went back downstairs. He hurried past his father, who lay sprawled on the sofa, wrapped in a dressing gown after his customary evening bath, a lager can clasped in his hand.

Although he did not intend to fish, Sebastian needed to speak to Hector after what he had discovered earlier that day. Considering the state Hector had been in, he only hoped he would not be too late. Whether he was likely to get any sense and cooperation out of the farmer was questionable, but he had to try.

'Start, you bugger, please,' Sebastian begged as the starter motor whirred and did not engage. He banged his hands on the steering wheel and glared at it. The wretched car had behaved itself all day but now, when he was desperate, the damned thing was determined to let him down. He jumped at a sharp rap on the side window, then wound it down.

'Where are you off to?' Vincent demanded, clutching the collar of his dressing gown.

'Just out with the lads.'

'What time will you be back?'

'I haven't the foggiest,' Sebastian replied. 'Probably after closing, unless we go back somewhere for a coffee.'

'Don't forget you've got work tomorrow.'

'I've got the day off.'

Vincent stared at him then grunted.

'Well, don't be too late, and don't make a noise when you come in.'

Sebastian watched the hunched figure scurry off.

'Don't you bloody let me down,' he muttered, at the dashboard and tried the starter again. As the engine coughed into life, he gave a sigh of relief, gunned the accelerator and headed off to the farm, the tyres squealing on the cobbles.

***

Smudger found it had all been so easy, almost too easy, so that he now felt nervous as to whether he had made a mistake or had left an obvious clue. The whole thing had been one big, really lucky break. Jez's call had left him with precious little time to do something, and he had fully expected there would be one complication or another to frustrate him. What an amazing coincidence that chance meeting had been!

Smudger got out of bed, leant over to the chair and thrust his hand into the inside pocket of his jacket. They were there. First thing, he would put them somewhere safe. Then he wondered if he should destroy them. No, best to hang on to them in case they might be needed, though he couldn't think why.

Once he had convinced the farmer that he was on his side, it had been easy to persuade him to hand over the document by telling him that he knew a guy who could turn the copies into something that would pass for originals. Had the farmer been sober, he would probably not have fallen for it. Hector had even agreed to keep quiet about the documents until the fakes had been made. Without anything to show, the farmer would have a hard job to make anyone believe that the document had ever existed in the first place. It would have been the farmer's word against his, although of course Smudger did not really want anyone to know about his involvement.

Of course there was always the risk that Hector had taken more copies, but Smudger very much doubted that. Anyway, that was academic now. Well, almost.

The exhilaration he had felt when driving away from the farm mellowed into one of satisfaction. He was sorry for the farmer, of course, but what had happened had been of his own making, pissed as he was. It had been enough not to do anything, just watch and do nothing, though he had almost been tempted to help the drowning fool. The man had started with a tirade about the land, which was only to have been expected, before he moved on to the map and the document. He even had the wretched things in his pocket! Even if they were copies, you didn't keep something like those in your pocket, did you? Come on!

'One more problem solved,' he muttered, and walked off to the bathroom.

***

The drive home was long and tedious. Even the relief of the toll road, a welcome break from the nose-to-tail convoy of slow-moving traffic through numerous road-works, was fleeting. Relieved to have at least missed the rush-hour snarl up through Hopestanding, Amanda finally parked in front of the cottage that had been her home since her arrival in Wisstingham and the world some twenty-two years earlier.

She pushed open the porch door, set her case down on the church pew bench then shucked off her shoes and padded down the stone-flagged passageway with a warning shout of,

'Hi, Nan, I'm home,' adding, in a low voice, in response to the silence, punctuated by snores, 'Nothing like pre-dictability.'

Asleep in the armchair in front of the unmade fire, her head lolled against the chair back, Nan showed no sign of movement other than the trembling of her lips on the exhalation of each snore. On the small table by the chair stood a depleted wine bottle and an empty glass. A further empty bottle lay by the table leg. Most of the pink cellular blanket that had covered the sleeping lady's legs now lay in a heap at her feet, but a corner was still precariously draped over one knee. An empty crisp packet lay on the dining table, next to a plate bearing a sandwich crust and an empty mug emblazoned with *Time 4 Tea*. On the floor by the kitchen doorway sat a shopping bag. Amanda peered inside it: three bottles of Merlot – screw-top, of course. Nan had a special opener for those, which lay next to her wine glass.

'A bit of one-dimensional shopping going on here, Nan,' Amanda murmured as she moved over to the old lady and gently rubbed her shoulder. 'I'm back,' she said softly.

'And about time,' Nan moaned. She wriggled into an upright position, blinked her eyes awake and glanced down at the table. 'I've been here on my own for days,' she complained.

'Three days to be precise, Nan. And what about Betty?'

'Yes, well, she called round but she doesn't count.'

'Each day, several times a day?'

'Well, I suppose so, but she's no help.'

'And the home help?'

Nan let out a low growl of annoyance.

'She didn't make the fire,' Amanda observed, with a frown.

'I told her not to. She doesn't do it properly.'

Amanda let out a tired sigh.

'And Hector? He's been round, hasn't he?' she prompted.

'There's been no sign of him,' Nan bridled and looked triumphantly towards the kitchen, into which Amanda had disappeared with the shopping bag and the lunchtime debris.

Her granddaughter's frowning face appeared round the door.

'I asked him to drop in,' she said. 'You were probably out, or asleep.'

'I've not been out at all,' Nan retorted. 'And if I was asleep he'd have come in anyway. He's got a key.'

Amanda was about to argue the case of the shopping bag but, in view of the empty bottles, thought better of it. Her frown persisted.

'Are you sure he didn't call in?'

The old lady slapped a hand on the side of her chair and glowered.

'I told you he's not been near,' she shouted. 'Why do you always have to argue with me? I'd be better off without you. Why don't you just clear off?' With her lips pursed, she darted rapid glances about the room as she scrabbled at the top of the blanket that Amanda had replaced over her legs.

Her grandmother's behaviour reminded Amanda of the day she had told her about the budding romance with Sebastian.

'You don't want to have anything to do with him,' Nan had snapped at her, and struck her chair. Amanda had tried to talk her round, but she would have none of it. Finally she concluded that Nan's hostility was born out of a fear that she would lose her granddaughter and the support she gave her. So no mention had been made of Sebastian since that day.

Amanda returned from the kitchen with newspaper and kindling, made the fire and went off to refill the empty coal scuttle. She lit the fire and went quietly back into the kitchen. All the time, her grandmother watched her work, all the while biting her lip. Then she stared at the fire in silence as it caught light. From the kitchen came the sound of pans being set on the stove for the evening meal.

After she had set the small dining table, on which she placed a posy bowl of flowers freshly cut from the garden, Amanda exchanged glances with her grandmother. She was fearfully conversant with what would now be acted out between them. It was not so much a mechanical rerun of something that had happened before, rather a drama into which they were both continually and inevitably drawn like some *Groundhog Day*.

Tears started to well in the old woman's eyes as she gazed at her granddaughter, who resented once more being unfairly cast as the guilty and negligent party. She knelt by the seated form, whose head was now bowed, the tears flowing freely down the pale, lined cheeks. Amanda took hold of the wrinkled hands and their contorted, arthritic fingers and looked up at the wet grey eyes.

'I'm sorry, Mandygirl,' Nan sobbed. 'I know I'm a stupid old woman who's just a liability. I'm holding you back in life. I shouldn't be here.'

'You're nothing of the sort,' Amanda murmured, her eyes also brimming. 'You're not holding me back at all. I love you and I always will. I'm sorry I left you. I just had to get away to think. Things haven't been good recently.'

The gnarled hands detached themselves and Nan gently brushed back a strand of Amanda's hair that clung to the girl's wet cheeks.

'I'm sorry, my dear. You're a good girl, the best there is. It's all my fault. I know it's the wine. I shouldn't drink it.'

'If you can't have a drink at your age, when can you? Just perhaps not quite so much, eh?'

Nan shrugged and Amanda produced a smile, albeit of resignation and acceptance of the unspoken inevitability that nothing would change and that they both knew it.

As the librarian stood in front of the kitchen stove, her eyes closed momentarily and she gave an ironic smile as she heard the chinking sound of glass on glass from the living room. She paused her cooking to phone Hector, only to hear the monotonous ringing tone, and cursed his steadfast refusal to set up his phone to take messages.

Puzzled at the lack of a reply, which was unusual for that time of night, Amanda decided she would drive out early the following morning to see him before she went to the library. After all, that was the way with farms. Even at that early hour, her cousin would be up, breakfasted and busy at work.

Chapter 13

Staring down at the body over which the pathologist was kneeling, DI Stone winced, reached into his pocket for the indigestion tablets and cursed the previous night's excesses.

Further along the jetty, which reached out into the lake, a fishing rod lay next to a battered wicker basket and a folding chair that lay on its side. A half-empty whisky bottle stood upright with an empty glass beside it. Submerged in the water, roped to a tall and stout wooden post, was an empty keep net.

The DI moved off to study them and slowly stroked the stubble on his double chin between finger and thumb. He winced again and rapped his chest with a clenched fist.

'So what can you tell me, Jack?' he asked, on his return to the pathologist, who had risen to his feet to signify that he had finished.

'Not much till I examine him back in the lab,' he replied. 'There's a blunt-force trauma to the skull, which looks to be consistent with falling against that post, but whether that killed him before he went into the lake, I can't say for now.'

'Any sign of other injuries or a struggle?'

'Not that I can see, but again—'

'Yes, I know,' Stone interrupted, with an impatient shake of his head. 'What about time of death?'

The pathologist gave him a tired smile.

'You know full well it'll have to wait till I get back, but I'd hazard a guess between 10 p.m. and midnight.'

Stone muttered his thanks and made his way to the patio where Amanda was seated on a bench, hunched over a mug of tea. Next to her sat a WPC, a notebook in her lap. As the librarian responded to his colleague's questions, Stone studied the young woman who had called in the discovery of the body. The WPC stood up as the DI joined them and he motioned his colleague to sit as he drew up a chair and sat opposite Amanda.

'Good morning, I'm Detective Inspector Stone,' he said, and produced his warrant card. 'I understand you found the deceased, Miss—?'

'Amanda Sheppard,' she replied.

'Can you identify the deceased?'

'Yes, he's Hector Middleton. This is…' She stopped to correct herself. 'This *was* his farm.'

'How did you know him?'

Amanda sniffed, her knuckles white against the mug handle.

'He was my cousin.'

The questioning continued.

Was the deceased married? Who was the next of kin? How many people worked on the farm? The farmhands who had already turned up were being questioned by another officer.

'And what was your reason for coming here so early, Miss Sheppard?' asked Stone.

Amanda glanced at him uneasily. The stern set of his mouth and his unblinking eyes gave nothing away.

'I was worried about him. I'd been away for a few days and he was supposed to call in and see my grandmother. She has, erm … difficulties. It wasn't like him not to call.

I tried to phone him last night but there was no reply, so I called in this morning before work.'

She glanced at the jetty, from which the body was now being stretchered to the waiting vehicle. The view blurred once more and she wiped her eyes. She could not dislodge the picture of how perfectly still the water had been as Hector's lifeless body floated face down on it in the lake, and how the chirping of the birds on such a beautiful day had seemed so incongruous. Stone's face remained impassive.

'Do you know what happened?' whispered Amanda. She didn't know why she was whispering. Perhaps it was in consideration of her dead cousin, who was now being driven away.

'We won't know that until after the post-mortem report. Until then, we'll keep an open mind. Was your cousin a keen fisherman?'

'Yes, very keen. He often fished at night.'

'Would you know if he fished alone or with anyone else?'

'Quite often with...' She faltered as thoughts of Sebastian surfaced. 'Sebastian Monaghan. He lives at Wisstingham Hall. His father is the estate manager.'

'Yes, we know of him,' Stone muttered, though the WPC still jotted the name down.

Amanda bent forward, her head cradled in her hands as she stared down at the ground. Never far away, the painful memory of the last time she had seen Sebastian resurfaced.

'Are you all right?' asked Stone, his tone more solicitous.

'Yes.'

'Was your cousin a regular drinker, do you know?'

'He liked a drink, but he didn't get drunk. Well, not often,' Amanda replied. She noted the officers' exchange of glances and wondered if she had said the wrong thing.

'And would you know of any regular visitors to the farm?'

'Not really. The farmhands could probably tell you better.'

'Can you think of anyone who might have wanted to harm your cousin?' queried the DI. 'Anyone he'd fallen out with, had a grudge against, or who perhaps had threatened him?'

Amanda looked up and grimaced.

'Do you think that he was murdered?' she asked.

'As I said, we're keeping an open mind. We have to examine all possibilities and investigate them, if only to rule them out. So, is there anyone you can think of?'

'No, though there has been a long-running dispute with Commander Fitzgerald up at the Hall over some land whose ownership has been contested for a long time.' She wanted to dismiss that as something that would have no bearing, but her suspicions about Alex's death still lingered. Perhaps it would be as well for the police to take an interest in the Commander.

'I assume you've been a regular visitor here in the past, Miss Sheppard?'

Amanda nodded.

'Then I'd like you to come along to the house and see if there appears to be anything out of place or missing,' asked Stone. They got up and walked to the front door. 'We found the door open when we got here,' he explained, 'but nothing seems to have been disturbed. You'll need to put on some coverings on your shoes and please don't touch anything.'

As they made their way through the house, its famili-arity and memories of previous visits, parties and family meetings came thick and fast as painful reminders to Amanda. Nothing seemed unusual, though… Nothing except the screaming fact that Hector … Hector was dead.

Stone gave Amanda his card and told her to call him if anything came to mind. She nodded, numbed against the reality of the day, and drove away.

An hour later, after she had broken the news to Nan, who had taken it better than she had expected, and the neigh-bour had agreed to stay with her until the home help arrived, Amanda left for work.

As she had expected and feared after a few days' absence from the library, she was immediately harangued by her staff with a barrage of questions and problems, most of which could have been dealt with by the application of a little common sense. Amanda was not inclined to share the details of the ordeal she had just been through and tried hard not to display any emotions, retreating at the first opportunity into the sanctuary of her office.

There, she cast her mind back to the events of the previous few days. Martin had been delighted to see her and she suspected his feelings for her were unchanged. On her drive north to the resort, Amanda had begun to have reservations about whether she was doing the right thing to stay with him, but he had assured her that his intentions were honourable and had been true to his word. His house, a large one on permanent loan from his parents, who lived in France, was close to the prom-enade.

They had strolled through Lytham, where Martin had taken her to his favourite pub, then later to a Mediterranean restaurant. From their reception by the staff, he was clearly a regular diner there.

''E's a mos' wunnerful man,' Mario the head waiter had assured Amanda, with his flashing smile, no doubt under the assumption that she and Martin were an item. However, throughout the visit Sebastian had never been far from her mind.

She was tormented by regret that she had refused to return Sebastian's calls and his attempts to contact her after she had seen him in the arms of that waitress. When he visited the library, Amanda had spotted him at the entrance, retreated to the archives, and given strict instructions that she was not to be disturbed – though disturbed emotionally she most certainly was. He had made another abortive visit when she had been out of the building altogether. Finally Sebastian had called at the house on an evening when Amanda had been out with an old school friend.

Then the calls had stopped, as had the attempts to see her, and she assumed Sebastian had finally taken 'no' for an answer. Perversely, she immediately found herself regretting that and, at times, even blamed him for not having tried harder.

Her thoughts returned to the morning's dreadful events, and unanswered questions stampeded through her mind. Had it been an accident or had someone killed Hector? If he had been murdered, did it have something to do with the documents? Had he been killed to shut him up and, if so, how safe was she?

Amanda began to wonder who else was aware of her

knowledge of the documents. From the few times she had been in the Commander's company, she had formed the opinion that he was a decent sort – but what if she was wrong? What if he was an out-and-out villain, ready to do anything to avoid losing some of his land?

She wondered how soon Hector's death would become public knowledge. It took no time at all for news like that to travel round the town. What if the press had already arrived at the house to plague her grandmother with questions? After all, Hector had had no other closer relations.

After a call to Marcia, Amanda told her staff that she was leaving for the day then hurried out of the building. Her resolve to be strong had faded fast, and she desperately needed to share her thoughts and fears with somebody. There was a lot to think about. She would have rung Martin, but he would now be in mid flight to Montreal. There was no one Amanda felt she could talk to or confide in. She felt so alone.

***

Selwyn executed a wide arc and brought the Jaguar to a halt in front of the Hall. He wound down the window, inhaled deeply and blinked his eyes closed for a moment, in the delight of being back home. Once out of the car, he stretched lazily and glanced up at the building's stone portico. After a pause to scan the grounds, he then unloaded the cases and started up the steps.

As he dropped the luggage at the foot of the staircase, Mrs Soames shuffled into view from the dark recesses of the hallway, followed and then rapidly overtaken by Mustard.

'What ho, Mrs S!' the Commander greeted her as he crouched to make a fuss of the dog. Hers was not a welcoming expression, however. 'Everything OK? You're looking pretty serious about something,' he observed.

'Welcome home, Commander,' the housekeeper said, her face as frosty as the tone of her greeting. 'Did you 'ave a successful trip and what time will you want dinner served?'

'It was fine, as far as any trip to London can be,' Selwyn replied. He straightened up as Mustard padded off towards the library. 'As for a meal, I'm ravenous, so as early as you like. Is 7 p.m. all right with you?'

Mrs S nodded, though there was not the shadow of a smile.

'Now what's the matter? I can see that something's upset you,' Selwyn challenged.

She shot a withering glance in the direction of the library, from where noises and muffled voices could be heard.

'Ah!' he exclaimed, and was fortunately saved by the ringing of the phone, which he gladly went to answer. After a brief conversation, he returned to the waiting Mrs S, her hands clasped neatly together in front of her and her lips tightly shut.

'That was Mayor Cheyney. She confirms that she and her colleague will be here for lunch tomorrow,' Selwyn explained. 'You hadn't forgotten, had you?'

Mrs Soames stiffened and gave a slight sniff, the meaning of which Selwyn knew only too well. Miriam had fallen dramatically from grace in Mrs Soames' estimation after their last touring visit. Her fears for his safety from 'that woman' had been well rehearsed previously and he did not intend to revisit them if it could be helped.

'No, I ain't forgot,' was her terse reply.

Hopeful of a temporary escape from her inevitable onslaught over the upheaval of 'the works', Selwyn moved to pick up his cases, but was distracted by a shout and barking from the library. Since he was not going to be allowed to ignore the housekeeper's steely gaze, Selwyn resigned himself to hear her out.

'It's them works and them workmen,' she grumbled, her arms now folded on the generous ledge of her bosom. 'Bin like that all the time: noise, dust, blarin' radios, barkin', shoutin', not to mention damage what'll need repairin'. Goodness knows what they're a-doin' of, but it's gettin' more than a soul can stand, I tell you straight, Commander.'

'Damage? What damage?' demanded Selwyn, now alarmed.

'Drillin' 'oles, they are, 'ere, there and everywhere. Place is like an Emmental cheese.'

Selwyn's brow relaxed.

'All part of getting up to date with technology, to be ready for when we open up the Hall. They'll put right whatever needs it,' he said, in an attempt to reassure her but conscious he had ventured onto further dangerous ground. 'For now, we mustn't let on to the mayor that the works have got anything to do with opening the Hall,' he stressed, and tapped the side of his nose.

This apparent distancing of the mayor appealed to Mrs Soames. She gave a quick nod, assured the Commander that he could rely on her being 'the soul of discretion' and, with a final disdainful look down the corridor, waddled off to the kitchen.

Selwyn found the library virtually covered with dust sheets. In the far corner, the lower half of a body in overalls lay on the floor. The upper half was somewhere below the floorboards. Alongside the hole, four cable reels spun slowly on metal spindles as their contents flowed into the hole. Mustard's supervision varied between staring at the reels and peering into the hole.

Selwyn watched the proceedings for several moments, then cleared his throat.

'Everything going to plan?' he enquired.

The upper half of the body emerged from the hole, its face smudged and hair dishevelled.

'Ah, Commander, you're back. How was London?' Sebastian asked while he stroked Mustard, who was trying to lick the workman's hand clean.

'Not bad. Managed to get done what I wanted to. Are you all right?'

'I'm good, thanks. The ground floor's nearly finished. We'll make a start on upstairs next week.'

'What state are the dining room and drawing room in?'

'They're bang on. Just the sensors to be connected and the plugs to fix.'

'I need to use them tomorrow. Got some guests for lunch.'

'No probs, we can get those done first thing.'

'Whatever else you've got on for tomorrow, it'll need to be as quiet as possible,' Selwyn warned. 'Certainly there's to be no indication that the work has anything to do with opening the Hall. Understood?'

'Got it,' confirmed Sebastian. 'We'll concentrate on the camera connections. They're all in place.'

Selwyn gave an appreciative nod.

'Good show,' he said. 'I'll catch up with you on Thursday for an update. As you were.'

His cases finally retrieved, the Commander had just reached the staircase when the arrival of a police car drew him to the window. As he watched two officers get out, Mrs Soames came swaying at speed from the kitchen, hands flapping wildly at her sides.

'Commander! Commander!' she wheezed, as she neared him. 'I've just 'eard that Mr Middleton, the farmer that came 'ere, 'e's been found dead at 'is farm. Drownded, from what folks are sayin'.'

Selwyn stared at her in disbelief. When the bell rang, Mrs Soames gave a start, shot a fearful glance at him then went to the door, muttering to herself. At the entrance stood DI Stone and WPC Pelman. Mrs Soames stared at their warrant cards, uncertain what she was supposed to do, and as she made to peer at them, they were whisked away.

'We're making enquiries about the death of a Mr Hector Middleton,' DI Stone explained to the Commander, once they were seated in the drawing room.

Despite having been there before, the WPC's attention wandered, together with her eyes, around the impressive room, then she was brought back to her notebook by the DI's cough and glare.

'I've just this minute heard the news from the house-keeper,' Selwyn replied. 'Terrible business.'

'I understand the deceased was known to you.'

'Yes, though we were very seldom in contact.'

'I also understand there was a disagreement between you about some land,' Stone continued.

Selwyn glanced down and tried to quickly order his thoughts. The ramifications of Hector's death and the possibility of the copies of the map and the transfer document surfacing had suddenly hit home.

'Commander?' Stone prompted.

'I'm sorry, it's been a bit of a shock to hear the man's dead. Yes, as you'll probably have noted, the Middleton farm is next to the estate. There's been a dispute over a piece of land that started years and years ago.'

'When was the last time you saw him?' asked Stone.

'I think it must have been about May. He came to see me.'

'What about?'

Selwyn shifted uncomfortably in his chair.

'It was about the land. He tried to persuade me to make it over to him.'

'He had something to offer?' Stone queried.

'What makes you say that?' Selwyn asked, his tone so defensive that the WPC looked up from her notebook.

'Well, there must have been some reason why he felt it was worth coming to see you if there'd been no progress over all those years,' Stone reasoned, and eyed Selwyn keenly.

'Er, no.' Selwyn coloured slightly, his mind still racing. 'He'd heard things were tight and thought if he made me an offer I'd snatch his hand off.'

Stone looked at him, puzzled.

'But if he believed the land belonged to him, why would he be prepared to pay for it?'

At a knock on the door, Selwyn's face relaxed.

Sebastian entered and apologised as he saw the police.

'Sorry, Commander, I didn't know you had company.'

'Do come in,' Selwyn said quickly, as Sebastian turned to go. The Commander offered a smile of apology to the two officers. 'Sorry, Sebastian's engaged on something urgent. It won't take a second, I imagine.'

'Sebastian Monaghan?' Stone enquired, and gave the new arrival a once-over.

'Yes,' Sebastian replied.

Stone turned to the Commander.

'I wonder if we might have a word with him while we're here?' he asked.

'Why certainly,' replied Selwyn. 'Have we finished?'

Sensing that the trail had gone cold, Stone confirmed that they had and asked the Commander to contact him should he remember anything that could be relevant.

Sebastian sat down as Selwyn happily departed. After Stone's introductory statements, Sebastian confirmed that he had just heard about Hector's death from Mrs Soames. He outlined his relationship with the dead farmer and their encounter in the pub car park.

'Was that the last time you saw him?' Stone asked.

Sebastian hesitated and allowed himself to become distracted by the memory of his first meeting with Amanda at Hector's barbecue.

Stone chivvied him.

'I said, was that the last time you saw him?'

'No, I went to the farm in the evening.'

The two officers glanced at each other.

'We've just spoken with your father, who claims you told him you were going out to see some friends,' challenged the DI.

'I changed my mind,' Sebastian countered irritably.

'Why did you go to the farm?'

'To see how Hector was. He was pretty drunk in the car park.'

'No other reason?' asked Stone.

'No,' lied Sebastian.

'And what time did you leave?'

'Around ten.'

'Can anyone vouch for that?' the DI asked.

'No, my father was in bed when I got home.'

'And how was Mr Middleton when you left him?'

'He was fine,' Sebastian replied. 'Well, he was still quite drunk but he was alive.'

'Did you see anybody else while you were there, or any vehicles near the farm when you left?'

'No.'

Stone sat back and fell silent. He stared at Sebastian. Then he rubbed his chin and looked across to the WPC. Sebastian looked from one officer to the other.

'I think that's all I have to ask for now,' Stone said eventually.

'Do you believe it was an accident?' asked Sebastian.

'We'll have a better idea after the post-mortem,' Stone replied. 'For now, we're just making routine enquiries. Thanks for your help. We may need to talk to you again. If there's anything else that occurs to you, please give me a call.'

Sebastian showed them to the front door, where Selwyn and Mrs Soames were hovering, then retraced his steps to the study, exhaling slowly and loudly.

'What do you think, sir?' the WPC asked, as she and the DI drove off.

'They're both hiding something, I reckon. Let's see what

the pathologist has to tell us,' he replied, his eyes focused on the estate's woodlands.

Chapter 14

Miriam Cheyney stooped to squeeze herself into the MINI Cooper that was Marcia Pincher's pride and joy and reflected on how much easier it was to get into the mayoral Mercedes and even her own BMW. She wondered why a woman of Pincher's size would choose such a car.

'It's like trying to get into a sardine tin,' she complained.

Marcia frowned, but did not reply.

'Are you sure you've got everything?' the mayor asked as they were about to pull out of the car park. 'We've got to be really polished about this.'

'Everything,' Marcia reassured her for the second time, though she nevertheless glanced in the rear-view mirror to check her briefcase really was on board.

The mayor wound down the window and lit up a cigarette.

'You don't mind, do you?' It was a statement rather than a question.

With a roll of her eyes, Marcia automatically wound down her own window but said nothing. She made no attempt to open the car's ashtray for her boss.

Although sensitive to Marcia's silent objection, Miriam needed the cigarette to gather her thoughts together. She had not seen Selwyn for several days, not since their return from what had been an informative tour of more stately homes. It had certainly been an enjoyable trip during which, and despite her resolution, she had found herself conjuring up images of him well beyond her comfort zone. When she woke that morning, Ms Cheyney had been positively unnerved to feel a thrill at the prospect of seeing him again. The man brought out all the wrong instincts and feelings in her.

The necessity for total secrecy had been drummed into Marcia before they set off. The mayor did not want to set any political hares running, certainly not among the council staff. If the Commander decided to terminate the lease, he would need to give the council the necessary three months' notice within the next fortnight. So, it was 'make your mind up' time for him. However, on the council's side, it would be essential for Miriam to demonstrate that her office and the planners had done all they could to fulfil their promises in the agreed run-up period. The Commander needed to be convinced of the financial viability of the scheme.

From the time Miriam had spent with Selwyn, it was clear that he hated to feel he was being pushed into a corner.

'Bad tactical judgement,' he had once remarked. His keenness to carry out the excavation was such that if the necessary permission for it to go ahead was not forthcoming, Miriam feared he might well follow through with his threat not to renew the lease.

She also knew that if it came to a council vote on such an ultimatum, things could easily go wrong. Her party only had a slim majority and some of her fellow members felt very strongly that they should not give in to blackmail, so the result could well be a defiant 'No!' Furthermore, the opposition would obtain considerable public support.

What Miriam could not gauge was just how important the council's support was to Selwyn. Or that of the local community. Nor did she know how much he could afford to invest to open the Hall, or if he would need a loan. If he did, the bank would certainly need to be convinced of the profitability of the project. Everything hinged on how attractive she and Marcia could make the project's viability appear.

A further and more personal uncertainty for Miriam, which gave rise to not a little insecurity, was Selwyn's true feelings towards her. Much as she tried to dispel such thoughts, they would not go away.

'How do you want to play this?' Marcia asked, after the cigarette stub had been jettisoned and the window wound up.

'I'll start with an overview of how I see the situation between the two parties then ask you to expand on the funding streams and grant availability, the timescales and the required outcomes. Then we'll need to draw the Commander out on his proposals, the revenue and the costs he's so far identified.'

'And the marketing strategy?' prompted Marcia. 'How far do I go with that?'

'Give him all the bullet points, but don't go into any more detail unless he asks. By all means spell out just what the marketing's financial value is. Above all, we need to reassure him that the council will support him all the way.'

By now, they had entered the gateway and started up the drive.

'Crikey! This is impressive,' Marcia exclaimed. 'Just

imagine how many cars you could park here and still have space for amusements and a restaurant-bar.'

'Yes, but for goodness sake don't mention things like that. He's pretty sensitive about the whole proposal, especially how it might detract from the estate and the quality of life he's been used to all these years.'

They parked in front of the Hall, the sole occupants of the space, since the Fellowes' vans had been banished to the garage yard. The sturdy doors swung open and Mrs Soames watched in stony silence as they mounted the steps.

***

The Pincher vehicle had not been the only place for private contemplation that morning. While he got ready for his meeting, Selwyn had also reviewed his options and strategy, fully aware that it was decision time. Since Middleton's death had increased his vulnerability, should the map and the transfer document be made public, Selwyn no longer had the relative luxury of time.

While uncertain of Miriam's feelings, he had decided not to take her into his confidence about the treasure, in case it would weaken his future negotiating position with her and the council, if the going got sticky.

Selwyn was hopeful that, with the information he had gathered and what the council could offer, the project would be feasible. In that case the decision would be simple. He could make the commitment and get on with the excavation.

But what if it didn't stack up? That would mean a parting of the ways, and time was now against him. He would not be able to wait for the council's decision on the excavation before he would have to give notice on the lease. Selwyn mostly feared the council's inability to provide enough information for him to decide on the project's feasibility. His only hope then would be to shift the responsibility onto the council, for having run out of time on their deadline. That would oblige him to give notice on the lease unless they immediately agreed to allow the excavation, while they continued to investigate. In that event, he could offer to commit to an agreement in principle.

'We'll just have to play it by ear,' he muttered to his reflection as he knotted his tie prior to his wait for the mayor's arrival.

***

Under the stern gaze of Mrs Soames, Selwyn and his guests retired to the conservatory for coffee. The discussion and negotiations started over a Buck's Fizz – the sensible Ms Pincher had opted for only the Buck – had gone fairly well and continued in the same manner through lunch.

It was during the dessert that Miriam momentarily lost control of the conversation. Distracted by the house-keeper's unfriendly stare, she began to ponder just what she had done to have fallen foul of the woman. As a result, Marcia pushed matters too far. Pressed to commit to a press release that day, Selwyn refused and withdrew into a shell of taciturn uncertainty, which left the mayor enraged, though for appearances' sake, she continued to smile on the flagging proceedings.

To Ms Pincher, matters could not have seemed clearer. The Commander had been favourably impressed by the upbeat information about available funding streams, for which it had been easy to demonstrate the project's suitability. He, in turn, had given a detailed overview of the works and logistics needed to open the Hall and seemed at ease with the costs involved. Marcia had therefore assumed both parties were keen to proceed.

When their host was called away to an urgent phone call, Miriam acted. With no attempt to disguise her annoyance, she instructed the departmental head to make her excuses and return to the office. Miriam would try to smooth things over and get the Commander's final commitment before she would make her own way back to Wisstingham.

Minutes later, a more relaxed Selwyn, with Miriam at his side, was sipping brandy, while they looked out over the woods.

'The wildflower meadow extends beyond those trees, you know,' he pointed out.

'As far as the Long Nessing road?' queried Miriam.

'No, it stops at the old quarry road, which is redundant now. That's crossed by the River Wiss, which flows into the lake then runs alongside the green.'

The mayor broke the ensuing silence.

'I'm sorry about Marcia. She's as keen as mustard but she isn't very politic when it comes to dealing with people.'

'That's all right,' Selwyn replied, though he continued to stare through the window.

She sensed his feathers were still ruffled and that an opportunity was slipping away.

'Although,' she continued, 'from what was said, even I thought you were happy to proceed with the project. Of course, if you've had second thoughts—'

'No, no,' he interrupted, and turned to her to place a reassuring hand on her arm. 'I won't let you down. I'm all for it, now we've agreed that the accommodation will be phase two, if it's workable. I just felt I was being railroaded.'

'Yes, I gathered that. From the time we've spent together, I think I've come to know you reasonably well.'

'And have you liked what you've found?' Selwyn asked. His pulse drummed in his ears as he once more felt a thrill at her touch.

She gazed at him, delighted in the warmth of his hand, and said nothing for several moments. The unsettling thoughts and emotions that had lingered as ghosts in her mind, since she had met this man, materialised once more. Now, though, she felt sure there was to be a resolution one way or another.

'Yes, I'd like to find out a lot more,' she murmured.

He gently clasped her hand.

'So would I,' he replied. 'You said you'd hold my hand through this project.' He inclined his head and kissed her softly on the lips, a scene lost to the witness of the world, other than the gardener who looked on from the patio.

***

'Good grief, it's busy tonight,' Amanda exclaimed on her return from the bar. She put the drinks down and handed her old school friend Kathy another bag of peanuts, which she immediately tore open while she studied the queue of hopeful diners. Amanda had already scanned the room for any sign of Sebastian, a habit she had not yet kicked.

'Anything more on Hector?' Kathy asked, between mouthfuls.

'Not really. The inspector said that, with a verdict of accidental death and because they had not found anything suspicious, they had closed the file. It appears Hector fell and hit his head against a post. They think he was probably unconscious when he fell into the lake.'

Kathy shuddered and Amanda's thoughts drifted to the school summer holidays, when she and her brother used to cycle to the lake. Invariably they would end up trying to teach their cousin to swim. Hector had been a dreadful pupil and would give up at the first mouthful of water, to desert them in favour of his fishing gear. Thereafter, he would sit happily on the jetty and watch his float as the two of them splashed around him.

'Do you think that's how it happened?' asked Kathy as she screwed up the empty packet.

'I don't know. I hope it was,' Amanda's sad expression was born not just out of the loss of her cousin.

'Why, what else could it be? You don't think he was killed, do you?' Kathy asked, with barely disguised excitement.

'No, the police don't think so. It's just me being morbid.' She had harboured doubts about Hector's death from the start, convinced that the documents had something to do with it. Her suspicion had fallen squarely on the Commander. To Amanda's knowledge, only he and Hector had known that the farmer had a copy of the documents. She had been tormented by guilt at how harshly she had spoken to her cousin when they last met, and regretted she had not taken more interest in what had happened between him and the Commander. Oh, how she had wanted to tell the police everything.

A roar of laughter erupted from the bar. Fred Ferris, evidently in good form, sat there in conversation with Clive, the landlord, their heads bowed together, probably over a joke. A waitress was busy setting more dining places at a recently vacated table in the snug and the bar itself was almost totally obscured by new arrivals, some being led to tables in the other bar, others determined to wait for one in the dining room.

As the last of the diners moved forward from the entrance, Amanda caught her breath. Sebastian. It seemed a lifetime since she had last seen him at Hector's funeral, though he had left immediately afterwards without saying a word. He now looked lonely and careworn. Oblivious to his surroundings, he sat alone and stared down into his glass.

'You're miles away,' Kathy commented, then turned to follow Amanda's line of sight. 'Oh, I see,' she added, with a wry smile, just as Sebastian, snapped out of his reverie, looked round and caught sight of Amanda watching him. She returned his hesitant smile and steady gaze, unwilling and unable to take her eyes off him.

'I don't know which of you is supposed to be Wyatt Earp,' Kathy muttered after several moments, 'but it's your shoot-out and I'll leave you to it. I've got to get back.' She swiftly drained her glass, said a quick goodbye, then left. Amanda glanced up at her in panic, which only increased when she saw Sebastian get up and approach her table.

'Hello,' he said cautiously. 'May I sit down?' She gestured to the empty chair opposite. 'It was bad about Hector,' he continued. 'I'm sorry. He was a nice guy.'

'Thank you. Yes, he was, and I'm going to miss him

enormously,' Amanda replied. She began to fear that was all he had come to say to her.

'How are you?' he almost whispered.

'I'm fine, and you?'

'I'm OK.'

'And what about your girlfriend?' Amanda regretted the question the instant the words were off her lips. A flicker of doubt crossed her mind when she saw his puzzled expression.

'I don't believe I've got one of those any longer,' he replied. 'The last time I saw her, she went off with another guy for a Chinese meal. They looked very cosy together.'

His piercing stare bore into her as he waited for her response. Confusion and a mass of conflicting emotions surged in Amanda's head, mixed with a glimmer of hope.

'My boyfriend ended up in the arms of a blonde in a cafe,' she countered, her voice wavering.

'You don't mean Gwen?' he spluttered.

'Yes, the girl you were kissing the night I came to look for you at the cafe.' The memory of the event fuelled the feeling of indignation Amanda had harboured since that night. Though the feeling had receded with time, it had never gone away.

Sebastian gave her an incredulous stare.

'I'd had a lousy day and she felt sorry for me. It was nothing. That's just Gwen. You can't be serious about that,' he retorted, his voice brittle 'Anyway,' he continued, 'if I remember rightly, that was after you'd gone out with that Martin bloke, *and* not for the first time.'

'What do you mean by that?' Amanda demanded, incensed partly at herself for having apparently misread the cafe incident. She cast him a smouldering look.

Sebastian's eyes were almost slits.

'I mean that wasn't the only time I saw you cosy up together – not to mention the time you went to stay with the bloke,' he snapped.

Amanda was taken aback by his assertiveness, a side she had not seen before. She should have been flattered at his evident jealousy, but he had pushed her too far.

'You've been stalking me,' she accused. Now incandescent, she jumped up and knocked over an empty glass, which rolled off the table. As it smashed on the tiled floor, those heads not already turned in their direction swung towards them to see the cause of the commotion.

About to reply, Sebastian was interrupted by the ring of his mobile.

'Blast!' he exclaimed as he turned away and put it to his ear. He uttered a brusque 'OK,' then turned to face his exasperated adversary. 'I've got to go,' he muttered, tersely.

'And not before time. Goodbye,' Amanda replied icily, fighting back tears.

He stared at her for a second but she averted her eyes, determined he should not see her cry. With a shrug, Sebastian turned and walked away.

As she watched him leave, Amanda felt a stab of regret that she had not disabused him of his belief about her relationship with Martin. She was certain there would never be another chance. She flopped back down onto her seat, completely crushed. Her head bowed as a waitress bustled around her and swept up the broken glass amid the hubbub of chatter from diners who now had no further interest in the spectacle.

***

'Hellfire! When was this?' Smudger asked, the mobile against his ear, his head shaking in disbelief.

'Must 'ave been a couple of days ago,' Ronnie replied.

'What was Harry doing in Holland?'

'Setting up a deal – but it looks like 'e was the one being set up, the bastards.'

'Who's in charge at your end now?'

'Me. We're goin' to 'ave to bleedin' lie low till the 'eat's off.'

Although it appeared that the problem was not connected to the antiques operation, Smudger knew it would only be a matter of time, and not long at that, before the Dutch police would contact the Met if they had not already done so. Then the police would start to poke about into Harry's other ventures and they would have to close down totally and pretty smartly.

I'll need to distance myself from Harry and Ronnie then be ready to get out as fast as possible if the net tightens, thought Smudger. However, that would not be before the next phase of his operation had been set up at the Hall. He would have his day, no matter what.

'So when do we move all the stuff from the barn?' Ronnie asked.

'Thursday night – but it won't be all of the goods. After that, I've got plans for some of it. If everything goes as I intend, we'll have nothing to fear. Just make sure you cover our tracks from your end. I assume you've already dumped the old mobile. Make sure you burn any paperwork you've got on this operation. Get rid of everything.'

'Yer teachin' yer grandma. It's all taken care of,' Ronnie assured him. 'What about the money? We need to settle up.'

'I'm still owed for the last consignment we shipped out,' Smudger reminded him. 'I'll sort things out with you on Thursday.'

Smudger's next call was to instruct Jez to put his other plan into operation.

Chapter 15

Selwyn stood at the base of the folly and looked out over the estate. With a total lack of interest in the view, Mustard cocked his leg and peed against the hefty timber door that had been fitted to secure the structure, on the recommendation of the police. The coroner at Penn's inquest had only just fallen short of criticising the way the folly had not been barred to the public. He had referred to it as a 'regrettable circumstance' when he recorded the historian's accidental death.

After he had padded around in irregular circles and sniffed the ground, the beagle suddenly stiffened, having spied a rabbit. As the creature fled the dog bounded off in pursuit, hurling bark after bark at his quarry.

'You wouldn't have a clue what to do with the darned thing if you caught it,' Selwyn murmured with a smile. He would wait a while in case Mustard returned after his inevitable abandonment of the chase, though it was more likely that the dog would go and sniff around the kitchen garden in the hope of a biscuit from the gardener.

In autumn, the folly had been Selwyn's favourite destination for walks with his dog. It was his thinking time. Now, after Penn's death, although he still walked there he was no longer inclined to enter it and climb to the top.

The ground was carpeted in shades of gold and amber as, day by day, more leaves fell. By tradition, those not already raked up for compost were eventually gathered into piles and burned on Boxing Day. Under the gardener's direction, the Fitzgerald family and staff lit then tended the piles of smoking leaves. Georgina's and Selwyn's role was to circulate with bottles of beer, wine and port, and ensure that no one's glass ran dry. Mrs Soames' task was to prepare a lunch comprised of huge platters of sandwiches, pies, warm sausage rolls and mince pies, set out on trestle tables covered with festive tablecloths.

Selwyn shuddered at the prospect of having to continue the tradition without Georgina or Felix. Were it not for his obligations to his employees and a hope that Sebastian would become increasingly involved, he would do away with the custom altogether. The loneliness he had felt for so long now crowded in on him again. Memories surfaced of earlier visits to the folly with Felix and Georgina. Then, with boundless energy, he chased the young child up the rise, and ensured the boy was always the first to reach the stone monument.

His family's laughing faces flashed before him but the fleeting happiness they brought was immediately swept away by more recent memories of the aftermath of Felix's stewardship of the estate. Some of the financial records and transactions still remained worryingly unexplained and unfathomable.

Among a number of the papers he had uncovered were notes in Lucian's handwriting. Unnerved by this communication from his brother, from beyond the grave, Selwyn had been unable to make sense of them. And it had prompted him to wonder, not for the first time, if Lucian really *was* dead and if not, where he could be and what he could be doing. Previously, when such thoughts had occurred, Selwyn had found it difficult to distinguish whether the sense that Lucian was still alive was a belief or merely a wish. However, such speculation always proved too uncomfortable, so as usual, Selwyn refused to dwell on it any further.

The smell of the stables that now drifted towards him on the breeze prompted new thoughts on the season's racing and Wisstingham Prancer's poor performance. If there was a crumb of comfort to be gained, it was that the other horses he stabled had all done well for their owners and hence the reputation of his business. Even Wisstingham Dresser continued to show promise, as Vincent had predicted. Nevertheless, barring a sudden miraculous improvement, Selwyn's mind was virtually made up to sell his half of Prancer to Vincent and lease the stables to him. That way the estate's finances would stack up better, and would enable him to take out a loan to open the Hall.

Selwyn climbed the rise and looked down on the lake garden. His last visit there had been Georgina's picnic. Now, he felt like an outcast from the place, barred by memories of times spent there with her and with Felix, either seated by the jetty or out on the lake. Such had been his sensitivity that, on the pretext of having to make a pressing phone call, he had left Miriam to explore the place on her own, during her tour of the estate.

And now the mayor was back in his thoughts once more. Their brief dalliance in the conservatory the last time he had seen her had been rudely interrupted by Mrs Soames. She had walked into what she thought was an empty room and uttered a shriek of surprise when she had seen their embrace. Before anything could be said, she had fled back to her kitchen. The moment of intimacy had progressed no further. Even the opportunity of a future meeting had been frustrated by Miriam's attendance at a conference in London.

Since then Mrs Soames' attitude to Selwyn, while no less affectionate and attentive, had changed subtly. In unguarded moments he caught her looking at him with an expression that he could only conclude was one of pity. He tried to avoid any mention of Miriam in the housekeeper's presence. When he did, Mrs Soames would introduce Georgina into the conversation and emphasise how well she had organised and run the household. Her clear implication was that the mayor was unfit to fill Georgina's shoes and that Selwyn was making a serious mistake.

Selwyn doubted if Mrs S could ever recognise how her feelings were probably driven by jealousy and a fear that her influence over her boss would be usurped by the mayor. She was also possibly fearful that her position as housekeeper might become untenable, or even non-existent, should the couple's relationship develop into marriage. Presently, Mrs S was blissfully unaware of a further trip that had already been arranged, to visit more stately homes, an excursion Selwyn eagerly anticipated.

Beyond, hidden from view by the trees that flanked the wildflower meadow, was the land that still exercised Selwyn's mind and aspirations. He was desperate to start the excavation, plus he was constantly fearful that the map and the transfer document would surface.

It was strange that Hector's copies had failed to materialise. Two sets of documents and two people accidentally dead, according to the coroner. Be that as it may, Selwyn still thought there was something not right. He did not believe in coincidences. He had been unable to figure out who else might be involved. Who would be prepared to murder for the sake of the documents – and what did they hope to gain by them?

If Penn's and Hector's involvement with the documents ever came to light, Selwyn himself would be the person with the strongest motive for having murdered the two men. The consequences of such an exposure did not bear thinking about.

The morning's walk and his thoughts had brought Selwyn to a physical and mental turning point. Ever since the loss of Felix and then Georgina, he had stubbornly clung to his rituals and routines as if they were a test of his endurance. He had tried so hard to shut out any feelings of self-pity for fear he would implode beneath them. Life had to go on and it was his responsibility to lead by example. He had castigated himself for any feelings of weakness or pleasure that were not in keeping with the duty he felt he owed to his dear departed. Now he realised this was not a sign of strength but of weakness. The real hardship was to face up to change and the future, to let go of the past. From tomorrow, things would change.

With Mustard still loose somewhere, Selwyn straightened his back, turned and started for the Hall.

***

With the customary twinge of apprehension, Sebastian entered the cottage and stooped to ruffle Pilsbury's ears. The dog's tail drummed against the kitchen door then, with a pause to give a brief lick at his young master's hand, the Labrador trotted off through the open doorway and padded across the yard.

Sebastian made his way warily from the kitchen into the living room. Vincent was stretched out on the sofa watching the racing on the television, an empty glass held at a rakish angle in one hand, a whisky bottle with its meagre remains, alongside on the floor.

As Sebastian gave his father a cautious 'Hello,' he braced himself for the response.

With a slight roll of his head, Vincent bared his teeth momentarily and grunted before he replied.

'You're back then, are you?'

With no expectation that Vincent would prolong the conversation, Sebastian made for the stairs. Since the day when Vincent had made a mess of the cottage, their relationship had steadily deteriorated. At best, Vincent now had very little time for Sebastian and maintained a surly silence when in his company, his conversation restricted to essential communication only. At worst, he was openly hostile and antagonistic. There were the odd days when he appeared to be in a very good mood and a completely different person altogether, but these were few and far between.

Sebastian had been unable to fathom the reason for the decline of the relationship and, after a succession of failed attempts to resolve matters which his father had stonewalled abusively, he had given up. The two men rubbed along abrasively, and avoided one another as much as possible. They lived in what seemed to be an uneasy truce punctuated by aggression, invariably initiated by Vincent.

'So what have you been up to today?' Vincent asked.

Sebastian paused and took a deep breath and wondered if this was going to be one of those rare occasions of meaningful conversation or if his father was about to pick an argument.

'I've been at the Hall, updating the computer records.'

'Really?' Vincent observed. He sat up and put his glass on the coffee table and positioned it with exaggerated precision. 'You seem to get on well with the Commander.'

'Yes, he's a good man. I like him.'

Vincent looked up at Sebastian with raised eyebrows and said nothing for several moments before he smiled to himself and shifted his gaze to the glass. Wary, Sebastian watched him in uncertain silence.

'As much as me?' Vincent asked, still focused on the glass.

'Well er, no,' Sebastian faltered, confused by a question that had led into totally uncharted territory.

Vincent thoughtfully fingered the glass.

'Things haven't been easy for you, I suppose,' he observed. 'I've not been a good person to live with.' The admission came as a bolt out of the blue.

'Well, I suppose we're none of us perfect,' Sebastian ventured. He wanted to say, 'You're dead right. Bloody impossible at times!' but that was not going to lead anywhere, so he settled for, 'You're a difficult person to read.'

'Bit of a closed book, eh?' Vincent replied, then looked up at Sebastian with the merest hint of a smile, before he returned his gaze to the glass.

Sebastian looked on uncertainly, but Vincent now appeared to be totally occupied with his thoughts.

'Well, I'd better start cooking tea, I suppose.' Sebastian excused himself.

'Yeah, on you go,' murmured Vincent. He looked up to watch him go and, as the young man disappeared into the kitchen, any semblance of happiness vanished from Vincent's face.

OCTOBER 2010

Amanda looked away from the spreadsheet she had stared at for the last five minutes, rose with a sigh and gazed around the office. She caught sight of a flower that had fallen from the pot plant, so she went to pick it up and throw it in the wastepaper basket. After another survey of the room, she flopped back down onto her chair and resumed the staring contest with the spreadsheet.

After days of battling with her hopes and fears for a relationship that now seemed withered on the vine, she had finally admitted to herself that she was hopelessly in love with Sebastian.

'You're going to waste away, Mandygirl,' her grand-mother warned her each day as Amanda picked at the meagre portions of food she served herself.

In her heart of hearts she knew she was more at fault than Sebastian, though his failure to contact her and their last disastrous meeting had convinced her that he really didn't care very much for her. Any man worth his salt and supposedly in love with a girl would make more of an effort. He had only visited the house once, when she was out, and after that had never tried to contact her.

The clock face to which she had now turned her atten-tion faded into the background, replaced by the vision of his face with the boyish grin that had first captivated her at the barbecue. That memory brought her back to the situation in which she now found herself. It was not an unpleasant one, though the reason for it was. The present challenge was what she should do about it.

A phone call earlier that week had resulted in Amanda's lunchtime presence at the offices of Grimston and Noblett. There, the partnership's corpulent senior solicitor had congratulated her on being the sole beneficiary of Hector's will. Although she had stepped in to try to ensure the continuity of the farm's business, which Hector's foreman had fortunately and expertly taken in hand, the librarian had never expected to become the farm's owner.

'It's not as if I know a thing about business,' she had foolishly admitted to Nan, who, when she heard the news and Amanda's admission, had gone into an anguish, wrung her hands and launched a salvo of questions and observations, all on the same doom-laden theme.

For once, Amanda was thankful for her grandmother's partiality to a drop of wine. A couple of glasses, together with Amanda's reassurances that the world had not yet come to an end, came into play in quick succession and partially settled the old lady's nerves and anxieties.

Now, in the confines of her office, the 'predicament', as Nan had labelled it, occupied Amanda's thoughts once more. She needed advice, but from whom?

Her deliberations were cut short by the appearance of Marcia Pincher, who carried a large folder, which she unceremoniously dropped onto Amanda's desk. With no heed for the niceties of introductory conversation, as was her wont, the boss launched straight into the purpose of her rare visit.

'Amanda, Councillor Cheyney has asked that this be

delivered to Commander Fitzgerald as soon as possible. I'm afraid I'm tied up at the moment so would you sort it out, please? They're layouts for the exhibition room and a list of suggested display items. If he wants to go through them with you, make a note of his observations. Otherwise just leave them with him.'

Amanda stared at the folder. This was the answer and opportunity she sought. Surely the Commander would be able to give her some advice if she approached him in the right way, especially if she offered a sweetener of the piece of land. That would surely get him on side. It might also give her the opportunity to discover whether or not he had found the documents among the papers Alex's aunty had handed him.

'That's fine. Just leave it with me, I'll get right on to it,' Amanda replied, with as sincere a smile as she could muster for her charmless boss. With a muttered and hurried thanks, Marcia left.

After a phone call to the Hall, Amanda wasted no time in setting off. She was received by a rather unfriendly-looking Mrs Soames, whose frown took on a puzzled aspect at Amanda's involuntary smile, the cause of which were two large smudges of flour on the housekeeper's cheeks. Tempted to ask the time of the next performance, the librarian followed the muttering Mrs Soames inside.

The reception the Commander afforded Amanda was thankfully more genial. He invited her into the drawing room, the splendour of which left her open-mouthed. Perched precariously on the edge of one of the chesterfields, she continued to stare about her. Selwyn could not help but smile as he watched her marvel at the furnishings, chandeliers and paintings.

Finally her eyes turned to the Commander and her mouth closed.

'It's gorgeous,' she murmured, lost for anything more eloquent to say.

'I'm glad you like it,' Selwyn replied, his smile even more genial.

As she smiled back at him, Amanda tried to decide whether or not this was a man who could have killed two people for the sake of two pieces of parchment. It seemed unlikely but she could not be certain, so she resolved to be very careful in how she approached him.

Minutes later, over the tea and scones that the slightly flushed but now clean-faced housekeeper had served, she watched the Commander leaf through the folder's contents, with a variety of expressions from pursed lips and nods of appreciation to the odd smile. Very much a schoolboy smile, Amanda thought. Someone with a similar smile immediately sprang to mind, and the thought instantly sent her spirits in a dive.

Finally, the Commander closed the folder and looked across at her.

'Thank you for bringing these, I'll have to go through them more thoroughly. Tea OK?'

'Excellent, thank you,' she replied.

He placed his hands on the arms of his chair as if to rise. The meeting appeared to be at an end.

'The library calls, I suppose,' she sighed, desperately trying to think how to introduce what she wanted to talk about.

Selwyn's arms dropped to the sides of the chair as realisation dawned.

'Of course!' he exclaimed. 'You're the librarian, aren't

you? How stupid of me not to have made the connection. Sebastian's talked about you a great deal.'

Amanda's hopes lifted. She desperately wanted to know what Sebastian had said about her. Maybe all was not lost – surely the Commander would not have mentioned him if he knew their relationship was over. But perhaps he did not know.

'Has he?' Amanda replied, but drew nothing more from her host. She had to move on. 'There's a matter that I hope you might be able to advise me about, Commander, if you'd be so kind,' she asked.

'I'll do what I can,' offered Selwyn.

She explained about her inheritance. Selwyn cut in to express his sympathies at Hector's death, though the gravity of his condolences was quickly followed by a change in manner and expression. The amiable smile had gone and his lips closed tightly. Under the piercing stare from his narrowed eyes, Amanda nervously fingered her chin.

'I wonder if you might be prepared to advise me how I can best manage the place,' she asked. 'I've no idea about these things.'

Selwyn eyed her warily.

'I'd be only too pleased to help,' came his affable reply. 'Have you had the chance to go through all Hector's papers yet?'

'No, not yet,' she replied, slightly puzzled by the nature of his question.

'Well, if you want me to go through the paperwork with you, I'd be happy to oblige,' Selwyn volunteered. 'Or anything else, of course,' he added hastily.

'Thanks. Also,' Amanda continued, 'I think it's time

to put an end to the tug of war over the disputed land. I don't intend to pursue that, and I'd be happy to sign something that relinquishes any claim on the land.'

Selwyn's face lit up in a broad smile.

'Thank you. That's very magnanimous of you. I'll give you as much advice and help as I can. Who knows, there may be ways in which we can work together to our mutual benefit. Will you move into the farm?'

'No. It would be too much of a strain for my grand-mother, so for now the foreman will look after things. I'll call in on a regular basis.'

'How about if I meet you there and we look at what systems are in place? It might be a good idea to have Sebastian along. We could meet with your foreman and find out exactly who does what. I also think it'd be useful for Vincent, our estate manager, to be involved. It would—'

Amanda's apprehensive frown brought him to a halt.

'I'm sorry,' he apologised. 'I'm not trying to bulldoze you. Of course, you must do whatever you feel comfortable with.'

'It's not that,' Amanda hastily assured him. 'I really appreciate your offer. I just think it might prove a bit awkward if Sebastian were involved.'

With knitted brow, the Commander thought this over for a moment before he nodded.

'I see,' he said slowly. 'Things are perhaps not what I thought, eh? All right then, we'll leave him out of it. Would you have any objection if his father, Vincent, was involved? He's first-rate and very knowledgeable.'

'No, I don't think so.' She felt this might be the right opportunity to explore her other concerns. 'I suppose I'll have to go through all Hector's files,' she sighed. 'I've only just finished going through Alexander Penn's stuff.'

Selwyn shifted in his chair.

'That was a terrible business,' he remarked.

'Yes. I agreed to be his executor but I never imagined it'd be so soon.'

'Executor!' the Commander exclaimed. 'Oh, I didn't know that. You must have come across some interesting documents in his files.'

'Very much so.' Amanda waited to see how he would respond to her baited reply. She watched his fingers tap on the arms of his chair.

'I don't suppose you came across anything relating to the estate?' Selwyn ventured.

'No, not really. I assume all that would have been in the folder you collected from Alex's aunty.'

Selwyn let out a disappointed 'Oh,' and they lapsed into silence, each mulling over the conversation and its implications. Amanda felt only partly relieved. While it appeared that the Commander had not found the documents among Penn's papers, she wondered just where they might be – a mystery that it now seemed had taken on a new dimension.

Since they appeared to have both exhausted their lines of enquiry, Amanda expressed her thanks and got up to leave. They arranged to meet at the farm at the weekend, and Selwyn escorted his new neighbour to her car.

***

In the Ferret & Wardrobe pub, tired but happy, Sebastian ordered a pint and sank into the little comfort the sofa's sagging upholstery still offered. The elation that had sustained him through a tiresome day had now given way to excited anticipation.

He had been racked by misery and sleepless nights since the last disastrous meeting with Amanda, such that he had finally called her the previous evening in a make-or-break attempt to rekindle their roller-coaster romance. After his previous disastrous attempt to see her, when he had been told that she was out, he had just about given up hope.

'She don't want anything more to do with you, so clear off and stay away from her,' were the words the stooped old lady had hurled at him on the doorstep on that occasion, before she went back inside and slammed the door in his face.

But now, here he was and everything was just great. Amanda had answered his call.

'I need to speak to you,' he said, after the quiet and cautious voice answered 'Hello.'

'I thought that was what you were doing.'

'Speak properly, I mean.'

'You mean you want elocution lessons?' she asked, then quickly added, 'Sorry.'

Sebastian smiled. He should have felt annoyed at her trivialising the conversation, but that was Amanda and it was so good to hear her soft voice again. He felt like a teenager about to organise a first date.

'Can we meet?' he asked.

'I'd like that.'

'How about the Phantom, tomorrow night?'

'That sounds fine. What time?'

'Seven?'

'Yes, seven it is. Sebastian?'

'Yes?'

'This isn't to return some late library books, is it?'

He sniggered.

'No, it's only the conversation that's overdue,' he replied.

'Then I won't bother bringing the fines box,' she purred. 'See you tomorrow.'

Chapter 16

Selwyn grimaced as he made his way to the pedestrian exit at the Hopestanding multistorey car park. It had been some considerable time since he had last suffered from heartburn, and today was definitely not the day for it to happen again. After all, this was a day to celebrate.

Shouldn't have had that extra helping last night, he thought. He rubbed his chest and decided that Mrs Soames really needed to come with a health and safety warning. In the stairwell he smiled, and his hand tightened on the briefcase handle as he recalled the reason for the lunch with Miriam. Nestled in the dark recesses of the battered case he had first used as a student were the final figures and the report that he and Sebastian had finalised for the opening of the Hall. Miriam had sounded delighted that it had all finally come together. Their last trip had been a great success in more ways than one: although by no means certain, Selwyn felt fairly confident about the answer he might expect to receive to the important question he intended to put to her over lunch.

At the Portman Street exit, Selwyn halted abruptly. His eyes tightened as he was hit by another stab of pain. After a short while he moved on. The ache was stronger now, and a feeling of anxiety had come over him. He began to feel dizzy and short of breath.

Then, ahead of him, Selwyn caught sight of Miriam, who was walking briskly towards their rendezvous. She was too far in front for him to call her, so he quickened his pace. As the pain increased, so did the dizziness. Everything in front of him blurred, and Selwyn's last view of Miriam faded as blackness engulfed him.

The briefcase fell from his grasp and the Commander reeled and crumpled to the ground, while Miriam strode blissfully on.

***

'I hoped I'd find you here.'

The voice both surprised and alarmed Amanda, who had been gazing abstractedly at the bubbles that rose in her glass. She looked up to see Martin, who smiled down at her.

'Martin! What are you doing here?' she demanded, her tone one of dismay. She did not return his smile.

'That's a fine way to greet someone who's travelled thousands of miles to be here,' he replied, oblivious to the unenthusiastic reception, 'I've come back to look at a home for aunty. They've got a vacancy.'

She rose and put her arms loosely round him in response to his warm embrace.

'I'm sorry,' she apologised, now almost in a panic. 'It's just that this isn't a good time. I mean, I'm…' Over his shoulder she caught sight of Sebastian who, as he entered the room, saw the embrace and halted in the doorway. With a parting glare at the couple, he turned abruptly, and before Amanda could say anything, he had gone.

'Oh no!' she muttered in dismay. Having disentangled herself from Martin, she pushed him aside and tried to get past him. In her rush for the door, Amanda collided with a man who had turned away from the bar with two full pints in his hands. Beer and glasses flew in all directions, followed by choice expletives from their bearer and those the beer had landed on. With a mumbled 'Sorry,' Amanda hurtled off in hot pursuit of Sebastian.

Unaware of the reason for Amanda's hasty departure, Martin assumed it had been down to his arrival.

'And don't bloody come back!' cried one of the damp and irate customers. Several pairs of angry eyes now turned on the bewildered Martin. Their owners clearly expected an offer of apology and reparation as they dabbed themselves down with anything to hand. Martin gave the moist audience a shrug to express his blame-lessness and a smile, intended to lighten the tension. Both fell short of their mark, so he opted for a hasty retreat.

'Is that it, then?' a member of the damp brigade demanded, as Martin passed by.

'I reckon so,' Martin replied as he hurried out and mentally struck the pub off his list of future watering holes.

Thank goodness there are two more in the village, he thought, as he looked around for Amanda, of whom there was no trace. With another shrug, and totally confused as to what he had done wrong, he resigned himself to dinner for one at Qwik Qwak and glumly set off down the road.

***

Sebastian ran pell-mell from the pub car park, accompa-nied by one or two choice expletives and unmindful of where he was headed. His illusions of what the evening had promised and his belief in Amanda's affection for him were now completely shattered. He could only see the encounter in the pub as Amanda's deliberate betrayal and humiliation of him.

Unconscious of how he had arrived there, Sebastian found himself in the graveyard, in front of his mother's grave. Automatically, he had once more gravitated to what had become his safe harbour during the recent turbulent and stormy times in his life. He struggled with the emotions that now coursed through him: anger at the girl who had led him on, then so publicly spurned him, despair at the loss of something so precious he had felt was within his grasp, and hatred for the man who had breezed into her affections and snatched away the woman he now knew he loved so much.

'It's a real bastard, Mum!' he muttered, as he dropped onto the familiar bench and stared at the slab of marble that only he ever visited.

'Yes, it is,' came a familiar voice. Its proximity startled him and he jerked round.

There at the corner of the church stood Amanda, panting. Annoyingly, the sight of her lit a fire somewhere inside him.

'Especially when the only man you want to see and be with rushes off without giving you the chance to explain,' she continued. Sebastian stood up to face her as she walked towards him.

'From what I could see, there didn't seem to be much need for an explanation,' he shot back with a scowl. She moved up even closer. Her wide almond eyes mesmerised him. Then she leant forward.

'Sebastian,' she said, quietly, 'if you're not going to stop being a grumpy boy, I'm going to have to spank you.' With her eyebrows raised, she stared into his eyes and gave him a mischievous grin.

His mouth gaped open for a moment. She had done it again – completely bowled him over. As he stared back at her, she leant forward, rose on tiptoes and planted a tender kiss on his lips. Then, with her face close to his, she pouted.

'You're just impossible,' he murmured, and lowered his face to hers. 'I just love you so much.'

'Of course you do,' she replied, and broke into a huge smile.

Again, he was taken aback.

'What about you?' he asked, urgently.

'Oh, I love you madly,' she whispered, as casually as she could, struggling desperately not to shriek with delight at his words. Then she brought her lips even closer to his and whispered, 'And only you.'

They clutched at each other, their kisses passionate and hungry. Amanda felt soft and warm against him, which made his pulse race even faster.

Amanda felt her legs begin to weaken. She was going to dissolve in his arms. They clung together, immersed in their kisses for several minutes, before they surfaced to the real world for breathing space.

'Martin's was a surprise visit. He's come to look at a care home for his aunty,' the rosy-cheeked Amanda eventually explained, as they strolled aimlessly, hand in hand. 'He's never been anything other than a friend.' She stopped suddenly, gently clasped the lapels of his jacket and put her face close to his. He expected her to kiss him but she said quietly, 'Of course, if I find there is anything between you and that coffee pusher, you do realise I'll have to kill you? Probably both of you.' She smiled and gazed into his eyes.

'Would you really have spanked me?' he asked.

'Not in front of your mother,' she replied with a smirk. 'But when I got you home…'

They chuckled at their unspoken thoughts and he slid his arm round her as they ambled on.

***

From the entrance to the stables, Vincent looked across to where a breathless Mrs Soames leant with one hand against the door frame of his cottage, her other hung loosely at her side as she peered through the windows.

'Been jogging, Beatrice?' he shouted, and set off across the yard.

Her head spun round. As he caught sight of the anguish on her reddened face, his smile faded. He quickened his pace as the housekeeper started to waddle towards him.

'It's the Commander, Vincent,' she panted, and grasped his arm for support. 'It's a right pickle and no mistake. ''E's proper poorly, at the hospital. 'Eart attack, they said.'

'Good grief!' Vincent exclaimed. 'Come inside. How bad is he?'

''E's in intensive care and unconscious,' she replied on being ushered into the kitchen, where she capsized onto a chair, a trembling hand clasped to her lips. 'They said it's no good goin' to see 'im at the moment. Where's Sebastian?' she demanded.

'No idea,' replied Vincent, who had now started to make some tea.

'What's best to do, Vincent?' asked Mrs S, who watched his every move as if he were an oracle.

He stared fixedly at the kettle and rubbed his chin, then looked round at her.

'Well, there's no family to tell, as far as I know,' he replied. 'I'm not right sure there's anything we can do for now. Where did it happen and when?'

'Some time this afternoon in 'Opestanding.'

'And do they think he'll pull through?'

'They just said 'e was very poorly and needed quiet and rest. We 'ave to ring tomorrow mornin', when they'll 'ave a better idea.'

'Can *you* think of anyone we should inform?' asked Vincent.

The housekeeper certainly could, namely the mayor, but she did not intend to tell her. Not at the moment. There was no way that scheming woman was going to get to see the Commander before his own housekeeper did, not if Beatrice Soames had anything to do with it. She shook her head.

'Then I don't think there's much we can do at present, Beatrice,' Monaghan reassured her, though she felt anything but reassured.

'It don't seem right to be just doin' nothin',' she protested. 'Lord above, the poor Commander's lyin' there with not a soul to comfort 'im, Gawd bless 'im.' Her shoulders began to shake and she reached for a hankie from her apron pocket. Her other hand idly picked at a stain on the apron, all the while her eyes cast down onto her lap.

'There's nothing to be done just now,' Vincent insisted. He poured out the tea and pushed a cup across the table. 'What numbers do the hospital have for here?'

'I've given 'em yours and they've got my 'ome one,' she sobbed. 'They've also got the one up at the 'All but I've told 'em it's no good goin' and ringin' there after five.'

'Then that should have it covered,' said Vincent. 'I don't intend to go out tonight.'

Mrs Soames looked up at him, anxiously.

'You must ring me right away, if they call,' she insisted. 'It don't matter what time. You'll do that, won't you, Vincent?'

'Of course I will. Now stop worrying.'

They finished their tea in silence, each preoccupied with their own thoughts. As the stables clock chimed the hour, Mrs Soames gave a start.

'Oh Lord bless us!' she exclaimed with a sniff, and gave Vincent another anxious look.

He shook his head at her in mock rebuke.

'Now, Beatrice, you just get yourself off home. There's nothing you can do here. And yes, I'll be sure to ring you if I hear anything,' he promised.

With a tremor on her lips, she rose and looked at him, uncertainty etched on her face. It was only after he had given her a nod and a further reassuring smile that she finally left.

Vincent watched her through the porch windows as she slowly shuffled back to the Hall. He continued to ponder and stare in the direction she had gone, long after she had disappeared. Then, having made a decision, he went inside to the phone and lifted the receiver.

***

With no change in the Commander's condition the following morning, the patient was still in intensive care and allowed no visitors. Vincent decided this was an ideal opportunity to do what he had in mind, though it was essential to get Sebastian out of the way for a few days. However, Sebastian had not come back home until after Vincent had gone to bed and, by the time he rose, Sebastian had already left the cottage. That he did not answer his mobile was not unusual.

'I'm just slipping out for a while. There's something I've got to do,' Vincent told the housekeeper over the safe distance of a phone call.

'Oh, Vincent!' she exclaimed. 'You're not going to be long, are you?' she pleaded. 'You'll have your mobile, won't you?'

'No I won't, and yes I will,' he assured her, then set off for Hopestanding.

***

The cheery expression Mrs Soames had assumed to greet the Commander instantly evaporated when she entered the side ward. There, sitting next to the bed, was the mayor.

Rigged up to a saline drip and various monitors, Selwyn turned his head to offer a welcoming smile to the house-keeper and Vincent.

'How lovely to see you both,' he croaked.

Mrs Soames broke into a smile, edged towards the bed and surreptitiously placed her box of grapes alongside the mayor's much bigger and more luxurious offering. Miriam extended her an indulgent smile.

The cat that got the cream, the housekeeper reflected sourly.

'Vincent, do please fetch a couple of chairs,' Selwyn instructed him with a vague gesture in the direction of the corridor. 'Miriam was just saying how bad news really does travel fast, Mrs S.'

The abashed housekeeper felt a pang of guilt at not having been the source of the news for the mayor. She was at a loss to fathom how *the Cheyney woman* had found out. However, Beatrice Soames was certainly not going to open up *that* can of worms. However, she did cast a glance at the Commander to gauge from his expression whether his comment had been one of accusation, but failed to glean anything.

'I'm only glad as 'ow you're still with us, Commander, and lookin' so 'ealthy,' Mrs S replied. Tears began to well in the corners of her eyes.

As Vincent carried in the chairs, Miriam rose and bent over Selwyn.

'I'd better go,' she said, in a stage whisper. 'There are only supposed to be two visitors per bed and I've had more than my fair share of time. I'll see you soon. Just rest and get well.' She kissed him lightly on the forehead and the housekeeper turned to glare through the window.

'They hope I'll be out in three or four days' time,' Selwyn informed his remaining two visitors during a lull in the subsequent conversation.

There was a noticeable broadening of Mrs Soames' shoulders at the prospect of the responsibility and control she would undoubtedly assume as the principal carer for their stricken chief.

'And I'll ensure you 'ave the best of care,' she promised, her spirits so uplifted that even Selwyn's short and distinctly unenthusiastic 'Hmm,' failed to dent them.

'You're going to have to take things easy for a while,' Vincent offered.

'I expect so,' the Commander sighed. 'They say I should do nothing for a week,' he grumbled.

'Then it's best we listen to 'em,' Mrs Soames concluded, in a tone that brooked no argument. 'I'll make sure of that.'

Selwyn groaned inwardly.

'How's Sebastian?' he eventually asked with affected nonchalance, hoping to have disguised his disappointment at the young man's absence. The visitors exchanged glances that Selwyn could not fail to notice. 'Nothing wrong, is there?' the patient asked.

'No, no,' Vincent cut in hastily. 'He's fine. I'm sure he'll be in to see you soon. He's just a bit tied up at the moment.'

Mrs Soames shot her colleague a questioning glance.

The conversation limped on, with occasional pockets of embarrassed silence. Selwyn's treatment, the weather, the lack of news from the Hall and various other tedious topics were covered and exhausted until the bell announced the end of visiting time, which generated three unspoken feelings of relief.

'Why didn't you tell 'im as 'ow Sebastian's off at those race meetings?' Mrs Soames reproached Vincent as they walked along the corridor.

'The Commander's got enough on his plate without having to think and worry about the stables,' Vincent replied.

'Does Sebastian know about 'im?' the housekeeper asked, her scowl resolutely fixed on the ground as she panted in her struggle to keep up with Vincent.

'No, I want Sebastian to concentrate on the job in hand. There's nothing he can do anyway. I'll tell him when he gets back.'

Mrs Soames gritted her teeth at Vincent's terseness.

'Well, I only 'ope as 'e doesn't 'old it against me for 'is

not knowin", the housekeeper muttered. She would have said more, but knew full well how low the relationship between Vincent and his son had sunk.

NOVEMBER 2010

'How do you fancy a trip to Cheltenham, all expenses paid?' Sebastian asked, and grinned at the screen of the tablet.

Amanda gazed fondly at him, soaking up his boyish enthusiasm.

'It's all a bit sudden. You've only just got back from your last jaunt. How's the Commander?'

'Due home in three days' time. He had complications so they've kept him in a bit longer. Nothing too serious, apparently. He's looking good.'

'So what's this about Cheltenham?' Amanda asked.

'Three days away from tomorrow evening. It's a race meeting. Father's asked me to go along with Wisstingham Prancer and the stable lads. He wants me to meet someone there who might stable his horses with us.'

'Why's your father not going? And what do you know about stabling horses?'

'Says he's tied up with something more important. Anyway, you'd be surprised what I've picked up. I know a smart filly when I see one,' Sebastian smirked.

'Cheeky boy. You'll be getting a short sharp visit from the smack fairy if you don't behave yourself. Anyway, what's a comely lass such as me supposed to do in Cheltenham? Wheel a barrow round to collect manure and feed the horses?'

Sebastian pulled a face at her and she laughed.

'I can think of something better you could do than that,' he suggested.

'I just bet you can, Sebastian, I just bet you can. However, despite your irresistible offer I doubt I could wangle the time off at such short notice, although I'll try. I'd better go now. There's an attractive young chap who's brought his books back late. I think I'm going to have to put him over my knee.' The librarian raised her eyebrows at the screen.

'Twisted disciplinarian!' Sebastian replied. 'You want to watch it. He may have secreted one of your hardbacks down his trousers.'

'We librarians know all the public's tricks and how to deal with them,' replied Amanda. 'Call in and I'll stamp your ticket for you any time.'

'There's an offer I can't refuse,' he retorted with a grin. 'I'd better go and check my books. See what you can do about Cheltenham and call me as soon as you can.'

***

'You've only got the next two days to do it in,' Smudger warned. 'He's due home some time on Thursday. Everything's got to be in place and working by Wednesday night.'

'Stop worrying, it's all in hand,' Jez reassured him. 'Will Sebastian be out of the way?'

'Yes, I believe he'll be gone from first thing tomorrow.'

There was a silence.

'Are you still there?' asked Smudger.

'Yes, I'm just working things out. I'll get the updates onto this machine after he's gone, then we're all set. You know it won't be *totally* foolproof. It never could be,' Jez warned.

'You've told me that a dozen times. Just as long as it's convincing enough.'

'Oh, it'll be that, all right. It'd take a great deal of digging down to find any flaws, and even then you'd need to know exactly what you were looking for.'

'OK. I'll be in contact again tomorrow night.'

Moments later, Smudger made another call.

'Ronnie, it's me. Any news of Harry?' The reply was not what Smudger wanted to hear. 'Well, I suppose it does give us some breathing space,' he replied. 'You need to send the package tomorrow, recorded delivery. Not from a local office. I'll be in touch and let you know how it goes. I'll be seeing you.'

Chapter 17

It was in her self-appointed role as the primary – and, if she had her way, the sole – custodian of the Commander's care and recovery that Mrs Soames insisted she accompany Vincent to the hospital to transport him home safely. The housekeeper was greatly relieved to hear that the mayor had not taken it upon herself to escort him or to be one of the party who came to liberate him.

In consequence, Mrs Soames' head stood more erect than usual as her generous frame slowly swayed its way down the hospital corridor. Alongside the new 'matron' of the Hall's recuperation centre walked Vincent, who had been relegated to the role of chauffeur, at least for this outing.

Any attempts at discussion with the patient on topics of a business nature had been strictly forbidden.

'We don't want 'im bein' upset with anything till 'e's good and ready,' the housekeeper had instructed the estate manager at least three times during the drive to the hospital.

With quiet amusement, Vincent observed her haughty profile as Mrs Soames presented herself to the nursing staff.

'I'll be the one looking after Commander Fitzgerald,' she announced stiffly to the ward sister who, although young-looking and moderately pretty, exuded the no-nonsense aura of her position.

'Then you'd better follow me and we'll go through his

medication, care regime and the exercise programme he's been allocated,' the sister replied curtly. '*You'd* better wait here,' she said to Vincent, with a curt nod, as she led the smiling housekeeper to the office.

Within an hour, Selwyn was being helped up the steps to the Hall by Vincent, while Mrs Soames plodded and panted ahead to open the doors. As she hurried back down to be near her charge, as much as she could ever hurry, the flustered woman was overtaken by an ecstatic Mustard, who whined in delight as he bounded madly up and down the flight of steps to greet his master.

'Get from under my feet, you silly 'ound,' Mrs Soames wheezed. About to topple backwards, she had to be steadied by Selwyn, who was heartily amused by the unfolding pantomime.

'There you go, Mrs S,' he said, her arm only released once he was sure she had regained her balance. 'Don't want you coming a cropper and having to return to the hospital, do we?' he cautioned her.

Her dignity badly bruised, she muttered a grudging thanks and looked daggers at the dog.

Once inside, Selwyn managed to resist the good lady's attempts to send him straight up to bed, and installed himself in the drawing room. During Mrs Soames' reluctant absence to make the pot of tea he had requested, he arranged to meet clandestinely with Vincent later that day.

'Need to chat about a few things,' the patient explained, before he enquired about Sebastian's whereabouts.

'He's at Cheltenham,' Vincent replied, without further elaboration.

Mrs Soames entered the room with a laden tray.

'I made one of your favourite cakes, to welcome you 'ome, Commander,' she announced proudly. Her happy expression then gave way to one of guilt. 'I know as 'ow you've got a proper diet to follow but one slice won't 'urt, I reckon.'

In the late afternoon, Vincent tapped at the drawing room door and guardedly poked his head into the room.

'All clear?' Selwyn asked in a low voice.

'It's all quiet out there,' Vincent replied and entered the room. He glanced up at the ceiling. The housekeeper had insisted she would quarter herself and sleep in one of the guest rooms.

'Just so as I'm close if you should 'ave any problems,' Mrs S had explained. Selwyn's protests that he would be quite all right had come to nought. However, on the positive side, she had eventually, and with much reluctance, agreed it would be for that night only.

Selwyn rose from his chair and, with a furtive, sideways peek at the closed door, went in search of the whisky bottle and two glasses.

'So how have things gone on?' he asked, once they were both settled.

'I can't speak for the office side of things,' replied Vincent. 'That's for Sebastian to fill you in on. But everything's steady at the stables.'

'So it's all quiet on the Western Front, then?'

'So far.'

Selwyn watched Vincent sip his whisky in silence while his eyes darted indiscriminately around the room. He seemed reluctant to meet the Commander's gaze.

'Is everything all right, Vincent?' Selwyn asked after a

while. 'You seem preoccupied.'

'Yes,' said Vincent, and finally looked at his boss. 'Everything's fine.' He showed no sign of elaborating.

'There's something. What is it, man? I've not known you all this time without being able to read you,' Selwyn said in a challenging tone. 'There's something afoot.' He sat back in his chair and folded his arms, his eyes still trained on the estate manager.

Vincent broke into a smile. Not a broad one, but any smile of late was a rarity for him.

'I've strict instructions to keep off anything to do with work or business,' he countered.

'I'm not a basket case yet,' Selwyn protested. 'Out with it.'

'It's nothing bad,' Vincent reassured him. 'It might turn out to be nothing. I was going to leave it till tomorrow.'

Selwyn let out a sigh of exasperation.

'Get on with it,' he ordered.

'Well, it could be some good news. We may have sold Wisstingham Biscuit to Sinclair. He said he would think about it over the weekend and, if he decided to go ahead, he'd send a holding deposit by bank transfer.'

Selwyn sat bolt upright and virtually slammed his glass down on the table. His wide eyes fixed on Vincent like a small child enthralled by a bedtime story.

'Crikey! That would be fantastic,' he exclaimed. 'At the original price, I assume?' he added quickly.

'Yes, the original price. I've not heard anything from him and I was going to get Sebastian to check the account when he gets back tomorrow then hopefully surprise you with the—'

'Bugger that, it won't wait till then,' Selwyn interrupted

and jumped out of his chair. 'Let's check it now.' They had just reached the study door when the grandfather clock chimed. 'Blast!' he muttered, then checked his watch. 'Mrs S will be serving dinner any moment. Daren't upset her now. I'd better leave it till later. I'll call you.'

Just over an hour later, there was a frantic call from the Hall.

'Vincent, get over here right away,' Selwyn ordered. 'I'm in the study.'

Minutes later, Vincent found Selwyn seated in front of the computer screen, his head clasped in his hands.

'What is it?' the estate manager asked.

Selwyn's ashen face turned towards him. His hands shook as he sought to grip the edge of the desk.

'Not only is there no deposit, the account's been vir-tually cleaned out,' he said. 'The deposit account's also nearly been wiped out.' He stared expectantly at Vincent. 'What the hell's been going on?'

'I've absolutely no idea,' Vincent replied, with a shake of his head.

Selwyn fixed him with an icy stare. He was about to get up but thought better of it and turned back to the screen. As he probed the account further with a rising sense of panic, his jaw suddenly dropped.

'Where's Sebastian? Get hold of him. I want him back here, *now*,' he barked, over his shoulder.

'What is it?' Vincent asked and tapped out Sebastian's number.

'All the money's been transferred into his account, the same one I used to make his payments for college.' Selwyn's voice was as cold as steel. He turned and glowered at Vincent, who, with the phone to his ear, waited as the call remained unanswered.

***

Marcia Pincher knocked on the door to Amanda's office and simultaneously barged into the room.

I don't know why she bothers knocking at all, Amanda thought, as her boss's ingratiating smile greeted her over another pile of large folders clutched to Marcia's generous bosom.

'Hi, Amanda,' the department head simpered. 'Hope I've not caught you at a bad time. I know your feelings about the exhibition but I really need your involvement in this.' She shuffled across the office and dumped her cargo onto a table.

'Thing is,' she continued, 'Mayor Cheyney wants the Commander to go through these before their meeting next week.' Ignoring the librarian's glazed expression, she ploughed on. 'They're the final exhibition layouts, exhibit lists and texts. The mayor's away for a few days and, since it seems you've clicked with the old boy, would you be a brick and take them over to him?' Her pretty-please pout of entreaty did little to advance her cause.

'How urgent is it?' Amanda sighed. She did not mind the task – to see the Commander again would be both pleasurable and useful – but she was not going to make it easy for this tiresome trollop who habitually put upon her staff.

'Oh, any time in the next twenty-four hours,' Marcia breezed.

Amanda smiled and replied that it would be a pleasure. The calculated insincerity of both her smile and her words were intended to register a point for future reference.

Her eager phone call to the Hall met with success. Mrs Soames, who was now the self-appointed receptionist, had taken a strong liking to her at their last meeting. The housekeeper had taken it upon herself to be the arbiter of who might or might not have access to her patient.

'Come along at eleven tomorrow, ducks. 'E'll see you then,' she confirmed.

***

DI Stone watched with growing uncertainty as his superior paced back and forth across the chief inspector's office.

'I hope to God we're doing the right thing, Roger. The shit will really hit the fan if we're barking up the wrong tree,' DCI Nelson warned, with a glance of uncertainty at his subordinate.

'It all seems to check out,' replied Stone. 'The Met say the photo looks to be the genuine article. It matches the stolen goods description they've got, and there's no doubt that it's the Hall in the background.'

'I smell something fishy,' Nelson announced. His puckered face looked as if he had literally done so. 'Whoever's sent us all this is clearly in on the operation. Why blow it all open? Strikes me they're either out for revenge or have set out to land someone up at the Hall right in it.'

'In which case, we could end up in the proverbial if we get it wrong,' Stone admitted.

'Quite. But then we can't just sit back and do nothing, not now the Met's involved,' the DCI argued.

Stone got up from his chair, wandered over to the

window and stared outside. The loose change in his pocket was once more on the receiving end of a good sorting.

Wouldn't be surprised if there's a farthing and a three-penny bit in there, the CI thought. DI Stone was not known to readily part with the contents of his pockets.

'OK, let's go for it,' Nelson decided. 'You'll need enough men to hit the outbuildings first and simultaneously. If you don't find anything there, concentrate on the Hall.'

'We're going to need some support from Hopestanding,' Stone warned.

'Yes, I know. Leave it with me. I'll run it by the super and get back to you.'

***

Selwyn spent a sleepless night tossing and turning. In his frequent waking moments, he tried to make some sense of his betrayal by the person in whom he had invested so much trust and faith. Earlier that evening he had felt so sick to the pit of his stomach that he had put a stop to any further conversation with Vincent and retired to his room.

Vincent undertook to go through Sebastian's personal possessions, to see if he could find anything that might shed light on what had happened and to report back the following morning. He had managed to make contact with one of the stable lads who had returned from Cheltenham, only to hear that Sebastian had not returned with them and that they did not know where he was. Further attempts to contact him had proved fruitless.

In the early hours, a bleary-eyed Selwyn crept down to the study to revisit the horror of his bank accounts.

Like people repeatedly searching the same places over and over again for a lost item, he refused to believe the evidence of his own eyes. He moved from one screen display to another in the vain hope that the figures would change. He found another account he had no memory of, into and out of which regular large amounts had been moved, the balance always left at the same low figure.

At breakfast, his grey countenance prompted Mrs Soames to recommend a day in bed for her charge. However, the stony silence and uncharacteristic scowl she received put an immediate end to any further approaches on that subject.

'Must be the pills 'e's on,' she muttered as she retreated to the safety of her kitchen. She began to regret that she had arranged the morning's appointment with the librarian.

No matter, she thought, *I'll tell 'er 'e's too ill to see 'er and rearrange the appointment.*

In the study, Selwyn stared ashen-faced in bewilderment at other files that he had discovered on the computer, files he had never seen when Sebastian had taken him through the system. Not being very computer-literate, his confusion mounted with every passing minute and every unwelcome discovery. There were galleries of photos of furniture, jewellery, ornaments and paintings, each with a reference number, the white backgrounds to the pictures always the same. Elsewhere he came across pages of article descriptions, each one again bearing a reference number and a price.

Although sorely tempted to ring the bank and alert them to the lost funds, Selwyn was determined to get to the bottom of the matter before he did so. His inability to believe what Sebastian had done played havoc with his self-confidence and rational thinking.

When he suddenly remembered the cheque books Selwyn tugged at the desk drawer, only to find it locked. He was about to go and search for his keys when there was a knock on the door.

'Come in,' he called, taken aback by the unsteadiness of his voice.

Vincent poked his face into the room, apprehension written all over it. He entered, his eyes staring up from under a lowered brow. There were no words of greeting or welcome.

'Well?' Selwyn demanded.

'I've finally got through to him. He says he's on his way back. I've looked through his things and it doesn't look like he's done a runner. I've checked that number and it is his account.'

'I thought it was,' Selwyn murmured.

'There must be some logical explanation—' Vincent's argument was cut short.

'I think things are very obvious,' Selwyn declared. 'Come and look at this.' He motioned Vincent over to the screen and clicked through the various files he had uncovered. 'What do you know of these?'

Vincent stared wide-eyed at the computer.

'Absolutely nothing,' he replied. 'What are they?'

'Well, either Sebastian's a closet antiques junkie or they're something of a more sinister nature. There's an account with some big amounts of money going in and out over a considerable period of time. How many accounts do we have?'

'Why are you asking me?' said Vincent, taken aback.

'Come on, man!' Selwyn barked. 'You deal with the stables and grounds. What accounts do we have for those?'

Vincent frowned.

'Well, there's the stables account, one for the quarry and one for the estate land. I deal with those and I can show you them right now.' He stared back defiantly at Selwyn, whose narrowed eyes glared at him.

'And is that it?'

'Yes. No, wait – there's the old Stables B account that you and Lucian set up, remember? But I don't have anything to do with that. I don't even know if it still exists.'

'Right, I need the statements for those accounts you deal with,' Selwyn insisted.

Several minutes later, as Selwyn pored over them, Vincent stood behind him silently. Satisfied with what he had seen, Selwyn turned and motioned Vincent to sit down. The demoralised Commander stood by the window and stared blankly out at the leafy trees and swathes of lawn, his tongue once more on the prowl.

'I'm going to try to be fair, Vincent,' he said eventually, 'though God only knows why. I want every penny returned to the accounts. I haven't informed the bank and I won't need to if it's all repaid. I'm going to need a full explanation from Sebastian. If what he has to say doesn't hold water, or if there's anything illegal about what's been going on, I'll have the police in like a shot.' He turned to face Vincent's expressionless gaze. 'Do I make myself clear?'

'Crystal clear,' Vincent replied, still without any sign of emotion.

Selwyn gave him a dismissive nod. After his manager had left, the Commander stared at the closed door and slowly shook his head in disbelief.

The room suddenly felt very stuffy and Selwyn badly needed some fresh air, so he made his way to the front door.

'I'm just popping out for a stroll, Mrs Soames,' he called, and was promptly joined by Mustard who brought, for the first time that day, a fleeting smile to his master's pale and haggard face.

'Suppose you want a walk too, do you, boy?' he murmured and bent to stroke the beagle before he reached for his duffel coat.

'All right, Commander, don't you be a-doin' too much. Wrap up warm,' came the housekeeper's warning instructions from the kitchen. Ordinarily she would have hurried out to see him but, from the mood he was in and the imminence of his eleven o'clock visitor, Mrs Soames thought it best not to detain him. He would hopefully be out of sight and earshot when the librarian arrived.

***

The Commander had only just stepped outside and taken several gulps of fresh air when he spotted a Land Rover coming up the drive. He frowned. For one awful moment he expected to see Hector and was acutely relieved when Amanda stepped out of it.

She gave him a quick wave and smile then went round to the back of the vehicle and emerged, laden with files and folders.

'Good morning, Commander,' she greeted him cheerily.

Her cheerfulness raised his spirits slightly. 'Sorry I'm a bit late.'

'Late?' he asked.

'Eleven o'clock? Mrs Soames said you'd see me at eleven.'

Selwyn glared in the direction of the kitchen.

'Did she, indeed? Are those for me?'

'Yes, they're from Mayor Cheyney for you to look over before your meeting.'

'I see. I'm afraid I wasn't expecting you. I'm off for a walk now.' Selwyn instantly regretted being so dismissive of the girl, particularly after her generosity over the disputed land.

Anyway, he thought, after a moment's reflection, *I might learn something useful about Sebastian.* 'Why don't you drop those things in the hallway and join me for a stroll?' he suggested.

'Yes, I'd like that if I'm not in the way.'

'Certainly not. I'll appreciate the company,' he assured her with a smile.

The walk took them in the direction of the lake. Selwyn decided to show her the garden there. Mustard could scamper around and chase the wildlife while they sat and talked.

'So how are things with Sebastian?' he asked, as they watched the beagle's antics.

'They're just fine, thank you, Commander,' Amanda replied, happiness in her voice and on her face.

Selwyn fixed his gaze on the lake.

'I seem to have lost touch with him over the past two or three weeks. What's he been up to?'

'He's been away a bit. I was with him in Cheltenham.'

Selwyn spun round to look at her.

'So he's back,' he exclaimed. The intensity of his reaction surprised her.

'No, I came back with the rest of the team,' she replied. 'Sebastian said there was something he had to do, so he set off elsewhere. He wouldn't say where, but he should be back today.'

'Indeed.' The Commander redirected his grim gaze to the lake. 'He's a hard worker,' he ventured, after a pause.

'Yes, he loves his computers, spends all his time with them. It's a pity he doesn't put his nose in a book now and then. Sebastian's bad for business, you know.'

Selwyn frowned.

'The library, I mean,' Amanda clarified.

Selwyn tried to smile and looked away again.

'Is there something wrong, Commander?'

'Yes, I'm afraid there is.'

'I'm sorry. Is there anything I can do to help?'

'It's kind of you to offer,' he replied. 'I'm not really sure.'

'Try me.'

'Try to understand that I'm not making any accusations,' Selwyn explained. 'These are just the facts. It's all very confidential but I believe I can trust you.'

As he recounted all that he had discovered, Amanda's previously happy demeanour ebbed away, to be replaced by shocked incredulity.

'I can't believe it,' she whispered. 'I just can't believe it of him. That's not the Sebastian I thought I knew. God! I can't have been so wrong. Can I?' She stared down at the ground, baffled.

Selwyn placed a comforting hand on her arm.

'Look, I need to hear his side of the story,' he said. His sympathy for the girl now almost superseded his sympathy for himself. 'There may be some other explanation for all this.'

'It sounds very doubtful,' she muttered forlornly.

'I'm sorry to have upset you with this, Amanda,' Selwyn apologised. 'Perhaps I shouldn't have said anything. If you see Sebastian before I do, please don't mention it.'

'No, I won't – and I appreciate your having told me. I suppose I needed to know. I'm so, so sorry.'

By now Mustard, who had chased much and caught nothing, trotted panting to the seat and nuzzled at his master's hand. Selwyn glanced at his watch.

'Goodness, I'd better be getting back,' he exclaimed.

By the time they reached the Hall, Amanda felt slightly more composed. She climbed into the Land Rover and drove off. Selwyn thoughtfully followed her progress until she was out of sight.

While Amanda had sensed the Commander's relief at having shared his troubles, she felt as if a chasm had opened up in front of her. The confidence she had felt in her relationship with Sebastian was evaporating and with it her confidence in herself and her judgement of others. The only conviction she was left with was that her trust in Sebastian appeared to have been grossly misplaced.

Chapter 18

After Amanda's departure, Selwyn had not even time to reach the kitchen to challenge Mrs Soames about the librarian's appointment before five police cars arrived with a cloud of dust thrown up in in their wake. Two more vehicles simultaneously made their way along the old quarry road, one headed to the quarry itself, the other to the old barn.

DI Stone mounted the steps to the Hall and rang the doorbell, then turned to survey the cars randomly parked below him. Their drivers and passengers now stood beside the vehicles.

Mrs S bustled past the Commander to the front door.

'Oh my Lord!' she exclaimed when she opened it and saw the vehicles and the sea of uniforms.

'Good morning, madam. Detective Inspector Stone again,' the DI greeted the disconcerted woman briskly, and held out his warrant card. 'I'd like to speak to Commander Fitzgerald, please.'

'Like as not you would,' she replied, her composure and housekeeper's determination now recovered. 'I'm afraid 'e can't be disturbed. 'E's been very ill. Just out of 'ospital. You'll 'ave to come back.' Mrs Soames gave a parting scowl at the uniformed officers before she made to retreat back inside.

'I'm sorry about that, but I'm afraid this won't wait. Who is there in authority that I can speak with?'

'Me,' she affirmed, and squared up to him.

They stared at each other until their stand-off was interrupted by a voice at the door.

'It's all right, Mrs Soames, I'm quite capable of dealing with this,' said Selwyn, and took up a position in front of the DI.

'Commander Fitzgerald, I should like to speak with you, please,' Stone said, with a triumphant glance at the retreating housekeeper as she now grudgingly departed for the kitchen.

As Selwyn led the officer down the corridor into the drawing room, a host of thoughts and questions ran riot in his brain.

Is it to do with Sebastian, or what I found on the computer? Is it about Hector or Penn? Should I pre-empt matters and mention what I have found? That there were so many officers present certainly boded ill. *A search, perhaps? Yes, definitely a search.*

Before Selwyn could offer his uninvited guests the courtesy of refreshments, Stone drew himself up to his full, short height and spoke.

'From information received, we have reason to believe that stolen goods may be, or may have been, stored on these premises or within the estate,' he announced.

Selwyn's drooping jowls and jaw testified to how gobsmacked he was to hear this.

'Accordingly,' the DI continued, 'I have here a warrant to conduct a search of the entire estate.' He withdrew the paper from his inside pocket and offered it to Selwyn, who stared blankly at it for several moments, before he stared back, equally blankly, at Stone.

As he stared, the computer images Selwyn had seen the previous day began to float through his mind.

'I don't know a thing about this,' he muttered eventually, and returned the warrant unopened and unread. 'I'm sorry, I'm going to have to sit down.'

'Please do so, sir,' Stone replied. The tone of his voice reflected his disdain for the upper crust. A republican at heart, the DI had no time for the Royal family, let alone the landed gentry. He resented how he had to pussyfoot around people such as the Commander who, as far as Stone was concerned, had been born with silver spoons in their mouths and were darned sure no one else was going to sup from them.

The DI knew he was on dodgy ground, banking on the discovery of something within the outbuildings to tie in with package of photos and documents that had been sent to the station. If he found nothing in the grounds, it would look a bit seedy to say,

'No sign of any stolen goods, sir. It must have been a set-up. Sorry to have troubled you.' What if the old boy, fresh out of hospital, had to be stretchered back in there? Or even worse, popped his clogs?

Selwyn regarded the unflinching detective, and again pondered the advisability of mentioning what he had seen. However, he had already denied any knowledge of stolen property. Was he, even now, an accessory after the fact if the police dug something up? He threw his arms up in the air.

'You'd better go ahead, then,' he capitulated. 'Just let me get hold of my estate manager so he can give you access to anywhere that's locked.'

He picked up the phone and within minutes, a puzzled-looking Vincent was being briefed.

'We'll start with the outbuildings first,' Stone announced,

once Vincent had arrived with a large bunch of keys in his hand.

Once the quarry buildings had been covered, the search party moved on, back down the road.

'What's that building over there?' the DI asked, pointing.

'It's an old barn.'

'What's it used for?'

'Nothing, as far as I know.'

Stone stopped and looked at him.

'What do you mean, "as far as I know"? You're the estate manager, aren't you?'

'That was young Felix's project. The Commander's son.'

'And where's he?'

'He died four years ago in a car accident.'

'Oh,' said Stone, his impetus momentarily checked and his tone more respectful. 'What did he do with the barn?'

'I'm not sure. I think he let someone use it for storage.'

Stone glanced at the officer standing next to him, on whose face the hint of a smile had appeared.

'Really? What sort of storage?'

'I've no idea. It was made very clear that it was none of my business,' replied Vincent.

'And what happened after he died?'

'I assume it came to an end. As I said, I wasn't involved.'

'Let's go and take a look, shall we?' said Stone.

'I'm not even certain I've got a key for the place,' Vincent said in a warning tone.

Stone gave him a broad smile.

'Oh, don't you worry,' he said. 'We're past masters at getting things open.'

In no time at all, the hasp was smashed off and the doors

thrown wide open. Stone noted the newness of the lock, for future reference. Inside, the barn stood in darkness and the lights did not work. It looked empty, apart from numerous tea chests stacked up in each of the far corners. On inspection, these proved to be empty. Stone inspected his finger after running it along the edge of one of the chests.

Clean as a whistle, he thought.

As the group made its way out to the road, the DI stopped and looked back. He gazed thoughtfully at the doors and the front of the building. Next he walked around it, then went back inside and looked towards the road. The rest of the party stared at him in puzzled silence. Next, he paced the length of the building inside and repeated the exercise outside.

'A bit of a Tardis in reverse, I reckon,' he said with growing enthusiasm. 'Maddox, take those boxes outside. Don't touch any of the metal surfaces.'

A few minutes later Stone muttered,

'Very clever,' as two doors were exposed in each of the corners. 'Someone's even hidden the door joints with overlapping planks.'

A buzz of excitement went round the assembled officers. The DI studiously watched Vincent's face as they pushed open the first door.

'Well, well, what have we here? Open flaming sesame,' Stone exclaimed, then chuckled and shone his torch as they entered the first of the spaces. They came upon a few pieces of fine antique furniture as they lifted the dust covers. On top of these were stacked vases, paintings, silverware and here and there jewellery boxes.

'Crikey!' muttered Vincent.

Stone rounded on him.

'Do you recognise any of this stuff?'

Vincent shook his head and scanned each item as Stone's torchlight moved from one piece to another.

'I'm beginning to understand how Howard Carter felt,' the DI quipped to one of his men. 'Set some lighting up and get the photographer and the fingerprint people down here, pronto,' he ordered. 'Get this stuff listed, and mind you don't touch anything without gloves on.'

'Maybe this is furniture and stuff from the Hall,' Vincent suggested. 'Do you have the authority to be doing all this?'

Stone looked up into Vincent's face and smiled.

'Oh yes, Mister Estate Manager, we've got the authority, all right.' He patted the breast pocket of his jacket and winked. 'Do you seriously think it would be appropriate to store all this beautiful furniture in these conditions for any length of time? I know the landed gentry can be eccentric, but come on. Just to be certain, though, let's get your boss down here to see if he can identify it, shall we?'

'He's in no fit state to walk down here,' Vincent protested.

'Who said anything about walking?' Stone asked in mock horror. 'We'll drive him in style. McBride, take charge till I get back,' he instructed, all the while he kept his eyes firmly fixed on Vincent.

***

'Please don't touch anything, sir,' Stone advised, some time later. He held out a supportive arm as the Commander reached out to steady himself on seeing the furniture and ornaments.

'Is this your property, Commander Fitzgerald?' the DI asked.

'I've never seen it before in my life,' Selwyn replied, shakily.

'That's funny, that's exactly what your estate manager said. There's some more stuff through here I'd like you to look at, if you would.' He led the Commander to the other room, where he repeated the question and received the same answer.

'Then I suggest we return to the Hall to continue this conversation,' said Stone.

Dumbfounded, Selwyn nodded silently.

'Have you any further need for Vincent?' he asked, as they returned to the police car.

'Oh yes, we'll need him for a while yet.'

Back at the Hall, Selwyn managed to keep the anxious Mrs Soames occupied and at bay as he instructed her to serve tea and biscuits not only for the DI and himself but all the police officers present.

'Don't you be puttin' your fingers on any of that there furniture, or anythin' else for that matter,' the house-keeper cautioned a couple of the officers on her way to the kitchen. 'I'm blowed if they're gettin' biscuits,' she muttered to herself when she was back in her haven.

Seated at a table in the drawing room, Stone took out his notebook and started to write. After a while he looked up at Selwyn, whose tongue was off on another dental crusade.

'I assume you have a computer on the premises,' the DI said eventually.

'In the study.'

'Is that the only computer?'

'I have a laptop. That's in there as well,' Selwyn replied wearily. As he got to his feet he staggered slightly and quickly sat down again.

Stone frowned.

'Are you all right, sir?' he asked, more out of duty than concern.

'Just a bit groggy. It must be the medication I'm on,' Selwyn lied. He sank back into the armchair and signalled the DI to continue.

'We'll need to take both computers with us for examination,' Stone advised.

'All right, if you must,' answered Selwyn. He wondered if the day could get any worse and whether he should mention the files he had uncovered on the wretched machine. No: that would be tantamount to an admission of guilt, and he needed to speak to Sebastian first and get his side of the story. He was uncertain just where the thread would lead to once he started to untangle it.

'In view of the nature of the items under investigation,' said the detective, 'I'd recommend that you give some thought to digging out whatever you can find to establish the provenance of the furniture, the ornaments and the paintings here at the Hall.'

Selwyn groaned.

'Perhaps there's an inventory with your insurance policy?' Stone suggested. 'Old photos, receipts, things like that?'

'I'll look into it if you really think it'll be necessary.'

'Yes, I think it may well prove to be necessary, sir. Also, I'll need you to accompany me to the station for a formal interview and statement when we're finished here,' Stone warned, and rose from his chair.

The disheartened Commander stared bleakly up at him and nodded.

'Now, I'd better go and see how my men are getting on. I'll be back shortly.'

'Officer,' Selwyn called out as the DI reached the door.

'Yes?'

'Please try to ensure that no one upsets Mrs Soames.'

'We'll do our best,' the DI replied. *Heaven forbid anyone should offend that horrendous Rottweiler*, he thought.

***

Seated alone and awaiting the inspector's return, Selwyn answered the phone. His spirits briefly rose as he recognised the caller's voice.

'I'm fine, but don't come over,' he urged.

'What's the matter? Are you all right?' Miriam asked, with a note of alarm.

'Yes, I'm fine. It's just that the police are here. There's a bit of a problem.'

'What sort of a problem? I'm coming over.'

'No, don't!' he insisted. 'You can't do any good and it will only complicate matters. I'll see you as soon as I can.'

'You've got me worried, Selwyn. Are you in trouble?'

'I may be, but it's not of my making.'

'What's happened? Why won't you tell me?' Now there was fear in her voice, something he had not heard before.

'I will tell you but I can't just now. I'm not even certain what it's all about. You may need to stay away from me for a while, for your own sake and for your position. I wouldn't want any of this mud sticking to you. I'll ring you as soon as I can.' Selwyn clenched his teeth, furious at how his whole life seemed to have been put in jeopardy through these developments.

'I don't care. I'm coming to see you and I don't care who knows it,' Miriam insisted. 'I'm not going to abandon you when things go wrong.'

'Now listen to me, Miriam,' said Selwyn, his tone abrupt and authoritative. 'You can do more good for me by standing well back. I'm probably going to need all the friends I can muster, especially those in high places. It's not going to do either of us any good if you're discredited by association. So do as I say and wait to hear from me, all right?'

The line was quiet for a few moments.

'OK. Goodbye, my dear. Please take care of yourself and call me, soon,' came Miriam's subdued reply.

***

'Vincent, what on earth's goin' on?' Mrs Soames pleaded, once the last of the police cars had driven away. She fidgeted with the strings of her apron and fumbled ineptly to tie a bow that she normally achieved subconsciously in a few seconds.

The Commander had had virtually no opportunity to speak with her before he was whisked away to the police station in the DI's car. He had merely told her not to worry and that he would be back soon. His optimism was certainly not shared by the DI.

'You'd better put a brew on and I'll tell you,' Vincent replied and seated himself at the kitchen table.

After she had poured the tea and rustled up some biscuits, the housekeeper sat subdued as Vincent brought her up to date.

'Come on, Beatrice, pull yourself together,' he chivvied her as she started to weep.

'I just can't believe it, Vincent, honest I can't,' the sobbing housekeeper stammered. 'Not Sebastian. There must be some mistake.'

'All this time I've been trying to tell you. He's not all he seems. As his father, I should know.'

Of a fashion, Mrs Soames thought, but kept quiet, though she was now inching towards considering the unbelievable.

'I'd better get over to the stables and see what sort of mess they've made there,' Vincent said after several moments' silence. He leant over and reassuringly patted the chubby hand that clutched a crumpled handkerchief and rested on the table.

'Oh my Gawd,' Mrs Soames kept repeating to herself, once she was alone. Finally, with a sniff, she hauled herself to her feet and dabbed her eyes. 'That's quite enough of that, my girl,' she murmured, roused herself and tried to smile. 'The Commander 'as a need of you and you ain't goin' to be the one to let 'im down.'

Through the hours that followed, she busied herself in the kitchen and made a variety of pies, cakes and biscuits, with regular glances at the clock and the occasional sortie into the hall to look out onto the drive through the window.

Finally, just as the housekeeper had gone to take Mustard for a quick walk, a police car drove up to the Hall and dropped off the Commander, who trudged up the steps.

On her return, Mrs Soames was just in time to see her boss disappear into the drawing room.

Better get to him before the whisky bottle does, she thought, if a little uncharitably. With that, she set off to offer her employer whatever consolation and refreshment she could.

***

'Hi, it's me,' Sebastian breezed into his mobile. His earlier attempts to contact Amanda on FaceTime had met with repeated failure.

'So I gather,' came the unfriendly reply.

'What's up, Amanda?'

'Have you seen the Commander?' she asked icily.

'No, I've only just got back.'

'How fortuitous for us all.'

'What's the matter?' he demanded.

'If you want to know, I suggest you go and see him. At the moment, I don't feel there's anything more to be said between us, Sebastian. Goodbye.'

Amanda ended the call, but not before Sebastian had caught her sob. He stared in total confusion at the mobile for a few moments, then pressed in her number again. There was no reply.

Sebastian hurried to the Hall, where he paused at the kitchen to look in on the housekeeper.

'Hello, Mrs Soames,' he called to the familiar back. The unsmiling housekeeper looked round and stared at him for a moment, muttered something then turned away and went off to the pantry. Nonplussed, Sebastian watched her retreating form then headed to the study. Finding it empty, he carried on to the drawing room and tapped on the door.

'Come in,' Selwyn called.

'Hi, I'm back,' Sebastian cheerily greeted the Commander, whose expression immediately became thunderous and, whose narrowed eyes fixed on Sebastian's.

'And about time,' Selwyn replied, his tone even colder than Amanda's had been. 'No, don't sit down,' he added. 'I'd prefer you to stand.'

Filled with alarm, Sebastian stared at Selwyn. His fingers rested hesitantly on the arm of the chair he had been about to occupy.

'What's the matter, Commander?'

'What indeed?' Selwyn replied as he rose and approached him. He stood close to Sebastian, and peered into his eyes. 'What indeed?' he repeated, then stepped back a pace. 'There are a few things I want to show you. I would have shown you on that smart new computer you so kindly installed for me, but unfortunately the police have commandeered it, and the laptop.'

'The police? What's happened?'

Selwyn continued to hold Sebastian's gaze.

'Yes, the police. It's been a very interesting couple of days. However, thanks to Felix's old laptop and my foresight to put things on a pen drive, all is not lost.' Selwyn stepped forward again and scanned from one eye to the other of the discomforted man.

'They teach you in the navy to anticipate the unexpected,' he murmured, 'but, my God, it would have been difficult to anticipate this. Come with me,' he ordered.

In the study, he motioned Sebastian to a chair in front of the open laptop and drew up a chair alongside him.

'What can you tell me about this?' Selwyn demanded. He clicked open an image.

'It's a table,' came the baffled reply.

'Remarkable! Mind like a laser. Here are some more.' Selwyn clicked from one image to another, all the while alert for Sebastian's reactions, which consistently appeared to be of total confusion. Then Selwyn moved on to the schedules.

'Is this some sort of sales literature?' Sebastian asked. 'Are they from an auction?'

'Possibly, but I suspect something more sinister. The thing is, what do you know about them?'

'Absolutely nothing,' Sebastian maintained.

'Then how do you explain their being on that shiny new computer you installed?'

'I haven't the foggiest,' Sebastian protested. 'Someone else must have put them on.'

'Who?'

'Well, perhaps it was Jez when he first set the machine up.'

'A thought that had occurred to me,' Selwyn countered. 'But how do you explain the fact that they weren't on there when you demonstrated the machine to me?' In the absence of an answer, Selwyn clicked onto a different screen as Sebastian started to bite his fingernail. The Commander brought up the old account used for the stables that Vincent had reminded him of.

'What can you tell me about this account and the transactions?'

Sebastian leant forward and peered at the screen.

'I've never seen that account before.'

'So what about those transactions?'

'I haven't a clue.'

Finally, Selwyn opened the statement for a different account.

'What about that transaction?' he asked, and jabbed the screen with his finger.

'I don't know anything about it,' Sebastian insisted.

Selwyn clicked again.

'You don't recognise your own account?' he bellowed.

'What?' Sebastian exclaimed, then stared at the screen open-mouthed, his whole frame rigid. 'That's just not possible,' he muttered, as he fumbled desperately through his pockets in search of his mobile. He tapped on it until he reached the display he wanted. He double-checked the account numbers then sat back, dumbstruck, disbelief etched on his face.

'I don't know anything about that, Commander. I swear to God I don't,' Sebastian spluttered, and caught his breath in his rising panic. He searched between the open files to recheck the statements. There, on the corresponding date, were entries for the money received into his account from the estate accounts and then, just after midnight, corresponding amounts shown leaving his account.

'Oh my God! This can't be right. It just can't be,' he blurted out.

Selwyn stared at Sebastian's account on the screen and went instantly cold.

'Where's it gone, Sebastian? Where's my money? It was there yesterday,' he shouted. 'Why have you done this to me?'

'I didn't do it! I don't know! I don't know anything about this, honestly,' Sebastian pleaded in panic, now on the verge of tears. 'I wouldn't do anything like this, especially to you. Not to you. Please, please, you've got to believe me.'

His plaintive face struck a chord with Selwyn, who had

come to trust the boy over the years to a point where he had even entrusted him to carry out his Internet banking. He fought down his rising terror at the loss of the money. Up to that moment, he had been confident it would still be in Sebastian's account and the transaction could be simply reversed.

Selwyn pressed him.

'Do you recognise the account where the money's gone?'

'No,' Sebastian finally answered after several agonising minutes, during which he cross-checked the account details against his standing orders and direct debits. 'The account means nothing to me.'

'If it wasn't you, who else would have the information and passwords to do this?' Selwyn demanded.

Sebastian furiously racked his brain.

'No one,' he eventually admitted.

'What about your father?'

'No. He doesn't know my login and password.'

Selwyn's head sank and he rubbed his forehead. Though everything pointed to Sebastian, his reactions were leading him to believe otherwise.

Believe or wish? he wondered. Yet, whatever had been going on, the antiques operation and the money from the account had to be connected.

Then there came a flash of clarity.

Of course! Some of the transactions surely went back to a time when Sebastian could not possibly have been involved.

'If you're not responsible for this, Sebastian, who could be?' Selwyn queried, determined to follow a path of systematic enquiry and a process of elimination. 'Purely from a logical point of view, the closest person would be your father.'

Sebastian thought for a moment.

'He's just not savvy enough to do this. He's virtually useless with computers.'

'Then what about that Fellowes chap?'

'Why him? He's too remote from it all. Anyway, why would he? He's nothing to do with the estate.'

Nagging at the back of Selwyn's brain was the timing of the start of the transactions, which was before Felix had died. Had this been the start of the affair, or had something been going on before that?

His thinking suddenly took off in a different direction.

What if Lucian had started this whole business? What if it had lain dormant and Felix had discovered it, resurrected it, then somehow involved Sebastian? He would need to dig out Felix's papers and statements, wherever they were. *And what of Lucian's papers?* There had been no trace of them after his departure. *Had his brother taken them with him or disposed of them? Had he left them for Felix to come across?*

There was a lot of digging to do, but Selwyn's first priority was to contact the bank immediately.

'Right now, I can't say whether I believe you or not, Sebastian,' he said. 'You must contact your bank right now and see if they can reverse the transactions. Do it from here. I'm going to call my bank. I'll be back in a minute. Needless to say, the police will want to talk to you pretty soon, so you'd best get to it,' he instructed, then left the room.

***

Later that evening, hunched in his chair by the fire, Selwyn sat and brooded. The firelight sparkled off the amber contents of his glass, and the whisky bottle was close at hand. The large escritoire was strewn with papers hauled from their dungeon trunk, which had been stored in one of the attic rooms.

The Commander's lips were set tight. His worst fears had been realised. Numerous entries in Felix's bank statements showed large amounts of money enter and leave the account. The eventual net balance had been a large one. In hindsight, Selwyn was surprised this had not registered with him when the balance had been transferred on Felix's death. He concluded it had been because of his preoccupation with Georgina's illness at the time.

The more Selwyn revisited the possibilities and permutations of who could be responsible for this cataclysm, the more confused he became. The evidence all pointed to Sebastian's involvement. Much as the Commander wanted to believe the protestations of innocence and his own doubts that it could be his young assistant, the evidence was damning. However, he did not believe that Sebastian had controlled and managed matters on his own – in which case, it had to be Fellowes.

A combination of Sebastian and Fellowes seemed unlikely, and Selwyn doubted that either of them could have masterminded or managed the antiques operation. Furthermore, when Felix had been in charge, Sebastian had been too young and had not been involved in the estate's affairs.

Lucian began to feature prominently in Selwyn's thinking. Had he set this up in the first place, and was he still alive and involved? Had he been controlling things from a distance, or was he close at hand?

Another scenario was of Vincent in partnership with

Felix, but Selwyn discounted this because the two had never been close or had much to do with each other. Also, with regard to more recent times, the relationship between Vincent and Sebastian was so bad that the concept of them working together was unthinkable. Anyway, despite his mood swings and attitude to his family, the estate manager had always been totally dependable and supportive, and his loyalty was unquestionable.

The telephone conversation with the bank was horrendous. Selwyn talked to machines, answered numerous security questions and finally had a conversation with a human being, who sounded very suspicious. The bank would carry out its own investigation and get back to him as soon as possible. In the meantime, the account was frozen and Selwyn would need to visit his local branch the next day to make temporary arrangements.

Sebastian had reported a very similar experience. If anything, his had been worse. He had been called to an interview the next day and his account had also been frozen.

***

Try as he might, Selwyn could not find one bright spot in the gloom that had descended upon him, that is until Amanda arrived at the Hall the following morning to collect the files and panels she had delivered.

'I understand the meeting with Mayor Cheyney has been postponed,' she remarked, as Selwyn led her into the conservatory. Narrow rays of sunshine streamed through the gaps in the louvre blinds.

'Yes,' he acknowledged, pleased to see this junior ambassador. Even the gloomy Mrs Soames managed to raise a smile for her as she served tea and biscuits, the ever-hungry and optimistic Mustard close behind her.

'Them scones are fresh out of the oven,' the housekeeper announced, then added a pointed, 'for those as are allowed to eat 'em,' and levelled a sideways glance at Selwyn.

'How are things, or should I not ask?' Amanda enquired, after Mrs S had gone. She looked anxiously at the Commander.

He considered the question in silence for a while. The desire to confide and to unburden himself was very strong but, although he believed Amanda to be totally innocent, she was very much involved with the person who was still high on his suspect list. Surely, though, the girl deserved to know? After all, what harm could it do? The damage was already done.

Piece by piece, Selwyn completed the jigsaw of the latest events and shared his suspicions while he observed the librarian's ever-darkening expression.

'I didn't know about any of this,' she murmured, when he had finished.

'I didn't think for one minute that you did,' Selwyn assured her. 'Anyway, I've no doubt it will all come out in the course of the police investigation. I only hope I'm left with a modicum of respectability at the end of it, though I wouldn't take any bets.'

'And those?' Amanda asked, pointing to the files.

'Unless the money's retrieved, the exhibition would be pointless – but please don't mention that to anyone. I haven't even talked to Miriam about it yet.'

Amanda crossed her mouth with her finger and offered him a sad smile. Even Selwyn's hopes for the excavation were financially dashed. In any event, now he would be unable to open the Hall, he certainly could not expect to receive any sympathetic consideration from the council.

They parted in mutual sadness, the Commander that this breath of sunshine had to depart, Amanda at the betrayal of this lovely, fatherly man and of herself by someone she had clearly never really known. Now that she had spent time with him and got to know him, her fears and suspicions as to the Commander's possible involvement in the deaths of Alexander and Hector had now completely dissolved.

Chapter 19

'Well that clinches it,' DI Stone declared, after he had reread the note he had just received from the Met. 'Let's wheel the Commander in again, McBride.'

A squad car was despatched and within the hour Selwyn was seated in the interview room across from the two officers, having declined to have a solicitor present. The evidence offered to him established that some of the goods found in the barn had been previously reported stolen. It also showed that the account from which numerous payments had been made into the estate's account was that of a known criminal.

'We've now established that the account, into which the money was paid, has only two signatories: you and a Lucian Fitzgerald, your brother,' Stone confirmed.

'I'd forgotten all about the account. I don't believe I ever used it.'

'Well, someone certainly has. When did your brother die?'

'Ten years ago.'

'These transactions are dated two years after that,' Stone observed with a 'pick the bones out of that' smile.

And before Felix's death, Selwyn noted, but he already knew that after he had spent hours delving into the old bank statements back at the Hall.

'I can't help you on that. It wasn't me. Someone else must have had access to the account.'

'Who?' Stone demanded.

'I don't know.'

'The bank says not,' Stone maintained. 'What about the photographs and descriptions we found on the computer?'

'They weren't on there when I first saw the machine,' claimed the Commander.

'When was that?'

'Two or three weeks ago. The computer had just been installed and Sebastian took me through the files he had created and already transferred. They definitely weren't on it then. They must have been added afterwards.'

Stone shook his head.

'The dates on the files are much earlier than that,' he confirmed.

'I'm sorry, I just don't understand what you're trying to tell me,' said Selwyn, his face lined with confusion and growing exasperation.

The DI explained in detail what the Hopestanding station's technical boffins had extracted from his computer. By the time he had finished, Selwyn had arrived at the unhappy conclusion that Lucian and Sebastian were the prime suspects – as well as his own son. Furthermore, it could only have been Sebastian who had put the files on the computer. However, he was determined not to point an accusing finger in their direction at that juncture. Doubtless the facts would eventually speak for themselves and lead the police to the right conclusions, so let this spiteful, fat detective do his own dirty work. He would get no help from Selwyn Fitzgerald.

**

Amanda paused for a moment at the front door. She took a deep breath and braced herself for what she expected to be yet another stormy homecoming. Not that there was anything to justify it, but lately Nan had delighted in picking an argument with Amanda, or anyone else for that matter, just for the sake of it. The dementia had worsened. Janice, the home help who covered while Amanda was at work, had warned that matters were coming to a head.

'Been looking for a home to lock me away in, have you?' Nan challenged Amanda as soon as she entered the room.

'Now, now, Mrs Sheppard, that's no way to talk,' Janice cautioned the old lady as she slipped on her coat and gestured to Amanda to step out of the room. 'This really can't go on much longer, Amanda,' she whispered, once they were in the hallway. 'She's so hostile and uncooperative. It's nigh on impossible. She really needs a different sort of care.'

Amanda sighed and shot a glance at the closed door.

'I can hear you're talking about me,' Nan shouted. 'Go, on, get off home, woman, and don't come back.'

Janice gave Amanda a shrug and patted her arm.

'I must go,' she whispered. 'Have a think about it and we'll speak tomorrow.'

As the front door closed, Amanda steeled herself and returned to the living room.

'What are you doing here?' Nan confronted her. 'Where's your mother? I want to speak to her.'

Amanda looked away in exasperation.

'Mum's not with us, Nan. She passed away years ago.' Nan gave her a blank stare.

'Oh,' she said. 'No one told me.' Her response to the news was devoid of emotion.

Amanda sank down onto a chair by the table. Her dreams of a possible future with Sebastian were now beyond hope, and she was also faced with the virtually impossible task of providing care for a grandmother whose mental health was in rapid decline. Either that or she had to find a home for her, a prospect the old lady dreaded.

As her vision started to mist over, Amanda turned away to hide her face. Nan stared at her impassively, then the expression on her wizened face melted as she noticed Amanda's shuddering shoulders. The old lady's preoccupation with her own aches, pains and mortality receded. Like the outlines of trees and fields that emerge from a vanishing mist, her mind started to clear to the point that she recognised her granddaughter's unhappiness.

'What is it, Mandygirl?' Nan coaxed.

Amanda glanced round quickly. She recognised in the nickname a sign of the old lady's lucidity. She rose and knelt alongside the frail, stooped form and took Nan's wizened hands, Amanda stroked the misshapen, arthritic fingers and smiled through her tears into the wrinkled face with its careworn smile.

'It's Sebastian,' she explained. 'He's done something pretty awful.'

Nan's face hardened.

'I told you not to have anything to do with him, Mandygirl.' Nan's old eyes narrowed in rebuke. 'Came from bad stock, he did. His father, Vincent, he's a real bad 'un. Always has been, always will be.'

A hint of a smile came to her wrinkled lips.

'Now that cousin of his, Lucian,' she continued, 'he was a one. Not a bad 'un like Vincent, mind, just a bit boisterous and easily led. Vincent got him into no end of trouble.'

'Not Lucian Fitzgerald?' Amanda gasped.

'Yes.'

'How do you know all this?'

Nan smiled at the innocence of the question.

'Why, bless you dearie, I lived in the same village then. Alstherham. Pretty place. We lived in Poppy Cottage. Lucian and his mother had Mole End. It was her brother's, really. That was just before I met your grandfather.'

'What about the Commander? Did he live there?'

'Oh no, he was here with his father, the old colonel. They didn't have anything to do with them,' replied Nan. She adjusted her position, eager to continue. 'The Commander never got to know Lucian. Lucian's mother left the old man when the boy was very young. Quite a scandal it was in those days. She took the boy with her, back to her old village.'

Nan's eyes shone with delight at this rare ability to remember so clearly.

'So,' she went on, peering ahead as if could actually see the images her memory conjured up, 'the mother kept very quiet about the incident. Had to go away in the end, thanks to Vincent,' she added, and pursed her lip.

'What incident?' Amanda asked.

The old lady seemed to ponder the question. Her face closed on her granddaughter's, her eyes darted conspiratorially from side to side.

'Killed him,' she whispered. 'They couldn't prove it, but he killed him. Deliberately. That were no accident, and everyone knew it.'

'Who?'

'Young Kenny Budd, God bless him, poor lamb. It fair broke his brother Joey's heart, it did. Joey was never the same after that.'

'What happened?' Amanda urged.

The old, milky eyes lit up. Nan felt invigorated as she enjoyed this fleeting chance to take Amanda on a tour of her museum of memories.

'Poor Kenny went down the well in the uncle's garden,' she explained. 'Vincent pushed him, of course. Claimed he didn't, but everyone knew he did. Lucian said he didn't see it. Said he'd wandered off, but he was blamed as well.'

'And Kenny?'

'Dead, of course, poor soul. But no one could prove anything. There was something very strange about Vincent after that. He could be good as gold sometimes, then he'd be the Devil incarnate. Really cruel and vicious. I suppose these days they'd say he had a split personality. He was very clever, though. Devious. He could fool anybody but he had a real bad streak. That's why I tried to steer you away from his son.

'Anyway, feelings against the families got so bad in the village that they had to move away. Went their separate ways. Later on, Lucian came to these parts to help look after the estate. Well, the old colonel was getting on by then. It was all kept very quiet. I'm not sure if even the Commander knows about it.' Nan turned her narrowed eyes to the window as if trying to discern something far away.

'Strange it was, how Vincent had a hold over Lucian,' the old lady murmured. 'He could make him do anything, almost like he had something over him.'

Nan stifled a yawn, closed her eyes and laid her head back. Amanda knew that sleep was only moments away and that it would erase any recollection of the conversation – and probably the events themselves – perhaps forever.

She was uncertain just what these revelations meant in relation to the events at the Hall. Maybe things were not as clear-cut as the Commander had thought. Amanda wondered if the information was important enough to share with the Commander.

'Funny how you remember things,' her Nan's voice piped up.

Surprised, Amanda looked at her.

'How do you mean?' she asked.

'Vincent,' Nan replied. 'The teachers gave him a nickname. 'Course, it wouldn't be allowed these days. Said he was always blotting his copybook, so they called him Smudger. Funny name,' she mused with a smile as her eyelids started to droop.

'Yes,' agreed Amanda, and wondered whether she should share all this information with the Commander, but decided that perhaps he had enough on his plate without her further intrusion on his time.

***

Selwyn leant forward to poke at the glowing coals in the fire and attempted once more to order his thoughts. He had trawled through every piece of paper he could lay his hands on, in an attempt to piece together sequences of events back to the time before Lucian's disappearance.

He lay back in his chair and closed his eyes, then suddenly they opened wide. Of all the nooks and crannies he had explored, there was one monumental omission: the drawer in the study, in which Sebastian kept his things. Several days earlier Selwyn had been about to find the spare key to it when the DI had appeared. Afterwards, he had forgotten all about it.

Moments later, as he rummaged through the desk drawer, he found some innocuous printouts of spreadsheets and routine correspondence then, tucked underneath, were some of the now familiar photos and catalogue pages. Selwyn let out a world-weary sigh, assailed once more by doubt and suspicion.

He delved further, then finally came across some sheets of paper that sent a chill through him.

'It's not possible. It can't be,' he muttered. He stared at his find then held the papers between his forefinger and thumb, as if someone had handed him some animal droppings. He did not want to hold them but neither could be bring himself to put them down. He recalled the last time he had seen them, when they had been handed to him by Hector Middleton.

Selwyn's head began to swim, and beads of perspiration formed on his brow. He rose and started to the door, the papers still in his hand. He made his way unsteadily to the library, where he locked the documents in the safe then sat down near the piles of documents and rolls of parchment that Penn had worked on, now abandoned in a corner of the room.

He tried to rationalise the implications of the find, the events of the last few months and what now seemed undeniably like Sebastian's treachery.

***

Vincent smiled as he reflected how well things were working out. The Commander was slowly crumbling in front of him. With a little luck, he would have another heart attack that might see him off.

As for Sebastian, the bastard had had plenty to say to Vincent since their initial row after his return from Cheltenham, but Vincent felt he had handled the boy like a pro. He complimented himself on a performance worthy of an Oscar. He had shown just the right combination of surprise, anger, disgust and contempt when he confronted the whelp and washed his hands of him, but drew short of throwing him out of the cottage. He could not do that. Vincent needed to keep Sebastian close to learn what was going to happen next, with the police and the bank.

His final move had totally wrong-footed the pathetic fool: he had turned on the fatherly concern and told Sebastian he would do his best to support him. That would ensure the bastard stayed close and confided in him.

'I'll try and speak with the Commander, though I can't say I'm hopeful,' Vincent had offered. 'At the moment he's adamant you're not to go near him or the Hall.'

'I just need to find out what's happened to turn him this way,' Sebastian had pleaded. 'He seemed to be coming round to believe me but something's happened. Amanda doesn't want me anywhere near her either, and she won't answer my calls.'

'I can't do anything about the lass but I'll see what I can do with the Commander,' Vincent had promised, though he had done nothing.

***

Now the time had come to raise the curtain on the final act. Vincent set off for the stables. It was time to clear everything out and make a call. He reached into the gap behind the wall board, retrieved the mobile, plugged it in and waited for it to come alive.

'I need you to do something,' Vincent said, when Jez finally answered. He gave a nod of satisfaction as he listened. 'So Sebastian's been on to you, has he?' Vincent asked.

His expression grew darker as he listened further.

'Look here, Jez, don't you go soft on me now. We're both in this too deep. Yes, I know it's hard on Sebastian but it's either him or us.'

He scratched the back of his head and started to pace as Jez talked. His eyes roved around the room but took nothing in.

'Now listen,' he finally interrupted. 'I've just thought how we can throw him a lifeline – but it would be better if it came from you. Get him round to the offices this evening.'

Vincent listened again.

'I'll tell you when I get there,' he replied to Jez's question. 'Get him round for eight and I'll see you about half an hour earlier. Don't mention I'm going to be there. Send me a text to confirm he'll be there.' He rang off.

He was about to retrieve the documents hidden in the stable before the police search when his other mobile rang. It was Selwyn, who sounded annoyingly more upbeat.

'Vincent, I need you up here right away. I've had a call from Sinclair. He says he's still interested in Biscuit. I said we'd ring him back immediately.'

Vincent pocketed both mobiles, put one on vibrate, then reluctantly set off for the Hall. He would shred the files later that evening when he returned to pick up the gun.

**

Selwyn gave a fleeting wave to Mrs Soames as she watched him through the kitchen window. There was a time when he could never have expected to come within sight but that she would immediately bustle over to him with a question or a morsel of advice. Now she watched him in silence when he set off on his walks, always with the same look of sympathy on her rosy face.

The habitual spring in his step long absent, he turned towards the woods but halted at the sound of crunching gravel on the drive. He doubled back and rounded the corner in time to see Miriam's BMW skid to a halt. She hastily got out and strode towards the main entrance steps.

'Over here, Miriam,' Selwyn called.

She stopped to look in his direction then hurried towards him.

'Selwyn, what's happened? What's going on?' She made to embrace him but stopped, hesitant as he raised his hands.

'You shouldn't be here. I told you to stay away.'

She stared at him in confusion, taken aback by his brusqueness.

'Why don't you want me here? What's going on?' she demanded.

Selwyn sighed and took hold of her hands.

'Being associated with me now is only going to mess

things up for you,' he warned. 'You'd better leave.'

'I'm not moving an inch until you tell me why,' she insisted.

'All right,' he conceded. 'Walk with me and I'll tell you.'

They strolled to the lake garden, where they sat down. He shared with her all that had happened. Alarm, shock and incredulity appeared on Miriam's face as the story unfolded.

'So I expect to be formally arrested and charged at any moment,' Selwyn concluded. 'The money's gone. There's no chance of opening the Hall. Once your council hear that, there's no way they'll let me carry out any excavations even if I could afford to. Not that that matters now, in the grand scheme of this whole mess.'

By now the trees silhouetted against the deep blue sky had reached their twilight shade of intense black. In the distance grey clouds slowly advanced, and with them a chill breeze.

As she plumbed the depths of despair and demoralisation that she had only experienced once before, Miriam stared out over the grey, choppy surface of the lake and tried to take in what Selwyn had said. In the fading light, he failed to notice her tearful eyes. To her, the Commander seemed very cold and distant. There was no hint of the warmth she had felt from him on the previous times they had spent together. Had he just strung her along to get the go-ahead for his blasted excavation? Doubt and suspicion seeped into her thoughts. Why was he being so stand-offish now? Why had he not taken her into his arms to share his dilemma and pain?

'No, I don't suppose they will,' she murmured, her head turned away from him.

Selwyn shot a glance at her then looked away.

'I'm sorry how things have worked out,' he apologised. 'It's best that you stay well away from me,' he added, with a harsh finality that brooked no further discussion.

Miriam turned to look at him, desperate to glimpse one spark of affection, but he stared back at her, tight-lipped.

'Very well,' she murmured. She rose then added quickly, 'No, I'd rather go alone,' as he got up to accompany her. 'I'm very sorry, Selwyn,' she said, choking back her tears. 'I hope it all turns out all right for you in the end.'

She so desperately wanted to tell him she would be there for him always but, out of pride, said nothing.

As Selwyn watched her recede into the darkness, he dropped back down onto the bench a broken man. Over the past few days, he had come to realise just how much in love he was with this elegant woman who he had been on his way to propose to, that wretched day. Now her dream for the Hall had been shattered. All he had to offer her was the cruel publicity and humiliation of being associated with a ruined man about to be dragged through the courts. Now the only honourable thing to do was to distance himself from her and give the lie to his true feelings.

In the gloom of the evening, he turned over in his mind how she had reacted to the news. His disquieting thoughts dwelt on the absence of any struggle on her part to keep him. For all her strong-mindedness, she had put up no resistance to his insistence that she should leave.

Shadows of doubt began to creep in. Perhaps her affection, which he had desperately hoped was real, had never truly existed. Yes, they had enjoyed each other's company, but doubts he had harboured as to any love she might feel for him now started to take shape. Perhaps any affection Miriam had shown towards him had been displayed to maintain his interest in her and her aim to persuade him to open the Hall.

Several minutes later, the sound of rustling leaves stirred Selwyn from his increasingly muddled thinking. He turned to see the beam of an approaching torch, then heard Mrs Soames' voice.

'The things one 'as to do round 'ere. What's 'e a-doin' of bein' out like this, in this wind, with 'im only just back from death's door?' it muttered. Then, more loudly, 'Commander, are you there?'

'Here, Mrs S,' Selwyn called back, and set off in her direction.

'Dear Lord, Commander, you might 'ave told me where you was goin',' the housekeeper puffed, 'with that woman,' she added, in an icy tone. 'I thought as 'ow you might 'ave come down 'ere. I saw 'er car was gone.'

He put his hand on her shoulder and steered her back towards the Hall.

'So what brings you out here?' he asked.

'That there librarian's just rung. Sounded all keyed up an' urgent, like. I said as 'ow she could come round right away.' Mrs Soames stopped and looked anxiously up at him. 'I 'ope I ain't done the wrong thing, Commander, only it sounded important.'

'Not as long as you're prepared to make me a nice coffee, Mrs S,' he replied, pleased to have something to smile about.

'That I shall,' she assured him, and gladly returned his smile.

Half an hour later, Amanda was shown into the drawing room. She felt less certain of herself than when she had phoned. It did not help that the Commander did not seem to be in a welcoming mood.

'So what is it that's so important?' Selwyn asked, with barely a hint of a smile.

Amanda hesitated.

'Well, er—' she began, but clammed up at the look of impatience on his face.

'Come on, Amanda,' he cut in. 'I've rather a lot on my mind at the moment and a few things that need to be done.'

'Well,' she resumed, then paused again to frantically decide how much to precis what Nan had told her. 'My grandmother knew both Lucian and Vincent when they were young and, to use her words, Vincent was "a real bad 'un". He was always getting Lucian into trouble.'

Selwyn's eyes widened. He stared at Amanda, his attention now fully focused on her.

'So how did he know Lucian?' he asked.

'They were cousins,' Amanda explained in surprise. 'Didn't you know?'

Totally taken aback, Selwyn merely shook his head and continued to stare at her as he grappled with the implications.

'So this made me wonder if everything's not quite as it seems,' she suggested.

Selwyn's thoughts darted between the possibilities her information had raised.

'So you think that Vincent could be involved after all?'

Amanda nodded.

'And what of Sebastian?'

'Perhaps he's been telling the truth all along,' she ventured.

'If it's not Sebastian, it must be that Fellowes chap,' Selwyn theorised. Then he shook his head. 'But that doesn't explain the money. And there's another piece of evidence I didn't tell you about.'

Amanda's shoulders sank. She seemed to crumple in despair.

'Honestly, Amanda, there's no one who wants to believe that Sebastian is innocent more than I do,' Selwyn tried to reassure her. He told her about the existence of the copies of the map and the transfer document and the meeting with her cousin.

'I know all about that,' Amanda admitted. She explained how the documents had come to her knowledge, how Hector had become involved and had copied them. Before she could finish, Selwyn held up a hand to stop her and went to retrieve the papers he had locked in the safe.

On his return he asked,

'Would you know if these are the ones?'

Amanda scrutinised them, then held them up to the light.

'Definitely. I recognise our paper,' she replied.

'I found them locked in Sebastian's desk,' the Commander said. 'He was the last person to see Hector alive that night, wasn't he?' Selwyn expected to see some sign of capitulation on Amanda's part, but if anything she appeared even more assured.

'There's no way Sebastian knew about these,' she affirmed. 'No way.'

'How do you know? Why did he go over to the farm in the first place?'

'I'd gone away,' she explained. 'He wanted to see Hector to find out where I was. He told me so when we patched up our differences.'

'And the documents?' Selwyn asked.

'I talked about it when we went to Cheltenham. He was gobsmacked. He did not have a clue about it.'

'And what if he was lying?' Selwyn challenged.

Amanda smiled.

'Sebastian's not that good an actor, believe me.'

'Maybe he is, if he's been involved with all this,' Selwyn argued, still unconvinced.

'Well, I don't believe it,' she declared defiantly. 'Not now.'

Selwyn stared about him, preoccupied by the jumble of permutations and combinations as to who might have done what. His reservations about Sebastian's innocence remained, though he was touched by the faith that Amanda had now professed.

'He has wanted to come and speak to me for the past few days, but I've refused to see him,' he admitted. 'Perhaps I should speak to him.'

Amanda wasted no time and rang Sebastian's number, but there was no reply. She stared across at the Commander then, on an impulse, rang another number.

'Jez, it's Amanda,' she said, when she got through. 'I'm trying to find Sebastian. Do you know where he is, by any chance?'

'He's probably on his way over here,' Jez replied.

'What for?' she asked, with a frown.

'I can't tell you. It's personal,' came the cagey reply. 'I must go, that's the door. I'll tell Sebastian you're after him, OK? Bye.'

'Jez!' she shouted as he cut her off. But not before she had heard him call into the intercom, 'Come up, Vincent.'

Amanda relayed the conversation to Selwyn, whose face clouded in suspicion. He glanced at his watch.

'I think things are best left until tomorrow,' he suggested. 'Then we can find out just what Sebastian has to say for himself.'

'It won't wait until then,' Amanda insisted. 'I don't like it. I'm going over there.'

'You'd do better to leave things alone,' Selwyn cautioned. 'You might involve yourself in something you'll regret.'

Amanda refused to listen to his advice and made a hasty departure.

Selwyn paced slowly from the front door back down the corridor, deep in thought. His conscience pricked him that he had allowed Amanda to go off on her own. He looked at his chair and pondered whether to sit down again or head off in pursuit of the librarian.

Or should I see the evening off with a whisky and simply go to bed? he asked himself.

Chapter 20

The front of Fellowes House stood in complete darkness except for a light in a solitary upstairs office. Even the feeble yellow glow from the street lamps on the edge of the car park petered out before it reached the building.

There were only three other cars in the car park when Sebastian drove in, one of them Jez's Porsche. The call had sounded vague and mysterious. Jez had refused to be drawn, other than to insist it would be in Sebastian's best interests to be there.

Although he suspected that Jez had been involved all along with the present calamity, Sebastian was desperate for some explanation and anything positive to pull him out of the mess he was in. He was effectively banished from the Hall and expected to be thrown off the Wisstingham estate, since his job there was now gone. He was anxious to know if he had a future with Fellowes – if he managed to escape a prison sentence.

The interviews with the bank and their experts had been cold and intense. The money that had been transferred into Sebastian's account was irretrievably lost. It had been moved simultaneously through several accounts and was now hidden somewhere abroad. There was the threat of possible legal action. Furthermore, Sebastian had been summoned to attend another interview at the police station the following day. The first one had left him feeling like a wrung-out lettuce and he had been left in no doubt that there were many more questions to follow.

The entrance door was wedged slightly open. Sebastian entered the dark silence, puzzled at this lack of security, which was a total affront to the company's philosophy. He stepped out of the lift and walked along the familiar gallery he had trodden so many times before. A motion sensor flooded his progress with light.

At Jez's office, Sebastian peered round the open door.

'Lights on but nobody at home,' he muttered. He thought immediately of Amanda, who would have made just such an observation.

He turned back towards the gallery and looked across the open central area to the galleries opposite. These were swathed in darkness. He looked over the edge of the parapet wall to the cobbled courtyard below, gasped and instantly drew back.

'Oh my God!' he exclaimed. There was a body lying on the ground, dimly lit by a nearby emergency exit light.

'Not a pretty sight, is it?' came a voice from close behind him.

Startled, he spun round to see Vincent, who stood with his back to the office.

'What the hell's happened?' Sebastian gasped. 'Who is it?'

'Who do you think?' Vincent stepped to the edge of the walkway and peered down. He took a torch from his pocket and shone it on the spreadeagled form. The unblinking eyes of Jez Fellowes stared up at them, his head haloed in a pool of blood.

Sebastian felt he was going to throw up. He drew back, his face ashen.

'What are you doing here?' he stuttered. 'What's been going on?'

'I don't know,' replied Vincent. 'Jez asked me to come. He wouldn't say why, just that it was important. When I got here, he was nowhere to be found.' As he talked, Vincent slowly advanced towards Sebastian, who fearful, started to back away.

'So what happened to Jez?' Sebastian whispered.

'He must have fallen, or perhaps he jumped,' Vincent replied. He continued to advance, his tone disturbingly casual. He stopped, as did Sebastian, and the two men eyed each other warily.

'It was you, wasn't it?' Sebastian accused.

Even at that stage Vincent could easily have brazened it out, but that would have left unfinished business. Quite a bit of unfinished business. He smiled as he recalled the events of the last half hour, and his eyes gleamed with elation and excitement.

'Fall, jump, push, it's all the same in the end,' he pronounced. 'He had to go. His job was finished and he was going to be troublesome. Jez had become...' He slowly enunciated the word 'unreliable.'

Sebastian felt compelled to glance towards the parapet. Vincent followed his gaze.

'In the end, he would have been unfaithful,' Vincent continued.

All the time he still edged towards the terrified Sebastian, who started to back away again.

'Just like your mother was. Now that's one thing I can't stand, you know,' continued Vincent. 'Mind you, Jez squealed like a pig when I pushed him over. Just like Kenny did. He was a squealer, was little Kenny. Ding dong bell, Kenny's in the well. And now it's ding dong bell, Jez is in the well.' Vincent sounded casual and abstracted, as if he was telling a story to a small child.

Sebastian stared at the maniac now so close to him, a person he could not recognise as the man he had grown up with.

As they stood motionless, the light went out. Vincent rushed forward, wrapped his powerful arms round Sebastian's waist and pinioned his arms. Then, with a tremendous heave, he started to lift his terrified victim off the floor.

Sebastian struggled and kicked out wildly. One of his feet connected with the parapet wall that he was being forced against. His other foot reached down in vain to touch the floor.

'It's no good struggling, boy,' Vincent hissed in his ear. 'I'm too strong for you. Just let it happen. It'll be over quickly.'

Sebastian kicked back from the wall. The two men staggered and fell against the opposite wall and he managed to break free. Sebastian made to bolt but Vincent pulled out a gun and aimed.

Sebastian froze and stared at the gun as if mesmerised by it.

'No, don't do that, you bastard. You just stay right where you are,' Vincent snarled.

'You're bloody mad,' Sebastian gasped. 'Where the hell did you get that from?'

'Friends from the Smoke, you little bastard,' Vincent hissed.

'I don't understand any of this,' the baffled son exclaimed 'and why do you keep calling me that?'

Vincent's features suddenly screwed up in rage.

'Because you *are* a bastard. The Commander's bastard,' he bellowed.

Sebastian's face froze in astonishment. A bombshell though it was, those few words instantly connected. Explanations suddenly flashed through his mind – Vincent's attitude towards him and the close affinity he felt with the Commander, which had been reciprocated until recently.

'How do you know that?' Sebastian demanded.

Vincent sneered.

'Well, you little piece of Fitzgerald shit, your dear departed mother told me, the whoring bitch!' Hatred blazed in his eyes. Then, suddenly and chillingly, his expression changed to a broad smile. 'I've played you and that toad Fitzgerald like fish,' he boasted.

'I don't understand. Why do all this?' asked Sebastian.

'You're a pretty dim bastard if you can't work that one out,' Vincent replied. 'Why the hell do you think? Revenge, of course. And money. When I've finished I'll have the lot. The estate, everything.'

Sebastian shook his head. His brain went into overdrive. He had to keep this madman talking while he fathomed a way out. This was a monster that he had never met before. There was not a vestige of the moody, monotone father he had known. Yes, Vincent had always been prone to rages, but here was pure insanity, a man totally consumed with hatred and erratic, violent emotions.

Knowing how far it was down the walkway to the stairwell, Sebastian realised he did not stand a chance of making it there before he would be shot, even when the timed lights went out again. Vincent blocked the way ahead of him. His only chance was to try and talk his way out of it.

'What are you going to do?' he asked. There was a tremor in his voice, much as he tried to sound calm.

'Well, for a start you're going to join your old boss down there,' Vincent replied, casually. 'The police can then decide whether it was murder and a suicide, or a falling-out between thieves that went wrong.'

Sebastian thought he saw a glimmer of hope.

'So if you shoot me, how's that going to be explained?' he asked.

The glimmer was instantly doused by Vincent's complete indifference.

'Well, it's either got to be your partner Fitzgerald who shot you, or another partner in the operation. No doubt the police will rule out the Commander, but they'll have him for the antiques. He's just stupid and honourable enough to take the blame for what his greedy and gullible brother and son did. Fitzgerald's awash with all that family loyalty and the officer and gentleman shit,' he snarled.

'You mean Felix was involved?'

'Of course he was. I introduced him to it. I had a great little number to start with, looking after stolen bullion until its owner came out of prison. The antiques followed.'

'And what if they do find the Commander to be innocent?'

'Then it's down to Felix, you and Fellowes.' Vincent shrugged and nodded in the direction of the yard. 'It could be a contract killing, of course. There're some pretty hard people involved in this. As for me, I'll just continue along as the not-too-bright-or-ambitious estate manager, who hadn't got a clue what his son or Felix were up to.'

'And if it doesn't work out like that?' Sebastian asked.

Vincent shrugged again.

'Worst case, there's that generous lump sum pension you kindly paid me. And my other little treasures, safely stashed away. You should have been more careful about where you left your confidential stuff. Not that it's going to matter now.'

'How did you find—?'

Vincent cut him off.

'This is all getting very boring, boy.' He waved the gun at the parapet. 'It's ding dong bell time for you, so be a good lad and just throw yourself over that wall.'

So this is it, Sebastian thought. He could hear the throb of his racing pulse thumping in his head. His hands began to shake – and the adrenalin surge was back. If he was going to go, it would not be from a fall. And if it was going to be a bullet, then he might as well try to rush Vincent. He had to play for more time.

'I really couldn't do that,' Sebastian said, annoyed at his shaky voice. 'I can't stand heights. I get dizzy in thick socks.'

'Nice try, Sebastian. Nothing like a bit of gallows humour, eh? The thing is, if you go over the side like a good boy, that's an end of it,' Vincent explained in his arctic voice. 'But if I have to shoot you that's not going to please me. In which case, I shall just have to make a real mess of your girlfriend as well.'

Sebastian shut his eyes at the horror of the thought.

'You bastard!' he exclaimed.

'No, it's you who's the bastard.' Vincent approached, the gun held high and pointed at his victim's head. His eyes were snakelike. The tip of his tongue played over his lips, venomously eager for the kill.

'Did you kill Alexander Penn?' Sebastian asked.

'Guilty as charged, m'lud.' Vincent smiled. 'Went down like a stone, the fat fool.'

'And Hector?'

'He was easy. Did most of it himself. More of a spectator sport, that one.'

'You're just pure evil,' Sebastian exclaimed. 'You actually enjoy killing people, don't you?' He felt a sudden chill at the realisation that he had lived with such a fiend.

'You're right. And it gets more enjoyable every time. I can definitely see how serial killers get a taste for it.'

With the gun still trained at his head, Sebastian ducked and lunged forward the moment the motion sensor light went out. Vincent had anticipated his move and stepped back. Sebastian went sprawling on the floor and let out a cry of pain as Vincent stamped on his back, located his head and gripped a handful of his hair then pulled his head back. When the light came back on again, Vincent was smiling down at Sebastian's shaking form.

'Oh well,' he said with mock sadness. 'You had your chance. It'll have to be a simple execution. I want you to die imagining what a mess I'm going to make of Little Miss Librarian. Up!' he barked, and dragged Sebastian onto his knees. 'Just like a dog,' Vincent muttered with grim satisfaction as he levelled the gun at Sebastian's head.

At that moment a scream rang out from the staircase. Sebastian opened his eyes to see Amanda, who stood at the end of the walkway. Transfixed, with her hand against the parapet, she gazed in horror at the spectacle.

Two seconds later, the crack of a gunshot shattered the momentary silence.

***

Ill at ease, Selwyn wandered listlessly from the drawing room into the hallway. He scanned the furniture and ornaments. They were so familiar that for many years he had scarcely noticed them. Only by their sudden absence would they be noted.

As his eyes came to rest on the portrait of his father, who had been a man of strong principles and quick decisions, Selwyn felt a pang of shame. He had allowed the girl to drive off into goodness knows what danger.

He had now come to believe that there was more to this than dealing in stolen antiques and the theft of his money. During all the recent revelations and interrogations, never once had Penn's and Hector Middleton's deaths been touched upon. They appeared to have been neatly boxed away as accidents. Preoccupied by his own problems, Selwyn had not given these events much further thought. Now the appearance of the copies of the map and the transfer document led Selwyn to consider the possibility of a broader, darker picture. At the moment the existence of the documents remained unknown to the police. He wondered what they would make of them. For now, the girl could be in danger and his priority had to be her safety.

He grabbed his coat and car keys and was about to leave when a thought occurred to him. He dashed upstairs, returned several minutes later then set off in pursuit of Amanda.

***

With a piercing scream, Amanda slumped to the ground.

Sebastian threw a terrified glance in her direction then, in a frenzied rage, thrust himself upwards and back against his captor. He flailed manically against the arm and the hand that had released its grip on his hair, while his other arm frantically reached backwards to grab at the hand and the gun.

As Vincent tumbled back against the wall, Sebastian threw himself with a bellow upon his assailant like an enraged animal. One hand was extended to grab the murderer's throat while the other grappled for the gun.

Vincent lunged his knee into Sebastian's stomach before swiftly bending his other arm under Sebastian's to fend it off. The movement sent his victim sideways to the floor.

He aimed the gun at Sebastian's head, and there was once more a wild gleam in his eyes.

'Two birds with one stone, eh?' he muttered.

A shout rang out down the passageway. Vincent's head turned in the direction of the sound. There stood Selwyn, horror-stricken, his hand held out in vain supplication.

Vincent grinned at him, elated that his hated boss would see Sebastian die. He squeezed the trigger. There was a click. He quickly squeezed again but there was nothing.

A shot rang out from Selwyn's direction.

Vincent ducked, looked up and tried his gun once more. As Sebastian started to rise, his face contorted with pain, Vincent aimed a kick at his ribs.

Selwyn started to advance towards Vincent, his gun levelled. Vincent lunged at Sebastian and sent him staggering backwards. Then with a snarl, he turned and ran towards the lift.

'Keep your head down,' shouted Selwyn, who stood against the parapet wall trying to take aim at the fugitive, as Sebastian tottered towards him and obstructed his line of fire.

There was the noise of the lift as the doors closed and it started to descend. Selwyn was tempted to race down the stairs in pursuit, but turned instead to join Sebastian, who was already kneeling by Amanda's motionless body.

**

Vincent jammed the lift door open with a chair, rushed over to the foyer's tinted windows and peered into the darkness beyond. All looked quiet. There were very few pedestrians in sight and the traffic was sparse.

A good sign, he thought. Had the police already arrived, the street would have been cordoned off.

He slipped cautiously out into the night and, with urgent steps, skirted the car park and loped along the poorly lit footpath to the nearby cul-de-sac, where he climbed into his Land Rover and drove off.

Within minutes, he had pulled up at the rented garage, a useful transit store and hiding place for the goods that he had acquired over the years. He slid up the creaking door, glanced around, then entered. Inside the garage was in darkness, other than for a thin shaft of light from a street lamp, which filtered in and glinted off the bonnet of his wife's old car.

Vincent felt around for the case and the shoulder bag he had dropped off earlier, as a precautionary measure, and dumped them onto the back seat, wincing in pain from the fight with Sebastian. He eased himself into the car, started the engine and the Clio crept slowly forward. After he had locked the Land Rover in the garage, he drove off into the night.

By the time the police marksmen had cleared the area and gained access to the office block after Selwyn's call, Vincent was long gone. As he drove, he reflected on the night's events and his next moves. He cursed Sebastian's luck, the arrival of the librarian and Fitzgerald, and finally, the faulty gun. By now he should have been home and dry. At best it would have been a case of a criminal partnership that had ended in murder and suicide, a case to be neatly wrapped up by the police. At worst, a contract killing that had ended up with more victims than intended.

By contrast, it had been a piece of cake to deal with Jez. He had lured him out of the office on the pretext of having a smoke, and it had taken only a matter of seconds to heave his light frame over the parapet.

Sebastian had been quite a different story. Vincent gave the lad his due: he was a fighter. It had felt strange to finally struggle to kill someone he had hated yet had lived with for so many years. The familiarity had somehow made it totally different to when he had dealt with Penn, Hector and even Jez.

The dream of becoming master of Wisstingham now looked to be at an end. Sebastian would probably inherit the estate in due course. Vincent comforted himself that at least he had the money, artworks and jewellery to fall back on. His partnership with Harry in the antiques and the other ventures had been very profitable indeed. Harry had been good to him, right from their first meeting as raw recruits in the army.

There was always another day and things were far from over, Vincent reflected, as he headed for his next destination and his next victim.

***

During the twenty minutes it took for the armed police response unit to arrive, Sebastian and the Commander knelt by Amanda. She was now conscious and shivery, and her face was deathly pale. Selwyn had made her as comfortable as possible, and applied a tourniquet to staunch the flow of blood while Sebastian went to scour the offices for something to cover her with.

'The wound's not too serious, by the looks of it,' Selwyn tried to assure the frightened couple.

'I thought I'd lost you. I thought I'd lost you,' Sebastian murmured, over and over.

'Such carelessness is going to land you in trouble one of these days,' Amanda managed to quip in a pained whisper.

'Are *you* hurt?' Selwyn asked Sebastian.

'I feel like I've gone a few rounds with Mike Tyson, but I don't think anything's broken.'

There was the sound of movement on both stairwells, then a shout of,

'Armed police, get down on the floor, arms stretched out!' Sebastian and Selwyn obliged as the dark silhouettes of armed black-clad men crept forward cautiously, then crouched.

'There's someone injured and the man you're after has gone,' Selwyn shouted.

The men moved up to them. They read the situation, then all but one of them moved off to search and secure the rest of the building. Several minutes later, when the office block had been declared safe, paramedics and the local police team moved in, headed by a grim-faced DI Stone.

'What the hell's been going on? Where's the body?' Stone demanded of the Commander. He paid scant regard to Amanda, who was now being carried away on a stretcher. 'And where do you think you're going, Sonny Jim?' he shouted to Sebastian, who had been about to accompany the stretcher-bearers.

'With Amanda, to hospital.'

'Oh, no, you're not, sunbeam,' the DI told him. 'Not unless you've been injured. Don't worry about her. She's in good hands. I've got some questions for you.'

Sebastian looked anxiously towards the now empty stairwell, then reluctantly turned to face the DI.

'The body's in the yard down there,' he pointed. 'It's Jez Fellowes. He owns the place.'

Stone walked over to the parapet, took out a torch, shone it down and stared at the body for a moment.

'Get the photographer down there and call the coroner in,' Stone instructed his subordinate. 'The SOCO team can start up here first, then you join me in reception. You two gentlemen had better come with me. I'll take your statement, Monaghan. The DC will take yours, when he joins us, Commander.'

As they followed the DI, Selwyn and Sebastian exchanged knowing glances. If previous experience was anything to go by, it was going to be a long and gruelling night.

***

The water slapped against the side of *Merryweather 2*, and the moonlight reflected off the concentric waves caused by the boat's violent motion moments earlier. The steel hatchway door slowly opened, and a figure cautiously emerged from the awning to peer into the surrounding darkness. A duck's quack and the distant hoot of an owl broke the silence of the night.

Panting from his exertion, Vincent stood silently on the deck, glanced around again then closed the door and slid the hatch cover forward. He stepped off and fastened the awning, then turned to watch the boat and listen for any sound from within. All was quiet.

Now it was the whites of Vincent's widened eyes on which the moonlight was reflected. On his face was a broad smile of excited satisfaction. He slunk down the towpath and the light from his torch swayed from side to side on the ground in front of him.

Inside the blackness of the boat, the bloodied and battered body of Clifford Caines lay motionless.

Chapter 21

'Oh my giddy aunt!' Mrs Soames murmured in dismay as she entered the room. Slumped in his chair was the Commander's crumpled form, the only sign of life the rhythmic rise and fall of his chest. In his hand, an empty whisky glass rested precariously at an angle. On an occasional table by the side of the armchair stood a virtually empty bottle.

The housekeeper waddled silently from the room and returned moments later with a blanket, which she spread tenderly over the sleeping form.

Selwyn stirred and his eyes blinked open.

'Mrs S, what are you doing here at this time?' he muttered, then narrowed his drowsy eyes to focus on the grandfather clock. 'You should be home with your husband.'

'Like as not I should be,' she replied in as severe a tone as she could manage, made difficult by the sympathy and affection she felt for her beleaguered boss. 'I couldn't settle, for worrying as 'ow you might be—'

Here she hesitated, and her eyes darted to the whisky bottle.

'Overdoin' things, as you might say.' This was not the first time Mrs S had found the Commander deep in his cups.

Selwyn rubbed a hand slowly over his face, stifled a yawn and cast her a guilty smile as he glanced down at the blanket. It had appeared at other times during the past few days when he had been found in his chair in the early morning hours.

'Why don't you sit a while?' he suggested. 'I don't suppose there's the chance of a mug of hot chocolate?'

''Appen as there might be,' she replied. 'Though it's 'igh time you were tucked up.'

This being the closest Selwyn was going to get to an enthusiastic acceptance of his invitation, he surrendered his empty glass and watched as Mrs S removed the whisky bottle and herself to the kitchen.

'I been proper worried about you of late, Commander, and that's no mistake,' she confided, as they later huddled over their drinks. 'And what with Vincent turnin' out the way 'e did an' all them policemen constantly 'ere, snoopin' and sniffin' around and asking questions, it's enough to put years on a person.'

Before Selwyn could reply, she leant forward and regarded him anxiously.

'Is a body safe 'ere, Commander?' she whispered. 'I don't mind tellin' you, I fair get the heebie-jeebies thinkin' as 'ow that monster might turn up 'ere. We could all be murdered in our beds.'

Selwyn gave her a reassuring smile.

'I don't think there's any chance that he will return. The police are on the lookout for him and, from what he took with him, it looks certain he's gone on the run.'

Mrs Soames' shoulders visibly relaxed, though Selwyn's expression became graver.

'What I do have to warn you about, Mrs S, is that there'll have to be some changes. I've no doubt you've heard through the grapevine that I've lost a lot of money, which the bank says is through my own fault. That means they've denied any responsibility for replacing it.'

The housekeeper's hand shot to her mouth.

'So,' he continued, 'there will have to be some significant cutbacks. Most certainly the Hall won't be opened to the public.'

'Does that mean you're goin' to be lettin' me go then, Commander?' the anxious woman asked.

'Heavens above, no! That'd be the very last thing I'd do, believe me.'

Mrs Soames heaved a huge sigh of relief. Her other hand searched out a crumpled handkerchief from her apron pocket, which she applied to the corner of an eye.

'Thank you, Commander,' she whispered with a sniff. 'This place 'as been my life. Other than my Reggie, of course,' she hastily added.

Selwyn swallowed hard.

'I couldn't conceive of life here at the Hall without you, dear Mrs S,' he said with a catch in his voice as he watched her sniff.

She smiled at him. Her eyes glistened.

'Then it's onwards and upwards, Commander. We'll see this through.' She stood up and relieved Selwyn of his empty mug. 'An' a good night's sleep is what we need now, I reckon,' she added, more as an instruction than a suggestion, with which Selwyn did not argue.

***

At the entrance, Meredith Jewson paused to look round the library. With some hesitation, he approached the reception desk, somewhat reassured by the infectious smile of the wispy blonde girl seated behind it.

'Can I help you?' she asked. Her appearance, charm and

the warmth of the question induced the bank manager to immediately regret his age and state of matrimony.

'I'm not certain,' he ventured. 'It's rather a strange situation. A bit of a long shot.'

'Don't tell me.' She grinned. 'You want to return a book you borrowed as a schoolboy.'

He eyed her warily, then returned her smile.

'Hmm, not quite that,' he replied. 'I've been given to understand that someone works here who is dealing with the affairs of an Alexander Penn.'

The girl frowned.

'I'd better get my boss, if you'll just wait a minute, sir,' she said. She rose and headed off in search of Amanda.

Minutes later, Jewson was shown into the librarian's office.

'Good heavens!' he exclaimed when he saw her arm and shoulder encased in bandages and a sling. 'What happened to you?'

'A clumsy accident. I wasn't quick enough. My shoulder blade, but it's healing well,' the librarian replied, and sidestepped the question.

Meredith explained how, on return from the isolation of his convalescence, he had learnt of his friend Alexander Penn's death and tracked down the man's aunt to a nearby care home, only to be vaguely informed that he 'needed the library person'.

Once he had seen evidence of Amanda's authority as executor, Meredith handed over the envelope Penn had left with him, which had languished in the dark recesses of his box in the bank's vaults.

Amanda thanked him and accompanied him to the

entrance, then hurried back to her office and tore open the envelope. There were the map and the transfer document, written in an ornate hand, and bearing seals and spidery signatures ... pieces of old parchment that could have such a profound effect on the life of the Commander and the wealth of Wisstingham.

Her initial feelings of euphoria at this unexpected delivery morphed into regret and doubt. It had fallen to her to be the temporary custodian of these treasures. Now it was her responsibility to decide what on earth to do with them.

***

Dark though the cottage was with its small leaded windows, a shaft of sunlight illuminated the kitchen table at which Vincent sat in contemplation, his hands clasped round a mug of tea.

He had arrived late the previous night, via the country lanes to avoid the drive through the village and past the only other cottage that stood nearby, which was a drab, neglected place, its gardens given over to long grasses and mostly weeds, its gimy windows hung with shabby curtains that stayed permanently closed. To the back of that cottage stood timber sheds and outbuildings in various stages of dilapidation. Were it not for the presence of occupied chicken coops at the end of the outbuildings, people might think that the place had long since been abandoned.

Vincent felt sure that no one had seen him arrive, nor would anyone know he was there unless they visited. The car was hidden out of sight and he had stocked up on groceries and provisions to last the few days he needed to hole up until Harry could make arrangements to get him across the Channel.

He shuddered at the thought of Harry and how things would be with him, now that he would be so much in his debt. Vincent had never had an inkling about Harry's true feelings for him, not until that drunken evening when they had celebrated the departure of the gold bullion and Harry had come on to him. How naive he had been! Even Ronnie had known.

Vincent was still furious about how his plans had been thwarted. He regretted having shot the girl only because if she were dead, the hunt for him would be all the more intense. What enraged him was that the two people he had most wanted to ruin and even kill were still alive and would now emerge unscathed.

He finished the tea and irritably pushed the empty mug away. All he needed to do right now was to lie low and get to France. There he would have time to work things out and plan what to do next. In the meantime there was still something he could do to make life as difficult as he could for Fitzgerald and, for the long term, his determination to permanently deal with Sebastian and the Commander remained resolute.

***

With Vincent at large, Selwyn insisted that Sebastian should move into the Hall, 'merely as a precautionary measure', he had emphasised to Mrs Soames, at least until the villain had been caught.

For the Hall's new resident, the word 'father' had become an emotive one. Sebastian no longer referred to Vincent in those terms. The fugitive had been relegated to *he* or *him*, or *Monaghan* if necessary, for clarification.

For days, Sebastian had tried to pluck up the courage to challenge the Commander on Monaghan's assertion about his parentage but there had not seemed to be a suitable opportunity. When there had been, his courage had failed him. That aspect of the night's happenings had been kept out of Sebastian's statement to the police.

Since then, he had felt awkward in Selwyn's presence, of which no doubt the Commander had been sensitive. Suspicion and uncertainty as to who really was his father constantly exercised Sebastian's mind, which he knew he would soon have to broach and resolve.

So, one evening when he put his head round the drawing room door and hesitantly asked Selwyn if he could have a word with him, it was a wary-looking Commander who invited him in.

'Certainly. Come and sit down, dear boy,' he said, his tone one of anxious anticipation rather than ease.

Sebastian decided not to beat about the bush and took a deep breath.

'That night at the offices, Monaghan told me that I was your bastard son. He also said that my mother had confessed it to him. Is it true?'

A look of shocked surprise appeared on Selwyn's face. He exhaled loudly and passed his palm across his brow as he considered his response. Once more his tongue was on the move as he paused to choose his words.

'There was never anything between your mother and me,' Selwyn assured him. 'She was a lovely woman and I was fond of her. Vincent treated her very badly at times, and I feel guilty for not having intervened. I gave her whatever sympathy and comfort I could.'

Sebastian swallowed hard.

Selwyn was about to wander off to the safety of his vantage point by the window but thought better of it. He glanced at Sebastian and gave him a hesitant smile.

'The truth is,' he continued, 'it's almost certain that Lucian was your father. Your mother confessed as much to me many years after he had gone.'

Stunned at this news, Sebastian stared at him for a moment. Then his gaze sank to the floor.

'She was so scared of what Vincent might do to him that she told Lucian she didn't love him and that the affair was over. It was your mother who forced Lucian to leave for his own safety, though she didn't let him know that was the reason. She swore me to secrecy and I told no one, not even Georgina. Your mother lived the rest of her life in fear. She dreaded that Vincent would discover you were not his son and what he might do to you if he found out. I tried to look out for you without arousing his suspicion.'

His head cupped in his hands, Sebastian stared at the floor. Images of his unhappy mother, the arguments between his parents and Vincent's hostility flooded back.

'The way he behaved towards me, he must have suspected something for quite a time,' Sebastian reflected.

'Believe me,' said Selwyn, 'although he was a good estate manager and all right with me – well, most of the time, anyway – I wouldn't have kept him on because of the way he behaved to you and Mary. But I needed to keep you both close so I played along with him. I'm sorry if I didn't do enough to protect you.'

Sebastian looked up. From Selwyn's expression, he seemed to be desperately in need of his understanding.

From his pocket, Sebastian took out the locket his mother had pressed into his hand before she died. He opened it and held it out to Selwyn.

'My mother gave me this,' he explained. 'When I came to take out *his* photo, I found another one behind it.'

Selwyn studied the photo and nodded slowly.

'That's Lucian,' he confirmed.

Sebastian stared at the Commander, his look so forlorn that Selwyn stood and placed a hand on his shoulder.

'One way or another, I'll make sure you're taken care of, Sebastian,' he promised. 'If you're amenable, I suggest we have a DNA test done to confirm matters beyond doubt.'

'Yeah, I reckon we should,' Sebastian agreed.

***

Amanda struggled with the Mazawat's stiff door and entered the cafe. She made her way to one of the tables at the back, hoping to attract as little attention as possible. The explanation of her injury to those not privy to the village grapevine, or readers of the *Hopestanding Chronicle*, had now been condensed to a few words of such generality as to avoid further detailed enquiry.

She glanced at her watch, smoothed the already perfectly flat tablecloth and adjusted the position of the cruet. Looking about her, the injured librarian smiled at the couple of elderly ladies who anxiously eyed her arm, then she checked the wall clock against her watch. The distance between the ladies' table and her own was thankfully enough to prevent them from making enquiries.

Having given her order to the civil but unsmiling Gwen, the librarian then gently tapped her fingers on the table.

It seemed an eternity before the door opened and Sebastian walked in.

He broke into a smile when he saw her.

'You should have let me pick you up,' he reproached her as he sat down, his eyes fixed on her injured arm. 'How is it?'

'It's fine. I needed the walk to give me time to think,' she replied.

'What about?' he asked, a note of alarm in his voice. 'We're good, aren't we?'

Amanda gave him a reassuring smile.

'Of course we are, you ninny.' She leant her head conspiratorially towards him. He took the hint and did likewise. 'It's about the missing map and the transfer document,' she whispered. 'The originals. They've turned up.'

Conversation was suspended as Gwen arrived with the order. When she saw the couple's demeanour, she refrained from any exchange of pleasantries with Sebastian and moved off.

'So what about them?' Sebastian asked. 'What's the problem?'

'What I should do with them?' she replied.

'Well, it's obvious. Give them to the Commander.'

'It's not as simple as that. I have to do what's right.'

'That *would* be right,' Sebastian argued.

'It's not so straightforward,' Amanda maintained. 'I'm employed by the council and it looks to be their land. I have to act responsibly. Also, I'm Alex's executor so I have to consider what he would have done with them.'

'I'm sure he'd have given them to the Commander. They're his property, after all,' Sebastian reasoned.

'Then why didn't he return them? He had plenty of

345

time,' she countered. 'Maybe he was going to give them to the council after he'd proved their authenticity.'

Sebastian scratched his head and sighed.

'The poor chap's had it really rough. You can't do this to him. It'd ruin him,' he pleaded.

'I have to do what's right,' Amanda insisted. She stared at him and yearned for him to understand her situation, but it did not appear this was going to happen.

Sebastian closed his eyes in resignation.

'OK,' he murmured. 'We're not going to let this turn into an argument. I love you too much to let it come between us. You must do what you think best – but please think carefully about the consequences.'

Amanda sipped her coffee and deeply regretted that the bank manager had ever found her.

'Anyway, there's something I have to tell you,' Sebastian said, to break the awkward silence that had fallen. He related the conversation with the Commander from the evening before.

As the story unfolded, a look of surprised relief spread over Amanda's face as she imagined the positive response she would receive from Nan when she told her the news.

'So there we are,' Sebastian said finally. He leant back in his chair, relieved that Amanda seemed easy with the revelation.

She craned her head towards him.

'I love you no less for that, nor could I, you little mongrel,' she teased.

'There's still no sign of *him*,' Sebastian observed, to change the subject. 'He's probably holed up somewhere in a holiday cottage or somewhere similar.'

Amanda just stared at him. Her eyes widened and her

mouth gaped open.

'What is it?' he asked.

'Of course,' Amanda exclaimed and got to her feet. 'Why on earth didn't I think of that before?'

'Think of what,' he queried, and also got up.

'We have to see the Commander,' she insisted.

'What are you on about?'

'Your father – sorry, Vincent.'

'What about him?' he asked, his frown now in danger of becoming a permanent feature.

'I think I know where he might be.'

Within a minute, they had hastily paid the bill and left the cafe, Sebastian with his mobile glued to his ear.

***

With much to think about, Selwyn set out on his morning stroll through the woods. Reluctantly, DI Stone had announced that, from the evidence he had, he would not presently continue to pursue further enquiries with Sebastian or the Commander. However, this was not before he had given Selwyn a hard time with his demand that he provide evidence of the provenance of many of the articles in the Hall. This the Commander had managed to do from old photographs, receipts and other pieces of documentation dug out from the family archives.

On a more positive note, Selwyn had met with a stroke of luck in the employment of a new and highly prized stables manager. On this basis, Sinclair had finally decided to stable his horses at Wisstingham, where the stable boy and Sebastian had gallantly stepped in to fill the gap left by Vincent. With his extensive knowledge of the estate, Fred Ferris had agreed to stand in until a new estate manager could be found. All in all, the day-to-day running of Wisstingham Hall seemed to continue fairly well. As to the estate's survival, that was a worry that Selwyn kept to himself.

His overriding concern was Sebastian. Selwyn thought that the loss of such a villainous and malevolent father should not have been a great one for the young man. However, to discover not only that he had meant absolutely nothing to Vincent but that the man positively hated him must have come as a shattering blow. Furthermore, there was the question of whether Vincent was indeed his father or not.

No doubt more than one person would already have said to Sebastian,

'You're better off without him,' but it was not for Selwyn to echo those sentiments. He was, however, determined to support the lad through thick and thin. As far as Selwyn Fitzgerald was concerned, Sebastian was now an unofficially adopted son. If the DNA tests proved that Lucian was indeed his father, that adoption would be made official.

The walk had brought Selwyn to the old barn, around which police tape still fluttered. The local press had had a field day reporting on all that had happened. Even a couple of the tabloids had run with the story and the Hall had been under siege from reporters for several days.

Selwyn had neither seen nor heard anything of Miriam. That she had not tried to contact him he considered was proof positive that he had misjudged her feelings for him. She had merely played on his emotions to get what she wanted. He had even been about to propose to her. It seemed that his heart attack had come at a most appropriate moment. Or had it? Without it, at least he would have been sure of the strength of Miriam's feelings.

He continued along the old quarry road and cut across the wildflower meadow towards the lake garden, where he lingered for only a few moments. The rowing boat still lay upside down on the jetty under its weather-stained tarpaulin. It made him think of Felix and ponder yet again on just what had happened when his son had run the estate – and how Vincent had figured in Felix's scheme. Where on earth was Vincent, and why had the police not apprehended him yet?

The Commander's thoughts turned to the hopes he had entertained for the excavation of the recreation field, which were now just a pipe dream. Two men had died because of the land. As for the missing money, the bank still adamantly refused to countenance any recompense, despite his solicitor's best efforts.

The gloom of his thoughts was temporarily dispelled by Mustard, wet from another unsuccessful duck chase. The dog bounded to his side and licked his hand. Selwyn scanned the distant hills, where brooding clouds blanketed their summits like a duvet, here and there following the folds in the hills, a little way down towards the lower ground.

At the sound of rapid footsteps Selwyn stiffened. Constantly on the alert since Vincent's disappearance, he looked around and tightened his grip on the walking stick that now habitually accompanied him.

'Mrs S said I'd probably find you here,' Sebastian gasped as he came to a halt, followed closely by a breathless

Amanda. 'Amanda thinks she knows where Monaghan might be.'

Before the Commander could reply, Amanda took over the conversation. She related what her grandmother had told her of Lucian's and Vincent's early days, and the Mole End cottage where Vincent had lived.

'Do you really think it's possible he's there?' Selwyn asked.

'That would explain where he went to when he used to occasionally disappear for a few days,' Sebastian chipped in.

'It sounds like the best we've got so far,' Selwyn acknowledged.

'Then we'd better tell Stone,' said Sebastian.

Selwyn grimaced at the mention of the name.

'No,' he replied, his mouth set firm. 'Vincent's got some explaining to do before Stone gets his hands on him.'

'Then I'm coming with you,' Sebastian insisted.

Selwyn was torn between not wanting to expose Sebastian to any danger and the possibility that he might well need some support in dealing with the monster that Vincent had become. On balance, he decided he could not put his new charge at risk.

Anyway, what was all that navy training for? Selwyn asked himself, with renewed confidence. He was surely more than a match for the man, deranged or not.

'Not sure that's a good idea,' he replied. 'You'd better stay here and man the fort.'

'Not likely. I'm not letting you go on your own,' Sebastian retorted. From the look on his face, it was clear that he was not to be shifted. Selwyn would just have to make sure he kept the lad out of harm's way.

'Then we'd better get going,' he conceded.

'I'll need a couple of hours,' Sebastian warned him, with a look at Amanda. 'There's something we have to do in Hopestanding.' A brief exchange of smiles between the couple suggested some personal and possibly secret commitment.

'Can't it wait? Selwyn asked, in exasperation. 'There's no time to lose.'

'No,' replied Sebastian, with another glance at Amanda ''Fraid not. It's too important,' though neither of them would say more.

'All right. But if you're not here by one thirty, I'm going.'

'By one thirty,' Sebastian agreed.

By half past two, after he had almost paced the polished surface off the hallway floor, much to Mrs Soames' frowning consternation, and after more glances at his watch than he would normally take in a week, Selwyn grabbed his overnight bag and made for the door. He bade the housekeeper farewell and left her at the top of the steps wringing her hands as she watched his car disappear from view.

Chapter 22

As the sun sank low in the sky, the Jaguar reached Alstherham. Since he had never visited the place before and did not know where the cottage was, Selwyn resorted to the local pub for information.

'Can't say as I recall that family. It'll be before my time,' was the landlord's unhelpful reply. 'George over there might know,' he suggested and called across to one of the regulars, who shuffled to the bar.

At Selwyn's question, George's eyes narrowed and he stared suspiciously at the enquirer.

'Bad business that, bad business,' he muttered. On being pressed further, George reluctantly told him where to find the cottage.

'Won't do you no good going there, anyhow,' George warned, as Selwyn headed to the door. 'The place is shut up, and has been this long time.'

**

Sebastian paced in exasperation while Amanda struggled to recall the name of the village her nan had mentioned to her.

'Anst, Alist, Aster…' she recited and paced up and down, her fists clenched in exasperation. 'It's on the tip of my tongue. How could I have forgotten it?' she moaned.

Confident Amanda knew their destination, Sebastian had texted the Commander to tell him they would soon be on their way. Now he felt a complete idiot at having to text again to ask where their destination was. It did not help that he had not paid attention when Amanda had told Selwyn the name of the village, earlier.

'Whereabouts was it?' he pleaded, as he threw himself into the office chair and started to thumb the pages of the road atlas on the desk. His exasperation at having missed the Commander by only five minutes was compounded by being clueless as to where to go.

'I don't know. I didn't think it was important at the time,' she retorted, her eyes screwed up in concentration.

'Then we'd better go and ask your nan,' Sebastian sighed. He sprang to his feet and snatched up the atlas.

'I doubt we'll get any sense out of her,' Amanda warned and followed him out of the study, her brow still furrowed.

***

Selwyn had intended to park some distance away from the cottage but, after he had passed a shabby-looking cottage, its curtained windows briefly lit up by the car's headlights, he rounded a bend and immediately came upon his destination. There was no light from within and the place looked totally deserted. He switched off the engine and studied the building, which was dimly silhouetted in the early evening darkness.

Selwyn switched on his mobile and was just able to read two messages from Sebastian before the screen went blank. He felt a fool for not having checked that the phone was fully charged before he set off and tossed it onto the passenger seat, then slid down in his seat to wait, just in case Sebastian should still arrive.

***

Their delight at having extracted the village name from Nan and being on their way at last was short-lived. Only minutes after he had texted the Commander to tell him they had set off, Amanda and Sebastian stood helplessly by the side of his stationary car waiting for the mechanic from Wisstingham Motors.

**

Time ticked by. One hour passed, then another, during which there was no sign of light or life in the cottage. Selwyn glared at his mobile then threw it down again. Another hour passed. The distant sky suddenly lit up with sheet lightning, followed by an ominous drum roll of thunder.

It was freezing in the car and Selwyn was cold, tired and distinctly uncomfortable. His patience was also frayed. If Vincent was in the cottage, he was probably asleep in bed. Before long it would start to get light.

Selwyn watched for several minutes more, then reached into the glove compartment and took out the gun. He gave an ironic smile as he remembered how DI Stone had threatened to throw the book at him the last time he had used it.

'Needs must when the Devil drives,' he muttered, while he checked for the second time that day that the chamber was fully loaded.

As the storm and thunder rolled in, his confidence that he would find Vincent inside had diminished. With no sign of Sebastian, he could wait no longer.

Selwyn cursed under his breath at the crackle of dry leaves underfoot as he crept towards the front door. He slowly twisted the doorknob, which was stiff and creaked as it turned. He pushed at the door and was surprised to find it unlocked.

With the revolver tightly clasped in his hand, Selwyn slid inside and peered into the blackness. With his left hand he felt his way along the wall and sidled against it, breathing more rapidly. Moments later, his fingers stopped against a door frame. He inched further on and found the door was closed.

It must lead into the front room, Selwyn calculated. Probably the darkened window he had watched from the car.

The drumming in his head from his pulse was even louder now. He paused to control his breathing before he crept beyond the door. His eyes had now become accustomed to the dark and he could make out two darker recesses on opposite sides of the end of the hall. Selwyn assumed that one would lead to the staircase, the other probably into a kitchen.

Which way to go?

He chose the left and turned the corner just as a figure moved silently from the shadow of the staircase on the other side. Selwyn felt certain the boom of his pulse must be audible. Beads of sweat had formed on his top lip, his mouth was dry and he was almost shaking from the rush of adrenalin.

At another closed door, Selwyn slowly reached for the handle. He started as he felt something cold and hard pressed against the back of his head. Then came Vincent's frighteningly calm voice.

'Careful, now, Fitzgerald. No sudden moves,' he said. 'How nice of you to drop in. The gun, please. Slowly, mind.'

Selwyn silently swallowed and slowly offered the gun over his shoulder.

He's like a ruddy cat, he thought. Vincent had crept up on him so silently.

'Have you mended that thing?' Selwyn asked. The barrel almost bored into his neck.

'Yes. Would you like to try it?' Vincent offered.

'I'll give that a miss.'

'I'll have to have a word with my friends about it when I see them,' Vincent commented.

Not if I have anything to do with it, Selwyn thought, before he said,

'You know what they say. Rubbish attracts rubbish.'

'Don't make it any harder on yourself,' Vincent hissed. 'Go on, open the door and go in.'

As he entered the room, Selwyn blinked when the light was switched on. But darkness immediately returned after the crashing blow to his skull.

***

The man wiped his dirty sleeve across his nose, sniffed, then peered through the windows of the Jaguar. Some of his dishevelled locks adhered to the wet window. He moved to look through the back window before he turned his attention to the cottage. His eyes narrowed as he scanned the windows. The gaunt frame stole cautiously past the front windows and disappeared down the side of the cottage. His head darted rapidly in unison with his eyes as they guardedly watched for any sign of life.

At the kitchen window, he stopped and slowly inclined his head to peep through. Inside, a man stood against the back of the kitchen door, down which a stream of blood had flowed. His face was also streaked with blood from the head and the nose. Around his neck, a rope stretched over the top of the door, which presumably was secured on the other side. From the glazed expression on the victim's face and the staring eyes, it was not certain whether he was alive or dead. His hands looked to be secured behind him and his feet were barely in contact with the ground.

In front of him paced a sturdily built man, a long kitchen knife in his hand. The malevolent expression on his face was the most frightening aspect of the horrendous scene. The attacker's eyes bulged. He alternated between enjoyment and hate as he talked then raged in front of his battered prey.

The onlooker, his eyes screwed up in concentration, studied the two men. He watched indifferently as the assailant suddenly moved forward and levelled the knife close to the victim's eye while he continued his verbal assault. Then he backed away and flashed a crazy smile. The whole spectacle was like some insane dance.

The spectator's frown gave way to a faint smile of recognition. He nodded his head, then slipped silently away.

***

Vincent had quickly secured the semi-conscious Commander against the door using a technique the dark recesses of his tortured mind had conjured up especially for such a day of reckoning.

'I wondered if you might think of this place,' he gloated. 'You're quite predictable. I knew if you did, you wouldn't leave things to the police. That wouldn't be your style, would it?'

His mouth pursed in hatred as he punched the Commander in the face.

'This is for fathering that bastard with my wife,' he hissed. 'That's how it felt when she told me.'

He paced in front of the groaning man, deciding what pain to inflict next as he remembered his dying wife's confession. His mouth curled cruelly and his hand shook as he selected a knife from the kitchen drawer.

'Yes, maybe I'll start with the eyes,' Vincent whispered, his face so close that Selwyn could smell his bad breath.

'Without them I'd still be able to see clearer than you've ever done or ever will do, you treacherous viper,' Selwyn whispered, and steeled his gaze into the glaring, blood-shot eyes.

Teeth clenched, Vincent exhaled heavily through his nostrils. He battled with his animal urge to immediately extinguish the life in front of him, to kill this hated cuckoo that, in spite of its predicament, still somehow manifested an overbearing supremacy. He could extinguish Fitzgerald's life instantly but he would still not have conquered him.

Consumed by his hatred, Vincent's mind flitted between the ways he could despatch and wanted to despatch the Commander. Whichever it was, it was going to be painful and the body would go into the well. It had such poetry to it: ding dong bell all over again.

He would have loved to throw Sebastian in there too. No matter. That was unfinished business he was determined to come back to after the boy had come into the estate. He would work it out somehow. After all, there was no real proof against Vincent either for the stolen antiques operation or for the deaths of Penn and Middleton. The girl might well be alive, and it was only the boy's word against his as to what exactly happened with Jez. Vincent was still convinced he had been too clever for them and that he always would be.

'You playing the lord of the manor, and me the lackey. *Droit de seigneur*, was it?' Monaghan accused, the rage coming on him again. 'You thought you could do just what you wanted.' He landed another punch, this time into Selwyn's stomach, then thrust his leering face close to the Commander's. Selwyn's eyes closed in pain and sweat trickled down his bloodied forehead.

'But I fooled you,' ranted Vincent. 'Ran rings round you.' He grinned triumphantly as he grabbed Selwyn's bowed head and slammed it against the door.

'Do you hear me, Fitzgerald?' he ranted. 'Ran rings round you and that other son of yours. And Lucian – they were both in on my rackets.'

Selwyn's groan brought a smile of satisfaction to Vincent. Again he thrust his face close up to the Commander's.

'Did you say something, cuckoo?' he teased. 'No?' He started to pace again, holding the knife at arm's length, but pointed at Selwyn.

'You and that ineffectual brother of yours, lording it over me.' Vincent's eyes darted around him, as if he was trying to keep pace with his thoughts. 'I was family,' he raged. 'Part of all that estate is mine. 'Then, then, the…' Vincent struggled with his rage. 'Then the ultimate insult. Cuckolded by you.'

Flying into another fury, he paced around the room. He furiously kicked the furniture and the walls then threw another punch, again into Selwyn's stomach.

The Commander cried out and tried to crouch down. He started to choke as his feet lifted involuntarily off the floor. He forced his feet back down again, all the while fighting for breath.

Vincent chuckled at the suffering he had imposed. His wide eyes gleamed. He closed in. The knife shook in his hand as he pointed it at one of the Commander's eyes, and watched the anguished face.

'You gave me a bastard. That bastard Sebastian,' he raged. 'I had to live with your whelp for twenty-three odious fucking years. And you took my wife's affection. She was mine.'

At the thought of his loss, he suddenly stopped and turned away. Tears welled in his eyes as he stared through the window.

Selwyn's eyes flickered open and he let out a sigh. Vincent approached the face that now cringed in expectation of another blow. He delighted in Fitzgerald's pain and evident fear.

'But I was cunning,' he whispered. 'Oh, so very cunning. I played along with all of you. Yes, and that whore of a wife. I plotted and schemed and looked after myself. I've done very nicely out of it all. I'll see you finished and then I'll have your son.'

He stopped and glanced away at the ringing of a mobile elsewhere in the cottage.

'Better get that. Don't go away,' he taunted.

When he returned, Monaghan's whole demeanour had changed. He looked dispassionately at the figure half-slumped against the door, then glanced at his watch.

'Well, Fitzgerald, we'd better not loiter any more. Things

to do. My transport's ready and I can't have you hanging around here all day.' Vincent snorted at his own joke. 'I reckon it's time you visited little Kenny's place. Ding dong bell, Fitzgerald's for the well.'

He walked to the rear door and opened it.

'We're going to have a little crawl down the garden. The well's still there. I checked it out. Your tomb awaits you,' he announced.

Vincent moved across and heaved the door. Selwyn choked as the rope tightened around his neck. With the knife between his teeth, Vincent unhooked the end of the rope, swung it over the door then quickly tightened his grip on it.

'On your knees,' he ordered, though Selwyn had automatically sunk down on them. 'Go on, get going.'

Summoning the little strength he had left, Selwyn tried to rise and turn towards his captor, who nimbly side-stepped and at the same time yanked the rope sideways. With a gasp, Selwyn collapsed completely. Vincent stamped his foot hard into the Commander's back, pulled the rope tight and jabbed the knife at his neck so the point drew blood.

'You're pathetic,' he sneered as Selwyn lay gasping. 'But I won't kill you in here. Carry your fat carcass to the well? Not likely! Get moving.'

Was it to end like this, to die humiliated? Selwyn wondered. He regretted so much, not least having failed to appreciate what a monster he had employed and trusted. Why had he been so gung-ho as to think he could bring Vincent to justice single-handed?

In these last moments, he had to tell him whose son Sebastian probably was. What could Vincent do to him that he wasn't already going to do? It would at least deny the man the satisfaction of closure and wrack him with a new uncertainty.

'Back on your knees and move!' Vincent barked.

Selwyn obeyed. His tormentor led, the rope held taut and ready to pull should Selwyn attempt to launch himself forward. In his weakened state, with Vincent's superior strength and the knife, Fitzgerald presented no threat.

Near the bottom of the overgrown garden, Vincent shortened the rope and swung wide. Still keeping the rope taut, he made his way behind his victim. They had arrived at a square-shaped shallow concrete surround to what was clearly a well.

'The first one's always the best,' Vincent muttered. 'Kenny went down squealing. I hope you're not going to disappoint, though I shall stick you a few times first.'

Still on his knees, Selwyn stealthily adjusted his balance then launched himself backwards and tried to gain his footing. The action proved futile. Vincent backed away but at the same time tugged the rope taut. With a cry and then a moan, the Commander fell to the ground.

Vincent let out a triumphant cry. His shining eyes now bulged, and the bloodlust was upon him once more. He rushed forward with the knife raised in both hands, high above his head. He moved to plunge it down into the prone form when the deafening sound of a shot made him freeze.

Vincent spun round to see a dishevelled man approach him carrying a rifle.

'So you're back, then, Vincent,' came a gravelly voice.

'Thought it was you.'

Vincent peered questioningly at him.

'Don't recognise old Joey, eh?' the man continued, all the while getting closer. 'Been a few years now since you killed my brother Kenny. I been waiting for you, I 'ave. Knew I'd get you one day, when you were back.'

Vincent glanced behind him and started to back away, past the well, as the tramp continued to advance. When he reached the tree he had been aiming for, Vincent dodged behind the trunk just as Joey raised his rifle. Another shot rang out and Joey cursed as the bullet missed its mark. Vincent pulled out his gun, aimed and fired. With a scream of pain Joey fell to the ground, where he writhed in agony.

By now, Selwyn had struggled to his feet. Vincent smiled as the Commander tottered towards him.

'The endgame, I think, Fitzgerald,' he said and raised his gun.

He spun round at the sound of a car screeching to a halt close by the cottage. Both men looked in the same direction. Selwyn's heart fell as Sebastian rushed round the corner of the building, followed by a frightened-looking Amanda.

Vincent's eyes lit up.

'Well, well,' he exclaimed, 'quite a family gathering. I'm really spoilt for choice. Perhaps I'll finish the Commander off first.'

Selwyn quickly sized up the situation. There was no way he could reach Vincent before he would fire, but best to go down fighting, he thought. As he was about to launch himself forward, Sebastian spoke.

'Yes, Monaghan, a real family get-together. The only person missing is my father.'

Vincent stared at Sebastian, a look of complete bewilderment now on his face.

'What are you talking about, gobshite? He's there,' he sneered, and gestured at Selwyn with the gun.

''Fraid not,' replied Sebastian, with greater confidence. '*Lucian* Fitzgerald was my father.'

Dumbstruck, Vincent instinctively lowered the gun as he grappled with this claim.

'No, no, that can't be. He was my cousin...' His incredulity now gave way to a whole new level of hatred. The insult of having been betrayed by Lucian, and his own fallibility in being fooled, was even more painful. 'You're still a bastard, boy,' he yelled.

He raised the gun and this time aimed it at Sebastian. Before anyone could move, he squeezed the trigger – but the gun did not fire. He squeezed again, with the same result.

Vincent spat out an oath and threw the gun aside. He drew out the knife and, with teeth bared, started towards Sebastian.

Selwyn moved to intervene. Fearing for the Commander's life, Sebastian shouted,

'You couldn't even get that right, could you, Monaghan?' and forced a laugh, to further antagonise the man, who took the bait. Vincent grabbed the rope and yanked it hard. With a cry of pain, Selwyn fell to the ground. Sebastian continued to walk steadily forward, while behind him, Amanda stood frozen in horror, her fists held against her mouth.

'I'll finish you off in a minute,' Vincent growled at

Selwyn. Sebastian was now almost upon him and Vincent raised the knife. As the blade sliced through the air, Selwyn summoned his last reserves of strength and kicked out his leg, which connected with Vincent's. Unbalanced, Vincent missed his mark and fell sideways. His upper body tumbled partly into the well, and one arm scrabbled frantically to find the concrete edge to stop his fall.

For a couple of seconds both Sebastian and Selwyn looked on motionless. As Vincent made to regain his feet, Joey struggled forward. With a yell of pain, he grabbed and lifted Vincent's frantically kicking legs and at the same time kicked the villain's arm away from its hold on the edge of the well. With a terrified scream, Vincent fell into the blackness. There was the sickly echo of a thud from far below, followed by a loud moan, then silence.

'You one of the Fitzgeralds, right?' Joey growled to Selwyn, as Sebastian and Amanda helped the two injured men back to the cottage.

'Selwyn,' the Commander confirmed in a hoarse whisper.

Joey stopped and turned to look at the well.

'And Vincent Monaghan,' he murmured, a grim smile of satisfaction on his hard, lined face. 'I've waited many a long year for this day.' His gaze remained fixed on where his brother's murderer had disappeared.

'I knew he'd be back,' he later explained. 'He inherited the place from his uncle, so he did. He's been before but he was careful, and I never got the chance to get near him. Didn't know he was here, till I saw your Jag arrive.'

***

'God, you look a mess!' Sebastian observed, when he collected Selwyn from the local hospital, three days later.

'Pity you didn't arrive a bit earlier. I wouldn't like to be standing in the rain for a bus you were driving,' Selwyn jibed.

'It's that wreck of a car you gave me,' Sebastian retorted, with a smirk. 'We had to abandon it and get Amanda's. Anyway, it's a good job your revolver didn't also go down the well. Stone would have had a real humour failure over that.'

Selwyn groaned.

'It's cool,' Sebastian reassured him and patted the rucksack. 'Got it safe and sound.'

After an unavoidable visit to the police station, they set off in the Jaguar. Selwyn gazed thoughtfully out of the window with not a little apprehension at being driven home by Sebastian. Amanda had gone on ahead the day before in her own car. Her shoulder was still strapped up, but fortunately she drove an automatic.

Other than the mobile, the police had come up with nothing of significance among Vincent's possessions. Once more in bad odour with the authorities, Selwyn had received a harsh dressing-down from the local chief inspector for his 'reckless and irresponsible intervention'. Threats of further possible consequences for not having alerted the police had been suggested, though the unofficial view was that Selwyn had already received punishment enough.

As for Joey, Vincent's death had been reported as an accident. Unless the post-mortem came up with anything else, it was unlikely the police would take any further action against him.

Chapter 23

'I needs a word with you, Commander, if you please,' Mrs Soames announced solemnly as she placed Selwyn's breakfast in front of him. He regarded the boiled egg gloomily. The weekend's stripped-down full English seemed a long way off. At the housekeeper's ominous tone, he put aside his newspaper and put on a smile.

'Of course, Mrs S. Do sit down and help yourself to a cup of coffee. It's always really excellent here.' Although she sat, the smile went unreciprocated and his compliment unappreciated.

This is serious indeed, thought the Commander. Usually, it was fairly easy to disarm the good lady. He adopted a more serious expression.

'What is it, then?' he asked.

'Fact is,' she began, 'I'm wanting to know 'ow things stand with Sebastian?'

'How do you mean?'

'Well, I mean, 'e ain't got no father now and 'is electricity boss is gone...'

'Electronics,' Selwyn corrected her.

Mrs S gave an impatient shake of her head.

'Well, 'e's gone, whatever 'e was, so what's going to 'appen to 'im?'

Selwyn leant forward and gently patted her hands, which were clenched together on the table.

'We're going to look after him, Mrs S,' he replied.

A smile of relief emerged on the rosy face as the housekeeper relaxed back into the chair, her hands now drawn back in peace onto her lap.

'That's what I was 'opin' you'd be sayin', Commander,' she said and gave him a nod of approval. 'And 'ow I was fully expecting you'd be sayin' it, too.'

'What I *can* say,' Selwyn continued, 'and I know Sebastian won't mind my telling you this, is that his dead boss's father has asked him to help run the company for a few months until he decides whether to keep it or not. It's a great opportunity for the lad.'

Mrs Soames' brief animation yielded to sadness once more.

'That poor man Jez. I can't say as 'ow I particularly warmed to 'im,' she confided. Memories of the days of dust and debris had instantly resurfaced. 'But it weren't right 'e should come to such an end. What did the police 'ave to say about it?'

'They're not saying much. I think they're taking on board Sebastian's statement about him having been murdered. I suppose it will all come out at the inquest.'

Mrs Soames rose.

'Well as long as our Sebastian's goin' to be all right,' she said, though her parting comment sounded more like an instruction.

'Who knows?' Selwyn ventured. 'If it works out, he could end up as the boss of the company. Anyway, there'll always be a place for him here.' At this stage he did not intend to impart the news that Sebastian might possibly be formally adopted. That would be too much for the good lady, and anyway it would have to await the results of the DNA test.

Now positively aglow, Mrs Soames thanked the Commander and bustled back to her kitchen. She even gave vent to a hum, though only when safely out of earshot.

What Selwyn had not aired were the other difficulties the estate faced. Although no charges had been made, he believed his reputation lay almost in tatters and with it, very probably, the council's and the community's regard for Wisstingham Hall. And in all of that there was some justification. Surely Lucian and Felix had made illegal gains, some of which had found their way into the estate's coffers. It did not matter that Selwyn had not known. Was it not possible that these sins might yet be visited on him and on the estate?

***

Amanda hesitantly knocked at the polished oak door. It seemed only a matter of days since she had last slammed it behind her. Since then, contact with Councillor Cheyney had been studiously avoided.

'Come in,' came the terse response. Once inside, the librarian approached the large desk. She glanced round to see if everything else in the room was made of oak. Her eyes came to rest on the person occupying the desk.

More like teak, that, I reckon, she thought.

For what seemed to be several uncomfortable minutes, the mayor continued to read the report before she glanced up and offered her visitor a brief, gratuitous smile.

'Good morning, Miss … erm…' Miriam said, feigning to have forgotten her name.

'Sheppard,' Amanda advised, and waited for the mayor to continue.

Instead, Miriam stared expectantly at her.

'Well?' she prompted.

Amanda's grasp tightened on the handle of the slim briefcase she held.

'I came across two documents about the Wisstingham estate,' she began falteringly.

'Which you thought might be of use in the exhibition,' the mayor interjected. Her face had assumed a stony expression.

'Actually, it's more—' Amanda tried again, but paused as Miriam impatiently pushed the report away and rose.

'Miss Sheppard,' she cut in, 'there will be no exhibition, nor any further mention of it. I've spent more than enough time on that project.' *And waking hours over that man*, she added mentally. She waved a dismissive hand. 'You may do as you think best with whatever documents you have, but please don't bother me with them.' The mayor resumed her seat and reached for the report.

Amanda pulled a face at the bowed head. Her thoughts flitted between the alternatives of her duty as a council official, to reveal the existence of the documents – which would bring kudos for the mayor and possibly benefit her own career prospects – and her present bloody-minded desire to see the bitch in hell first, and the moral obligation to return them to the Commander.

'I believe we are finished, Miss Sheppard,' the voice from the lowered head advised. 'Good day.'

Amanda flushed crimson, and her grip tightened further on the briefcase.

'Things so hardly gained, so easily lost,' she murmured as she turned to leave the room.

Miriam glanced after her with a curious frown, then continued to read.

Amanda closed the door with sufficient force to make

a statement, though it could not be called a slam. As she passed through the outer office, she gave a tired shake of her head at the mousy secretary. Then, she made her way out of the building, smiling at the power that Wisstingham's leading citizen had just bestowed upon her and the way her conscience was now salved.

***

The funeral was a very quiet affair. Only Sebastian, Amanda, Selwyn and Mrs Soames were the mourners, though a contingent of the more inquisitive Wisstingham residents lurked far enough away from the crematorium so as to not be expected to enter for the service.

It was perhaps just as well that none of the party noticed the black Mercedes parked a discreet distance away from the crematorium. Its two occupants watched, from the arrival of the coffin to the departure of the mourners. In the driving seat, Ronnie did not observe the tears that ran down Harry's cheeks, as he sat in the back.

After the cremation, Selwyn invited the small party up to the Hall, where Mrs Soames had laid on a simple but delicious spread. There was, of course, nothing to celebrate. Under the circumstances, perhaps the greatest thing to be mourned was not Vincent's death, but rather the sadness and pain his actions had caused. The wake certainly seemed to do nothing to dampen Sebastian's and Amanda's spirits.

Fortunately for Selwyn, his housekeeper's eagle eyes had spotted the reason for their happiness. After a discreet whisper to her boss, who needed a moment to overcome his surprise, the two of them homed in on the young couple to shower them with congratulations on their engagement.

'That was why Sebastian stayed on at Cheltenham and sent me back with the others,' Amanda proudly explained as they admired her ring. 'I'd seen it in the shop and said how much I liked it.' Her adoring gaze gave way to a mischievous smile. 'I hope this sneakiness is not going to become a regular thing,' she whispered in her fiancé's ear. 'You know what I might have to do if it does.'

***

'There's a Reverend Venables and a man in a wheelchair wantin' to see you, Commander,' Mrs Soames announced at the library door. The surprise in her voice matched the expression on Selwyn's face as he looked up from the plan he had been engrossed in.

'We weren't expecting them, were we?' he asked.

'No, you weren't, Commander, but I hope you can spare us some of your valuable time,' said the vicar, who had squeezed round the housekeeper and thrust his head into the doorway while ignoring the housekeeper's scowl.

'I said as 'ow you should wait in the 'all—' she began.

'Show our guests into the drawing room, would you please, Mrs Soames?' Selwyn quickly interrupted her. He followed the procession down the hallway. Mrs Soames indignantly led the wheelchair pushed by the vicar, a rucksack slung over his shoulder.

Once seated, Venables introduced Clifford Caines.

'What happened to you?' Selwyn asked the bruised and bandaged invalid.

'Vincent Monaghan,' Caines replied darkly.

'You know he's dead, don't you?'

'Yes, I read about it. I can't say I'm sorry or surprised.'

Selwyn eyed the man cautiously.

'How did you know him?' he asked.

Caines related how Vincent had blackmailed him – without explaining what he had done in the first place – and then had coerced him to become a courier of stolen goods to France.

'I never really knew what all the goods were. Some I reckoned were paintings. Others were small packages, which I assumed were jewellery. Sometimes there were envelopes, and sometimes small but heavy boxes, always well sealed.'

The Commander leant forward and stared intently at the invalid.

'And what happened to them?' he asked.

'There was a house I had to leave them in. A neighbour had the keys. Monaghan would go there from time to time. It seemed he lived quite another life over there.'

No wonder he was so interested in attending the French race meetings, thought Selwyn, *and was away for days at a time.*

'I heard about the trouble he's caused you and thought the least I could do would be to try to help you,' Caines continued.

Selwyn stared unmoved at this possible co-author of his predicament.

'Why shouldn't I just hand you over to the police?'

The vicar rose.

'The man's throwing himself on your mercy, Commander,' he pleaded. 'He was an unwilling participant and I think he's been punished enough. He may never recover the full use of his legs.'

'Nor I mine,' Selwyn replied drily. 'What's been done has just about ruined me and the estate, so I'm not feeling very charitable about things, Vicar.'

Caines bowed his head.

'Then let me appeal to your better feelings of humanity, Commander,' the vicar implored.

Selwyn snorted and gave Caines a cold stare.

'All right, then let's bring some pragmatism to bear,' Venables suggested. 'There may be a chance to recover some of what you've lost if Monaghan salted *everything* away in France.'

This struck a chord with Selwyn. One of the most baffling things had been the failure of the police to find anything of significance among Vincent's belongings, such as another mobile phone, bank cards or financial items. Only his current account had come to light, which held precious little. The mobile recovered at the cottage, which Selwyn had had the foresight to look through before the police took possession of it, had only con-tained two UK numbers. There had to be more.

'If you're able to find any of the goods, you might at least derive some benefit,' the vicar argued. 'I would assume that those items of high value may well attract a reward. If you were to just alert the police to what had happened and they were to involve their French counterparts, I doubt if you would see any benefit at all. You'd probably not hear anything more about it. What's more, if your money was tied up in Monaghan's financial affairs, you could probably say goodbye to that as well.'

Selwyn rose and took up his thinking position by the window, his tongue once more on its travels. After a tense silence he turned to study the two men.

'You're guaranteed Clifford's total cooperation,' Venables assured him, to which Caines nodded meekly.

As Vincent's sole heir, Sebastian would be able to unlock more doors in France than the gendarmes might, Selwyn reasoned to himself. The possibility that the stolen money might lie in an account there was a prospect at which he brightened.

'Very well, I'll take up your offer,' he consented.

'I kept notes and diaries,' said the greatly relieved Caines. He nodded to the vicar, who unzipped the rucksack and placed some small notebooks on the coffee table.

Selwyn eyed them with interest. No doubt these would never have come to light had he declined their assistance.

'I'd like to get started on this as soon as possible,' he said.

'Then I think my job here's done,' the vicar declared. 'Clifford's staying with me for the present so, if it's all right with you, Commander, may I suggest it would be easier to meet at the vicarage?'

With a time agreed for the following day, the trio made their way to the door, Selwyn impatient for the morrow. He watched as Venables guided the wheelchair slowly down the ramp that had been originally installed for Georgina.

On his return to the drawing room, Mrs Soames was already there to collect the empty crockery. She eyed with undisguised curiosity the small pile of books at the corner of the table.

'A good meetin', then, Commander?' she asked, relieved to note the Commander's much-improved humour.

'Possibly a very good one indeed, Mrs S,' he replied with a wink.

She had scarcely left the room before there was another ring of the doorbell.

'They must have forgotten something,' Selwyn murmured as he rose from his chair.

'Saints preserve us, there's not a moment's peace,' exclaimed Mrs Soames as she scuttled down the hallway with the laden tray. ''Old yer 'orses. I'm comin',' she shouted.

A minute later she reappeared, followed by Amanda, who carried a large envelope.

'I have an early Christmas present for you,' the librarian told Selwyn, eager to see his reaction when he opened it.

***

It was the best night's sleep that Selwyn had enjoyed for a long time. Up and breakfasted, he was seated in the study and staring in happy disbelief at the returned map and the transfer document, when Sebastian burst into the room. That Amanda had made what he believed to be the right and only decision was a source of joy and satisfaction to the new acting manager of Fellowes Electronics. She had thought better than to disillusion him about how little his contribution had been in the decision-making process, or to mention the encounter with the mayor.

'What'll you do with them? Burn 'em?' Sebastian asked as he eagerly perused the map, over Selwyn's shoulder.

'No, I won't do that. I'm still undecided. For now, they'll go away somewhere safe. At present, there's something more pressing to discuss.' He described his meeting with Caines and the vicar, while Sebastian stared at him in amazement. 'So, if anything's to be done, it's going to be very much down to you as the only heir,' Selwyn concluded.

'I'm good with that. When do we start?' Sebastian was barely able to contain his eagerness.

'Just as soon as you can get some leave.'

'That shouldn't be a problem. I'm owed some already and the place closes over Christmas until after the New Year. I'll just need a few days to get some things sorted out before then.'

'I don't know what we'll unearth,' Selwyn cautioned. 'It may be something or nothing.'

'A bit of a treasure hunt, then,' Sebastian suggested.

They grinned at one another in their shared excitement at the prospect.

Selwyn placed his hand on his nephew's shoulder.

'Yes,' he replied, 'not the one I'd had in mind, but that may still come later.'

***

'Are you sure you've got everything?' Selwyn asked, as Sebastian deposited their suitcases by the front door. 'You've got all the certificates: birth, marriage, deaths, haven't you?'

'Yes,' came the tired reply.

'Been flappin' round like a mother 'en all mornin', Mrs Soames muttered under her breath, then zipped a box of sandwiches into Sebastian's rucksack.

The sound of an approaching car put paid to any further interrogation about Sebastian's packing.

'Can't be the taxi, surely?' Selwyn remarked with a frown. 'It's far too early.' He opened the front door and looked out. He took a sharp intake of breath and felt a distinct palpitation, as he watched the BMW convertible came to a halt. By now Sebastian and Mrs Soames had joined him, but, after she had glimpsed the car, the housekeeper gave a sniff and abruptly returned inside.

'I'll need a few moments,' Selwyn murmured aside to Sebastian as Miriam got out. Butterflies were now flapping about wildly in the Commander's stomach.

Sebastian took his cue and returned inside. A smile played on his lips.

At the foot of the steps, the mayor looked up at Selwyn, her brow lined with uncertainty. The very sight of her instantly banished any intentions Selwyn might have had to feign a continued lack of affection for her. Although he appeared to have been exonerated from the criminal aspect of recent events, things were not much different to when he had last seen her. Mud sticks, and the potential damage to her position and reputation by association with him were just as real as before. Nevertheless, after his struggle to resist contacting her for what seemed an eternity, he admitted defeat.

He hurried down the steps to greet her.

She anxiously scrutinised his face.

'Selwyn,' she greeted him, in a whisper.

'Miriam,' he murmured, now with a sparkle in his eyes as he reached for her hands.

'I couldn't keep away any longer,' she admitted.

'It won't do you any good with your colleagues,' he warned, delight lighting up his whole face.

'To hell with that! It's not important,' Miriam replied.

'Meaning I am?'

'Yes,' she said, softly. 'Though I hope my feelings are reciprocated.'

'There's never been any question about that,' he replied softly.

He pulled her gently towards him and kissed her. After several moments, she reluctantly pulled away from him.

'I can't stay,' she murmured. 'I've got a meeting.'

'Just as well, I suppose,' Selwyn replied. 'I'm off to France with Sebastian. I'll tell you all about it later,' he added, in answer to her look of surprise. 'There's lots to talk about. I'll ring you tonight.'

'Make sure you do,' she smiled.

He waved her goodbye, his hand still poised in the air after the car had disappeared from view. Then, smiling, he made his way up the steps and into the Hall, once more humming *The Waltz of the Toreadors*.

Acknowledgements

My appreciation goes out to my late, much-loved sister Lynette, for her invaluable comments on the manuscript and her no less valued encouragement.

Thanks also to Ted Rhodes for his valued comments and advice on police matters and also to Catherine Cousins and her team at 2QT for their great support in the publication of this book, which is much appreciated.

About the Author

Nigel Hanson enjoyed a varied career, starting out as a civil engineer and later branching into project management for major British companies, both in the UK and Saudi Arabia.

From there he became the commercial manager for a group of Lancashire-based engineering companies, eventually leading to the role of general manager of a major UK desalination plant company.

For the last thirteen years of his career, he took a totally different path and became Blackpool's first town centre manager, eventually succeeding in creating the first Business Improvement District in the north-west.

Since retirement, much of his leisure time has been spent on what he always wanted to do in life – writing.